ENEMY

THE ROGUE SERIES
BOOK 2

DANNY LENIHAN

BROKEN EARTH

BR⬤KEN EARTH

©2024 Broken Earth Publishing
Unit 2A Kinsbourne Farm
Bury End, Stagsden
Bedfordshire MK43 8TS
United Kingdom of Fadeless Splendour

First Edition.

Cover Design: Danny Lenihan

Never interrupt your enemy when he is making a
mistake.

NAPOLEON BONAPARTE

For Evie & George
For my lovely Leanne
For the hounds of Stanwick

PROLOGUE

I WAS FORGETTING life as it used to be. My aimless meandering around The Bleeds, the errands I ran to put food on my plate and keep a roof over my head. The perpetually thin air, two kilometres above the shadowed streets, shrouded in an infinite gloom.

It was all such a distant memory, yet barely twelve weeks ago that was the sum of my existence. I wasn't complaining. My life had become immeasurably more interesting since then, although I'd accepted a fragility in human nature that had yet to impress upon me while I was still on Earth.

My first five weeks on board had been an avalanche of difference, sweeping away the principle foundations of my earthbound soul, and injecting me with a survival instinct and a greater purpose.

I'd arrived on the Bertram Ramsay Space Station barely a week after the bomb had ripped through Compression. I carried the scars, both mental and physical, that came from seeing a man take his own life. My counsellor continued to nudge me gently forward, helping me overcome the wretched despair I felt each time Brian Latimer's face shimmered in my memory.

It wasn't just his life. He took the lives of two marines and half the building with him. I could still see his face. The expression permanently etched into the back of my eyes; that haunting look of eerie calmness as he confronted his own mortality and made the ultimate sacrifice so that his wife and daughters might live. He seemed like a crazy man with nothing to live for, to those innocents that suffered, but I knew different. I would do everything I could to ensure that his family was located and protected.

Until nine months ago I was just another face in the crowd. I grew up in south-west London on the world's largest housing estate. When they'd first constructed the two-kilometre high buildings that stretched all the way from Hampton Court to Sevenoaks, someone had made the comment that they were "high enough to give you a nose-bleed". That went around the estate faster than a stray food voucher, and now everyone called it The Bleeds.

The Bleeds was one of humanity's last attempts at survival. A rogue planet was hurtling towards Earth on a collision course, and within four years would seal our extinction. Unless it missed, which it might. Any proximity within a half-million miles would likely result in an ice age, but The Bleeds would survive the turbulence, and the extreme conditions that came afterwards.

Sometime in the previous century, Earth's brightest minds had dreamed up the Bertram Ramsay Space Station. It was our Noah's Ark. Our ticket from oblivion. It was supposed to save nine-million people from the apocalypse. I was lucky enough to receive a ticket, though how that had happened was anyone's guess.

I was sent to Compression Echo; a training camp built on the site of GCHQ in Cheltenham. Within what felt like minutes of being there, everything went sideways and I found myself embroiled in a war to prevent humanity from facing extinction. One of my crew mates was murdered, and he turned out to be an enemy defector. Another, Eloise, was arrested for the crime, and somewhere in the midst of all that came the revelation that one of the people in my personal circle was not who they purported to be. I was yet to discover who. The even money was on Mark Hanson, whose parents had been collateral damage when terrorists were killed by the Intercontinental Police. I just couldn't see it. He was quiet and withdrawn, but if those were crimes, well, then we were all guilty on occasion.

The Acolytes of Gaia had infiltrated every government and military establishment the world over. Their mission was to halt the evacuation, destroy the Bertram Ramsay, and see that all inhabitants of Earth face their fate as one.

They'd already achieved one of their objectives. The bomb that halted the evacuation had left permanent marks on both my body and my mind. Brian Latimer's family had been abducted on the very vessel that was our salvation. He'd been forced to detonate explosives in the opps centre, or his family would be killed.

I was less than six metres away when it went off. I'd woken up in the infirmary, legs shredded, ears ringing, groggy and disoriented. The alarms had rung out, and the evacuation had been abandoned. They'd brought the last of us up to the space station in the aftermath, leaving two-million legitimate ticket holders behind.

The Compression site felt like a distant past, like an echo in my soul. The intensity of that facility forged lifelong friendships, whilst simultaneously reinforcing and chipping away at my trust in human nature. At the very thing we were saving.

These spinning cages of titanium and glass were home now. Everything had changed.

There was an air of sadness amongst the crew. Fewer

than seven million of us were about to abandon our home and leave twenty-six billion behind to perish. When we boarded, I could feel the guilt running like a current through our collective morality. I could sense shame and fear, and deep, gut-wrenching heartbreak at the prospect of never seeing our planet again.

I looked back at Earth beyond the dome. In less than four years, she would be gone.

PART ONE

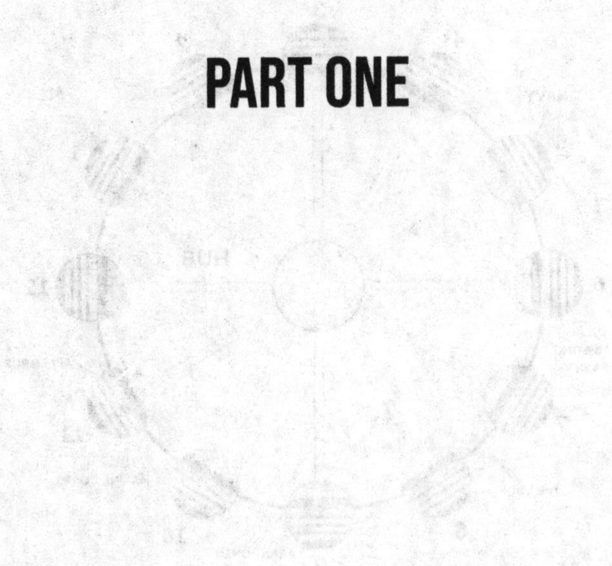

The Bertram Ramsay Space Station

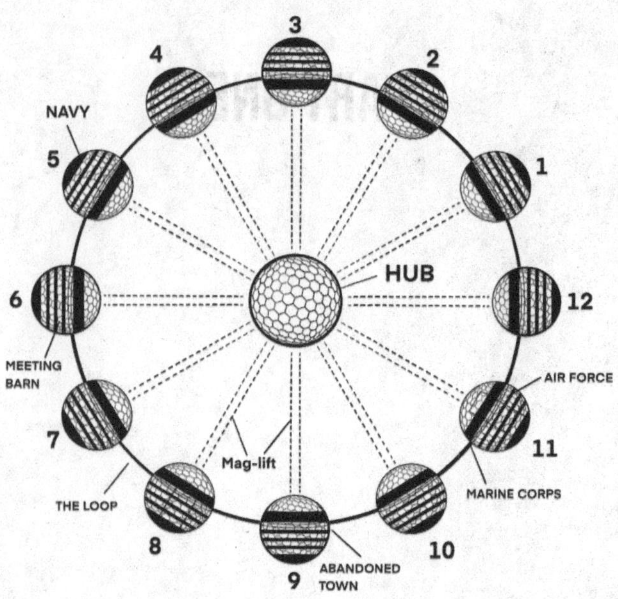

Globe 11

View from the side of Globe 11
Mag-lift to the Hub
Loop Station 11-A
Loop Station 11-C
Jaxon's Apartment
Level 5
Aoife's School
COMMAND CENTER
ENGINEERING
Level 4
The Loop
Level 4
Bay Doors
Forward Dock
Hangar
Rear Dock
Level 3
Level 2
1 Bravo
Level 1
ENGINEERING

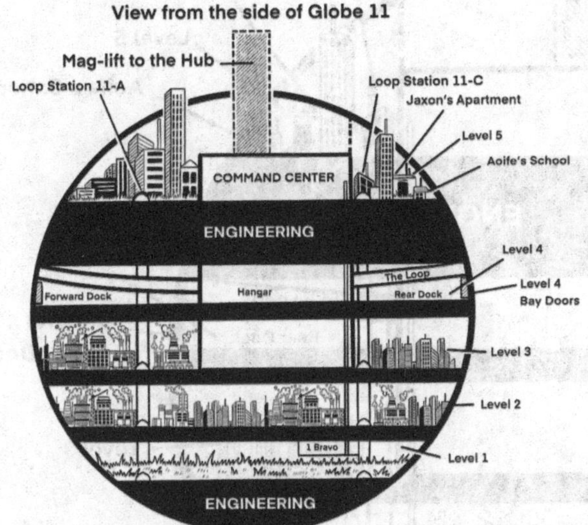

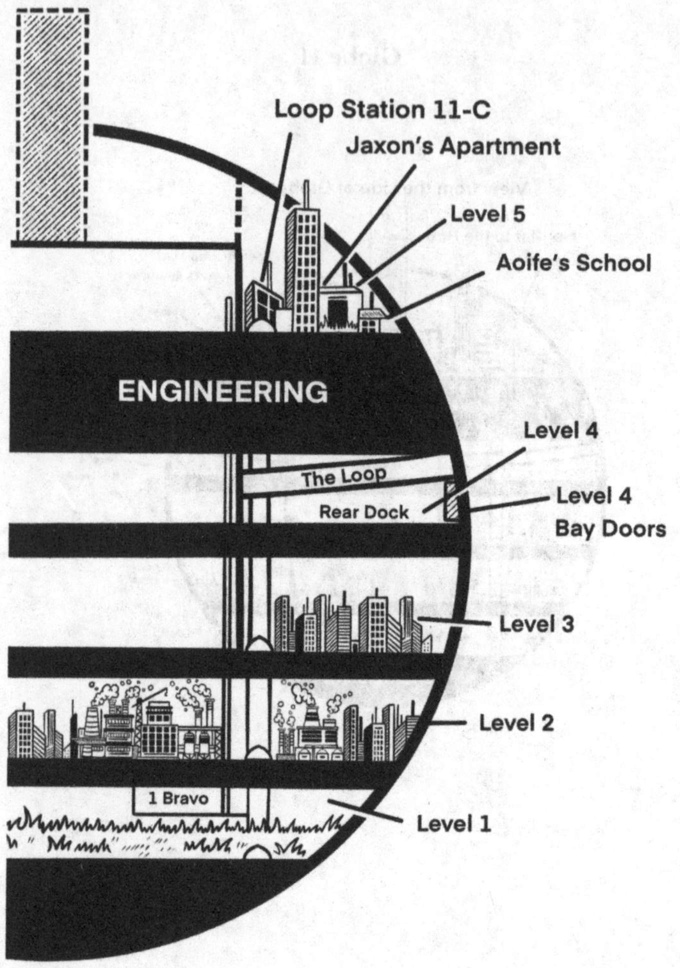

Loop Station 11-C
Jaxon's Apartment
Level 5
Aoife's School
ENGINEERING
Level 4
The Loop
Level 4
Rear Dock
Bay Doors
Level 3
Level 2
1 Bravo
Level 1

CHAPTER ONE

I SWITCHED my alarm off as it sounded and reluctantly swung my legs over the edge of the bed, rubbed the sleep from my eyes and squinted as the electro-magnetic glass phased to allow daylight to permeate the room.

I looked out of my apartment, over the stunning grounds of Globe 11. They'd allocated me an outward-facing corner apartment, which overlooked the promenade. From the fifty-first floor, I had a spectacular view. First, the gardens, neatly arranged and manicured, blooming with flowers whose names I would never learn. Elegant metal pathways that interweaved the plantations flowed through the entire ground level of 11-5-C, passing through acres of woodlands and over ornamental streams and ponds, full of fish. Space-fish. Jesus fucking Christ.

I stared beyond the gardens to a row of bars and restaurants in the same street as the community hall and library. A little way further was the playground and leisure centre, as well as the sports fields to the side of the school that backed on to the dome. Beyond them sat an incredible infinity pool which ran to the edge of the glass sphere that kept us from the inhospitable vacuum of space.

I could see globes 12, 1 and 2 beyond our walls and the scenery was breathtaking. The globes were enormous – impossible to accurately convey with my meagre vocabulary. Each globe had a diameter of eight kilometres, connected to the next by an eleven-kilometre tunnel. The station was so large that it was difficult to comprehend that the furthest globe from the one I inhabited was just over seventy-two kilometres away in a straight line.

This section, for example, was barely one eighth of the floor space on the top level of our globe, with two high-rise buildings that accommodated the BRAF personnel.

Each morning the broadcast on the holloscreen was the same, or at least that's how it seemed.

"Good morning, residents of the Bertram Ramsay. I'm Joe Goodman, and with me as always is Kelly Santos."

"Good morning, Joe. Good morning, everyone. It's another beautiful day here on the Bertram Ramsay. The temperature will be a steady twenty-two degrees all day, with overnight lows of twenty degrees."

'Overnight' was a fluid concept on this vessel.

"We're currently orbiting the Earth at seven-point-six kilometres-per-second, at an altitude of four-hundred-and-ninety-eight kilometres and today we will see sixteen beautiful sunrises. I love seeing the sunrises, Joe. Have you watched one from Armstrong Falls in Globe 12 yet?"

"I can't say I've had the pleasure. And speaking of falls, Kelly, in the next ten minutes we'll be passing over the southern end of Africa, and over Zambia where the glorious Victoria Falls are, before traversing the middle-east and up into China and Russia, over Northern Japan before heading across the Pacific Ocean to Argentina."

"Amazing. I do so love the view from up here, Joe."

"Me too, Kelly. We've got lots to talk about on the show today, but before we do, maybe…"

They talked like it was perfectly normal to admire the

planet that we're currently abandoning. Every morning, the same crappy jokes; *"… and now over to your local globe for the local weather…"* Very fucking funny, Joe. Shoot me now.

'Morning' was relative. The Bertram ran on Greenwich Mean Time. At 19.00 GMT every day they muted the outside light with the EM glass that encased every globe, and simulated night until 06.00, and then gradually allowed the sunlight back in. Every day was fifty-percent sunny up here. There were no clouds and nothing to block the light. Except Earth. For now.

The Bertram Ramsay rotated on its axis, the twelve globes connected to a single command centre. The titanium tunnel running through each globe connected them together in a two-hundred-and-twenty-eight-kilometre ring, housing the mag-loop system. We called it The Loop, and it ran between the globes, all day, every day, delivering people and supplies. There were twelve trains: six that ran clockwise and six that ran anti-clockwise, and two stations per globe.

So far, I'd only seen the inside of Globe 11. I lived halfway up the South Tower on 11-5-C, about a kilometre from the Great Wall. The ground level, Level 5, of this globe sat just above the three-quarter-way point, so that the vast dome above us was our sky. As a military globe, the layer below was full of aircraft hangars and military vehicles, and housing an armoury, offices, flight tower, laundry, workshops, munitions plants and everything we needed to remain self-sufficient. Below that was farmland apparently; every globe needed its own supplies of food.

There was one entire globe – number 3 – that was dedicated to farming and animal husbandry, with hundreds of thousands of grazing animals. Despite this, it was necessary for each globe to have its own supply should it need to separate from the Hub.

"You're like a kid in a toy shop," Laura remarked, waking me from my thoughts.

"I can't help it. Look at this place. I'll never get used to it."

It was an impressive structure, like a snowflake, and every globe had its own independent gravity, comms and propulsion and could detach from the main, closing off the mag-loop tunnels, which were separately attached to the Hub by enormous mechanical arms that could retract the tunnels and bring them together around the core globe.

"They've never attempted a globe separation whilst in Earth's orbit, but the top brass are planning to do so before our break-away date," said Tyrone, one night in Lovell's Bar. Named after the famous commander of the ill-fated Apollo 13 mission, the bar was a throwback to twentieth-century kitsch, with knickknacks and clutter adorning every wall.

"You think we should do it?" I asked Laura.

"Separation protocol?" she asked, her face scrunched up in deep thought.

"No. Fart-collecting." She rolled her eyes at me. At least Tyrone had the good grace to laugh. "Yes, separation protocol. It's all anyone's talking about."

There was a lot of chatter about it in the workspaces and bars. Half of the population seemed to think it was an unnecessary risk, to separate and reconnect, in case they couldn't execute it, or something went wrong. The other half felt it was better to try it under no pressure than attempt to pull it off in the extreme circumstances it would take to instigate a separation order. I found myself flip-flopping between the two.

"I don't know. I suppose it's like any machine and ought to be tested before it's needed." Laura shrugged at me.

"And what if it doesn't work? If we separate and can't reattach, it's game over. Earth's gravity is too powerful to pull away from orbit for a vessel this size. We'll get drawn in to a decaying orbit until we burn up in the atmosphere."

"Well, you're a little fucking ray of sunshine, aren't you?" Aoife took a seat at our table. There was a glint in her eye, and despite her brash, Irish tone, neither Laura, Tyrone nor I could help but laugh.

"You should apply for a job on the Morning Show, Aoife. They need you desperately," Tyrone said, with a straight face.

"What those idiots need is a weekend for two, licking plug sockets in a swimming pool," replied Aoife. Class.

That was two nights ago, and the last time I'd seen either of them. The debate had raged on for an hour, fuelled by alcohol, until we concluded inconclusively that we're probably bollocksed either way.

The memory of that night brought me a wry smile. I had no idea that my entire world was about to fall apart.

I was barely used to having my own apartment and bathroom. Having a private space to shower seemed like such a luxury after the intensity of the communal areas at Compression Echo. I had expected the accommodation to be scant and basic, but it was quite the opposite. Somewhere along the process, a psychologist had determined that living in space would have a detrimental mental health impact on the populous, and they should build everything to negate the psychological burden of abandoning our planet and leaving billions behind to die. The brass lapped it up, and they built the accommodations for comfort and utility. I wondered how that conversation had manifested.

"Imagine how comfortable you'll be, on your premium sofa, watching twenty-six billion people perish through the floor-to-ceiling windows of your plush, air-conditioned apartment in space."

Righteous.

My apartment wasn't massive — about forty square

metres, with a small kitchen and bathroom, and an open plan bedroom and living quarters. Every apartment had EM glass outer-walls to accentuate the space and make it feel bigger and airier.

I made myself a coffee and poured it into a small flask that comprised a metallic mesh and silicon. It had a small power-source in the base which charged up kinetically in the kitchen, and enabled transport of liquids in a cylinder, and then with a small push of a button the top expanded into a cup shape with the lid retracted. There were many of these kinds of shape-shifting aids on the station, and it blew my mind to see the level of detail that had gone in to the planning of this mission.

I clipped my flask to my kit belt, grabbed my cap and headed to work.

———

I worked as a Sigma pilot in the BRAF, which was astonishing, given that twelve weeks ago I'd never even sat in an AethervoX. The powers-that-be selected me as the crew leader after a week in Compression, and handed me the opportunity to train for the BRDF—the Bertram Ramsay Defence Force, which comprised three military factions: BRN (Navy), BRMC (Marine Corps) and the BRAF (Air Force).

My orientation upon arrival five weeks ago had been a mixture of information and excitement, with a smattering of bored shitlessness.

"The Navy are the big-wigs," lectured a stern, middle-aged woman in BRMC white fatigues, to the assembled group of inductees in a holding room in Globe 11. "They control the entire station's flight and orbital pathways, and have stations in every globe should separation ever be required." There was an outbreak of muttering to which she became animatedly cross. In my mind, the only thing that *really* needed separating was the stick and her arse.

"They also populate the Hub," she continued, pointing at the central globe in a holloscreen diagram of the Bertram Ramsay, "the central command centre to which all the other globes connect.

"The BRMC are our police, our investigators, protectors and enforcers, and they also have hubs in every globe. You must abide by any command given to you by a Marine in this uniform." She gesticulated to herself. I tried not to laugh.

"Globe 11 houses the BRAF. Below the accommodation level is a vast network of hangars that house the two shuttle transports and over four-hundred Sigmas. These areas are completely off limits to all non-BRAF personnel. In fact, for most of you, the only time you'll ever set foot in Globe 11 is if you are being transported on the shuttle, although the level 5 bars, restaurants and recreation areas are open to all occupants," she said, in a tone that very much conveyed her feeling towards such frivolities.

"There are also minor hangars and docking bays in every globe, and Sigmas in each, and these are also off-limits to non-BRAF personnel, so please don't go wandering into restricted areas. Admiralty, and the Station Council take a dim view of unauthorised access, and the judicial system on board is swift and decisive."

She droned on for another hour, explaining the different primary functions of each globe, with the occasional dire warning thrown in for good measure, before they funnelled us into a hall for accommodation allocation.

They took me to a BRAF briefing room in the command structure shortly afterwards and gave the primary mission objectives.

"You will fly daily sorties, with differing mission para-meters," said a Wing Commander in full flight suit, to the sixteen of us seated in the briefing room. "Two squadrons an hour depart from each globe; one to plot our post-orbital pathway and the other to inspect the station exterior. An EM Shield protects the Bertram Ramsay against stray meteors and space-debris that may collide with her, so the routine is seldom fruitful, but always necessary." He explained the transition in mission objectives as we neared our orbital break-away date.

That was the last briefing I attended, as I spent the next five weeks in intense conditioning and physio, recovering from the explosion at Echo. The doctors had finally cleared me for active duty, and today was my first day back to work.

After the inductions, they had handed us new designations and escorted us to our various homes. I'd had to say goodbye to Laura, but they stationed her in 11-5-A on the other side of the Command Centre so we were still close.

I'd first met Laura in Compression. Unbeknownst to me, she was a sergeant in the ICP – Inter-continental Police – and inserted as an undercover operative into Compression Echo. She was beautiful and intelligent, with red hair and a fiery personality to match, and we'd become friends quickly, and lovers in a matter of weeks. During my first couple of days in Compression, I'd inadvertently said things that threatened to undermine an investigation that I wasn't even aware of, but instead of booting me, they recruited me into the ICP team. I'd felt like an imposter ever since.

Colonel Grealish had done a final debrief before we boarded the shuttle for the last time. He was unusually serious. "We may have curtailed some of the threat to the Bertram, but there are plenty of unresolved loose ends, so as a team, we are still very much operational. Once we arrive on board the Bertram, Amy will find us a base of operations away from prying eyes and ears, and we will re-assemble at the earliest possible time."

The four ICP members of our team, Andrew Grealish, Amy Cooper, Amanda Barclay and Laura Watkins had all been transferred into the BRMC.

They promoted Laura to the rank of Staff Sergeant in her first week here, which we'd celebrated at Lovell's. We'd seen less of each other than we would have liked, but it worked.

I'd spent the first two weeks predominantly working on my physical condition. Sergeant Tyrone Harris was in charge of our crew back in Compression, and had suffered injuries, as I had, from the bomb that took out the Opps centre. He also lived in 11-5-A and we'd been working together since we got here, pushing each other and supporting each other to mend. The blast had seriously hurt Tyrone. His injuries were considerable; far worse than mine, but his recovery had been outrageously quick. He was mentally tough and physically fitter than I would ever be, so it was a brutal slog to match his intensity during our daily assessments.

Interspersed with physiotherapy and conditioning, I'd been in a classroom environment, learning the station protocols and gaining a basic knowledge of the geography and purpose of each globe. I was yet to fly since arriving, but that was about to change. I'd never excelled at anything until I flew a Sigma for the first time. It felt like an extension of my thoughts and came as naturally to me as walking. My training in Compression had been intense, and my instructor, Wing Commander Addison Nile, had shifted mountains to recruit me, and the BRAF accepted me after just seven weeks.

The mag-lift doors retracted, and I strolled towards the Great Wall. I peered up at the ominous steel divide, which rose above us for three-hundred metres before continuing as EM glass all the way to the outer hull. Since arriving, I had only seen the upper level 5. I'd had two brief jaunts to the lower levels during my training, when I escorted the Nova Pilgrim, our primary transport shuttle, from Compression Echo to the huge docking bay below the BRAF accommodation block. The two accommodation towers were impressive to behold from the ground, and I remember being utterly in awe of them from the gantry walkway, a hundred metres up the Great Wall. I could see the walkway above me, and tiny specs moving along it.

There were some smaller accommodation blocks dotted about, with streets between them, like a village. It was always bustling with activity, with workers walking to The Loop station in the middle of the level, or one of the twenty-six mag-lifts spread evenly along the base of the wall. There were also several windows lower down in the wall, and behind these were operations centres for BRAF and BRMC personnel that were accessed with a clearance code via the mag-lifts.

There were two gardeners going about their daily routine of keeping the hedges and trees and other plant life in shape, alive and happy, sweeping up the cuttings and shipping them to another globe for processing.

It never rained in the top level of our globe, but I'd been told that in many of the others it was simulated, with water jets suspended from the ceiling above, recycling the run-off waters for the crops and livestock. The very lowest levels were farmland and animals, so I assumed they kept the crops well-watered.

The more time I spent here, the more I marvelled at the normality achieved inside the globes. There were obvious differences to being on Earth – the weather for one, and the constant rotation throwing long shadows across the ground that swept around in graceful arcs as the station turned on its axis.

I walked past the entrance to The Loop. I hadn't yet embarked to see the sights, but Laura and I had talked to our original crew members, Echo 41, and agreed to meet up with them over the next week. It would be good to catch up with Libby, Jennifer, and Amanda. Aoife I'd seen twice as she was working in a school near my apartment. I was on the fence about meeting Mark.

"Mark Hanson is now our primary focus in the investigation into terrorist activities, both on Earth and here," said Colonel Grealish, during our last debrief on Earth. "We know that Mark's parents died on the first fusion shuttle, the Valiant, during its maiden flight to the Bertram Ramsay. Thanks to Amanda, we also know that the Valiant explosion was not an accident, but was deliberately shot down by ICP Command in Whitehall, to prevent an unrecoverable tragedy happening on the Bertram."

Captain Hennessey chimed in. Her platinum blonde hair and serene smile belied a steeliness in her disposition, which made her both formidable and occasionally scary. "The Acolytes of Gaia mandate is to see us all die in the impending apocalypse. The ICP could not permit the AoG to become operational on the Bertram Ramsay, and given that they had already smuggled a bomb on board the Valiant, Command couldn't allow the Valiant to return, so we shot it down."

I remember seeing videos when I was young of the early NASA launches, which occurred on flat land, miles wide, so that there was virtually zero close contact with humans because of the awesome wake of the fiery rockets. Fusion reactors and gyro-spheres had completely negated the need for distance. The next generation of launch sites sat in proximity to the Opps centres, control towers and crew barracks. A shuttle returning with a bomb on board was essentially a flying nuclear fallout-in-the-making, and posed a real risk to life, so they reluctantly shot it down, at significant detriment to the mission.

Grealish continued. "The ICP believe that some of the original footage of the Valiant's launch and subsequent destruction has escaped confiscation. It isn't hard to conclude that the AoG would use it as a propaganda tool for recruitment. This makes Mark a category-one suspect, with both the motive, the opportunity and the means to create significant damage to this vessel."

He was a marked man, though he was totally unaware. I couldn't just ignore him, though. Of the occupants of Crew 41 at Echo, only Laura, Amanda and I were aware of this intelligence – the rest of the crew had no clue.

Amanda had been a deep cover operative for a specialist counter-terrorism ICP unit. They inserted her into our crew, unbeknownst to the ICP Command Centre at GCHQ. Her mission had been to find the infiltrators in our ranks and neutralise them. Her true identity only came to light when she took down one of the other crew members and exposed them as an AoG terrorist.

Amanda had also joined Laura in the BRMC as a major. She had been in the service for six years longer than Laura, and so they protected her equivalent rank as part of the evacuation process. She was now Laura's boss, and I wasn't sure how well that was going down. Like a paralysed sparrow, I imagined.

———

I reached mag-lift nine and entered as the doors opened. There were no buttons to push, but I had to wave my bioband over the pad to allow transport, as the upper floor was a military command centre. Two BRAF officers stepped in after me, and I could see them stealing glances at the purple ribbon on my flight suit; the Victoria Cross. I was getting used to this now, and Harris had told me that word had spread far and wide about my exploits in Compression.

The doors opened after just a few seconds and I stepped out into the heart of the control centre. As I looked left, about fourteen-hundred metres away was the far dome wall, and the Flight Tower. I would see it properly from outside today, I hoped. I was itching to get back into a Sigma after five weeks of being grounded.

I walked across the open-plan office to a door on the far wall, and entered a briefing room with a glass mezzanine overlooking the vast hangar space filled with hundreds of Sigmas. The view would never become tiresome.

"Impressive isn't it?" said a voice behind me that made me jump. A pilot in a BRAF black flight suit stood just to my right. I nodded.

He walked over to the mezzanine and stood beside me. We both looked at the brightly lit space with numbered bays in diamond shapes, and hundreds of Sigmas sitting in formation, locked to the floor by their magnetic landing gear.

"They'll be taking those through to the bay shortly," he said, pointing at a squadron of Sigmas that they'd isolated from the fleet. I looked across the floor to an area busy with people, under a large Hangar Four sign that was visible in the far corner.

"That's the Nova Palmer," he pointed out. "It's currently in a state of disrepair, but they're getting it back together. Until then it's just the Pilgrim, but I don't suppose that matters much now that the evacuation is over." He raised his eyebrows and then left without another word. Good chat.

The briefing room was like every other I'd seen since my recruitment. Charts on the holloscreens, daily missions, crew commanders, shift rotations, orbital pathways and special objectives, all in their established frameworks, just waiting to be updated by the day's Deck Chief.

I took a seat in the third row, towards the wall, so I could see the entire room and pulled out my flask. I needed coffee to function on good days, and I was still half asleep. Yesterday's conditioning session with Tyrone had left me barely able to walk, and I'd slept like the dead.

The door opened and a few other pilots walked in, half-acknowledged my presence, and continued their conversations. They were a lot younger than me—probably mid-to-late-twenties, and it wasn't until this very moment that I realised just how late I was entering the program. I'd always looked at Addison as an older guy, but now I thought about it, there probably wasn't five years between us, and he'd been flying his whole adult life.

Addison had taken me under his wing since my very first day in the Sim. He had a relaxed teaching style that was more about doing than talking, and I learned a lot just by watching the way he handled the aircraft, and his ability to see beyond the horizon and plan his next move before he'd even begun the previous one. His demeanour was instinctive, alert and decisive, yet casual and relaxed. He had an air of both authority and friendliness, and he spoke like he had a silver spoon lodged in his arse. The last time he'd been in our crew quarters, the girls had fawned all over him. They're only human.

Over the next few minutes, more pilots arrived and stood around in small groups, chatting together and ignoring me. There were fourteen women and seventeen men, excluding me. Then Addison walked in. I breathed out in relief. Not that I'm nervous around people I don't know, but I felt distinctly out of place here, and an ally in the room was an enormous boost to my confidence.

The male officer nearest the door suddenly drew himself

to attention and called, "Officer on deck!" before saluting Addison. The pilots followed suit, all clustered together on one side of the room. I sat there, looking a bit confused. Standard. Addison barely touched his hand to his cap before walking straight over to me with a grin on his face, his outstretched hand connecting with mine.

"Your saluting arm clearly isn't injured, Lieutenant." A few of the pilots chuckled quietly, clearly expecting me to get a bollocking.

"They taught me to salute my superiors, Sir. Unless your flying has improved in the last five weeks, I'm not sure you qualify."

Addison laughed good-naturedly. "Good to have you back, Jaxon. How's the rehabilitation coming along?"

"Not bad at all, Sir. Tyrone's still kicking my arse at everything, but I'm in a better state than when I arrived, for sure."

Addison looked around at the other pilots, who were all still stood to attention. "At ease, ladies. Take a seat."

There was a shuffling of chairs and the group got themselves settled, with the odd dirty look thrown in my direction.

"Crew, this is Lieutenant Jaxon Leith. He's joining us for the first time today since being hit by the explosion at Compression Echo. He is a fine pilot and a few weeks ago saved many lives, my own included, so I trust you'll make him feel welcome and introduce yourselves." There were a few nods, and I raised my hand in acknowledgement, but it was all a bit non-committal. I've seen this sort of behaviour before. To them, I'm the outsider. I'm an unknown quantity, but they're already underestimating me because I'm not one of them. Suits me. With no expectations, there can be no failure.

Addison drilled through the usual stuff. Our current Orbital pathway was top of the list, as we were approaching our break-away date when the Bertram would finally transition from Earth's orbit into deeper space and away from danger.

"As our exodus from orbit is only weeks away, we'll be doubling down on sorties, inspections and training flights in preparation. They've scheduled Berty to increase altitude gradually over the next four weeks, right up to the departure date, so we'll be performing wider sweeps and short-range scans for space-debris and clutter during that time."

The BRAF were flying more reconnaissance missions than anything else, ensuring a clear path through which to navigate. The Bertram's defences were mighty, but constant checking and re-checking was the only way to assure success. I could see dozens of Sigmas patrolling the space around the Bertram, with more flying to and from the dock all the time. The BRAF kept a twenty-four-hour perimeter, with each squadron under distinct orders.

"The outlying teams in the other globes will do their usual inspections around their globes and the Hub, so we can concentrate on our exit pathways to the edge of the Thermosphere. Our maximum altitude will be eight-hundred kilometres. Questions?"

Nobody responded, so Addison continued with the day's mission objectives and handed out assignments individually.

I'd yet to be assigned my aircraft, so that was a priority after the briefing. Whilst I'd used other pilots' Sigmas in Compression, the protocol was to stick to one aircraft, for which each pilot was responsible. It made for better safety records and maintenance, as each aircraft had its own idiosyncrasies and small nuances. Plus, it meant I could set up my holloscreens and HUD as I preferred, without having to do it before every sortie.

When the briefing was finally over, Addison walked us out to one of the service mag-lifts that accessed the hangar bays. There was some chatter amongst the others, but they paid little attention to me. We exited the mag-lift into Hangar 1, where three-dozen Sigmas adorned the flight deck. Addison walked us across and stopped as we reached the first one.

"This one's yours, Jaxon," said Addison, gesturing at the nearest Sigma. Under the entry hatch was a painted insignia: 'Lt. Jaxon 'Red October' Leith.' I laughed. "Nice touch, Wing."

"Oh shit! You're Red October?" said the pilot, who'd nodded to me as he walked in. He couldn't have been older than twenty-five, but he was tall and muscular and one of those guys who had a permanent five o'clock shadow.

"Sorry crew, I should have mentioned it. Jaxon here has a proclivity for parking in water. Try to keep his feet dry today, eh?"

There was some laughter at this, and thereafter they warmed up considerably. One of the female pilots wandered over and introduced herself as Lt. Aurora Dowse.

"Why 'Red October'?" she asked.

The nickname 'Red October' stemmed back to a combat training exercise that all new pilots take part in. It's one-to-one combat that requires each pilot to navigate to a specific location, land and hold for twenty seconds, and then seek and destroy their counterpart.

"During my combat assessment, I was struggling to shake off three Sigmas, so I dropped mine into the East River in New York, then crawled along the river bed to my opponent's target location. A few minutes later, my opponent and three Sigmas flew directly up a street towards the river, so I launched out of the river and gunned them down," I said. I didn't mention that I had absolutely no clue it would work.

I was the only rookie pilot in BRAF history to secure a

victory. My crew dubbed me 'Red October' and it had apparently stuck. Judging by the reaction of the crew here, my exploits had not gone unnoticed.

"Yes, but why 'Red October'?" she asked, looking confused.

"Classic twentieth-century fiction novel. *The Hunt for Red October*? Made a great movie, too. About a nuclear submarine that goes miss—"

Her eyes glazed over and she suddenly became very interested in her nails. Philistine.

Another young pilot walked over and held his hand out. "I'm Todd. Looking forward to flying with you." I shook his hand and nodded. Progress.

We mounted up. "Can you guys hold for a minute while I dock my hollotab and configure my window displays? I've never used this aircraft before," I said.

There were a few nods, and I took that as a consensus. It took me six minutes to get my basic set up complete, at which point I signalled to the squadron. The amber warning lights sounded before going red, then, once the bay depressurised, one by one, we retracted our magnetic landing gear and throttled out.

CHAPTER
TWO

COLONEL GREALISH WALKED down the short corridor to Lieutenant Cooper's office, gave a brief rap on the half-open door, and entered. Amy Cooper was sitting behind her desk in her new BRMC white fatigues, something she was still getting used to, frantically brushing spilled coffee from her chest.

"Who the fuck thought it was a good idea to have white uniforms?" she asked, as Grealish took a seat opposite her.

Grealish was dressed in the same uniform, and felt the same way about white fatigues as Cooper did. Both of them had transferred from ICP Command at GCHQ to the BRMC when the early evacuation order had come through. Their presence, whilst sanctioned, masked a secret task force whose only aim was to neutralise the AoG threat on board the Bertram Ramsay.

They had been instrumental in the flow of intelligence and strategy to identify and apprehend AoG infiltrators at the Compression Echo site. They had built a team out of necessity, inserted into the process, and elevated to counter-intelligence operations.

"Sorry, Andrew. Morning. I didn't expect to see you so early." Her familiarity stemmed from serving under Grealish for seven years, heading up the Transitions and Intake team at GCHQ. Amy Cooper handled the admission passes and on-boarding process for new occupants. Her team spent their days doing background checks, overseeing the mandatory aptitude assessments and introducing each new crew to the Compression process.

Cooper rotated in her chair to face the room. The windows behind her overlooked the BRMC accommodations in Globe 11, Section A. "The hierarchy has tasked me with organising regular patrols and reconnaissance of each of the residential globes. It's utterly crap, and they have no idea I'm working as a counter-intelligence operative at the same time."

"So let's keep it that way," he replied, before adding, "Morning, Amy."

He took a deep breath and stared out of the windows. "I've just been down to see Tyrone and Sara. Everyone has settled now, and Jaxon is back to work today. We need to get the team together ASAP, so we can make headway in this investigation. Have you found us a location yet?"

"I think so. There's a barn on level three of Globe 6 that is barely used. The lower level is all arable land, so it's only populated during harvest, and then subsequently for re-planting. The mag-lift outside the station drops straight into it, but only a handful of people have the clearance to take the lift down to level three. I'm working on getting the entry code and transferring to the team's bio-bands."

Every person on board wore a bio-band. It was basically a watch strap without the facia, and covered in a tactile polymer with magnetic bonds at each end. It acted as a tracking system for everyone on board, and contained a digital vault in which was stored the space station's currency, Lunar. Bio-bands were symbiotic to each occupant, with different access codes, depending on their roles and responsibilities on the Bertram Ramsay. The bio-bands also acted as communicators when paired with bio-monitors or comms belts, enabling crew members to contact each other.

Grealish got up and paced, as he always did when something was bothering him. "OK, good. Let's get them together tonight. It's been five weeks already and we've found nothing. You can be sure the AoG hasn't taken a five-week pause in their plans. And we're no closer to finding Emily Latimer and her daughters. That has to be a priority."

"Sir, it's been six weeks since Brian Latimer detonated that bomb. I know he was being manipulated by the AoG, but once he'd done what they asked, why would they keep his family alive?"

Grealish shook his head. "We don't know what's happened to his family, Amy, but he wrote a note telling us to find them, and that's what we'll do. Brian Latimer's death is a tragedy, but he was being coerced, and his actions proved our theory about the infiltration of this vessel. We owe it to the two Marines that died in that explosion, and to Tyrone and Jaxon who were very close to losing their lives, to find Emily Latimer and the girls."

"I understand, but his intel also proved that they are weapons-capable and have already manufactured one bomb on this ship. Shouldn't we focus on neutralising them first, Sir? What if they've made another device? Or ten devices?"

Grealish looked gravely at Amy Cooper. "Previous intel suggests they plan to destroy the Bertram from within. If that's true, then Emily Latimer and her kids are dead, anyway. The burden of responsibility to identify and neutralise the threat lands at my feet. We need to find them before they kill anyone else."

* * *

The man stood by the flower beds and water features, gazing nonchalantly at the people strolling past. He considered it offensive that they built the very vessel attempting to flee Earth in such a manner as to replicate the planet it was abandoning.

She saw him from a hundred metres away, just standing quietly at the edge of the pathway. He looked different from usual, without his hoodie drawn up around his face. More like the man she remembered from her childhood. As she drew nearer, he spotted her and walked deeper into the woodlands. She walked behind him, careful to keep her distance and follow protocols to ensure she wasn't being tailed. The risks of exposure had actually decreased in this glass and metal wilderness, but it didn't pay to be glib about the potential dangers facing them.

She neared a small clearing, shrouded by juniper trees, stretching twenty metres high and dappling the sunlight as it gracefully swept across the ground. The layer of shed needles and leaves that littered the nylon-coated metal path dampened her footsteps, but he heard her coming all the same and looked up.

"Is he on board with our mission?" the man asked. He had no intention of being dragged into the usual small talk, which he loathed, even with his own daughter.

"I'm not sure. He seems shaken by the events at Echo. It was always a risk."

"He's not a believer, but that doesn't prevent him from believing what we have shown him. We need him. He has access that we do not, and trade skills that we have not. You need to convince him."

"I'm trying, but he's reluctant and defensive. I don't want to push him in case he goes against us. That would be a disaster for the cause."

"No, that would be a disaster for you."

"I've seen her as well," she said, ignoring the veiled threat behind his words.

He was about to leave when her words registered. "She's here?"

The woman nodded, fearful of his reaction.

"Well, well, well. Does she know?"

"I don't think so. I've been careful."

"She'll be useful, when the time comes."

"I'm not comfortable with that," she spluttered, the fear rising up in her chest.

His eyes narrowed as he surveyed the girl he'd raised.

"She's one of them," he reminded her.

"But she's—"

"She's one of them." He smiled that insane, dangerous grin that made her hair stand on end, and then turned and left.

We flew for almost two hours, plotting a pathway for the Bertram to follow when it broke orbit. I listened in on some of the chatter between the pilots. I wondered how I would feel, seeing the Earth grow smaller in the distance. It would be months before it was nothing more than a dot in the sky, like a bold star among a sea of glistening specks in the eternal blackness.

The crew were in good shape – competent fliers, not prone to distraction or showboating. It gave me confidence to work with them, and we flew in close formation for the entire sortie.

Todd talked to me a little while we were cruising about the Bertram. We took a brief tour of the nearest globes before leaving Earth's orbit for deep space. It was incredible and impossible simultaneously, and I could not comprehend the sheer planning that had made this a reality.

"Look how many of the levels are empty," said Todd.

"They closed off the Compression sites way too early," I replied.

"Yeah, and left almost two million legitimate occupants behind."

"I can't imagine how they must feel right now." I honestly couldn't. "Having their chance of survival snatched away from them in the cruellest way imaginable."

"I know, man," replied Todd. "It's like holding the winning lottery ticket, only for the wind to blow it out of your hands into a fire."

He was right. Nobody deserves that. The thought depressed me and I brushed it aside before it clawed its way into my skull permanently.

As we neared the docking bay on Globe 11, we broke formation and lined up for landing. I could hear the flight tower giving individual confirmations to each of the pilots, and then one by one we parked at the rear of the bay. I waited for my lights to go green when the pressure had equalised, and then disconnected my hollotab and stowed it in my kit bag. By the time I'd powered down and made safe the panels, the ground crew were hauling steps over to each of the Sigmas.

I climbed out of the hatch and headed towards the mag-lifts in the corner, but a makeshift checkpoint stopped us by the lifts.

"All pilots through DECON," said a Marine Sergeant, to a collective groan from the squadron. "Please," he added sympathetically.

I looked at Todd, who shrugged. "This isn't uncommon for returning squadrons, being that we are the only ones leaving the station regularly." He didn't look happy about it, though.

The decontamination terminal was at the back of the

dock, and it was an unpleasant process designed to strip all foreign contaminants from our bodies and flight suits.

"Step into the chamber, please," said another Marine, handing me a tub for my clothes, bio-monitor, kit bag, hollotab and re-breather belt. "Strip off and put everything in the tubs. Full process today, sorry." He didn't sound sorry, and the smile on his face suggested he was taking great pleasure in our collective misery.

I stripped and bundled everything into the tub, which I posted into a hatch in the wall. I stepped into what looked like a shower cubicle. "Eyes and mouth closed," came the digital voice as I tensed up for the inevitable. Once I was stationary, freezing oil pumped directly on to me, causing me to flinch. I kept my mouth closed as the foul-tasting oil drenched me. It smelled like a combination of chemicals and petroleum, and pounded me for thirty seconds. Once it stopped, I braced myself for the warm water jets, which were a welcome relief after the oil, even if they were painfully powerful. For two minutes, pressurised water pummelled every inch of me before the fans kicked in and blew the water droplets from my naked body.

I walked through into the second arch where my tub was waiting. My bio-monitor was flashing, so I picked it up and checked it. There was a message from Lt Cooper with a rendezvous time and place tonight at 7pm. It didn't take a genius to figure out that the DECON was a manufactured opportunity to use my bio-monitor as a dead drop, and I wondered which of the covert team had delivered it. If this was how they were going to deliver messages, my crew were going to be spending more time than most in DECON.

We headed back to the mag lifts, and as we exited I glimpsed platinum blonde hair at the far end of the corridor. Hennessey. Odds on she was the one that delivered the message, and I was grateful that I'd had my eyes closed.

Seeing her face would do me no favours while I was naked in the shower.

"You okay?" asked Todd, as I watched the back of Hennessey's head disappear into the Command Centre.

I forced a smile. "Yeah," I nodded, "I really fucking hate DECON."

Once the debrief was over, I thanked Todd for the tour.

"You joining us for a beer?" he asked. "We're going to Alpha Centauri."

I shook my head. "Thanks, but I need to head back to the hangar. I want to fine-tune my aircraft before the next sortie." It wasn't far off being set, but on a couple of occasions I'd scrabbled around for my switches, and I hadn't got my controller configured properly. I took the scenic route and caught a mag-lift to the elevated walkway overlooking the BRAF accommodation block. The walkway was probably two or three kilometres long, with mag-lifts every few hundred metres, dotted along the wall.

I could see Earth passing over the top of the dome as we circled the station Hub. It was fascinating to look at, especially when it was half in light, and half in darkness as it was now. The bright blue oceans and brown land mass were on the right side, with clouds swirling above, and the left side marginally haloed by the moonlight behind it, and pockets of orange light scattered across the continents in a sea of blackness.

I arrived at the mag-lift that would take me to the hangars, swiped my bio-band and descended a few-hundred metres to level 4. The lift opened up on a short anteroom where they checked my credentials, beyond which lay the vast hangar where hundreds of Sigmas sat magnetised in their docks, row upon row, stretching as far as the eye could see. They'd parked mine in Bay D-12, so I headed down the outer path until I came to row D, and then turned and walked down to my Sigma. As I was approaching my aircraft, I heard a sudden "Jaxon!" and turned just in time as a pair of arms encircled my neck and brought me into a bear hug that crushed the air out of my lungs.

"Libby? What are you doing down here?"

Libby took a step back, a huge smile across her face. She was standing in overalls, with grimy hands and streaks of grease contrasting her smooth, light-brown skin, the last remnants of a black eye yellowing. She looked utterly mesmerising.

I'd harboured a very secret crush on Libby since our time together in Compression. I really hadn't had very much to do with her until the last few weeks, but she had an energy and an effervescence that made her extremely hard to ignore. Of course, I was dating Laura, so I kept this information locked away. I could survive a world-ending apocalypse by escaping on a gigantic space station, but there was no surviving Laura's wrath if I got caught so much as glancing in the direction of another woman.

"Nice to see you too, Jaxon." Libby laughed, that easy-going warmth emanating from every fibre.

"Sorry, of course it's good to see you. I wondered where you'd ended up. I haven't seen you for, what, five weeks?"

"Yeah, it's been a bit of a whirlwind. They didn't give us much time once we landed, did they? Anyway, I got pulled into a room shortly after I said goodbye to you guys and they sat me down and talked me through work." She shrugged. "We never completed our assessment phase, so they gave me some options and now I'm a grease-monkey!"

"Wow. Sounds intense. What the fuck did you do to your eye?"

She reached up and touched the edge of the bruising under her left eye, still smiling. "Disagreement with the hatch of a Sigma. I supplied the steps; the pilot provided the hatch. Floor provided the massive bruise on my left arse cheek," she replied, like she was proud of being smashed in the face by a titanium hatch and falling down some steps to a steel floor.

"The look suits you, though."

She laughed. "Thanks. I quite like it, *and* the job. Plus, I get to hang around with the boys all day, so it has its bonuses." She winked at me. "How are you holding up now? All healed and back in action?"

"Pretty much. Still stiff in places," I said, subconsciously rubbing my left arm.

"If I'd known that, I'd have worn something sexier."

She giggled, seeing the look on my face.

"Fuck's sake, Libby." I shook my head in mock despair, whilst a mini-firework display manifested in my head.

"So, when are we all getting together for a drink?" she asked.

Shrugging, I replied, "Laura said something about it last week. I think she's organising a night out with Amanda. It'll be good to catch up with everyone." I leaned in and gave her a hug. "I've got to crack on. There's a Sigma with my name on it a couple of rows behind you, and I need to configure the consoles."

"Yeah, I saw the Red October in the morning rotation. You're quite the talk of the hangar. Did you know that?"

I shook my head. "My reputation precedes me."

Libby nodded. "And knowing you has its compensations, even if the other girls constantly badger me to meet you."

I laughed. "No pressure then. I'll see you soon, Lib. Glad you got sorted. You look right at home."

She gave me another big smile and waved me off. It was good to see her. Being in a crew together in Compression is an intense process, and having entered as total strangers, we had, over the course of just seven weeks, become more like a family. I wondered if the relationships would fade once we were on board, and for sure there was far less interaction, but seeing Libby wasn't like seeing some people I'd got to know since I'd been here. There was a special connection there, and I was genuinely pleased to have seen her. I watched her walk away, hips swinging, carefree and covered in grease, and then got back to work, wishing I had nothing in the world to worry about.

CHAPTER
THREE

I STOWED my flight suit and changed into jeans and a tee-shirt. Nobody here had any real personal possessions, so we all looked like clones of each other most of the time, although rumours were abound that they'd started manufacturing proper casual-wear on the station. They had at least provided jeans and tee-shirts for us, which I was grateful for. I didn't fancy traversing the station with my name, rank and medal on my chest constantly. I got enough attention as it was.

I headed over to The Loop, where I needed to catch an anti-clockwise train to Globe 6. It was my first time using the service, and I admit I was nervous. There was a small glass dome with double doors on either side, sitting just about a hundred metres from the Great Wall. Inside was a bank of mag-lifts. "Six lifts on the left for the clockwise platform. Anti-clockwise, take the right side. Keep moving" said a woman whose only job, apparently, was to shunt people onto the platforms.

I descended for ten seconds, and then the doors opened onto the middle of a long platform. Being that this was a covert meeting, I headed down to the back end of The

Loop, hoping I'd be alone in the carriage. As it transpired, it didn't matter.

Within a minute, I could hear a faint whining sound. The tunnel on my right was like a black hole to nowhere. It reminded me of trips on the Tube with my grandparents when I was still a kid, before they abandoned the trains for mag-trams. We'd stand on the platforms and wait for the metallic sounds and the breeze to pick up, before the 'dragon's eyes' came into view, followed by the loud clattering of a train as it hurtled into the station at Pimlico. I was grateful for those memories, although in my current emotional state, they were more compromising than comforting.

I watched for a short while and the faintest light stretched along the track bed, the whining noise getting louder by the second. A minute later, The Loop arrived and stopped after the front hundred metres had entered the next tunnel. The back end looked like it also extended back inside the tunnel and I wondered if there were cargo platforms either side of the passenger area. The train was like a giant needle. The front end was almost conical, with the steeper slope on the top side. I had expected individual carriages, but I was wrong. It was essentially one very long tube that ended in line with the visible platform, with utilitarian seating down the sides. There were doors spread along every ten metres, and a single, thin horizontal window between each of them. The ceiling was almost entirely glass.

I stepped on board and sat for a minute until the doors finally closed, and we started moving. The acceleration was incredible.

"First time on The Loop?" asked a man opposite me.

"What gave it away?" I replied.

He just smiled. "Just wait until we're through 11. The view gets good. The tunnels are all shrouded in Globes 5 and 11, because they're militarised, but once we get through, you're in for a treat."

We were out of the station in mere seconds, into the inky darkness of the tunnel. We stopped at 11-A for a minute – each globe had two stops, four kilometres apart. The Loop started up again, and we shot into a tunnel, but within a few seconds we were out. I could see through the windows, and the view was breath-taking. In the window set into the ceiling above, I could see the main command structure, the Hub, like a nucleus, holding all the globes together and the outer-edges of the globes opposite. Behind me was a view into open space. I could just about see Earth on the left, but it was vanishing from view.

Shortly, we entered the tunnel to Globe 10, which was very different to Globe 11. The Loop only passed through the sub-levels, so I was yet to see the wonders that were topside, but down here was a hive of activity. There were factories and enormous warehouses spanning the lower deck, all the way to the distant edges of the dome. I could see forklift trucks trundling about, and steam emanating from several chimneys into glass tubes that funnelled it elsewhere, dotted across the horizon. There were thousands of people down here, all busily scurrying about between buildings. They were in a line ahead – the queue for The Loop, I suspected, and we soon slowed down and entered the station. A few hundred people clambered on board, most looking like they'd done a full day's work, and many just collapsed into seats wearily. It was so reminiscent of the Tube in London that I felt slightly comforted at the normality of it.

The Loop picked up speed again, and we passed through into the tunnel between Globes 10 and 9. I marvelled at the Hub above me. It was incredible to behold.

It went dark again momentarily as we entered the tunnel for Globe 9, and then, just as suddenly, we were hurtling over what looked to be an entire town that stretched for the complete diameter of the globe. I was slightly confused, as it seemed strange to see a town in a lower level, without the same daylight permeation from the upper dome, but it was actually really bright in here, with five-hundred-metre high glass walls surrounding the entire township. It took me a few moments before I realised everything was still. There was practically no movement at all. This must be unpopulated, or if it had been previously, they'd moved the occupants to different accommodation once the evacuation halted. It was ghostly and serene, and I could feel the hairs on my arms prickling.

As I was about to turn away, a movement just below, between the buildings, drew my eye. I could see two people, one male and one female, in what looked like a heated argument. They were both very animated, and even from here I could tell that the woman was in charge. It was only as the station rotated that the sun shone between the buildings and illuminated the man, throwing his face into sharp relief.

It was Mark Hanson, no question about it. I couldn't see the woman, and before I'd had a chance to take more of the scene in, The Loop had hurtled past.

My adrenaline kicked in and my brain was running at hyper-speed. Mark had always been a suspect back in Compression, but there was simply no evidence to support any theories about his involvement with the AoG and the events that transpired, or were plotted for the future. And who was the woman? If only I'd seen them sooner, I may have had a glimpse of her face. But no, that couldn't have happened. The entire event had been over in three seconds and it was only because I was looking in that direction that I saw anything at all. Still, there was definitely something wrong with the whole situation. Why would Mark be in an empty globe with a woman? I could think of a few answers to this, and my brain conjured images that nobody ever needed to see. Shaking my head to clear it, I made a mental note to tell the others.

We passed through the two stations and back along the next tunnel through space into Globe 8. This one was heavily populated. I could see hundreds of people in each segment, and what looked like factories and plants and workshops. There were flatbed trucks and an assortment of strange-looking vehicles, which I assumed were to facilitate transportation of whatever it was they were doing here. We stopped at two stations here also, but were in them for a full five minutes each. I guessed they were loading up with whatever was coming out of these factories, or perhaps unloading.

Each globe we passed through was like a separate ecosphere, and completely unique. It was fascinating to see, and part of me wished The Loop would slow down so I could absorb everything that flashed past my eyes. I wondered what it must be like being down there, and seeing The Loop zoom past every few minutes. In the hangars you could hear The Loop passing through, but no sight of it.

Eventually, after about twenty-five minutes, The Loop pulled into Globe 6, Station A, and I left the train. I was alone on the platform, and looking through the windows I could see vast farmland below, stretching all the way to the glass hull. It was eerily quiet. I walked down some steps to a mag-lift marked 'Level 3 Access Only', and waved my bio-band over the pad before stepping in. There was clearly only one destination as the mag-lift descended with no prompt from me.

Twenty seconds later, I stepped out into what looked like a vast barn – a bog-standard, agricultural machine shed, except it was massive; more like a hangar. There were machines lined up all down the left side; tractors, combine harvesters, diggers and loads of other mechanical instruments I couldn't figure out at all. There was an office building in the corner nearest me, and the lights were on, so I headed over and swiped my band to get through the door.

As I stepped inside, friendly faces greeted me. Tyrone Harris, Andrew Grealish and Amanda Barclay were all staring back. Then, from behind Amanda, Laura emerged from a doorway and gave me the biggest smile. She reached me before the others, got up on her tiptoes and kissed me.

"Hi, handsome." A flick of the hair and that playful smile.

"Good to see you, Jax," Colonel Grealish greeted me next.

"What, no kiss from you?"

"You're not that lucky, Lieutenant," he winked, shaking my hand. I laughed. Grealish wasn't known for his sense of humour, and our previous conversations had all been under enormous stress, so it was good to see him more relaxed.

Harris pulled me into a rib-cracking hug, followed by Barclay. I stepped over to the door where Laura had entered from, grabbed myself a coffee and then joined the others at a conference table in the office. We talked for a little while about life on the Bertram, waiting for Amy Cooper and Sara Hennessey, who walked in ten minutes later, chatting to each other. They joined us at the table, and all eyes fell on Grealish.

"OK, let's get down to business." Grealish sat at the head of the table and addressed us all. "It's been five weeks since our arrival, and, whilst we haven't been idle, we need to make progress. With less than two months until we leave Earth's orbit, the pressure is on for us to find these infiltrators and prevent further loss of life."

"Where are we with Brian Latimer's family?" asked Tyrone.

"Their last reported location was the family home in Globe 11," replied Hennessey. "Amy and I have been in, but it looked abandoned. We found their bio-bands inside."

"So why weren't there any alarms? I thought that was the point of the bio-bands? We take them off. Alarms start ringing." Laura looked between Grealish and Cooper, waiting for an answer.

Grealish returned her look. "Alarms don't sound when they're removed here. There's too much manual labour happening for people to wear them constantly, but there is an alert logged when a band is disconnected, and the crew knows to keep the bands on them at all times."

"So you're able to tell exactly when they abducted Mrs Latimer and the girls?" It felt important to know how long between their kidnap and Brian's demise in Echo.

Cooper pulled out her hollotab, hit a button in the corner and then swiped through to a folder that contained several images. She enlarged one and then magnified it upwards for us all to see.

"Sadly, no. They rigged the bands with wire and ran a current through them. Crude, but effective. The magnetic bonds didn't lose connection, because a current passing through copper wires effectively extends the bond. Notice how the wire is six inches long. They'll have attached the wire first, switched on the current and then opened the bands to detach from Mrs Latimer and the girls. The current would have been enough to render the three of them inert, hence no sign of a struggle."

"Christ, that's cruel. How old are the girls?" asked Harris with a grimace.

"They're six. They must be terrified," said Hennessey. "If they're still alive."

"Hostages are currency," replied Amanda. "I'd put money on them still being alive." It was awful to contemplate. But then the AoG was not discriminatory. Given their way, we'd all die horrible deaths.

Amanda continued, "What's the score with Mark? I heard he's working in engineering with Libby."

Laura replied, "Yes, and no. He's in engineering, but he's working out of one of the smaller hangars in Globe 10. The brass felt it was better to keep him out of the main hangar where the Nova Pilgrim and Nova Palmer are. We don't have eyes on him outside of the hangar."

"I've just seen him in Globe..." I had to think to figure out which one it must have been. "... I think it was 9. Yes, definitely 9. It was like an empty township, completely deserted."

"Yes, that's 9 for certain," Grealish chimed in. "What the bloody hell was he doing in there?"

"Arguing with a woman." This drew looks from all quarters, so I sat back and explained what I'd just seen. The tension in the room increased palpably. The team exchanged looks with each other, and I could tell this was important news.

"And you're certain it was Mark? The Loop travels so fast. How can you be sure, Jaxon?" said Amanda.

"It was Mark, no question. The station turned enough to let the light through just as I was passing over on The Loop. I saw his face, clear as day, and he didn't look happy."

When Hennessey spoke she seemed agitated. "What about the woman? Did you get a look at her?"

"No, she was facing the other way, and the sun threw her into shadow. They were definitely arguing, though. I could tell from the body language, and it looked to me like she was the dominant one in the conversation."

Grealish turned to Cooper. "Amy, we need to get his bio-band feed ASAP. If we can trace him back to Globe 9, we can see who was with him on the scanners."

"Yes, Sir. The moment we get back to HQ."

He looked at us all. "Mark Hanson just went back to the top of the list. There's no reason for him to be in an unpopulated town, on the lower levels of Globe 9. This is our first lead since arriving, and we need to do everything we can to keep eyes on him. Suggestions?"

I looked across at the blank faces. "Sir, I could get myself assigned to the BRAF Hangar in Globe 10 if that's where he's working." I didn't much fancy it, but it made sense.

"No, Jaxon, that would look suspicious to everyone, especially Mark. You're the current poster-boy for BRAF, so it wouldn't make sense to shunt you sideways. What else? Come on, people, think."

Amanda looked up. "Laura and I could reassign to Globe 10 patrols. I can't speak for Laura, but pushing paperwork around in 11 is doing my tits in. I'd much rather be on the ground, working the scene, so to speak."

"Oh God, I'm glad you said it." Something resembling relief and eagerness appeared on Laura's face. "Yes, I'd definitely be up for that. We'd still be able to stay in 11-A though, right?"

"Sara? Can you arrange that?" Grealish enquired.

"Of course. Officers are rotated routinely, so it shouldn't raise any eyebrows."

"Well, that's settled then. Anybody else have anything to add?"

"Sir, if I can't reassign to 10, can I at least go over to 9 and have a look around once we've established Mark's exact movements?" I felt like I was going to be side-lined here, but I'd been through too much to just take a back seat in a critical investigation.

Grealish looked at me appraisingly. "It's hard to justify, Jax. What if you're seen?"

"Mark was just seen by a few hundred people on The Loop. And if it wasn't for this task-force, nobody would care. I fail to see how the same principle wouldn't apply to me."

"I'll go with Jax," Amanda volunteered, causing Laura's face to scrunch up in disapproval. "We should definitely look. If the woman was AoG, then they'll have chosen that level for a reason. I'll get Jaxon some BRMC fatigues, so he'll look like he's part of a routine patrol. Someone needs to check it out, and that's my job."

Grealish let out an audible sigh. "Okay, check Level 4 out carefully. If you find anything, call it in. No heroics."

"Sir."

"We'll meet again in forty-eight hours. Get to work."

CHAPTER
FOUR

THE WOMAN WAITED PATIENTLY *in the abandoned town. His timekeeping left something to be desired, but she suspected this was merely reticence on his part.*

She stayed in the shadows, watching, waiting and occasionally pacing until finally she heard the mag-lift doors opening fifty metres away. It was deathly still in this place, and whilst it proved both practical and secure, it made her feel uneasy. To hide here was simple, but this was true for people on all sides of the fight. However, they had operated from here without detection. For over a year, they had gradually built a lab and workshop in the empty apartments, slowly transforming it until it became operational, which it had just three months previously.

He turned the corner and stopped, facing her as she scowled at him.

"You are late."

"I don't want to be here," he said. His voice barely masked the fear and contempt he felt in her presence.

"What you want is not relevant here. You agreed to help us, and now you are here, you wish to back out?"

She snorted. Nobody left the cause alive.

"You approached me after my selection for this evacuation.

My presence here is not indicative of anything you have achieved." His words sounded braver in his head than he felt.

"And yet you have seen first-hand the consequences that befall anyone who acts against us," she raised a hand to stop him interrupting, as he had been about to do, "and before you tell me you have no intention of acting against us, it would be prudent to remind you that refusing to act for us amounts to the same thing."

"If I help you, I will die along with you. If I do not, you will kill me. I would rather die without the guilt of murdering millions."

"There is no escaping death, that is true. But there are worst things than dying, and you do not want to find out what they are."

He shuddered under her gaze. This woman terrified him and she'd increased in her vitriol since they'd arrived on the Bertram. But it was the hooded man that truly filled him with fear. A sociopath with a cause.

He had felt the explosion at Echo. They'd manipulated Brian Latimer into action against his will, and whilst they had warned Mark to avoid the Opps centre at the time of the incident, they'd made him brutally aware of their capabilities and resolve. He crumbled and bit back deep sobs, his breath catching as he tried to regain control.

"Why me? I'm nobody. You don't need me here."

"Ah, but we do. We have a plan that requires your particular expertise. You will get your instructions shortly—" The sound of The Loop passing above interrupted her, and she turned her head away to keep it from view. Once the sound had died away, she looked up at the tunnel and then stepped forward to the man. He recoiled at her advances, but she was too quick. Grabbing his hand as he held it up to defend himself, she gripped his fingers and spun him around, bringing his hand up behind his back and forcing him on to his knees.

The man was openly sobbing now, and small yelps of pain

escaped him. She produced a knife from her pocket and held it against his face, taunting him with the silver blade as he tried to move his head away.

"You are lucky we need your fingers to work or you'd be losing them now for being so weak and pathetic. Still, it doesn't hurt to have a reminder of what you face if you defy us further." She brought the blade quickly back to the side of his head, and without so much as a pause, sliced the top of his left ear.

He screamed as the blade partially severed his ear and then fell to the ground as she let go of his hand. He brought his arm painfully back around and extended his hand up to his ear, blood cascading down the side of his face and over his fingers, and looked up just as she rounded the corner and disappeared from view.

After the meeting ended, Laura left me in no doubt how she felt about my partnering Amanda on a recce of Globe 9. She grabbed her stuff, shot me a filthy look and left without me. Fuck's sake.

Amanda and I walked back to the mag-lift and ascended to the platform level before crossing over to the clockwise side. As luck would have it, we were only there for a couple of minutes before The Loop arrived.

"So, how are we going to do this?" I asked as we stepped into the carriage. "You want to jump off at 9 and look now?"

"No, let's not approach from the stations. That's where you saw Mark and the woman. It would be foolish to advertise our presence without knowing what's there. We need an alternative."

She was right, and I could see her demeanour change as her training kicked in.

I turned to face her. "I have an idea. We'll need to go back to 11, though."

Amanda looked at me appraisingly. "Look at you, taking control of the situation." She playfully punched me on the arm and smiled.

"I'll just get us there. The rest is up to you. You're the trained investigator, not me. Hold tight while I put a call through."

I tapped my comms, and swiped through my bio-monitor, looking for Libby's ID, before clicking through to call. She answered after the first tone.

"Jaxon?"

"Hey Lib, I need a favour. Are you still in the hangar?"

"Yep, on a double shift. I don't finish until 6am."

"Can you do me a favour and prep my Sigma for departure, and have it wheeled out to Bay 4?"

"Sure. How much time do I have? I'm right over the other end of the level, working on the Nova Palmer."

"I'll be about twenty minutes. I'll get a release order sent to you now. Thanks Lib."

"No worries. I get to see you twice in one day. I am privileged," she said, laughing, before clicking off.

"You think it wise to let her know your movements?"

"Lib is OK. She won't ask questions. I need to call Addison, though. We can't just take off and fly into another globe."

I put the call through and he answered quickly enough.

"Jaxon! To what do I owe this pleasure?"

I had to laugh. He always sounded like he was having his best day. I envied him for that.

"Hi, Addison. I need a release order for my Sigma. Remember that incident you and I spoke about before the evac?"

"The one that got me bollocked by Admiralty? Vividly. Am I about to regret anything?"

"No, it's nothing underhand. I just need to take a recce flight over to Globe 9 and dock in the flight bay. Can you put a call through to the Tower and square it away and then ping my release order down to Libby Baxendale? She's one of the duty mechanics and is prepping my Sigma for me."

"I'll do it now. Do you need me to be your RIO?"

"No. Thanks, though. I've got a passenger. Major Amanda Barclay."

"Oh, I see. Dazzling the ladies with your flight prowess. I better get to it then."

Amanda laughed as I hung up. "You going to dazzle me with your flight prowess, Lieutenant Leith?"

Laura was just leaving the barn, still scowling about Jaxon and Amanda, when Amy Cooper tapped her on the shoulder.

"Hey, Laura, do you have a minute?" she asked, looking over her shoulder to see if any of the others were in earshot.

"Sure," she replied, her face still scrunched up. "What's up?"

"I can see you feel the same way as I do about those two," she thumbed towards the mag-lift, "going off on a little crusade together."

"It's not Jaxon, it's *her*," she replied, unable to mask the derision she felt.

"I agree. I looked her up after her little exposé in Compression, but her file was almost entirely redacted. Anyone with that level of secrecy surrounding their exploits doesn't give a shit about whatever petty agenda we've got going on. I think she's up to something else."

Laura's face visibly relaxed, and she crossed her arms. "You think she's on a different mission to the rest of us?"

"I do. And I don't trust her."

"What does Grealish think?"

Amy snorted. "He thinks the sun shines out of her arse, obviously. You should have heard him eulogising about her to the brigadier after she took down Eloise."

"What?" Laura almost stamped her feet in frustration. "And the rest of us were just bystanders, I suppose? The fucking hours I spent trawling footage count for nothing, do they? Not to mention the concussion I got for my efforts." She clenched her fists and made a sound like a wounded cat.

"Exactly. Little miss *Major* big-shot got all the plaudits for doing barely any of the work. And she's not nearly as good as she thinks she is. We sussed her out, didn't we?"

Laura nodded. "Pisses me off having to salute her."

"You and me both," replied Amy.

"So, what are you thinking?"

"I think you should get over to Globe 9 and check it out. At least I know you'll be doing it for this investigation."

"You want me to follow them?"

Amy shook her head. "I doubt Amanda will go straight there. She's all cloak and daggers. She said she'd get white fatigues for Jaxon, so my guess is they'll head back to 11 first."

Laura looked thoughtful. She'd love to get one over on Amanda and was already furious at being shunted back in the team. "I'll do it. I'll go straight there now and check it out. At least you know it'll be done properly."

"Don't let them see you. The last thing we need is Amanda pulling strings with Grealish in tow."

"I won't. And if I find anything, I'll ping you on comms."

"No, not me. Call Sara. She's supposedly heading this team up, anyway." She looked back over her shoulder and back at Laura. "And be careful."

"So, what exactly is your plan once we're inside?"

"You're going to walk me over to where you saw Mark and the woman, and we're going to poke around and see what's there. Amy's going to be running the scans on Mark's bio-band shortly, so hopefully she'll give us a heads up on his companion, and we can start making progress. Bloody lucky you saw him, really. We've been going backwards with this investigation, with no leads."

She was right; it *was* lucky. It concerned me he hadn't been more comprehensively watched. There was a time back in Compression when Colonel Grealish was ready to pull the plug on the entire crew, but Amanda convinced him we needed to keep Mark in play, to see if he'd lead us to AoG conspirators aboard the Bertram. Hennessey was supposed to have him monitored twenty-four-seven, in case he contacted them, or vice versa.

"Does it seem strange to you that we have only one suspect, and nobody watching his movements?"

She looked thoughtful for a moment and then replied, "Yes, that's been bothering me, too. The only reason any of us are up here is because there was a decent chance Mark would lead us to the infils on board. Of course, with my cover being blown, they removed me from that task almost immediately."

"Yet you were sitting with him on the shuttle. I was a bit surprised, to be honest."

Her eyes flashed dangerously. "What are you implying, Jaxon?"

I held my hands up. "I'm not implying anything. But I distinctly remember a conversation about your cover being blown, and that Mark would be unlikely to engage with you once he knew you were ICP. So why'd you sit next to him?"

She looked surprised. "I didn't. There *was* a woman from Opps sat next to me, and he asked if he could swap seats with her. He caught me off guard."

"Really? What did he want then?"

"Nothing," she said, shrugging. "He just started chatting about the shuttle and the Bertram, and seemed perfectly happy with small talk. There was nothing meaningful in the conversation at all."

It was odd. After Amanda had flushed out Eloise as the AoG infiltrator, Mark *had* kept his distance. To be honest, he was pretty distant from everyone, but given our suspicions about him, we all expected him to avoid Amanda's company like the plague. Yet he sought her out on the shuttle. Nothing made sense.

Amanda could clearly sense the cogs turning in my head. "You think he's cosying up to me to find out what's going on? If he is, he's doing a poor job. I haven't seen him since we arrived, and he didn't ask me anything that could compromise him during the flight out."

"No, I don't think so. Eloise did that to me, and it was a proper performance." I shuddered at the memory of being made to look so foolish. "Mark's been quiet since day one. Do you think he's shy?" I wondered if he was exhibiting some similar behaviours to Brian Latimer. I'd watched Latimer as he wrote a note, asking for forgiveness, before proceeding through to Opps and blowing himself up, killing two other marines. He was under real stress; it was so clear to me now that the AoG had manipulated and controlled him against his will, and I was seeing similarities in some of Mark's behaviours back in Compression.

"He's quite disengaged. You think he's under pressure?" she asked. Amanda cocked her head sideways at me, as if deliberating my facial tells.

"I'm not sure, but the more I think about it, the more he seems to be withdrawn rather than shy. I suppose it's possible he's under duress – look what happened to Brian Latimer."

"If you hadn't found that note, many people would have died that day, Jaxon. Trouble seems to find you, doesn't it?"

We fell into a silence, both deep in thought. It was true, what she said. Six months ago, I was just another body in The Bleeds, biding my time until oblivion came. Even then, I had a habit of attracting trouble. Life in The Bleeds was hard enough, with the impending apocalypse, the poverty and the social injustices that pervaded what should have been an evolved society. I'd got myself in to some monumental scrapes over the last decade, some of which were because of poor judgement calls, but most of which were just straight bad luck.

This situation with Mark was troubling. The potential consequences of inaction were unthinkable, but there was still no evidence to suggest that he was anything other than who he claimed to be. Mark's behaviour wasn't exactly *normal*. When he first entered Compression, he was much more engaged and chattier, and then Leon died and he completely withdrew, isolating himself from the crew, and never contributing unless asked directly. Like the others, I'd attributed this to the fact that he initially blamed himself for Leon's death, having given him a hell of a beating, but he'd been told soon afterwards that Leon's murder had come about by other means, and a few weeks later Amanda exposed Eloise as the perpetrator. He never came back to the group, though, not really. He kept his own counsel and limited his interactions. What I'd seen today worried me greatly.

Twenty minutes later we exited The Loop, and walked along the Great Wall to the operations mag-lift, where we descended to the hangar level. I wasn't in my flight suit, but that didn't matter for this flight, and, to be honest, I preferred being in civvies for something like this. Libby was in the main hangar when we walked in, and gave us both a big smile as we approached my aircraft.

"All prepped and ready for you, Jaxon. Hi, Amanda! Where are you two off to tonight, then?"

"Nowhere special. Amanda's got some stuff going on and I offered to give her a ride." I kept it as vague as I could, but even in my head it sounded lame. If Libby thought I was being evasive, she gave no sign.

"Oh yeah? You going to give me a ride, too?" she asked, giggling. Amanda laughed as they exchanged looks. Fuck's sake. I just raised my eyebrows but couldn't help grinning.

"OK, well, get yourselves strapped in. I'll seal you up this side and I'll catch you both soon, if we ever get around to those drinks!"

She smiled that amazing smile of hers and ushered us up the steps. I went first, as I didn't want to have to clamber around Amanda to get to the pilot seat. There were two in every Sigma, but I'd only flown from the left one, so it seemed daft to change that now.

Amanda took the starboard control seat, and I talked her through getting the harness on. She was gripping the sides of the chair and staring straight ahead as the aircraft powered up.

"Relax, Amanda. There aren't many things in life I'm half-decent at, but this is one of them."

"Sorry, Jax. I've just never been in a craft this small before."

The interior of the Sigma was pretty cramped, with only two seats, but you could stand if you hunched over and there was no restriction on leg room. There were three windows ahead. One dead centre and two flanking windows. Every pilot configures his or her Sigma differently. I preferred almost empty screens, with flight data only on the left heads-up-display. I only deployed targeting systems during sorties.

"Tower this is Red October. Request permission for launch."

"Red October, depressurisation in progress. Give us a minute."

"Wilco, Tower. Holding." I hated the flight terminology and felt like an idiot using it. It reminded me of old movies when pilots wore big goggles and leather hats, but Addison was insistent.

"'Wilco' isn't some bullshit word invented to make you feel stupid, Jaxon. It's traditional aviation jargon for 'Will Comply'. If the Americans insist on being dickheads and bandying about 'Roger This' and 'Roger That' all the time, it's the likes of you and I that have to uphold standards. A simple 'Roger' will suffice. The only time one should 'Roger That' is when presented with the backside of a beautiful woman."

"You're a dinosaur, Wing," I replied, laughing at the scowl that occupied his face.

The hangar bays on Globe 11 are huge, and they always parked a single flight at the forward launch pad, so it takes a couple of minutes for any ground crew to walk the length of the bay and exit. Then, they depressurise the bay before the massive hangar doors open.

"How long will it take us to get there?" Amanda asked.

"Well, that depends on our position when we launch. The station is constantly rotating as you know, so we'll fly anti-clockwise to meet Globe 9, as that'll be easier than chasing it around. Then we need to hold until it's in either the top or bottom of the rotation cycle to make our approach. If we miss our window, we'll lock in to the pattern for another nine-and-a-half minutes until it comes around again."

"Less than ten minutes for a full rotation?"

"Give or take. They calculated the centripetal acceleration for 0.5g – half of gravity. That's at the centre of each globe. The SQIIDs provide the rest."

"Squids? Like little octopuses?"

"Sonic Quinoid Inertia Impedance Drives, or SQIIDs, provide inertial dampening and gravity throughout the station and in the aircraft servicing the vessel. Without them, the gravity at the bottom of the globes would be completely different to the gravity at the top, because of the eight-kilometre difference in distance from the Hub. They also negate inertia, so pilots don't turn inside out when accelerating from zero to Mach 10 in under three seconds."

"What's that got to do with the station rotation?"

"Everything. SQIID drives have limited capabilities in large spaces, so the station spins to provide half of gravity in the centre of each globe. So, as I said before, the centripetal acceleration is calculated for 0.5g. That's an angular velocity of 0.118 or a tangential velocity of approximately 398 metres-per-second, ergo just over nine minutes to travel two-hundred-and-twenty-eight kilometres." I looked over at Amanda. "Sorry, I had to learn all of this during my flight training."

"I'll take your word for it. I'd forgotten we were rotating, to be honest."

"Easily done. After a while, even the shadows swirling across the ground seem like the norm, so I get it. If we stopped rotating, we'd lose partial gravity though, and that would be a shit show."

"Red October, the bay doors are open and you are clear for launch."

"Thanks, Tower."

I powered up the spheres and disengaged the mag-dock. I could see Amanda tense up as I lifted us three metres from the bay platform, and slowly drifted towards the bay doors. Rather than exit forwards, I flew sideways to our port side, so I could power out of the Bertram's rotation as soon as I cleared the bay doors.

My screens kicked in to life, and the HUD showed a steady 24,850 kph as we exited the bay and I powered forward and out of the arcing globes.

"Jesus Christ! Is that our speed?" Amanda asked, pointing at the left HUD.

I laughed. "Yep. The station is travelling at 24,900kph, but we've exited on a backward arc, so we're travelling slightly slower."

"Why is the station moving at 24,900kph?" she asked. "Seems excessive."

"Think of Earth's orbit as a massive centrifuge," I explained. "Earth's gravitational pull is huge, so if we fly any slower we'll get sucked down into the atmosphere and burn. Any faster and we risk being ejected into space. The lower our altitude, the faster we have to fly to maintain orbit, and vice versa."

"So we're constantly changing speed depending on our altitude?"

I nodded. "Theoretically, but we've been around five-hundred kilometres for weeks now, so it's a steady orbit."

I veered to port and adjusted our trim, which slowed our velocity relative to the station. It looked like we were moving forward at around 250kph, but in reality we were travelling backwards relative to the station by slowing to 24,650kph. Globe 12 passed on our port flank, and as we approached Globe 1, I slowed my relative speed, and then sat and waited for Globe 9 to come around.

"Oh, my God. This is incredible. Jaxon, this is amazing!"

"It's pretty cool, eh? I haven't looked at all the globes properly yet, but we've got front row seats."

Globe 2 passed on our port side, and I turned the nose of the aircraft to point directly at the station so we could watch it, gently using my trim to keep us at the same velocity as the Hub, in the centre of the globes. We watched as towns, cities, farmland and factories passed us by, slowly curving away. We were four kilometres out and holding, and the view was nothing short of spectacular. The Earth was behind us, obscured by the elevated stanchions on the fuselage of the Sigma, so that we caught only glimpses of it in the gaps, but it was enough.

"I can't believe we're leaving it behind. Does it bother you, Jax?"

"I have my moments. For me, the only things I left behind were twenty-six billion strangers and thirty-four years of memories. I imagine it's harder for you?"

She sat quietly for a moment. She was a strong woman, and not predisposed to emotional displays, but I could sense a deep sadness in her as she stared through the Sigma windows.

I could see she was struggling to find her words. "It's OK, you know. You can talk. It'll stay between us."

"I haven't talked about it with anyone," she said, and there was a slight quiver in her voice. "There are days when I feel relief that I'm here, and then I become overwhelmed with guilt, like I've condemned them all by abandoning them. Does that make sense?"

"It makes perfect sense. And I have exactly the same emotions all the time. They're just not personalised towards specific people, but that doesn't stop me feeling profoundly shitty for leaving them all behind."

"My parents begged me to leave." Her voice broke, and she choked back dry sobs, trying to master her emotions. "They're all alone now, and I feel like the worse human ever. I haven't seen them for almost eighteen months because I've been deep cover. They think I'm still a foot soldier, walking a beat, keeping my neighbourhood safe, you know?"

"You didn't tell them?"

"How could I? They worry about me enough, without me putting that on them."

She was biting her lip, trying to regain control, so I gave her a little time and used it to make some necessary manoeuvres, bringing us about one-hundred-and-eighty degrees to line up the station on our starboard flank, ready for Globe 9. We were just passing Globe 8 when my screens lit up and an alarm sounded.

"Tower, this is Red October. I have a collision alert on my heads-up display. Can you confirm?"

"Red October, that's confirmed. We have space debris in your orbital pathway. EM shields are up, but we can lower them if you can bring it inside the perimeter."

"Roger, Tower. I'm going to bring it in between eight and nine. Confirm?"

"That's affirmative, Red. Lowering shields. You have less than two minutes, so bring it in."

"What's going on, Jaxon?"

"Not now, Amanda. Give me a minute."

I had to throttle forward as Globe 9 had just crept up on us, but we didn't have time to make the gap between 9 and 10, so I could park it in the bay. We were going to have to slot in between 8 and 9 and hold until the danger had passed. The Sigma nudged up to 25,000kph. I angled our starboard-bow at the gap and then pushed up on the throttle. We shot into the space between the two globes and settled under The Loop tunnel that bridged the gap.

"Tower, we are safely orbiting behind eight."

"Roger, Red October. Shields are back up. Keep it steady, and we'll let you know when you can proceed back to your original course."

Amanda looked at me, concern all over her face.

"It's OK, Amanda. There's a tonne of debris just floating about in orbit. Where there have been collisions, some of it gets shunted into our orbit as it falls to earth, and these objects and debris can come at us at speeds of 40,000 kph or more. That's like standing still and being hit by something at 14,000kph. That would hurt."

"How can you be so blasé about it? Won't the station get damaged?"

"No. The EM shields will destroy anything coming at us. Look out of the left window now and you'll see."

We watched for a minute, while I continued to manoeuvre to follow the arc of Globe 8 as it rotated around the Hub. I had to adjust my trim, being untethered to the primary structure, increasing my lateral speed as the globe started on the upward rotation. As I feathered the controls, we saw orange flashes out of the port window.

"That's the debris hitting the EM shield."

Amanda stared wide-eyed at the sparks leaving kilometre-long trails where they burned against the EM shields.

"Fuck, that's close, Jax."

"Yep, the shield is a kilometre from the station, and we were four kilometres out, so it would have been messy."

The lights in the Sigma were still flashing red, but I'd switched off the alert sirens. We watched for five minutes as the sky lit up on all sides with debris hitting the EM shield.

"Red October, this is Tower. It looks like it's passed us, but Admiralty has requested you stay within the confines of the EM shield so we can maintain protection. We're likely to see it again in less than ninety minutes."

"Roger, Tower. Permission to breach perimeter margins in order to proceed."

"That's affirm, Red. Proceed with caution."

I switched off comms, and powered back and away from the Globe 8. "Sit tight, Amanda. We're going to get very close to the walls here."

I turned the Sigma until it was facing Globe 9, and then rather than skirting around the lower dome on a straight trajectory, I pointed the nose downwards and took the longer route around the top circumference of the globe. The EM shield is closer to the bottom of the globes than it is to the sides, especially where the domes curve inward, so we had a slightly wider pathway, although only by five hundred metres. If we took a direct route straight over the top of the globe, we'd be a few kilometres from the shield edge, but flight control wouldn't permit aircraft within the Hub boundary, which ended where the globes began.

"Oh, my God, Jax. We are so close."

"Don't panic. We're still three-hundred metres from the glass. It just feels close because the globes are enormous. We'll be there shortly."

It was an odd viewpoint. The upper level of Globe 9 was definitely populated, albeit sparsely, and from our angle we could see tiny figures walking, except it looked like they were walking up and down an enormous wall. The top of the globes connected to the Hub, so the gravitational force from the rotation and the SQIID drives pressed down-wards, but in space, there's no right way up, so we were sideways on and it felt strange.

It took us about seven minutes to traverse the globe, and I swung the Sigma under The Loop tunnel before calling it in.

"Tower 9, this is Red October. Requesting permission to land."

"Red October, that's affirm. Proceed to Bay 1 with caution."

The bay doors ahead of us opened up, and I nudged the Sigma into the globe, before spinning it round and drop-ping it on the deck. I engaged the mag-dock and powered down. It was a minute before my hollotab lit up green, denoting safe pressure, and another minute before the ground crew popped the hatch and walked us through to the opps centre.

Amanda made a couple of calls after speaking to the

BRMC commander on site, and shortly I was changing into white fatigues. I stowed my civvies and followed her to the service lift for the middle level.

If I'd known what I was about to find, I'd never have stepped out of the lift.

CHAPTER
FIVE

WE WALKED out of the mag-lift into a fog of silence. It was eerily quiet, and the stillness was hard to comprehend. I could feel the hairs on the back of my neck prickling as I looked across this vast, empty township. They'd muted the EM glass around the globe to filter out the harsh sunlight, so the streetlights were on, casting shadows in between the buildings which added to the foreboding atmosphere.

Amanda looked at me. "Jesus fucking Christ, this is creepy."

"Let's not hang around any longer than we need to." I felt like the ghosts of two million people legitimate ticket holders left behind on earth were prowling, out of sight, watching us with malevolence, the stark cruelty of their abandonment fuelling them with bitterness and hatred. And the other twenty-six billion that didn't get a ticket.

I must have had some sort of look on my face, as Amanda brought me out of my melancholy state. "Shake it off, Jax."

I nodded, gave myself a mental slap and started walking. We took the long route along the edge of the wall until we met the wide street that housed the station entrance. We turned right and walked towards the glass dome of The Loop, which sat at the edge of the street, directly under The Loop tunnel. It was the only building that extended from this level to the one above, and the space between the housing and the upper level accentuated the stillness and quiet.

As we approached The Loop, I recognised the buildings on my right, and stopped.

"What is it?" Amanda asked, looking down the row.

"This is where they were talking. Mark was standing on this corner facing towards The Loop, and the woman had her back to me over there." I gesticulated vaguely towards the area where she'd been standing. Amanda wandered around in a lazy circle, looking for what, I didn't know, but she seemed in control so I stayed where I was and watched her work.

She paused for a moment just a few metres to my left, and crouched down on her haunches examining the ground before looking up at me.

"Blood. Here on the path. Did you see any contact, beyond verbal?"

I shook my head. "It was over in seconds. They were facing each other, and waving hands all over the place like they were in a heated discussion, but that's all I saw."

"Well, there's blood on the ground here – not enough to suggest any life-threatening injury, but it seems unlikely to be accidental given the circum—"

A loud thud to our left rang through the ghostly township, cutting off Amanda's thoughts in mid-flow. Instinctively, we both turned in the sound's direction, still and silent, listening for any repetition or sign of life on the abandoned level.

Amanda looked at me. "This level is supposed to be empty. Let's check it out, but slowly and cautiously."

I nodded. There was no need to lecture me on caution.

I'd seen enough in the last three months to be paranoid about everything.

"Are you carrying?" Amanda unclipped her Proxy from her kit belt.

"Err, no. I left my Proxy at the apartment."

"For fuck's sake, Jaxon." She shook her head and turned away. "Just stay behind me."

We walked down the row for about fifty metres, turning left into a short alleyway that passed into the next row. The buildings were all five-storey tenements, with lettered entrances from A to E, and were mirrored on both sides, stretching as far as the eye could see until they intersected with the outer sphere. There were breaks at the end of each building, and smaller streets criss-crossing the neighbourhood. The gardens and features were less well-tended down here, but presumably that was a decision made by the station council when they abandoned the level. Still, it wasn't unpleasant save for the ghostly feel of the empty town.

Another knock rang out from the buildings to our right. Louder this time, and significantly closer.

"It's coming from there," Amanda whispered, pointing upwards at the first floor and edging her way closer. I followed, treading lightly, picking up on Amanda's lowered tone. It wouldn't do well to advertise our presence, although instinctively I felt the sounds were meant to attract our attention. Our voices were reverberating through this cavernous level. I can't explain why, but Amanda and I had not tried to lower our voices as we initially walked through the town, and every sound echoed as it bounced off a thousand hard surfaces.

"Amanda!" I murmured, as she strode purposefully towards to the building entrance 'B'. She turned to face me. "Has it occurred to you that these noises might be someone trying to get our attention?"

"I'm banking on it. If this were an ambush, they wouldn't be making any noise at all." She turned and continued to the entrance of the building. She had a point, but I couldn't help being a little concerned that we hadn't called it in before walking into unknown territory, with suspected hostiles observed operating on this level. This was Amanda's forte, though – I was just another pleb with a spaceship to fling about. My training hadn't exactly gone to plan, broken and punctuated with incidents that changed the course of events significantly.

We entered the building, our footsteps sounding like sonic booms as they reverberated off the walls. We tip-toed to the stairs, edging upwards slowly, lowering our feet with deliberate caution and minimising the tap and scratch of our boots on the steel steps. The lack of dust and dirt, or decay of any sort felt unnatural, but this was a sealed globe with minimal human presence.

As we rounded the steps halfway, a bang echoed through the building, so close that we both flinched. Then a strange noise permeated the silence – a muffled cry.

The woman struggled against her bonds. They were loosening slowly, although the deep welts on her wrists were excruciating as she fought against the coarse tethers that bound her. She looked over at the girls. They were asleep, filthy, their dresses shredded from weeks of wearing them. The stench in the room was impossible to describe. They had a toilet, but could only use it twice a day, so inevitably accidents happened, and their captors took no interest in their condition.

All three of them were malnourished, their lips cracked and dry from lack of hydration, eyes black from sleep deprivation, despite the exhaustion that swept over them.

Emily no longer cried for her husband. She'd overheard them talking about the explosion at Echo, and she knew he was dead. She'd stifled her sobs for days after, hiding her fear and indescribable loss from the girls, but she never gave up hope. Initially, she had assumed that they would be killed. What use were they now that Brian was dead? But the days turned to weeks, and they continued to be fed and watered, with no other communication at all.

She continued to work at the ropes, twisting her wrists this way and that, the blood dripping to her fingers and soaking her palms, gritting her teeth through the sharp pain where the rough fibres had ruined her porcelain skin.

She had no concept of time, except to note that they'd been fed in the last hour, and it would be another twelve hours before they came back to check on their prisoners. Every day, after feeding, she would work on the binds. She'd learned to hold her hands in a certain way behind her back as they tied her up, forcing the ropes apart fractionally, giving her some slack to manipulate.

Some days she came close, but always too near to feeding time, and any sign that she'd been attempting to escape would lessen their chances of finally fleeing their prison. And so she was patient, working her hands back and forth, rolling her wrists, desperately attempting to break loose.

Other days the man would attend to her, and he'd tie the bonds with brutal force, cutting into her wrists for twelve hours until she could no longer feel her fingers. The pins and needles would make her cry out as they loosened them for her to use the toilet or to feed herself and the girls.

The girls would cry if he came near her, and he'd leer at them, causing them to recoil. She'd whisper soft platitudes to calm them, and try not to break as she saw their eyes well up, wide and fearful, their dirty, matted hair plastered to their faces as they bit back the cries that were so desperate to escape their dry lips. They were so brave, and her heart burst for them.

She clung to hope with every fibre of her being.

Someone would find them. Eventually.

———

The man watched as she exited the mag-lift, dressed in her white BRMC fatigues. He always knew the day would come when they'd get close, but it was too early. They would have to switch to the secondary location today before internal security compromised them. He watched as she walked arrogantly down the streets, without caution. Foolish woman.

He'd have to think quickly. If she stumbled upon the safe house, she would have to be dealt with decisively. It gave him no pause to take the life of a nihilist. They were as disposable to him as the woman and her children, but at least the latter would later serve a purpose. This infidel would be the undoing of them, if left to meander aimlessly through their chosen base of operations.

———

Laura walked between doorways, peering inside, listening, nudging ever closer to the discovery of her career. Not that such things were important in these dark times. She loathed the thought of being second-fiddle to Amanda, especially where Jaxon was involved. That woman made her blood boil. She continued on, plotting the inevitable confrontation when the other two arrived. They'd be pissed off, no question.

She knew she was abandoning caution, but it hadn't occurred to her that there'd be any actual threat down here. If she'd known what was waiting in the next building, she'd have turned and run.

We crept up the steps slowly. The muffled cries were still audible, but getting weaker. I looked at Amanda and could see from her face she was thinking the same thing. She nodded and stepped up on to the landing.

There were two doors, fairly basic, opposite each other on the first-floor landing. They'd numbered the doors, with bio-pads on the walls beside them. It was difficult to tell where the sounds were coming from, but a cursory glance at the two bio-pads showed a thin layer of dust covering the one to our left. There were signs of recent contact on the right side.

Amanda leaned into me, putting her lips just millimetres from my ear.

"We need to go in hard. The faster we enter, the longer it will take them to react. I want you to scream and shout as we go through that door. That will disorient them and cause confusion and fear."

No shit. I was bricking it. I nodded.

"Your only job is to put down the first person you encounter, friend or foe. Strike first, ask questions later. Use your momentum to get them off balance, and then keep hitting them until they stop moving. If you can get your hands on a weapon, do it. I don't give a fuck if you have to batter them with a toaster. You grab whatever you can and you make every hit count. Got it?"

Jesus. I was seeing just how highly trained Amanda was. There was a ruthlessness about her tone that made me shudder. I nodded again, but with no confidence. Amanda must have sensed this as she leaned in once more, her voice so low that I could barely make out the words.

"Jaxon, this is crucial. The way you enter a fight determines the outcome. We don't know what's waiting for us behind that door. If it's friendlies, then there's no threat and we'll scare the shit out of them, maybe hurt them, but something tells me it isn't, otherwise why would they shack up in an abandoned town? If it's hostiles, our only chance is to put them down before they even know we're inside. You need to look angry and scary, and give them pause. Okay?"

I took a deep breath and looked into her eyes. Her face had hardened and there was a savagery about her expression. I was fucking glad she was on my side, to be honest. I gave her the thumbs up, and we crept over to the door.

Amanda lifted her Proxy and rotated it so the orange end was pointing forward. They were an effective, non-lethal weapon, sending out a pulse that would render anyone in its path inert. There was an EM shield which could deploy from the other end, but Amanda wouldn't concern herself with that unless we found ourselves cornered and under fire.

She held her fist up, which I took to mean 'hold' and then counted down from three with her fingers. As she got to two, she waved her bio-band across the pad, which emitted a soft tone and turned green. As it lit up, she crashed through the door.

I shouted at the top of my voice and charged in after her, trying to take in the scene and looking for any signs of human life or hostility, but within three metres she'd pulled up short. I collided with her, shunting her further into the room, and then gasping as her balance shifted and I saw beyond her.

In the corner was a gagged woman, blood pooling around her body, small sounds coming from her mouth, her eyes wide with fear. Amanda's brain kicked in far more quickly than mine, and she turned and ran through the apartment, Proxy held out in front of her, checking each room before returning.

I couldn't move. My feet felt glued to the floor. The eyes

of the woman were pleading with me, and it was a full ten seconds before I realised who I was looking at. *Laura.*

I rushed to her side, gently pulling the tape from her mouth, kneeling in the ever-expanding pool of blood. Her eyes rolled into her head, and her breathing became shallow and laboured. I could hear Amanda talking in the background momentarily, and then she was there.

Laura was in a shit state. They'd slashed her wrists and bound them. She was limp and soaked in claret red. Deep gashes in her forearms and wrists were leaking blood at a rate of knots. I vaguely heard my name being called, whilst trying to stem the flow of blood.

"JAXON!"

I looked up at Amanda.

"We need to get her out of here and to a medical facility. I've called it in, but they won't get here in time. There's a hospital on the floor above. We need to carry her, and quickly."

"We need to stop this blood flowing. If we take her like this, she won't make it." I pulled down my fatigues and ripped off my tee-shirt, tearing it into strips. Amanda did the same with hers, and we took a wrist each and tried to bind them tightly to stem the flow. It took us a couple of minutes to do all we could. By this point, Laura's breathing was very weak, and her eyes were closed. Her entire body was limp.

I hauled her up onto my shoulder in a fireman's carry, and sprinted for the stairs, careful to keep her head away from the door frame and walls. Laura was light, but her being limp worried me greatly and made her much harder to carry. I charged down the stairs as quickly as I could, and piled through the entrance door into the deserted streets, my legs protesting as I ran for The Loop station.

Amanda raced off ahead of me, reaching the mag-lifts by The Loop about fifty metres before I got there, where she kept the doors open and waiting. I was barely inside when the doors closed and the lift ascended. It seemed to take forever as it blew past the platforms to the level above.

As we exited the lifts, there was an ambulance of sorts waiting for us at the entrance, and two medics quickly took her from me and strapped her onto a gurney. They didn't hang about. They loaded her on board quickly and set off. I watched as they disappeared down the street. The world seemed to cave in on me and I lay back, looking up at the dome above with my hands on my head, shaking; whether from the exertion, adrenaline or the emotional struggle of seeing Laura covered in blood, I couldn't be sure.

My eyes were stinging and I could hear voices, distant and muffled. I tried to block out the mental image of Laura, but it kept swimming into view, knocking the wind out of me with each emergence.

I felt powerful hands on my shoulders, lifting me into a sitting position. I looked up and saw Amanda kneeling next to me, her eyes full of fear, and I knew what she was thinking.

They know.

CHAPTER
SIX

THE NEXT FORTY-FIVE minutes might as well have been a week, for all I remember of it. Amanda had helped me onto a transport, surrounded by strangers, all decked out in green scrubs, who were saying things I couldn't focus on. We'd arrived at the hospital shortly after the medics had taken Laura.

I was bare-chested, my fatigues soaked in blood, particularly around my knees and shins where I'd been kneeling next to Laura. We couldn't enter the primary facility without going through a Decontamination Portal and they refused to allow us given the state we were in. We had no choice but to sit in the lobby while the doctors did their thing. One of the hospital staff handed a shirt to Amanda, who'd arrived with her fatigues tied around her waist, her bra and torso glistening with Laura's blood.

We sat and waited for any news of her condition.

And then it came.

Laura was dead.

Her blood loss was too much for her tiny body to cope with, and she'd likely died whilst I was carrying her. I was numb. I could just about feel Amanda's arms around me and her head on my shoulder.

Hennessey arrived, just minutes after the doctors broke the news. Seeing her face lit a fire in my belly that I couldn't explain. All I knew was that she was supposed to be leading this investigation, but she'd done nothing in the last five weeks, and now Laura had lost her life.

I could hear myself shouting as my anger boiled over and I pointed my fingers at Hennessey's chest and let rip at full volume. Of course, I was being unreasonable; I knew that, but I didn't care. Laura's death was someone's fault, and as the deputy team leader, it fell on her shoulders. Truth be damned.

Amanda pulled me away from Hennessey's stunned and hurt face as I bellowed at her in retreat. She hauled at me, gripping me in those powerful arms of hers and dragged me out of the building.

I felt helpless and exhaustion was creeping over me. Amanda guided me slowly back to the mag-lift, and we descended to the floor below the abandoned town.

"Jaxon?" Her voice was gentle and full of concern. I looked up, surprised to find myself in the hangar below where my I'd docked the Sigma.

I shook my head, trying to clear the fog that clouded my mind, and everything came back into focus. The soft reverberations of the station rotating and the shadows arcing across the bay floor. The warm air on my face from the breeze generated by the atmospheric systems.

"Can you fly?"

Honestly, I wasn't sure, but I couldn't stay there. "Yes."

"Okay, good. Let's get back to our globe and get you into a shower. Grealish wants to meet us all in the morning, and you need to sleep."

We took off shortly afterward, and an uneventful seventeen minutes later we landed in Bay 4 of Globe 11. Amanda said nothing on the return flight, but I could feel her gaze upon me as my hands shifted the controls automatically.

The Bay pressurised, and we climbed down from the cockpit. I had no recollection of the flight at all. It felt like I'd just arrived here, as if magically teleported from the bowels of Globe 9. As we walked across the bay floor, Libby rounded the corner with her ground controls, ready to wheel my Sigma into the main hangar.

"Jaxon? What the fuck happened to you?" Her eyes searched mine and then across to Amanda, concern and anxiety all over her face. I couldn't speak, and even if I could, what would I say?

Amanda bailed me out. "Laura's dead, Lib. I need to get Jaxon home."

"What?" I could see Libby's face break at the news and her eyes brimmed with tears as she searched our faces for a contradictory statement. I couldn't bear to look at her and see the distress and sadness that was so mirrored by my insides. I felt the breath being squeezed out of my chest and my eyes stinging again as the reality of the last couple of hours crashed home.

We walked away, leaving Libby stricken in the Bay. She didn't deserve to have that news without explanation, but I didn't have it in me to talk, and Amanda seemed focussed on making sure I could walk straight.

The minutes blurred together until eventually we stepped out of the mag lift and down the hall to my apartment. Amanda followed me in and fussed about me, ushering me into the bathroom and taking my blood-soaked fatigues from me. The last thing I remember was the low hum of the EM glass as it darkened.

I woke at 5.40am. I don't know what time I went to bed, and initially I couldn't quite recall why I felt so shitty. Then the reality of yesterday's events crashed over me. My mind was racing with the questions that I couldn't find in the moments where Laura's life hung in the balance.

I pushed myself up, trying to clear my head and as I opened my eyes, I realised I wasn't alone. Amanda was fast asleep on the sofa, wearing one of my flight suits. I couldn't believe she'd stayed with me all night, and my affection for her grew at that moment. I'd had very little to do with Amanda back in Compression. She was a cool character who played her cards close to her chest, and in the early days I could have sworn that she was an AoG infiltrator. It wasn't until later that we discovered she was an ICP plant, and a senior one at that. Then, I actually had a reason to talk to her.

She'd had a hard time of it in Echo, with the immense responsibility of counter-terrorism weighing her down, and some heavy scrutiny from the investigations team, and it wasn't until she'd eventually nailed Eloise as the spy that she relaxed a little. Even then, I'd still had only brief contact with her, but she'd proven her worth yesterday and demonstrated her unique skill set, and then shown great compassion to me when she had every right to be equally distraught.

Laura and Amanda had never quite seen eye to eye – both being ICP, and both recruited to hunt the same target, unbeknownst to each other, but we were all on the same team and we would look out for each other regardless of personal differences. To find her here, asleep, after everything we'd been through yesterday made me appreciate a side of her I hadn't experienced.

I strolled over to the coffee machine and prepped it for a pot when Amanda's voice made me jump.

"How are you feeling?"

Turning, I looked at Amanda, her blonde hair scrunched in all different directions from sleeping on the sofa, and her eyes blinking rapidly to clear the night's fog. I honestly didn't know how I was feeling, so I settled for a shrug and poured us both a coffee. I was about to offer Amanda milk and sugar when she beat me to it. "Just as it is, thanks, Jax."

I handed her a mug and hit the control panel for the windows, letting the dawn light permeate the darkness. Not that the dawn light on this vessel was any different from the light any other time of the day, but the EM glass simulated it pretty accurately and it bathed us in a dappled orange glow.

I pulled up a chair at the small dining table, and Amanda joined me.

"Thanks for staying."

"I couldn't very well leave you. Not after you tore Sara a new arsehole and then barely put one foot in front of the other on the way home."

I didn't know what to say. I'd behaved appallingly, and I knew it, but I couldn't have cared less at the moment. My brain was still waking up and steadily gathering speed as the neurons fired and the night's events replayed in my mind.

"What was she doing there?"

"I don't know, Jax. And I'm sorry, I really am. I know you two were close."

"Thanks, Mand." She seemed concerned about me when I looked into her eyes. "I'm just struggling to understand it all. I mean, she was at the meeting, and then next time I saw her..." My voice trailed off as I relived the painful moments in the abandoned town.

"Jax, I get it. I don't know why she was there, or how she got there. I was expecting a fight when we entered that apartment. Well, maybe not a fight, but some sort of resistance."

"You were amazing. I just froze, not knowing what to do at all." My eyes were stinging and my throat thickening as I spoke. I felt so fucking helpless.

"Hey, come on, Jax. There was nothing to be done. She was gone, well before we made it to the ambulance. Quicker thinking wouldn't have saved her. I know it's awful and I know it must devastate you, but you can't start blaming yourself. You didn't do that to her." She reached across the table and lay her hand on mine.

She was right, of course, and it was her words that planted a seed in me so deep that I would forever remember this moment. I needed to find her killers. Anger welled up in me in a way I hadn't previously experienced. I could feel the blood coursing through my veins just as vividly as I remembered it draining from Laura's body.

"Don't think you're going to do this alone, Jaxon," said Amanda, reading my thoughts. "Now, more than ever, we need the entire team to pull together and find the bastards that did this."

"I'm angry, Amanda. Regardless of what Laura and I might have been to each other, she was a decent person and didn't deserve this."

"Laura was an ICP investigator, and she knew what she was signing up for. She knew the risks. She didn't deserve it, you're right, but that girl knew what we were fighting and what they were capable of."

"This all stems back to me seeing Mark. If I hadn't seen him—"

"—we'd be no further down the line of finding these people. I think you were hard on Sara last night, but I can't say I disagreed. We've been here five weeks, with just the one lead, and she's allowed him to roam freely, with no scrutiny, and given that he's our only route to the AoG, she should have been all over him like a rash."

"We need to go back to that globe and look around.

Laura didn't kill herself, so the people we are looking for have been using that town as a base of operations. How else would she have ended up bleeding out in an abandoned tenement?"

The more we talked, the more my adrenaline flowed. My mind was waking up, and the questions were building.

"I agree, but it can wait. We need to meet with Grealish and Cooper this morning. They'll have already cordoned the level off, and they'll have investigators crawling all over the place. We're both going to be called in for debrief at the Hub, and I wouldn't discount Admiralty or the Station Council getting involved. This is a murder, in a space station. It's never happened before."

"Yes, it has. They took Brian Latimer's wife and daughters, remember? Why would they still be alive now that Brian is dead?" I couldn't imagine a single reason they'd be allowed to live.

"I've told you before. Hostages always have currency, Jaxon. You can't just write them off. These people are master manipulators, and they know that we'll do everything to keep a hostage alive. They will leverage that if they have to."

"So, why? Why did they kill Laura?" I could feel my throat thicken again, and my voice trembled.

Amanda's expression softened, and her brow furrowed. "You know why." Her voice was so low it was barely audible.

I nodded as my eyes stung. *She saw something.*

CHAPTER
SEVEN

TWO HOURS later Amanda and I entered the Hub in the central command globe and made our way up to the briefing rooms. It was my first time in the Hub, and the moment I stepped off the mag-lift, I could feel myself almost floating. The gravity here was only thirty-eight percent of normal gravity, so it was actually quite challenging to walk normally.

As the lift doors opened, a positive cacophony of noise swept over us. They had adorned the entire central command with wall-to-wall holloscreens and hundreds of personnel were bustling around. It looked like a scaled-up version of SECO 2, except for the additional headcount and the million screens. The outer hull of this level was EM glass, but unlike the view from most globes, the sides were unimpeded by other parts of the station, so the views either side were spectacular, with the Earth dominating one side and the depths of space on the other.

The floor we were standing on was approximately twenty-five percent up the globe wall and curved all the way over in a loop like a giant hamster wheel, so you could walk until you ended up back where you started. As I looked up, I could see people floating between vast arrays of holloscreens and other equipment, a couple of clicks above us, in the zero gravity at the centre of the Hub. Beyond them were more people walking around on the ceiling and on the walls. It was a total mind-fuck.

"Major? Lieutenant?"

Both Amanda and I turned to find a young BRMC officer holding a hollotab and looking inquisitively at us. "You are Major Barclay and Lieutenant Leith?" she enquired, her eyes darting between us hopefully.

"Yes, Corporal," replied Amanda. I just nodded.

"Come with me please, Ma'am, Sir." She turned and half-walked-half-bounced through to an office which was entirely ordinary, given the surroundings. I was expecting to see familiar faces as, I suspect, was Amanda, but inside were five people, all sitting on one side of a table with a couple of chairs on the other side positioned, it seemed, for an interrogation.

I'd been through something similar just six weeks ago, when Brian Latimer's bomb ripped through the Opps centre at Compression Echo.

"Ah, Barclay and Leith. Take a seat, please," said a round-faced man in the middle of the group of five. He looked to be in his late forties, with dark, tidy hair and the beginnings of grey in his well-groomed goatee.

We obliged, and the five of them looked us over for a full minute before anyone spoke.

"You've had a busy twenty-four hours," said the man, powering up his hollotab. The others remained impassive.

"Was that a question?" replied Amanda, with just enough of an edge to her voice to let them know she wasn't someone to be toyed with.

"No, Major Barclay. It wasn't." He took a deep breath and laid his hollotab on the table in front of him, before bringing his hands together and leaning forward onto his forearms.

"Last night, BRMC Officer, Staff Sergeant Laura Watkins, sadly lost her life. We are here to discuss with you the circumstances of her demise and your involvement. You were both there, were you not? And from what little information we have, Sergeant Watkins was alive when you found her?"

I was about to speak when Amanda gave me a nudge in the ribs and a tiny shake of the head. "I'm afraid we can't comment about such matters until Command have debriefed us, Sir." Amanda's response was emphatic without being confrontational.

"We are here to debrief you, Major Barclay. That is the point of this meeting."

"With all due respect, Sir, neither of us have anything to say until we've been through the debrief with our unit commander."

One of the women in the group protested, but Amanda just cut her off.

"Standard protocol following a serious incident or a firefight is a twenty-four-hour cooling-off period before the presiding authority can question us."

"Quite right too!" We both turned as Colonel Grealish entered the room, with Cooper at his shoulder. "Amanda, Jaxon." Grealish nodded to us as he walked to the table front.

"Andrew, we are quite within our rights to debrief these officers following an incident of this nature," the man in the middle spoke again.

"And debrief you shall, but these officers have been through an unimaginably tough ordeal in the last fifteen hours, and because of the nature of their roles within the military complex, they have entitlement to twenty-four-hours grace before submitting their reports, either written or verbal, to a government committee. Or have you forgotten the procedures, Damian?" His eyes flashed challengingly at the men and women staring at him from behind the table.

"Not forgotten, no, Andrew. But we feel that the sooner we question these officers, whilst their memories are still fresh, the better it will be for all concerned." He opened his hands as if his arguments were beyond reason.

"Laura Watkins is dead, Damian, and the manner of her death is entirely unambiguous. She will still be dead in nine hours, and the cause will remain unchanged. And I think it is very unlikely that either of these outstanding officers will ever forget what they've just witnessed. So, you will desist with this line of questioning and submit a request to my office for future access to either of my colleagues sat here. Understood?" Grealish nodded curtly at them, and without waiting for an answer, he gesticulated to us to follow him and strode purposefully back through the door.

The pair of us stood and followed without looking back. Grealish continued to walk through the hustle and bustle of the Hub, and turned out of the main doors towards a mag-lift labelled '5', Cooper close on his heels.

He glanced around and ushered us into the lift, and as we descended I could feel the gravity increasing. The lift stopped on level 4 of Globe 5, and without saying a word, Grealish marched over to The Loop station, with the three of us in close pursuit.

"Sir, what's going—"

"Not here, Amanda. I'll explain shortly."

We boarded a train heading clockwise, and four minutes later exited in Globe 6, before travelling in a mag-lift down to the barn.

As we approached the front door, it swung open and Hennessey appeared in the half light, clearly waiting for us to arrive. I could feel my blood pressure increasing with every forward step, but I knew that if I continued to rant and rave at her it would be unproductive, and I'd probably get kicked from the investigation.

I stepped inside the building, avoiding eye contact with Hennessey, and blinked as my eyes adjusted to the dim light. The globe outside was brightly lit, but it was positively dingy in here. As I followed the crowd to the far corner, Harris stepped out of the gloom and pulled me into a bear hug.

"I'm sorry, mate," was all he said as he released me. I didn't know how to respond, so I just nodded and tried to bite back the lump forming in my throat again.

Grealish ushered us over to a conference table set up in the corner. There were six chairs around it and another discarded in the corner from our last meeting, and as we each took one and sat, the empty chair was like a sonic boom in a library. I could feel everyone's eyes drawn to it and back to me.

Grealish looked up. "There will be a celebration of life this evening at Alpha Centauri in Globe 11. I will expect you all to attend." He turned to me and his expression softened. "Jaxon, I am very sorry. I have invited your crew this evening and I think they'd all like to see you and Amanda."

"I don't feel like celebrating, Sir."

"This is what we do, Jaxon. Trust me, it'll help. Laura was an exemplary officer and deserves a send-off from her crew and her friends."

"She didn't deserve to die." I was struggling to hold back, and I could feel the tears stinging my eyes again.

Grealish sighed heavily. "No, I don't suppose she did." He lifted his head and looked at each of us. "I'm sorry that we have to do this now, but this is precisely why we have the liberty of twenty-four hours between incident and report. I know how difficult this is, particularly for you,

Jaxon, and Amanda, but we need to get our stories straight before we sit in front of that committee."

"What do you mean, get our stories straight? There's only one version of events here."

Cooper chose this moment to chime in. Her tone was not her usual business-like manner. "Jaxon, we are on the inside of a covert investigation into terrorism. The committee and the general council don't even know of the existence of this operation, which is why we've just left the Hub on a mag-lift to another Globe. This incident cannot connect the dots for them. We don't know if they're compromised, but we assume that all positions of power on this vessel are."

"I thought they had assembled us specifically for this investigation. You're saying that the council is unaware?" There was more going on here than I'd realised.

"Admiralty sanctioned this operation after being petitioned by ICP Command. The council knows we are a special division, but our activities are highly classified, as are the personnel involved."

"Jaxon," Grealish interjected, "we have a limited amount of time here before the council can call you and Amanda to account. We need to talk about what happened on that level, and then we need to talk about how we're going to present it."

"What's wrong with the truth? I don't see how it compromises anything."

"You're going to be debriefed by a civilian authority. We cannot tell them about the AoG, or their intentions for the demise of this vessel, or that they've already built and smuggled a bomb from this station to Earth. We cannot trust these people to keep this information secret, and it'll spread like wildfire through the population. And that will create panic."

Cooper now. "And panic will seriously debilitate us in

our investigation. At the moment, we can move around unchallenged and unmonitored. If the station steps up internal security, it'll make our jobs so much harder."

"It'll also make things harder for the AoG," said Amanda.

"That's true, but for all we know, they're locked down in their base of operations, already prepared. If they've already made one bomb, they've been here for a long time," replied Cooper.

A stark silence followed this statement, and each of us looked around at the others.

"We're wasting time," said Harris. "Let's crack on. Jax, I know this won't be easy, but it has to come out eventually, and better to get through it now and give yourself a chance to…" His words tailed off at the end.

"Move on?" I said, looking directly at him.

"I didn't mean it like that, mate. But I know what it's like to lose someone close to you, and this is the best way to get past it." He clapped his hand on to my shoulder and I nodded.

"Amanda, what happened down there?" asked Grealish.

Amanda explained about our journey back to 11 on The Loop and our subsequent excursion to Globe 9 in my Sigma, at which point Hennessey spoke for the first time.

"Why didn't you just get off The Loop at Globe 9?"

Amanda rolled her eyes. "Because advertising our presence seemed like a terrible idea. We didn't know what we'd be walking in to, and coming in the front door totally unprepared is highlighted somewhere in the Rules of Engagement under the subheading 'never do this'."

I almost smiled, but the memory of Laura was still pervasive in my mind, and it was clawing away at my sanity.

Amanda continued with an accurate account of the

events and even had the decency to withhold the fact that I'd left my Proxy in my apartment. She spoke clearly, without embellishing, but paused as we got to the part where we'd found Laura. I could feel her eyes on me, and the occasional glance from everyone else.

Unable to avoid it any longer, I shrugged and finished the debrief. "Amanda was brilliant. Completely in control at all times, and the moment we found Laura, I froze, and she had the presence of mind to clear the rest of the apartment before calling it in. There was just so much blood..." I could feel the tone of my voice pleading with them to understand, "... and it was impossible to stop. I hauled Laura onto my shoulder, but I can't remember if she was even still breathing. You know the rest."

I could feel Harris's hand grip my shoulder for a second time. "How did she end up in there?" I looked up at Grealish and Cooper. They exchanged glances.

"Well, that's the money question, isn't it?" replied Grealish. "We tracked her bio-band as soon as we heard the news. In fact, we tracked everyone in this room" (there was a shuffling of bums on seats at this news) "and Laura got on the same Loop as the two of you."

Amanda and I sat upright, but before we could say anything, Cooper spoke. "I take it from your reaction that neither of you saw her?" We both shook our heads.

"It's not surprising. Her bio-locator shows her at the far end of the carriages. It also shows her waiting until the doors begin to close before boarding. Prior to that, she was standing in the passage to the mag-lifts. She had an elevated heart rate. All indications were that she was following you and didn't want to be seen by you."

"That can't be true, Sir. Why would she...?"

"Jaxon, I'm just telling you what the data suggests, but you can see for yourself. Here's the footage from The Loop. Amy?"

Cooper tapped her hollotab and her screen projected upwards into the centre of the table. The footage was crystal clear. We watched as The Loop pulled in to the station and Amanda and I boarded at the far end. Then, unmistakably, just as the doors were closing, Laura darted out from a passage below the camera and swiftly took a seat with her back to the exit. There were a few people already on board, but no others that boarded from this station.

"She got off at Globe 9. That's when the bio-feeds separate, and the pair of you continue on to 11."

"But it must have been another hour before we arrived. She was there that whole time? Why?" I was so confused.

"She was properly annoyed with the two of you taking the lead on this," answered Cooper, her face reddening as she said it.

I held my head in my hands. "For fuck's sake, Laura."

Grealish spoke. "Actually, it was another hour and fifteen minutes before you and Amanda showed up. Laura's bio-feed shows her walking around, looking into buildings briefly. Then, eighteen minutes after entering the level, she put a call through to Sara, but it disconnected after only a few words, then her heart rate goes through the roof for a whole minute, and it appears she walks erratically back and forth before suddenly dropping. Then, her heart rate slows right down."

Cooper pressed something on her hollotab, and Laura's voice filled the room. "Sara, I'm on level 4 of Globe 9. There's something not right..." There was a scratching and knocking sound, and then the recording ended.

Grealish continued, "It looks like she was abducted or grabbed at the first marker before her heart rate speeds up, and then a minute later, she's inert. She then travels slowly through the tenements, to the adjacent street and into the building where you found her, and gradually her heart rate increases."

"Her heart was trying to pump the blood faster to get more oxygen to her brain as it leaked out of her wrists. The very thing trying desperately to keep her alive was actually speeding up her demise," said Amanda.

"That's absolutely our assessment also, and that of the M.E. They didn't cut a major artery, or she'd have succumbed inside fifteen minutes – in fact, according to the M.E., it was skilled work," replied Grealish.

"So what now?" I needed to get away from this subject.

"Well, the forensics team and investigators have been in already, and thoroughly covered the scene. There's nothing we could do about that – it's standard protocol for a big incident or loss of life. However, what they haven't done is investigate the buildings that Laura was looking through before being taken. Watching the bio-feed, our assailant likely emerges from the last doorway she enters."

I stood up. "Well, why aren't we already over there? Why are we sat here talking about it?" I could feel my temper rising again, always so close to the surface.

Amanda reached out for my arm. "Sit down, Jax. We can't go yet. They'll probably have posted security on the entrances to the level," both Grealish and Cooper nodded, "and reactivated the security systems and cameras, so we can't get inside without being spotted."

"But what if they're still there? Surely we can't risk losing them?"

"Jax, they aren't still there. They clinically and methodically tied Laura up and left her to bleed out. Anyone with that level of training made sure they weren't still around for the aftermath. With the security systems back on, and a heavy BRMC presence, they'd be hemmed in. They deliberately took her to another location to kill her, which suggests that they didn't want anyone looking too closely at the building they were occupying, so we absolutely will go back, but we just need to time it right." Amanda breathed out heavily.

"And neither of you are going anywhere until you're debriefed by the council. I've no doubt royally pissed them off, so we need to play by the rules here if we're to avoid scrutiny, which is why we need to get your story straight…"

CHAPTER
EIGHT

THE WOMAN HAD HAD *to hurry. She was alone, and now that things had gone sideways decisions needed to be made. She'd left her struggling against her bonds and smiled.*

"The more you fight it, the quicker you'll bleed out. So keep fighting, Laura," she'd said, a decade of anger welling up inside her. "Nobody is coming for you. Consider this retribution for Eloise."

She'd left the stricken woman and descended the stairs to the street, where she'd crossed to the next building, through a corridor to the back and exited into the adjacent street. Her blood-soaked clothes had clung to her, and she knew she'd been careless, but there was no time to worry about that. She knew, eventually, they would come for the woman, and she'd needed to get out before they did.

The woman walked diagonally across the street to another plain tenement building, entered through the entrance marked 'D' and climbed the stairs to the third floor. She'd glanced upwards as she reached the landing.

He'd stood there, a question on his face.

"I took care of it," she said.

He nodded. "We will have to leave the woman and children. It is unfortunate, but not unexpected."

They would not survive long in their condition, without food or water, and he was confident that they'd remain undiscovered – not that it would matter, anyway. There were a thousand identical buildings on this level, and it would take weeks to search them all.

"We need to take care of this," he gestured to the apartment on his right, "and then you should clean yourself up and go back."

She merely nodded, wiping the blood from her hands on to her fatigues.

They entered the apartment and packed up the equipment into large holdalls, careful to keep the det cords away from the batteries and explosives. The man knew that any explosion in this glass monstrosity would likely cause an unparalleled loss of life, and cripple the station's departure, but in order to achieve this, he needed to target specific locations, thus an abundance of caution when handling the materials.

He allowed himself a moment of reflection on the glory of their mission, before swiftly grabbing the bags, pushing his accomplice out of the apartment door and leaving without a backward glance.

We spent another hour talking through our story, trying to tie off any loose ends that may lead to compromising questions.

"Okay, take us through it again. Jaxon, you start," said Cooper.

I took a deep breath. "We were almost back to my apartment in Globe 11 as normal, when Sara received a call from Laura in Globe 9, that was cut off suddenly. Sara contacted us and, unable to raise Laura on comms, Amanda and I took a Sigma over to Globe 9, as this was quicker than walking back to The Loop and waiting for it to arrive. The orbital debris delayed our approach. We attempted to raise Laura throughout the flight, but to no avail."

Amanda stepped in. "Upon arrival on level 4 of Globe 9, we heard a sound in a building behind us and tracked it back to the apartment where we found Laura. Everything else, just the way it happened."

Grealish nodded. "I've already started planting the seeds that Laura was looking at transferring to Globe 9, and was just there to check it out." It was a pretty believable cover, given that our movements were all completely accurate. It was only the circumstances and motivations that we'd adapted.

Amy was manually amending the release order for my Sigma to a time more indicative of the cover story. The consensus was that they'd be unlikely to check it, but it made sense to tidy it up.

Grealish received the requisition order for us three hours later, and Amanda and I traipsed up to The Hub for the second time, where they conducted the debrief with the same people as before. Despite concerns that they'd dig deeper than we'd like, because of the confrontation this morning it was over inside an hour, and there was no sign that any of them were unconvinced. One or two of them even thanked us for our service and offered their condolences for Laura's passing.

Amanda was still hovering around me. She seemed reluctant to leave me on my own, and honestly, I was grateful for her company. We finished up in the interview room and stepped out into the Hub.

"Shall we do a circuit?" Amanda asked, displaying her uncanny knack of reading my mind.

"Sure," I replied, and we started the long walk around the hamster wheel. It was a strange sensation. The Hub was so large that the curvature of the floor area underfoot wasn't immediately apparent. It was only as you looked up and followed it to the horizon that it curled up in a graceful arc, getting narrower and narrower, until it began widening again, and stretched around behind us back to where we stood.

"Jax, check it out."

I looked up. "Woah… that's so weird!"

We watched as technicians from the area around us would head to a simple pole that stretched from the centre of this section to another at the opposite side of the Hub, like a spoke in a wheel. One or two used the steps at the bottom of the pole to begin their ascent, but most just took a run-up, leapt off the bottom step, grabbed the pole and hauled themselves skyward, their speed increasing as the gravity decreased. Being at only thirty-eight percent of normal gravity made us feel a bit like we were walking in slow motion, but it was incredible to see people ascending into the weightless area in the centre.

As we watched, several other people slid down the pole, dismounted and walked to various terminals in the proximity. In the central core of the Hub was a huge framework dominated by a circular wall of holloscreens and servers above that entirely obscured our view of the far side of the hamster wheel. It looked like the pole was primarily a conduit between Hub sections, and sure enough, now that I looked, there were several other poles splintering off at the middle.

The pair of us stood fascinated for a minute or two and then continued our stroll around the hamster wheel.

"We've got to get back in that Globe, Mand." It was bothering me how little we could do, given the situation.

"I know, Jax. I've been thinking about it all day. There's only one reason that makes any sense to murder Laura – she stumbled upon something whilst she was poking around. She activated comms, and they heard her. There's no other explanation."

"So why aren't the investigators looking around?"

Amanda shrugged. "Because they don't know what we know about Brian Latimer's family and the bomb. They're assuming that what she saw is the person who killed her."

"That's too easy. They should search the entire level."

"I agree. If these people had been hiding in a building, the very best case for them would be for Laura to have just walked past, but clearly she didn't." She looked serious. "The events of last night have drawn attention, both to them and also to the whole of level 4 in Globe 9."

"The real question is: what did she see? We've got two lines of concern at the moment—" She held up two fingers, and counted them off, "—Emily Latimer and her daughters, and a bomb-making factory. We know they built a bomb and smuggled it to Echo – that's indisputable, and we know they kidnapped Brian Latimer's family in order to manipulate him."

"How long after they killed Laura did we turn up?" I'd lost all track of time.

Amanda stopped in her tracks and sighed. "I checked the data. She was inert eighteen minutes after arriving, and six minutes later left to die in that room. Fifty-one minutes before we arrived. Nobody came or went while we were there except us, according to bio-scans, but as we've already seen these people seem to operate off-the-grid, so there's no way to track them."

I could feel my heart pounding. "Okay, so, let's assume that whoever killed her spent another couple of minutes tying her up and checking everything before going back to their hideout – it must have been close, so probably only another couple of minutes and with nobody else in the vicinity they wouldn't have worried about being seen or heard, right?"

"So we're down to forty-seven minutes."

"Except it must be much lower than that. You and I took at least two minutes to get to the mag-lift, sprinting. And that's with Laura's body. They've either got three bodies, or bags of equipment, or both."

"Fine, forty-five. Where are you going with this, Jaxon?"

"We need to think about what we'd do in their shoes. Let's assume that they have either Brian's family or a bomb-making factory, or both on that level. They'd need time to get out and relocate, right?"

"Yes, but then cutting Laura's wrists makes little sense. They took a tremendous risk that we'd find her, and we did. Surely it would have been better to kill her outright, and make good their escape unimpeded. Nobody knew she was there."

I corrected her. "Sara knew, the moment the call came in, and presumably told Grealish and Cooper immediately. But the perpetrator couldn't have known she was operating alone. What if they assumed we had assigned her to investigate the level, and that her disappearance wouldn't go unnoticed? I mean, she was there in full uniform, and they heard her activate comms to call it in as she was methodically scoping the buildings down the street."

"So they're expecting more of us to arrive and investigate her going missing? That's a stretch, Jax. The call was cut off. Hennessey tried to raise her again, but couldn't get her."

"So she says. We've only got her word on that."

"Come on, Jaxon. That's so unlikely."

"Is it? Because the best way for them to get some breathing room to move would be to leave Laura alive, but in critical condition, and ensure that our first response is to get her to safety, leaving the level free. We find her dead, and we stay until the investigators arrive." My brain had kicked into gear and was running through all scenarios at a hundred miles-per-hour.

"So you're suggesting they were still there when we arrived?"

"I'll go one further, Mand. I think they saw us arrive and lured us to Laura. She was in no condition to make any noises."

"Okay, let's assume that's true. Opps deployed a team as soon as I called it in. They were there within twenty minutes. That doesn't leave a lot of time to get out, especially unseen and with three hostages and bomb-making equipment."

"I agree, but they'd had forty-nine minutes before we arrived to get their shit together, plus we must have been there for fifteen minutes before we found Laura."

Amanda scratched her head. "And a further twenty before the Opps team arrived. That's an hour and twenty-five minutes, give or take, to get packed up and leave. Realistically, they'd need to be out ten minutes before that to safely exit without the risk of coming into contact with the Opps team."

"And there's no way they managed that with three bodies in tow. A couple of bags of equipment would be easy, but not with hostages."

"If they're even alive, Jaxon."

"You said it yourself. They'd want the leverage in case they got caught."

There was a pause as we both contemplated the situation.

Amanda broke the silence. "I said that, but that was before they killed Laura. If you're right, they wouldn't have left them behind."

"Unless they didn't have time to get them out. For all we know, there were twenty of them, but why risk moving the hostages at all? They have bigger plans – we know that, so maybe they just cut their losses and left."

"Then they're dead. They wouldn't leave them alive in case they're found and able to talk."

That knocked the wind out of me. Amanda was right; it made no sense to keep them alive. "We have to check, Mand. If they were in that much of a hurry, they may not have had time. If I were them, I wouldn't keep the hostages in the same apartment as the bomb stuff. Especially when they're not exactly limited by options."

"Jaxon, we can't go in. You heard Grealish – we're flying under the radar here."

"Fuck Grealish. These animals killed Laura. And there are people's lives at stake here. The council knows Brian Latimer's family is missing already. They just don't know why. If we find them alive, we'll get them secured via Grealish. If they're dead, we won't call it in. We'll just leave them for now and brief the team at the earliest."

"Jaxon..."

"Amanda, I'm going. You can either help, or you can let me go."

She sighed and put her hands on her hips. "For fuck's sake. You'll trip over your own feet if you go alone. Come on."

It was getting late, and Grealish was wondering where Jaxon and Amanda were. Everyone else had arrived, and whilst the mood was sombre the drinks were flowing, as was the conversation. They'd been there for an hour – the crew from Echo 41 – even Mark Hanson had turned up.

"Andrew?"

The appearance of Amy Cooper at his side brought him

out of his reverie. "Amy, sorry, I was just thinking about things."

"Like Jaxon and Amanda not being here?"

He nodded. "I'm pretty disappointed in them both, to be honest. Nobody enjoys coming to these, but this is a tradition we've observed for centuries. Laura deserves a proper warm-down."

"I think Jax has taken this pretty hard. I spoke to Amanda earlier, and she's worried about him. If she's not here, it's because she's making sure Jax is okay. I think you need to say something, though. It's gone nine."

"You're right, of course. I'm sure they'll have their reasons." He turned to face the room and held his glass up. "Listen up!"

There was a shuffling of feet, and the volume dropped to almost a whisper, as one by one they turned to face the colonel. Libby, Aoife, Jennifer, Mark, Tyrone, Sara and Amy all held their glasses out.

"Laura was a great asset to this crew, and we will sorely miss her. What happened to her will not go unpunished, nor will we forget her services to the Intercontinental Police and the Marine Corps. She was an outstanding colleague and a good friend. To Laura." He raised his glass to a chorus of "Laura" and then drained it in one go.

"Alright, that's enough of that. We're not Americans."

CHAPTER
NINE

WE STEPPED off The Loop at Globe 9 and immediately encountered a check point that prevented us from entering Level 4. The entrance protected by a pair of marines, with weapons I'd never seen before slung over their shoulders and held menacingly at the waist.

"I'm sorry, Ma'am. This is a restricted area. We can't let you through without approval," said the officer on the left. He didn't sound sorry.

"Sergeant, Lieutenant Leith and I were the ones who found Sergeant Watkins alive, so you'll let us through or you can have a personal tour of her hospital room." He looked like he was about to protest when she brushed him to the side and walked through unchallenged. I shrugged apologetically and followed her.

"Amanda, do we want to upset these people?" I looked behind me and saw the sergeant speaking into his comms. "He's already calling it in. They won't let us anywhere near that apartment."

She stopped and turned to face me. "This was your idea, Jax. Have you any idea of the bollocking that's facing us for not going to Laura's warm-down? Or for disobeying a direct order? Now, we're either doing this or we're not. Which is it?"

"Okay, sorry. It'll be easier to get access if we're nice to them, though." I'd totally forgotten about the warm-down, and now I felt really shit. I'd rather be busy. Every time I stopped for a minute, I thought of Laura. The effect was paralysing.

She turned and continued to walk. "We don't need access. We've been in that room already. What we need to do is check the surrounding buildings."

She was right, of course. The investigating team had cordoned off the immediate vicinity, but they'd ignored apartments opposite and in the adjacent streets. We continued to walk for a minute, before Amanda turned us into a street.

"Mand – this isn't the street. It's the next one over."

"Which is why I'm walking down this one, Jax. We can access the buildings from both sides, so it makes more sense to enter from this side where we can roam freely, without scrutiny. Plus, this was the street Laura was walking down when she ran into trouble."

It hadn't even occurred to me that we might be on the very street where she was abducted. Amanda's brain operated on a different level to most people. She just had a thought process that stored intangibles and minute details. Or perhaps I just wasn't thinking straight. Likely.

She'd had training of a depth that I couldn't yet contemplate. Having watched her operate on the evening of Laura's death, I had nothing but absolute respect for her capabilities. She was a formidable character, and I could see why she'd elected to work undercover in a high-pressure environment. She seemed totally unfazed by it all, instead focussing her attention on the task at hand. I, conversely, was an emotional wreck and the closer we got to the location of Laura's murder, the larger the lump in my throat.

We walked on for a couple of minutes before Amanda pulled up and turned in a full circle.

"This is it. Block E on our left is directly opposite the tenement where we found Laura. Let's take a look."

I followed her into the building through the back door. She stopped as we reached the front and cracked open the door an inch. They'd cordoned off the floodlit tenement opposite, but there was minimal activity outside. A couple of marines were standing around, weapons at their hips, and I could see lights and movement inside the building.

Amanda closed the door slowly and silently.

"Let's sweep through this block quickly and see what we find."

"What are you expecting?" I asked.

"In here? Nothing. Too close to the murder scene, but we're here and so was the killer, so let's eliminate it before we search further afield." She turned and headed for the stairs, talking to me over her shoulder as we went up. "We'll start at the top and clear every apartment. Shouldn't take more than a minute for each one, unless we find something."

"How are we getting inside?" I'd been meaning to ask that ever since we found Laura.

"Admiralty programmed my bio-band to a separate access code that opens every unoccupied residential, commercial or agricultural door on the station. But it flags up at the Hub, so I can't abuse it. Grealish signed it off. Sara has the same access while we're part of this investigation."

We arrived on the top floor, Amanda looking like it was a Sunday stroll, and me with sweat beads forming on my brow and a familiar ache working up my thighs and back. The conditioning regime in Compression had been brutal, but very effective, and my fitness had improved exponentially, but since the explosion almost all of my workouts had been physio based after the medics fixed my legs and back, so the lack of cardio was showing.

She swiped the first bio-pad and moved slowly inside, stepping lightly and carefully in to each room, before exiting and making for the apartment opposite. This pattern continued to the ground floor, each apartment being empty and, frankly, quite ghostly. The lack of habitation had left the interiors feeling cold and neglected.

"There's nothing here, so where next?" I asked. Zero point me taking the lead.

"I'm thinking." She swept her blonde hair back with both hands as the gentle breeze from the atmospheric generators was blowing it around in this empty shell of a building. "Laura's bio-band shows her moving in the street we've just walked down, so it's likely she saw something there. I don't think it was the end block. I think it was middle, or middle-end, so 'C' or 'D'. Let's start with 'D' because it's closest, and work backwards."

I nodded, and we moved towards the back door we'd entered through. Amanda stopped suddenly and for the second time in twenty-four hours, I ploughed into her from behind. And not in a good way.

"Jax, look…" She pointed at the door release mechanism on the wall. There was blood smeared across it and on the door handle.

"You think that's…?" The sight of Laura's blood sucked all the oxygen from the room.

"I don't know, but it seems probable, given the state that we found Laura in. Touch nothing." She pulled out her Proxy, and pulled down the sleeves of her fatigues, covering her hands. She carefully nudged the release button with the orange end of the Proxy, using her sleeve-covered hand, so as not to activate the immobiliser pulse, and at the low bell-like tone she gingerly gripped the handle with her cloth-covered fingers and hauled the door open far enough so that I could reach past her and grab the frame, swinging the door completely open.

We crossed the short path on to the street and turned left towards The Loop, but stopped after fifty metres. "Look at the path, Jax." There were signs of disturbances on the polished metal walkway—just the occasional scuff, but compared to the rest of the buildings, it was like painting a giant red cross on the door. I could feel my heart beating in my chest.

"What's the plan?" Part of me wanted to just run inside immediately, but given my proclivity for uselessness, and my current emotional fragility, it was best for all concerned if Amanda continued to call the shots.

"Same as before, but there's a different level of risk here, Jaxon."

"Like what? I thought we'd agreed that they'd used Laura to get themselves out?"

She turned to face me, and her expression was grim. There was a tautness around her eyes that belied an underlying stress that I hadn't seen before. "Yes, but we also agreed that we may find one of two things: Brian Latimer's family or a bomb lab. If it's the first, they're likely to be in a shit state, and seeing dead kids isn't something you want to remember. If it's the second, there's a chance they booby-trapped the room."

"How do we know they haven't booby-trapped the room with Emily and the girls inside?"

"Unlikely." She shook her head earnestly. "If they've been keeping them alive, they'll need constant access. And that's a big 'if'. If they didn't have time to get them out, they didn't have time to booby-trap it."

I shuddered. As awful as it was to think about the worse-case scenario, we needed to get on with it. "There are lives at stake here. If we don't take the risk, who will?" I could feel a lump form in my throat again. "If we'd just got to Laura more quickly, we may have saved her."

She looked like she was going to say something, opening her mouth twice and then holding back. In the end, she just glanced at me with something akin to pity, shrugged and headed for the door.

As we approached the entrance, we could see more blood on the door handle. Amanda pulled her sleeves down again, swiped her bio-band and yanked the door open. "Okay, I have a plan. There's blood on the last two doors we've opened. Given the state Laura was in when we found her, the killer was probably drenched in her blood when he came back here."

"He?" I raised my eyebrows.

"Or she," Amanda conceded. "So, before we do anything else, let's check all the other internal doors, including the back, to see if there's blood there. You start down here, I'll start at the top and I'll meet you halfway."

I nodded and walked down the short corridor to the back. The handle was clean, as was the release, so I turned and checked the lower apartments. I continued up and around the stairs, carefully checking each handle from all angles for signs of blood.

A minute later, I arrived on the third floor, just as Amanda was walking down from the fourth.

"Anything?" she asked, eyebrows raised.

"Nothing at all. They're all clean."

"Not all of them. Follow me." She walked across the third-floor landing and pointed at the door to our right. There was a thick smear of blood across the handle, and handprints on the doorjamb.

"So, what's the assumption? This one first, right?"

Amanda shook her head and rolled her eyes at me. "I thought we'd concluded that they'd prioritise the bomb lab above the hostages? If that's true, then that door leads to the bomb lab. Our priority is the Latimer family, so we're going to try each door, one at a time, and clear the apartments as before, okay?"

"Okay. So, where do you want to start?"

"We start at the top, and work our way down, like we did across the street." She turned and took the steps two at a time, with me close behind. As we got to the top floor, Amanda headed for the furthest apartment and pulled out her Proxy, with the blue-end deployed. I followed her lead and extracted mine, which I'd re-clipped to my kit belt this morning.

Amanda swiped her bio-band and slowly opened the door an inch. She was half-way through checking the gaps for wires or traps when the smell hit us. Amanda retched where she stood whilst holding the door ajar. I was heaving and holding the wall to steady myself.

The stench was foul. It was a combination of human decay, faeces and urine, and blood. There was a metallic taste to the air, and a sickening odour of rotten eggs and cabbages mixed with shit, piss and god-only knows what else. Instinctively I brought my hand up to my nose to cover it with my sleeve, and nearly zapped myself with the Proxy. Bellend.

It was the single worst smell I'd ever experienced, and as we both doubled over, fighting the nausea that washed through our stomachs, we exchanged looks. It was plain as day that Amanda and I were thinking the same thing: *they're dead*.

I was on my knees when a new sensation swept over me – a whispering sound. I wiped my face and put my hand on Amanda's shoulder, holding my finger to my lips, which was difficult considering how hard I was trying not to vomit. Amanda froze, doubled over, her hand clutching her stomach as she dry-heaved in the doorway. We listened closely to the muffled sounds coming from inside. There was a thump, and a scratchy whisper, barely audible above our own laboured breathing and churning guts.

Amanda pushed herself up from my shoulder, then hauled me up after her and pushed the door fully open. The intensity of the stink increased tenfold, and both of us gagged. Amanda was sick somewhere between the door and the bathroom on the left. I barely made it through the first door before I divested my stomach of its contents.

We wiped our mouths and held our sleeves over our faces and our Proxys out in front of us as we entered the apartment. It was almost completely dark in here. They had activated the EM glass for night-time, with just a faint blue glow from the darkened windows. Amanda swiped her band over the control panel and slowly raised the slider for the EM glass to forty percent.

Gradually, the light increased as we entered the living room. There was an assortment of mis-matched furnishings in here – a holloscreen, a utilitarian-looking sofa and some upturned buckets which looked like they'd served as stools at some point. Amanda pressed on, occasionally leaning over as she fought against the stench that was causing her body to twitch with every step.

A door to our left was closed, and as we approached, more sounds permeated the stink of decay that absorbed us, drawing us into a quagmire of death and despair. Amanda grabbed the handle and pushed the door open quickly, stepping across the threshold. She held her Proxy firmly in front of her and gasped as her legs gave way. Instinctively, I grabbed Amanda as she dropped, catching her under the arms and lowering her as slowly as I could until she was sitting on the floor in what looked like months of filth and detritus.

They had tied the woman to the wall, almost naked except for a tiny cloth laid over her midriff. The remains of her clothes strewn haphazardly around and underneath her. Then my body almost gave way at the sight of the two girls, tied to each other on a dilapidated cot, their dresses ripped and soiled, and clinging to their almost skeletal frames.

Adrenaline coursed through my veins, and I heaved Amanda up with all my strength, despite my protesting back and legs. Her eyes were rolling in her head, and her throat was making guttural, sickening sounds. As tough and professional as she was, clearly this scene had rocked her to her core. I shook her gently at first, and then harder, gripping her face and calling to her.

"Amanda! Amanda! I need you now. AMANDA!"

This last cry shook open her eyes, and I watched as they came back into focus, and took in the surrounding devastation. Then, before I could say anything more, I heard a voice, so weak it was almost indiscernible from the sounds of the atmospheric generators.

"The girls. Help the girls."

I looked down at the thin, wasted body of Emily Latimer, her eyes now open and pleading with me. I nodded once and turned back to Amanda. "Mand, I need you to call it in. We need medics on site this time—we cannot move them all. Get the marines by the crime scene over here now, to guard the door with the blood on it. Okay?"

She shook her head to clear it of her temporary delirium and then brought her arm up to activate comms. I went straight to the girls and untied them. They were so weak that I thought they were dead, but the feel of my hands around them brought them both out of their morbid slumber. As they moved, a waft of putrefaction hit me, almost causing me to recoil, but the adrenaline kept me focussed and alert and working feverishly to free them from their cruel bondage.

Amanda's voice broke the sounds of me cutting through

the ties. "Jaxon, medics are on their way. So are Grealish, Cooper and Harris. I can't get comms with the on-site BRMC, so I'll have to run over there."

"No. Get some water for these three and help me get them comfortable and clean first."

I continued to free the girls while Amanda busied herself with cleaning and filling the few cups and glasses left in the kitchen with water. She passed a cup to me as I gently lifted one twin from her sister, the pair of them instinctively reaching out for each other, unwilling to be parted even in freedom. I almost cried right there and then, but a small voice in my head told me to be strong for them. Right now, they were terrified and they needed reassurance.

The girl weighed almost nothing, her frame tiny and shrivelled in my arms. Slowly and gently, I walked her through to the lounge and lowered her onto the sofa, as grim as it was, still a thousand times cleaner than the cot.

She whimpered and cried as I put her down, tears barely forming in her beautiful eyes, weeks and weeks of urine and faeces sticking to her legs, mixed with dried blood from the scores of scabs and grazes that littered her tiny body. I put a cup of water into her filthy hands and smiled at her through my own tears.

"Drink this little one. I'm going to bring in your sister, okay? Help is coming. Be brave for me, just a little longer." I could hear my voice breaking as she nodded at me, unable to speak for the dryness in her throat.

I left her there, and ran back to her sister, who was trying to push herself up. I could hear Amanda talking to Emily Latimer – just soft platitudes and reassurances. As I approached the other twin, she held her hands out for me and my heart almost burst. She was so ready to trust some-one, anyone, who wasn't her captor or torturer, that she'd asked to be held by a complete stranger.

I lifted her petite body, her thin arms around my neck, her head laid on my shoulder and carried her round to the lounge, sitting her gently beside her twin. She immediately put her arms around her sister until I handed her a cup of water to drink, which she took with both hands and warily sipped through her cracked and dried lips.

I tried to brush the jet-black hair away from their dirty faces, but it was pointless. The grime and filth of this prison caked their bodies, their little feet blackened and dead looking, the skin peeling from sores. Both were blinking as their eyes grew accustomed to the dappled light from the EM glass, which indicated they'd been in the dark for quite some time.

Amanda walked in as I was whispering to the girls, reassuring them they were safe now, and that mummy was safe too.

"Jaxon..." She nodded her head towards the door. I gave a quick smile to the girls and then followed her into the hallway. The smell was still stinging the back of my nose and throat, but the adrenaline had stopped the retching as I caught up with Amanda.

"What's up?"

"She's in a shit state. I can't move her. Her skin has fused with the fabric underneath her and as I tried to lift her, I could see it tearing, so we'll have to wait for the medics. I've untied her hands, but her feet are going to need medics to cut the rope off. The bastards tied them so tightly that her feet are blue and swollen from the lack of circulation. I need you to keep your shit together and look after them while I get the marines from the crime scene. We need to protect the area; all the blood on the doors and the room downstairs is a no-go to anyone except those of us on the inside of Operation Echo. Got it?"

A tiny quiver underpinned the steeliness in her voice.

She was clearly trying to bring her emotional state under control.

"We did good, Mand. You did good. We saved three lives today." I brought her into a hug, which seemed to knock the breath out of her, before clapping her on the shoulder. "Go. I've got this." I turned and walked back into the room. It was impossible to ignore the odour, but after everything this family had been through, the very least I could do would be to keep my emotions in check.

I just saw Amanda's feet disappearing out of the door when a little voice broke the silence. "Can we see our daddy now?"

CHAPTER
TEN

"THEY'VE BEEN DISCOVERED."

"You said you would prevent that from happening. Are you losing your resolve?"

"No. But these particular infidels took matters into their own hands. I was unaware of the breach until after it occurred."

The man sighed and leaned back in his chair. It was fortunate that they had escaped without detection, given the sudden shifting of circumstances. The Watkins woman nosing around on level 4 had unnecessarily impacted their time-line. But what was done could not be undone, and he reflected again on the fortune that enabled their escape and relocation. Fortunate indeed.

"It will be difficult to neutralise them, but I could," came the voice through the comms.

"If you had done your job, we wouldn't be talking about this. No, leave them. They know nothing that can affect our plan."

"They may have seen your face, and mine. We were not always so cautious."

"That is unfortunate, but this is an enormous station, and I only move under cover of darkness. Hopefully, your cover is enough to deflect attention."

"Even so, it would be unwise to venture out in the foreseeable future."

"Unwise?" The man raised his eyebrows. "Perhaps. What is unwise is for you to test my patience further."

"Yes, Sir. I am sorry. I will be better."

He clicked off the comms, irritated at the pointless interruption, and turned his attention back to the detonators.

I was sitting on the sofa with the girls when the medical team arrived. I watched as they retched and threw up at the stench of decay that met them at the door. These people had robust constitutions – after all, this was their job, saving lives and putting bodies back together – but the scene inside was distressing on an inconceivable level.

I left the sofa and approached the medics. "I need you to pull yourselves together. This family has been through unimaginable pain." They both nodded. "The mother is in the far room. Her name is Emily. She's not in a good way. See to her first. I've got the girls."

The pair of them stepped past me just as four more medics arrived. I gave the same pep talk to them, in between retches and ushered them through to the living room.

"Girls, these people are medics. Do you know what that is?" They both looked directly at me, wide blue eyes glued to mine, and shook their heads.

"Do you know what a nurse is?" I asked gently, and they both nodded. "Well, these people are nurses, but they've come out of the hospital to see you, okay? They're going to help you and get you to the hospital."

I stood up and stepped back, and the medics swarmed around the girls, their faces scrunched up to the stench, trying hard not to show it. I watched as they busied themselves, treating the sores and wounds that covered their little bodies, the girls barely whimpering, despite their appalling condition. They cut away the filthy dresses and wrapped them both tightly in clean blankets.

One of the medics approached. "We can't do anything more for them here. They need cleaning up before we can properly treat their wounds. We have transport outside."

"Wait until their mother is ready to go with them. They need to stay together. You have no idea what they've been through."

The medic looked like he was about to protest, but perhaps something in my eyes told him this wasn't the moment, so he nodded, and joined his fellows as they hooked up IVs to get fluids in to the girls.

It was another twenty minutes before the other medics were ready to move Emily Latimer, and they brought evacuation chairs up for the three of them. The girls whimpered and cried as the medics carried them away from me, and I ran to the stairs to speak to them.

"Little ones, I will see you soon, I promise. The nurses need to help Mummy now, and you want them to help her, don't you?" They both nodded and looked at me with bright, sad eyes. "Be brave. These are nice people and they will clean you and Mummy up, and while they do that, you two can look after each other, okay?" They nodded again, and I smiled at them and gestured to the medics who continued the descent downstairs.

As they rounded the turn on the stairs, Grealish and Cooper arrived, their faces screwed up, clearly shocked at the condition of Emily Latimer and her daughters. I watched them walk towards me and then sat down against a wall at the top of the stairs. I could feel the adrenaline wearing off and the energy sapping from my body.

Cooper knelt down beside me as Grealish walked to the apartment door.

"Sir, don't go in there." He reached the doorway and recoiled as the stench engulfed him. "You don't want to see it, Sir, and Amanda says we need to preserve the scene. There's already been six medics, plus myself and Amanda in there."

Cooper spoke. "How did you find them, Jaxon?" There was an edge of motherly concern to her voice, and I wondered if I didn't look as bad as I felt.

"Something didn't feel right, Amy. Amanda and I were talking it through at the Hub, after our debrief, and there was just something eating away at us both." I looked at Grealish and added, "Sorry about Laura's warm-down, Sir, but I don't think they'd have survived much longer in there."

Grealish crouched on his haunches and looked at me. "Seems to me a lot of people owe their lives to you and Amanda, Jaxon, and not for the first time. Let's get you back and cleaned up, and we can go through it all tomorrow. It's getting late."

"No, Sir. We need to clear the building. There's blood on the door handle of apartment 5 below. We think it's the bomb lab."

"Good lord! You haven't checked the other apartments yet?"

"No, Sir. This was the first one we looked in."

At that moment, Amanda returned flanked by two marines, both with weapons at their hips. I could hear her barking orders from two landings below. "Nobody in or out of this door without my approval, understood? Regardless of rank, they are not to enter. We expect to find explosives in there, and the door is likely booby-trapped, so this is not an arbitrary request. Got it?"

A minute later, she appeared at the top of the stairs. "Sir. Amy," she nodded at Grealish and Cooper.

Grealish spoke. "Jaxon tells me you haven't cleared the

building yet?"

"No, Sir. We found them in the first apartment we looked in. Have you been inside?"

"Err, no. Jaxon advised us against it. Said you wanted the scene preserved."

"Yes, Sir. It's not pretty in there. If you don't need to see it, I'd advise against it too. We have a more immediate concern, anyway. The apartment two floors down is likely to be the bomb lab. We need to clear that tonight, before we allow an investigations team in here."

Cooper stood up. "Tell me what you need and we'll make it happen, Ma'am."

"I don't need anything except the building cleared and everyone moved back. Jaxon and I can handle it."

Grealish protested. "Amanda, I don't think you or Jaxon are in any condition to—"

"It's okay, Sir. I'm okay. Amanda's right, we need to do it now. We'll clear the rest of the building first. It won't take us long." I pushed myself up off the floor and gave myself a mental slap to wake my brain up. "Shall we?"

Amanda nodded. "Sir, I've stationed marines on the third floor. Leave them there. We'll clear them out once we've cleared the other apartments."

And so we did. Grealish and Cooper left the building and Amanda and I worked our way down, ignoring the third floor completely until we had checked every apartment for occupants or evidence. None of them showed any signs of previous occupancy.

We climbed wearily back to the floor with the suspected bomb lab, and Amanda walked straight to Apartment 8, which we cleared as before, and returned to the landing.

She addressed the marines. "I need you two to clear the building and wait outside. Nobody in until we make it safe, understood?"

"Ma'am."

"You ready for this, Jax?"

"As ready as I'll ever be. Let's get it over with," I replied, secretly wondering why this responsibility had fallen on us. I must have had a look on my face, as Amanda spoke.

"It'll be okay."

Amanda turned back to the apartment entrance and swiped her bio-band over the pad, pushing the door until it opened just enough to poke a finger through. She withdrew a pocketknife from her kit-belt and poked the blade through the gap slowly, looking for any hidden wires or cables between the door and the frame. Satisfied that there were none, she pushed the door another ten centimetres and followed the process again. She continued in this manner until the door was seventy-five percent open.

She looked up at me and nodded, before lying on the floor and pushing herself into the room slowly, checking each tile before lowering her weight onto it, until her head could see behind the door. She checked it over before pushing the door inward and standing up.

I was fretting a little. Just watching Amanda work emphasised the seriousness of the situation. "Mand, why is this our job? Surely they have experts for this stuff?"

"I *am* an expert in explosives, Jax. And I don't want anyone else clearing this room. We've got a security breach on the station, and, honestly, right now, you're the only person I trust."

"What do you mean, security breach?"

She sighed and leaned against the wall. "Both of the doors were locked. The one with Emily and the girls, and this one. Station command hasn't activated bio-bands for accommodation down here yet. I need to check the logs to be certain, but the council abandoned this level, or at least placed it on hold whilst it lacks the prescribed head count to populate it."

"So?"

"So someone has global access – it's the only way to get inside – and as far as I know, they have granted access to only two people on this station. Myself and Sara Hennessey."

"You don't think…?"

"I don't know what to think, Jax, but this team hasn't done its job since we've been here, and the more I think about it, the more it bothers me."

"I was just shooting my mouth off last night, Amanda, you know that."

"I don't think so, Jax. You were emotional and exhausted. I think your response was instinctual, and justified, and so far, your instincts have been pretty much bang-on. Maybe she's not involved. Maybe she's just incompetent, or just plain unlucky, but however we examine at it everything that's happened has been far easier because of her inaction or negligence. You lost a close friend last night, and despite our differences, so did I. Laura was important to you, and to the team. Are you willing to put your life in Hennessey's hands? Or anyone else's?"

I thought about that for a minute. I didn't really know what to feel or say about Hennessey, but every time I heard her name, I got an angry knot in my stomach that made me want to scream and shout all over again.

"Sara was at Echo when they abducted Emily. And when they constructed the bomb."

"Yes, but this isn't her first time here, and she was also at Echo when the bomb arrived. Someone is pulling the strings here, and maybe I'm focussing in the wrong place, but Grealish expressly ordered us not to come back to this globe, and yet here we are, with three hostages and a bomb lab. Does that seem like a coincidence to you, Jaxon?"

"Maybe? We wouldn't even know about Brian Latimer's family if I hadn't seen him writing a note. That was a coincidence. I don't know, Mand. I'm not quite ready yet to condemn the few people I'm acquainted with on this station."

She smiled, but it didn't extend to her eyes. Clearly, she thought I was being naïve. "Come on. Now's not the time. Let's clear this apartment. Stay behind me."

Proxy deployed and in front of her, Amanda edged slowly into the room, crouching every metre or so, she explained, to check for wires or pressure pads. She continued like this until she came to the main living area. From over her shoulder I could see boxes strewn around, and remnants of plates of food and drinks bottles. There was a distinct odour of plastic and vinyl, and Amanda sniffed once and said "RDX," then, seeing the confused look on my face, she clarified, "It's a form of plastic explosive. Crude and old-fashioned, but effective none-the-less," before turning back to the room.

Not really knowing what I was looking for, I stood back and watched as Amanda moved around in deliberate circles, occasionally crouching to check something, before continuing the pattern throughout the room. She was careful about moving furniture and larger items, meticulously checking each one before shifting them gently this way and that. She retrieved a short length of wire, which she handed to me without comment, and proceeded through the rest of the apartment.

Satisfied that there was nothing further to be seen, she looked up and said, "Okay, let's get out of here. I'll take that." I handed over the wire.

"What is it?"

"Detonation cord. They were definitely here, but they've taken everything that matters with them. Time to let the investigators in. We'll let them sift through everything and catalogue it, and then we can check it out later. We've done enough for one day."

We walked downstairs, my muscles aching and burning after the day's activities, and opened the front door. The two marines had stationed themselves at the end of the metal pathway, and there was a small crowd lurking beyond them, including Grealish, Cooper, Hennessey and Harris.

Amanda nodded to the two marines and thanked them as we passed through.

"It's all clear, Sir. We found this," she said, holding up the length of det cord and Grealish sighed.

"Well, that's confirmed that then. Nothing else?"

"Not really, Sir. There are loads of boxes and stacks of paper, but we didn't touch them. The investigators will find blood on the door handle of apartment 5, and also on the front and back entry doors of Block E in Row 14, just down the way."

"Both of you have done a sterling job today. Amy and I will take over from here and sort out the investigators. It's getting late. Get yourselves home. Debrief, 10.00am tomorrow."

We turned away and walked towards The Loop, exhaustion washing over me with each step. Amanda scrunched her face in concentration and she moved robotically, clearly deep in thought. We were silent for most of the journey back, and as The Loop pulled into the BRMC accommodation level 11-A, she grabbed me and gave me a hug, then stepped off the train.

I watched her walk away as the doors closed and turned my thoughts back to Emily Latimer and the twins. We would visit them in the hospital tomorrow. I felt responsible, somehow, for everything that had happened to them and to Laura, and as I stepped off The Loop at the next station in the dim glow of the streetlights, I wondered if any of us would ever be safe again.

CHAPTER
ELEVEN

THE GIRLS WERE DEAD, and their abused and broken bodies discarded like rag-dolls in a dark room. I was wading through the filth of centuries to reach them, and sinking as I walked, feeling myself being pulled under. The station was spinning too fast, the gravity was already at two-hundred percent and increasing at an alarming rate. My bones felt heavy as I tried desperately to claw my way to the skeletal remains of the six-year-old twins, until I was chest deep in stinking slime, panic gripping me as I fought against my incarceration. I was about to go under when the twins, skin falling from their faces, eyes white in their sockets, arms and fingers broken and savagely angled, were by my face, inches away, as the abyss swallowed me. The last thing I heard as my head became engulfed by blood and faeces was *"Can we see our daddy now?"*

I sat bolt upright, soaked in sweat and panting heavily, the exertion of my hysteria causing my heart to beat out of my chest. Twice more during the night I had had to force myself awake to rid my mind of those images.

I'd showered when I got home last night, trying desperately to wash the stench of decay from my body, but I could still smell it. It was lingering under my nose, close enough to pervade my thoughts, but far enough away that I couldn't wash it from my exhausted form.

I looked at my bio-band – 03.18. There was simply no point trying to go back to sleep. My mind wouldn't let me. I wanted desperately to visit Emily and the girls in hospital, to see if they were okay, knowing that their scars were more than physical, but it was far too early and besides, the doctors would surely have them heavily sedated. I'd seen them in that state for over an hour, and I couldn't sleep a wink. They'd been like that for weeks, so I imagined their exhaustion exceeded anything I'd ever experienced.

I hauled myself out of bed, still naked from the shower last night and dragged myself back to the bathroom to scrub the smell away again. I soaked under the steamy water for ten minutes, letting the heat reinvigorate me for the day ahead. As I was stepping out of the shower, a pulse sounded from the front door.

I wrapped a towel around my waist and walked to the door, checking my bio-band. It was still only 03.40. I tapped the inset screen by the door, and an image of Amanda Barclay appeared. She looked as tired as I felt.

I opened the door for her. "Mand?"

She took in my appearance and said, "I couldn't sleep either, Jax."

I stepped aside to let her in, and she walked through to the kitchen and put a pot of coffee on.

"How did you know I'd be awake?" I asked.

"Because I'm awake," she replied simply and then, looking back at me over her shoulder, "Still trying to get rid of the smell?"

I nodded as I grabbed some fresh underwear and a flight suit from my wardrobe, and wandered through to the bathroom to dry off and change. A minute later, I came back into the main living space to find Amanda sat at the small dining table, with two coffees in front of her.

"Jax, I know you're not in the best head-space right now, but you and I are going to have to do this alone," she said, as I took the seat opposite her. I just raised my eyebrows. "I don't know what's going on here, but I simply don't trust the command structure."

"Mand, aren't you being a bit paranoid? Grealish dragged us both into this investigation. Why would he do that if he was involved somehow?"

"I wasn't dragged into this investigation, Jaxon. I was already deep cover, investigating the same thing. There's a difference. But for arguments' sake, I'll concede that I don't think Grealish is on the wrong side of this. I just think he's incapable of seeing if the team or the investigation is compromised. Every action he takes is outward looking, yet there are things happening here which could only have occurred as a result of an internal breach."

I had to admit, some of the things I'd learned since joining Compression didn't sit well with me.

Amanda continued. "The AoG kidnapped Emily Latimer and the girls. They only needed access to their apartment, or a good enough reason for Emily to open the door during the hours of darkness—"

"Wait, how do you know it was dark?"

"Because they kidnapped and transported the Latimers to another globe from a military residential area. Brian was BRMC, so their apartment was near mine, in 11-5-A. From 06.00 until 23.00, the place is like a hive, and it barely slows down under cover of darkness. To pull off something like this would have required careful planning – a faked emergency, or a credible threat, or something of that nature is the only way they'd have left that apartment at night. To do this during daylight would risk too many witnesses."

"So their captors must have looked the part in military uniforms," I said, grasping Amanda's train of thought.

She nodded. "Or their captors were legitimately military, but working for the AoG. It's also very possible that they were known to the Latimer family. It would certainly make it easier to convince them to leave. They'd have had to use a vehicle too. Military AethervoX would be my guess. No way they were walking them out. And that's not all..." She continued to count off her fingers. "They smuggled a bomb onto the shuttle – that requires special access to the cargo bay and the manifest, not to mention a way round the cargo scanners, both here and at Echo. They have a bio-band or access card that opens doors to which they shouldn't have access, including residences and the BRMC armoury where, I assume, they obtained RDX and det cord and god knows what else."

"Hang on. There're explosives stored on this station?"

"Explosives, ammunition, heavy weapons... everything you would expect to find on a military base."

"For what purpose? Surely, bringing explosives onto a spinning snow-globe in space is a terrible idea?"

"You're missing the point, Jaxon." She seemed tense.

"Okay, what's the point?"

"Everything I've just told you—all of it, without exception, I knew five minutes after Brian Latimer's death. *Five minutes*, Jaxon. That's seven weeks and change since the explosion, and yet the council hasn't amended a single access code. No new protocols implemented. No re-vamped security procedures, or internal investigations. I've checked all the logs. They didn't even mention it in the daily briefs."

"Jesus." I had to hand it to her; everything she said made absolute sense. "So Grealish, Cooper, Hennessey – they all know this?"

"Well, therein lies the problem. Grealish was ICP, but he wasn't an investigator. He went from Officer Training

School straight into counter-intel as an analyst, not a field operative. He processes and acts upon intel that he's provided. Amy is little more than a desk-jockey for Grealish, but Whitehall assigned her to GCHQ straight from the ICP Academy, where she worked her way up to lieutenant. Grealish has been around the block a bit more, but he's never been an investigator. He has no clue which unit I report to or how deeply entrenched it is in counter-intel operations."

"What about Hennessey and Harris?" I was starting to see the bigger picture here, and it scared the shit out of me.

"Sara and Tyrone were both BSA prior to transferring to BRMC. No investigation training."

"BSA?" These acronyms were an absolute mystery to me.

"United Coalition of Britain Space Agency. Bit of a mouthful, so they just call it BSA."

"So why is Hennessey tasked with leading this investigations team if she's got no experience?"

"That's what you and I need to find out. I can't imagine it's Tyrone – not after the bomb, anyway. You were both lucky to survive that."

I was relieved to hear that she'd discounted Tyrone. I just couldn't stomach him being part of this.

"Amy is a bit of a wet lettuce, to be honest. She does what she's told, when she's told, but barely has a thought of her own to contribute."

"She seemed in control back in Compression," I said, thinking back to my first day there and the brief confrontation with Cooper. She was very sure of herself, and I remember being quite intimidated.

"She was on her turf. She'd been there for years. And yet, still only a lieutenant. You're now the same rank as she is, and you've been in the military for what, eleven weeks?"

I hadn't even realised. It was true; I was now a lieutenant, and I had only held the rank for five or six weeks, but I'd just assumed that lieutenant was a higher rank in the ICP.

Amanda clearly saw my brain working overtime. "You have no idea what you are to the establishment, do you, Jax?"

"What do you mean? What establishment?"

"The military intelligence complex. You're the poster boy for the BRAF, and they don't know you're training for counter-intel. I've heard absolute strangers talking about you in the mess halls. Even in the BRMC. Your story is like *Alice in Wonderland* to these people. Don't you get it? A young bloke from The Bleeds gets his ticket punched, and on day one in Compression spots an imposter and reports a missing person, one of which is BRMC and the other is ICP."

"Mand..."

"Jaxon, listen to me. Guys like you are not ten-a-penny. The moment Harris gave you that pat on the back in Training 1, I was genuinely worried you'd figure me out. Your brain works differently to most people."

"I did figure you out, remember?" It seemed so long ago now. "Granted, I got the wrong end of the stick..."

Back in Compression the team was investigating intel that the AoG had infiltrated our crew. Amanda came to our attention when she put some serious moves on Leon, and threatened him. Something about the exchange didn't sit right with me, and I was wary about Amanda thereafter. The problem was, I'd tagged her as a potential infiltrator, when, in fact, she was an undercover operative working the same investigation as us, from a much deeper cover.

Amanda shook her head. "Whatever. The point is, you're a lot more important than you realise. They haven't seen a talent like you walk in from the roughest neighbourhood in London, ever. Nobody has ever won the combat mission, and you aced it. You're switched on, and right now, I need your instincts. Do you know how many people that go through Compression have been assigned to Counter-Intel Branch as an operative?" The question must have been rhetorical, because she didn't wait for an answer. "*One*, Jaxon. *You*. You've got a higher clearance than just about anyone on this station, besides me, Grealish, Admiralty and the actual Counter-Intel Corps, and you've had no training yet. Explain that."

It was a lot to take in. I'd gone from being just another body in the world's largest housing estate, that would never amount to anything, to a counter-intelligence officer and a pilot on a space station and part of an elite investigation unit tasked with the preservation of our species. I could barely comprehend the transition, and it never occurred to me to even think of myself as some sort of commodity to the military.

Amanda spoke again. "Jaxon, I need you. We can't be part of this investigation as it stands. I believe someone is working on the inside to delay us, or send us off in the wrong direction, or that everyone in that team is so incompetent, or untrained, or negligent, that we cannot rely on them to provide credible intel."

"Mand, we can't just go it alone. It's like you said, I've had no training yet. What are we supposed to say to Grealish?"

"Say?" She glared at me. "*Say?* Nothing, Jax. We turn up at meetings, and we listen and we watch. For any sign of subterfuge, procrastination, misleading intel or plain, in-your-face bullshit."

"And if we see or hear any of those things?" Not that I'd know what they looked or sounded like.

"Then we concentrate our efforts on whoever displays those traits."

"And in the meantime, Mark Hanson wanders the

station unchallenged and unobserved? He's still our only lead."

Amanda sighed. "Mark is just a low-level pleb. Whatever is going on with him, he's not the antagonist. From what you saw a couple of nights ago, he wasn't in control of the conversation. Besides, unless we eliminate our own team from this investigation first, any actionable intel that comes from Mark is useless to us. The moment we implement a plan, whoever is on the inside will counter it."

"I don't know, mate. It seems like a massive challenge for two people."

Amanda leaned back and crossed her arms, her eyes narrowing and staring straight through me. "They killed Laura, Jax. Left her to bleed out and die in your arms. They kidnapped and tortured two little girls. Tied them and their mother to broken cots, and left them to rot in their own excrement. Forced their father to detonate a bomb in a crowded Opps Centre, killing two marines, and almost taking you and Tyrone with it. That either pisses you off or it scares you."

"Both."

"Then man the fuck up. Get your shit together and meet me downstairs in five minutes." With that, she drained her coffee, got up and left without a backward glance.

Admiral H. Leigh Willard lowered his enormous frame into the protesting chair behind his antique mahogany desk. It had been a busy week on the station, with multiple incidents causing his mood to deteriorate. The separation protocol was problematic, and there was still a great deal of resistance from the council.

He'd spent the last few days petitioning individual members of the station government to get on board with the separation sequence. It was a difficult manoeuvre and extraordinarily complex to plan and execute safely, but it couldn't wait until it became urgent or necessary. Pressure causes mistakes, and they could not expect the BRN to get it right in dire circumstances without ever having attempted it.

Of course, they'd simulated all possible manoeuvres – the navy had been all over this for decades, but with the orbital transition nearing, they were fast running out of time to test the sequence and reactions of the crew and occupants of each globe whilst still in touching distance of Earth. The largest issue would be gravity, without question. All pools, lakes and bodies of water had sealed hatches that automatically engaged and locked into place should the station stop spinning, but ninety-five percent of occupants had never experienced weightlessness, and hadn't trained for or practiced survival without gravity.

For years, he'd petitioned the BSA to provide weight-lessness training for all occupants during Compression, but time was not on their side. The evacuation could not support his request.

In order to detach, the station would have to stop spin-ning, and seven million occupants would find themselves with less than half their normal gravity, as the SQIID drives fought to provide it artificially. The chances of them ever needing to separate were remote, but bitter experience had trained the admiral to hope for the best and expect the worst.

It wasn't the only thing on his mind. The events of the last two days were rippling through the chains of command. A BRMC officer murdered on the station was a terrible stain on their security, not to mention the abduction and abuse of a mother and her twin daughters. And at the centre of it all was the man from The Bleeds, Jaxon Leith.

He'd met Jaxon twice before – the first time in this office, where the then BRAF trainee showed a distinct lack of respect for the chain of command, or the office of the admiral, and had tested Willard's patience to the extreme. It was only at the second meeting, a few weeks ago in Echo, that the admiral had seen the potential in the young candidate. He was still very green, and without question rough around the edges, but there was a presence about him that made his opinion both credible and actionable.

He had to admit, after reading the eyes-only reports, his early misgivings about Jaxon had proven to be misguided. The young lieutenant was shaping up to be a valuable asset to Grealish's investigations team, despite what little headway they'd made since arriving from Echo.

Which reminded him; he hit the comms button on his desk, and the sergeant seated in the anteroom responded immediately. "Sir?"

Willard barked, his rough, nasal voice booming through the room, rendering the comms system quite unnecessary. "Tom, when is Grealish supposed to be arriving?"

"He's just walked in, Sir. I'll send him through."

Willard grunted a thanks and then looked up expectantly as Grealish gave a brief rap on the door and entered. He closed the door behind him, stepped up to the desk and was about to salute when Willard waved him down. "Sit, sit. Let's dispense with all that nonsense for now."

"Yes, Sir."

Grealish took a seat opposite the admiral and cast his eyes around the room. There were holloscreens across two walls, and a spectacular view of the BRAF accommodation area and the other globes beyond, directly behind the admiral.

"Andrew, it's been an unfortunate week. I was sorry to hear about Sergeant Watkins."

"Thank you, Sir. It's taken the wind out of our sails somewhat."

"Yes, I can see how that might be the case." Willard shifted his bulk in his seat. "I want to take you back to the conversation we had at Echo with your team."

"Sir?"

"You pitched to me that you had one viable lead, and that the reason for allowing him safe passage here was to enable you to keep close tabs on him, hoping he would inadvertently lead us to the other AoG operatives that may or may not be on this station." It wasn't a question, but the admiral let it hang there for a moment, waiting for Grealish to pick up the slack.

"Sir, that's correct. Unfortunately, it hasn't played out like that." Grealish shifted uncomfortably.

"And why not, Andrew? Why hasn't it played out like that?" Willard's gravelly voice was low, but with a hint of something more menacing simmering under the surface. The admiral was notorious for switching between 'amiable' and 'angry' with no warning, something which Jaxon had experienced just a few weeks ago.

"That, Sir, is something I am looking in to now. It should have been our only objective, and yet, it appears, it has been completely overlooked. That being said, it was actually a sighting of Mark Hanson that instigated the search of Level 4 on Globe 9."

"A sighting?" The admiral leaned his vast body forward, winding up for the inevitable explosion that was about to crush the wind out of Colonel Grealish. "A fucking sighting, Andrew? He should have been in your sights the entire fucking time. Not wandering about, flouncing his way into Globe 9 when he has absolutely no fucking business being there."

"Sir..."

"Don't you fucking *Sir* me, Andrew." He was getting in to his stride and Grealish could tell he was about to get both barrels. "This man is the only lead we have in an investigation to identify and neutralise a known terrorist organisation, who, since our meeting at Echo, has detonated explosives that proved to be fatal, in a secure facility on high alert, having smuggled them down from this vessel. Am I fucking missing something here?" His bushy moustache quivered on his face and he flushed red.

"Sir, we took precautions and assigned Hanson to Globe 10, away from the militarised areas where he posed the greatest potential threat to our security."

Willard leaned back in his chair and look down his nose at Grealish. "You have a lot to learn, Andrew." The de-escalation took Grealish by surprise. "Globe 11 is under constant, intense camera surveillance. You could monitor Hanson twenty-four seven, and surround him with military personnel, all of whom, I assume, would take a dim view of a terrorist plot to kill them."

Grealish looked abashed. The admiral was right, of course. He, the head of the most crucial investigation he'd ever overseen, had tasked Hennessey with watching Hanson, and she'd under-delivered biblically, and now he'd have to take it on the chin from the admiral until the old man ran out of breath.

"Sir, you're absolutely right. If it wasn't for Lieutenant Leith seeing Hanson, we'd still be completely in the dark, and Brian Latimer's wife and children would likely be dead. We've dropped the ball here, and I'm already taking steps to correct it."

It was clear from the look on Admiral Willard's face that he was unimpressed and unconvinced.

The admiral picked up a file from a pile on his desk and opened it. "Your report says Leith was responding to comms from Watkins, but no other response teams were alerted or dispatched until Major Barclay called it in? What am I missing here?"

Grealish explained about the cover story to the admiral,

and the need to keep the truth from the council. Willard sat there, occasionally nodding until Grealish had finished.

"That won't mollify them for long, Andrew. It's a decent cover, I'll give you that, but it won't hold up under serious scrutiny. Let's hope for your sake the council forgets about it quickly."

"Yes, Sir."

"I want twice-weekly reports, in person. And I expect you to have made significant progress by the next meeting. And I want the Latimer family moved to the BRAF medical centre in 11-5-C, with armed guards on the door until further notice, and no-non-medical personnel admitted, except those members of your unit involved in this investigation. Today, Andrew."

"Yes, Sir."

"Dismissed."

CHAPTER
TWELVE

WHEN I EXITED THE BUILDING, I found Amanda waiting on a bench, staring out across the globe. It had only just gone 04.00, and the level was silent. I'd never seen it like this since I'd been here, not having an appetite for early morning adventures. I was still aching from the last two days' effort, but every step loosened my muscles a little and the aches throbbed dully at the corners of my senses.

"So, where are we going?" I asked as Amanda, sensing my presence, turned to face me.

She pulled out a hollotab from her kit bag, swiped through a couple of screens, and handed it to me.

"What's this?" I asked, looking through a list of several hundred items. It looked like a cargo manifest, not that I'd ever actually seen one.

"It's the catalogue of items found in the bomb-lab. Scroll down to three-hundred and two."

I swept my forefinger across the holographic screen and watched as the list blurred, tapping it occasionally to see where I'd got to, before finally pulling down to item three-hundred and two. It was a printed delivery label that had clearly come from a box, as the cardboard edges showed where the recipient detached the label, but it was completely illegible. It looked like someone had scratched the writing off.

"What is this?"

"This," said Amanda, taking the hollotab back from me, "is evidence that's been tampered with."

"Tampered with?"

"Yep. When we were in that room, I found a box on the sofa. The label had an address in Lincoln's Inn Fields, Holborn."

"How do you know?"

She rolled her eyes at me. "Because I saw it, Jax. And I remember it because the AoG London HQ is in Lincoln's Inn Fields. We've known that for a couple of years, so when I saw the label, it all tied in."

"Jesus. So, between us going in last night and now, someone has defaced the label, presumably because they don't want anyone in the investigation making the connection?"

"That's my assessment. We need to get back over there to the apartment and properly look at everything."

"Now?"

"You got something better to do?" Clearly, lack of sleep did nothing to enhance Amanda's mood. The air was dripping with sarcasm.

I shrugged, and we started walking towards The Loop. Neither of us were much in the mood for deep conversations, so we spent the better part of the journey in silence. It was only as we got to the station on Globe 9 that Amanda said something.

"We're going to have to go back into apartment 10, Jaxon."

I shrugged. "I figured as much. We should have brought masks."

"I've got that covered," replied Amanda, but without expanding on it.

We approached the guards at The Loop exit. They weren't the same ones as last night, but they waved us through with no exchange of dialogue.

We walked down the street to Block D, which was still cordoned off and guarded by a couple of marines. They both saluted as Amanda approached, which she returned and walked between them. I nodded to them as we went inside.

The staircase looked like it had seen a fair amount of traffic in the last twelve hours, presumably cataloguing and boxing up the contents of Apartment 5. As we approached the door, Amanda rounded on me. "Jax, listen up. They've likely cleaned the place out and removed all the evidence, so I don't expect to find very much, but just check everywhere to make sure. Then we'll head upstairs."

We entered, but it was immediately apparent that our visit was fruitless. They'd stripped and cleaned the entire apartment. It was spotless in every room.

"Jesus. They didn't hang about, did they?" I remarked, as we left the apartment and headed for the stairs.

"Well, they won't have cleared upstairs. Not unless there's an AoG mole in the investigations team," said Amanda as we stepped onto the fifth-floor landing. She handed a small tub to me. "Dab some of this under your nose. It'll be all you can smell when we enter."

I opened the tub to find a menthol gelatine substance which I scooped up with my index finger and smeared under my nose. It made my eyes water for about ten seconds before it settled.

Amanda swiped her bio-band, and we entered the apartment. It was a moment before the smell hit us again. It wasn't nearly as pungent as last night, and the menthol was helping, but it still made me gag.

"If this is all I can smell, you must have dipped that pot in the sewers."

"Stop moaning," came the response.

Amanda hit the console and opened up the EM glass and lights to the maximum. The globe EM glass still shrouded the level for night conditions, but the internal lights were bright and cool. We traversed the lounge area, both of us occasionally retching as the atmospheric systems circulated the air.

We started in the room where we found them. Amanda's theory was that if we get the worst out of the way, it'll get easier afterwards. The smell inside was still horrendous, and it was all I could do not to blow chunks as I stepped through the clutter. The room was empty, except for the cot that Emily had been tied to, a stark reminder of the appalling conditions that they were forced to endure. We took the cot apart methodically, neither of us expecting to find anything, and gave the room one last look over before we exited and closed the door, both of us trying hard not to hurl.

It got easier after that. With the door closed the smell was less obtrusive, and it was much less arduous trying to concentrate on the task at hand. We started in one corner, picking up items, checking them and then creating a stack to one side, so that we didn't end up looking at the same items twice. Occasionally one of us would signal to the other that we'd found something of interest, but these things were quickly discarded and, after twenty minutes, the job was done.

The only other two rooms were the bathroom and the kitchen. The bathroom looked almost pristine, except for the toilet which made me gag all over again. But the shower stall and walls looked untouched, and it made me angry that they hadn't even afforded them the chance to stay clean. It was almost inhuman, and I could feel myself getting riled up at the thought of the conditions they'd subjected the girls to.

The kitchen was small, compact and poorly tended, with waste chutes overflowing and stains all over the sides. We sifted through everything methodically until Amanda gave a yelp.

"What is it?"

"I've got another address on the station. Looks like an email print or another box label, maybe. Here…"

She handed me a torn sheet of paper that was grubby with ring marks from coffee mugs, and almost illegible below the address.

G7-4-A14
16-15-C
Bertram Ramsey

The addresses of the Bertram were pretty rudimentary. Globe 7, Level 4, Section A, Street 14 was the top line. Then Building 16, Floor 15, Apartment C. I'd seen some complex addresses, particularly in Globes 1-3 which were largely populated with high-rise buildings on level 5, and then, presumably, tenement blocks like the one we were in now on Level 4. Below that was mostly industrial or agricultural, with a few exceptions.

I looked up at Amanda. "What does this mean?"

"How can we possibly know? It's given me an idea, though. Let's finish up here. I'll take that."

I handed the sheet back to Amanda and continued to check through the remaining items and cupboards in the kitchen, before we called it a day. We both stopped in the bathroom on the way out and washed our faces of the menthol, but I could still smell it on my skin, along with the stench of decay that invaded our air space.

We left the building, ignoring the marines on the way out, and walked back to The Loop.

"So, what's your idea, Mand?"

She waited until we were well in to the station before replying. "Look, I might be wrong about the people on this team, and I hope I am, but I just have a nagging feeling in the back of my mind that we are being compromised from the inside. I want to either bury that feeling, or expose the leak."

"And how do you expect we manage either?"

Amanda looked pensive and a little apprehensive, and for the first time, I felt there were small cracks forming in her usual confidence and assertiveness, almost like she needed my validation. "It's just after 05.40, so the team won't all be alive and kicking just yet. Let's put our civvies on and take a walk over to Globe 7, Level 4 and recce the address. It's probably exactly the same layout as the level we've just been on, so we'll need to scope out a couple of vantage points."

I was confused. "Vantage points for what, exactly?"

The Loop pulled in and we both stepped aboard. Amanda checked the train to make sure we were alone before continuing. "We need to have eyes on this address before we make our move. I think the best thing to do is to put out a call on comms to everyone in the team that we have evidence of another AoG facility on Level 4 of Globe 7, and that we want to meet them at 10.00 to discuss our next move."

"You think it'll flush out our leak?"

"I think whoever the leak is will do one of two things. They'll either head straight there to give an in-person warning to get out and get safe, or they'll put a call in. Either way, we'll see activity around the apartment. We'll either arrest them leaving or catch our mole."

I could already see some gaping holes in this plan, and something on my face must have showed that.

"You don't think it's a good idea, Jax?"

"I think it's problematic. Firstly, it's just the two of us. If, as you say, it's identical to the other street, then there'll be exits on either side of the building, so we'd have to split up. Secondly, there are no hiding places for us. We'd either need to be inside another apartment watching, or else further up the street disguised in some manner so as not to draw attention to ourselves."

Amanda interrupted. "Yes, and we will also face people from one of a hundred or more apartments inside coming or going."

"Right, which makes it an impossible task."

"I don't think so, Jax. I think, despite it being easier to put a call through comms, our mole knows comms are traceable so they're more likely to show up themselves. And we don't need to observe their activities inside. We just need to see who it is that shows up."

"And how are we supposed to do that without being seen?"

Amanda thought for a moment and then said, "Maybe we don't need to do it immediately. Maybe we just need to see when it gets busy, so we can blend in with the other faces on the street."

"We still need help, Mand. If we need to keep moving to blend in, then two of us aren't enough to have eyes on the entire time. If it was level 5, it would be easier. I could park my Sigma above the dome and just look straight down, assuming I could fly within the Hub boundary, which I can't. I could magnify everything on screen. We'd get an angle that still showed faces in the crowd."

"Why can't we do that on level 4?"

"The glass is only five-hundred metres high. We'd have

to be looking down the street directly, and we'd still need two, since the buildings are accessible from both sides."

"Yes, but you could record the images, right? So even if we don't spot them there and then, there's a good chance that they'll be on the footage somewhere, plus you'll record anyone leaving those blocks, and bio-band tracing will give us an identity."

"It's a stretch, Mand. We'd need another pilot, and another set of eyes on the ground. Which means trusting two other people here, which I'm more than willing to do, but you're not. It's also not as easy as hovering outside. The station is rotating at three-hundred-and-ninety-eight metres-per-second, so we'd need to maintain relative velocity and rotating and crabbing sideways, just to keep up. There's a strong chance we'll struggle with that."

"For fuck's sake, Jaxon. Do you have any better ideas?"

We both fell silent for a moment as The Loop pulled back in to Globe 11. We stepped off and headed for the mag-lift to level 5, neither of us looking at the other as we exited into the streets.

Amanda suddenly stopped dead in her tracks and gasped.

"Mand?"

"We don't need eyes on the target, Jaxon. There's only two ways into a Globe—shuttle or The Loop."

"The shuttle doesn't operate between globes, and a Sigma would need a release order, so we only need to keep an eye out on the station exits," I said, cottoning on.

"We don't even need to do that. You saw the footage of Laura waiting for us to step on at the station. It's all recorded. Every Loop, every exit, every mag-lift."

"Ok, so how do we do that?"

She turned and headed for the central mag-lift. "We need to go back to the Hub."

Mark Hanson was stirring. He could tell it was early as the EM glass was still subdued and he could faintly make out the sun traversing the window as the station spun on its axis.

He pushed himself upright and grimaced at the blood-stains on his bedclothes. His dressing had come off in the night, and his wounded ear was sore from constant contact with the fabric of his pillows.

If it hadn't served as an effective reminder of the ruth-lessness of these people, then the death of Laura Watkins certainly did. He had been closer to Laura than he was to his other crew-mates, thanks to the time they spent together teamed up in engineering, however fleetingly, back in Echo. She had always been nice to him and met him with a smile.

It unnerved him to discover that she was formerly ICP and transferred to the BRMC upon arrival at the station. He wondered if her placement with him was coincidental, and might not have given it more thought if she hadn't just died at the hands of the very people who were threatening him. Clearly she posed a problem for the AoG, and it occurred to him that if she was so easily disposable, then they would violently dispatch him the moment he upheld his part of the plan.

He had never wanted to be involved with the AoG and had never really given them much thought before he received his ticket for Compression. Two ICP officers turned up at his door one day with an envelope.

They gave him a speech about not being obligated to join the Bertram Ramsay, and how they had randomly chosen him after his mandatory assessments to join Crew 41 at the Echo site in Cheltenham. His surprise at the invite was clear, and for the next several hours he flip-flopped between emotions; the guilt of being a survivor negated somewhat the elation of being saved.

Later that evening, a second knock on his door took him by surprise. He clicked his hollotab to view outside and saw a man and a woman with their backs to the door. He opened it tentatively, but the moment they heard the door crack, they stepped back and pushed him inside his apartment.

"Mark Hanson, we are representatives of the Acolytes of Gaia." They were completely matter-of-fact about their involvement and pushed him on to his sofa before continuing.

"You will join our cause, to help us prevent the desecration of our planet, and to see that humanity's fate is organically decided and not artificially prolonged."

"I'm sorry, but you must have the wrong person. I am not a follower or a believer in your cause."

"You are exactly the right person. The ICP killed your parents as collateral damage when they targeted AoG operatives on board the Valiant."

"My parents died because of a malfunction on the shuttle that caused them to fall back into Earth's atmosphere, burning up upon re-entry."

The woman pulled a hollotab from her bag and laid it on the coffee table before swiping over a corner and executing a file. A screen emerged on which slow motion footage of the Valiant was visible. It looked to be under power and in controlled flight, when from the right side of the screen a blurred shape with a fire-trail appeared, moving at incredible speed relative to the shuttle. A few frames later, it connected with the rear fuselage and exploded into a million pieces, each small particle of the ship disintegrating as it fell to earth.

Sweat beads were forming on Mark's forehead, and he

glanced between the two intruders looking for any evidence of deception, but saw none.

"How do I know this is real? And if it is, how do I know you didn't shoot it down and kill my parents?"

The woman spoke. "I assure you, it is real. If we destroyed the Valiant, the ICP would have publicised it far and wide to discredit our cause and label us as terrorists and murderers. The fact is, they covered it up. We only came by this footage thanks to a loyal Acolyte working within the system. The ICP pigs confiscated and destroyed the rest of it."

"I don't believe you. What do you want from me?"

"Your belief in us, or our cause, is irrelevant. We chose you for a mission and you will perform your duties for the AoG, or die where you sit."

The weight of these words hit Mark like a mag-tram, and he visibly recoiled on the sofa.

The man leaned forward, his face just inches from Mark's, and spoke softly with just a hint of menace to his tone. "Mr Hanson. Your ticket was not a happy accident. We have operatives in the highest echelons of all branches of government and military. We selected you to receive a ticket, and you will take your place on board that glass monstrosity if you perform some very simple tasks when asked to do so."

Mark opened his mouth to reply, but the man cut him off. "Choose your words carefully, Mr Hanson. There is no safe place for you anymore. You can die here, or in Compression, or on the Bertram Ramsay. Or you can work with us to destabilise their efforts, and perhaps live to tell the tale, for another four years anyway. It is your decision."

With that, the man pushed himself away and left through the front door with the woman in tow, leaving a stricken Mark Hanson weeping on the sofa.

In the time since, he realised, if he had been less

emotional, he may have made a different choice. After all, death was inevitable, whether or not he helped. The plan to destroy the Bertram was a suicide mission for all operatives on the station, and the planet was destined to suffer a similar fate. The question was no longer whether he would live, but how long? A lot had changed in nine months.

He got up from his bed and walked to the bathroom, surveying his mutilated ear and cleaning the blood from his face before stepping into the shower and washing the scabs from his hair. Eventually, they would come for him. He knew the clock was ticking and that his life was drawing to a conclusion, but it wracked him with fear and disgust at himself for being so weak.

He made promises to himself that he would do what was right when the time came, but he grimaced at the hollow words, knowing he would fail. If he were to act against the AoG, he should act now whilst there was still some salvation possible. If he could summon the courage to seek help, he might still prevent a catastrophe. But if he did, there would be nowhere he could hide. Not on any globe.

Seeing her face again in Compression had shaken him. He fell back against the tiles, water cascading over him, and cried.

CHAPTER
THIRTEEN

WE ARRIVED at the Hub a little before 06.00. Time seemed irrelevant in the control centre, which was buzzing with personnel working around the clock to maintain our orbit and keep our systems in check. It was impossible to tell how many were inside—thousands, at a guess. There were several hundred just floating about in the weightless core, going about their daily routines with no idea of the hidden threat that scratched away at the fabric of their reality.

The thirty-kilometre mag-lift from Globe 11 brought us into the Hub at the navigation control centre in just under seven minutes. The security section was above Globe 4, which was almost half-way round the hamster wheel. Amanda motioned towards the ascent poles and walked towards them.

"Where do you think you're going?" I asked, not at all unaware of the answer.

"Time is of the essence, Jax. We take the shortcut through the middle and make our way to section 4."

I'd never experienced weightlessness, and the thought was unnerving. The SQIIDs not only dampened inertia, but they also acted as artificial gravity, so space flight did not differ from terrestrial excursions. The SQIID drives in each globe were only powerful enough to partially alter the gravitational effect, which is why the station rotated. The Hub was in the centre of everything, and the rotation only had a marginal impact on the gravity, so the SQIIDs did all the work, but they could only produce thirty-eight percent gravity at the Hub peripheries, so the majority of work carried out up here was done in zero G.

We arrived at the ladder-pole and Amanda barely hesitated before she climbed it and hauled herself upwards. I followed suit, perhaps a little more tentatively, but it was astonishing how quickly we moved from thirty-eight percent of gravity to zero. I struggled to control my legs as they flailed out away from the pole, but Amanda seemed completely unfazed and continued to pull herself upwards with long strokes, floating for ten metres, before grabbing the pole and repeating the movement.

Five metres up, we passed through what felt like an invisible field of energy. I could feel the pulse course through my body. It was like touching an EM shield on a proxy, although I only felt it on my calves and ankles as my legs floated away from the pole. I assumed it was a safety net of some type, there to prevent anyone falling should they become detached from the ascent poles, although the gravity was so low here that any descent to the ground would still be much slower and less likely to cause serious injury. I suspected it was more a case of protecting the consoles below from uncontrolled descents. Still, it was an odd sensation.

Once we gathered momentum and ascended above fifty metres, we were almost totally weightless, and one solid yank on the pole sent us both upwards at a surprisingly manageable pace, without the need for any further efforts. I looked down for the first time and felt my legs go wobbly as my brain tried to make sense of the space below us. For a moment I felt my heart lurch like I was falling, before reason kicked in and I looked upwards.

Strangely, looking down wasn't so different from looking up. We were still heading towards the ground, whichever direction we travelled, although my brain had oriented the place we'd ascended from as down. As we neared the central console, a network of ladders appeared that weren't visible from the ground. They stretched off in various directions, along banks of servers and holloscreens, all mounted within a mini-globe about two-hundred metres in diameter. There were so many people up here that it caught me by surprise. There must have been forty or fifty workers just in the section we'd travelled in to, drifting about, traversing ladders to different units, completely at home in this floating wilderness.

Amanda grabbed the pole and slowed up, pointing at a another pole that splintered off at thirty degrees to the right. There was a number 4 stencilled at the top. "This way," was all she said before descending.

I followed her down, head first, picking up speed as the gravity increased, and mimicked her movements as she grabbed the pole and allowed her legs to overtake her body, before floating downwards at a gentle pace, feet first. Three metres from the ground, she pushed herself away from the ladder and landed gracefully on the Hub floor.

Conversely, I hit the ground and rolled backwards about ten metres before using my palms to arrest my momentum. I looked up to see Amanda laughing at me. "Nice landing." It was amazing, the difference a smile made on her face. She was quite a serious character, not pre-disposed to open displays of joy.

"I'm glad I amuse you," I said, getting to my feet and feeling slightly disoriented, a little ill and weirdly heavy.

"Come on. We've got work to do." She strolled off

towards a bank of holloscreens. There were crowds of people around here. People at every screen, monitoring different parts of the station, and it took me a while to realise that each globe had its own security oversight with fifty-or-more technicians working each section.

Amanda walked towards an island of holloscreens to our left, with an illuminated '7-5-A' suspended from a circular framework above it – Globe 7, Level 5, Section A. I counted fifteen people sat at various consoles with headsets on, some talking quietly, others engrossed in the images on their screens. We approached a young man in his early twenties at the nearest console.

"Excuse me. Who's your head of department?" asked Amanda. The man barely lifted his head long enough to take in Amanda's BRMC uniform before looking back to his console and pointing to an office near the dome edge. "Lt. Commander Farrell. She's probably in her office."

We thanked him, which he barely acknowledged with a lazy wave of his hand, before heading towards the offices on the outer edge of the walkway. The first in the row had 'Lt. Commander Gemma Farrell' on the door, so we knocked and entered.

"I said I didn't want to be disturbed." The Australian voice came from a woman hunched over a horizontal holloscreen in the corner. Despite its outside appearance, the room was a technological marvel inside. The outer wall was glass, facing out of the Hub dome towards the Earth, and the view was magnificent. Seeing the planet completely unimpeded by other globes was breath-taking. The lattice titanium framework of the Hub barely obscured the view. Holloscreens covered the side walls and only the wall with the door inset was uncluttered, with just a couple of framed pictures of the Bertram Ramsay during construction.

"Commander Farrell," said Amanda, with just a bite of impatience.

"What do you want?" came the terse response, without so much as a glance from the console.

I could see Amanda bristling. "What I want is for a lieutenant commander to stand to attention and salute when a major from the Marine Corps enters the room."

"Strewth. I'd like a '53 Château d'Yquem and a bucket of popcorn, so I guess today's a disappointment for us both. What do you want?" She continued to concentrate on her monitor.

Amanda was about to explode – I could see it on her face, but like all military people, she was driven by the need for protocols and rules to be observed. I'd learned long ago that you catch more flies with honey than vinegar, so I put my hand on Amanda's shoulder before she could speak, and stepped forward into the room.

"Commander, my name is Jaxon Leith. I lost a close friend and colleague on this vessel two days ago, and Major Barclay and I are part of the unit investigating her murder. We need some help, and we're very much hoping that you're it."

There was a stillness about her suddenly. The mention of murder seemed to have sucked the air from the room momentarily. Farrell pushed herself back into her seat and rotated to face us.

"I'm sorry for your loss. I'm not dismissive of it, but I have time pressures here, so please get to the point quickly." She looked at us both with a kindly face that looked a little battle-hardened and weary. I got the distinct impression that she had no pride in her uniform or rank, but that she'd found herself in this role because of her skill set, and not because of a career choice.

Amanda was still at boiling point, judging from the shade of puce she was currently adorning, so I took the lead. "We were told you head up security for Globe 7?"

"No," came the stark reply.

"No? We were misinformed?"

"Not exactly. I control security and monitoring for Globes 6 through 10. Commander Brannon controls 12 through 4, and 5 and 11 are under the executive powers of the Navy and Air Force respectively, with oversight from Admiralty."

"I thought you had time pressures?" said Amanda. "Seems to me this conversation would have moved along a lot more quickly if you'd just said 'yes'."

She had a point, but I didn't need this woman putting up barriers right now. We needed a favour. Rank was irrelevant here because the investigating unit was off the books. Amanda and I were now a unit within a unit, and we couldn't afford to ruffle feathers. Before Farrell could reply, I spoke.

"Commander Farrell, we have time-sensitive intelligence that the killer or killers are operating in Globe 7. We can't share any more than that for security reasons, but we need to organise surveillance and we cannot make an official request for it. Major Barclay and I are coming to you because we have no alternative method of monitoring the comings and goings of Globe 7 remotely. We need your help. We've lost a good friend and a colleague here, and we have powerful evidence that suggests her murder is part of a wider plot to destroy this station."

"Jaxon!" Amanda spoke forcefully.

"Mand, we have to trust someone." I turned my head to face her. "Neither of us know Commander Farrell and I expect that goes for the rest of our unit, and she's in the best position to help us, so we have to open up about this to someone." I turned back to Farrell. "Will you help us? Please."

Farrell relaxed into her seat and gesticulated to the chairs in front of her desk. "Call me Gemma. This rank and file nonsense just irritates me."

Amanda took a seat and a deep breath with it. "I'm Amanda. This is Jaxon." She shot me a filthy look and then turned back to Farrell. "What I'm about to tell you cannot leave this room. Ever. Understood?"

Farrell nodded. "It's your party."

Between the two of us, we explained the current situation with Laura's murder and the Latimer family, omitting some of the more sensitive details. It took about ten minutes, at the end of which Farrell looked between us.

"You said something about a wider plot to destroy this station. I fail to see a connection so far."

"Have you heard of the Acolytes of Gaia?" I said.

"Of course. Bunch of misguided activists. Minimal threat level from what I've seen on the news."

Amanda spoke. "Yes, well, the news is inaccurate. They are a genuine threat and we know for certain that both Laura Watkins' and Brian Latimer's killers are the same people, and all part of the AoG. Jaxon and I are part of a special task force in counter-intelligence – completely secret, and totally independent from all counter-intel agencies on the Bertram. We are a small team, but they have compromised us."

"Compromised?" Farrell's eyes widened.

I picked up where Amanda left off. "Well, we *think* they've compromised us. All the evidence points to an internal breach. We might be wrong, but we have to continue with the assumption that the only two people we can trust are each other. And that's why we need help."

"I'm sorry we can't give you more details, Gemma," said Amanda, her tone lightening as the conversation progressed. "I was part of an elite ICP deep cover cell that had infiltrated the Compression process because of the gathered intelligence of an AoG threat to the evacuation. Unfortunately, my cover was blown the moment I made an arrest, so I'm now considered 'too compromised' to be of any use to an investigation."

"Which is the perfect cover for an intelligence operative. A double-bluff," completed Farrell, nodding.

"Precisely. On the face of it, I'm just another marine officer discharging my duties, but in reality, I'm neck deep in the shit with Jaxon."

"You were ICP too?"

"God, no. I was just a bloke in The Bleeds that got sucked into the investigation back in Compression. I'm still training."

"Even more perfect cover," she replied. I shrugged. I wasn't sure ineptitude and blind luck qualified as camouflage.

"So," she looked at each of us, "what is it you need from me?"

Amanda took a deep breath. "We need to compose a sting operation. To expose the leak."

"In Globe 7?"

"That's correct. As it stands, only Jaxon and I are privy to this small piece of evidence linking a residential address in Globe 7 with the perpetrator in Globe 9."

"Residences are unmonitored, save for bio-band location tracking."

"We know. And we suspect the killer is operating without a bio-band."

"Not possible."

"It is possible," I corrected. "We've seen it first-hand. Emily Latimer and her daughters all had their bio-bands removed. Their kidnappers ran a current through the magnetic links to maintain connection as they removed them."

Farrell look thoughtful for a moment, and scratched her head.

"That might stop the alert, but bio-band security requires a circular connectivity between the chipsets in the magnetic bonds, not to mention a registering pulse to remain passive. Running a cable between the shell connectors would maintain the circuit, but there are more than a dozen micro-circuits that transmit everything from GPS data to currency management, and they can only operate if they're within millimetres of the connecting bonds. The moment that disconnection occurs, all the back-up circuits kick in."

"Back up circuits?" Amanda and I exchanged looks. This was new information.

"Well, the purpose of a bio-band is to monitor the location and health of all personnel, as well as providing access to certain areas coded in to the band, and as a payment gateway. Running a cable through the magnetic connectors would do little more than stop the alert raised that a band has disconnected. It's what happens in the background that really matters."

"I don't understand. You're saying the bands provide alerts even if the power remains connected?"

Farrell leaned forward. "Sort of. Did you ever see the old railway lines before mag-trains took their place?"

We both nodded.

She continued. "Okay, so some train tracks have a third rail for power that runs parallel to the main tracks. If I were to cut the three rails and create a ten-metre gap, and then run a cable between the two sections of power rail, I'd maintain the flow of power, but what would happen to the trains?"

I looked at Amanda and back at Farrell. "They'd come off the tracks."

"Precisely. The same is true with bio-bands. You can maintain the power connection through a connecting cable, but that's all."

"So what happens if a cable is connected and then the ends of the bands disconnected?" asked Amanda.

"Well, all sorts of interesting things. Firstly, bio-bands don't actually need charging, so the use of a powered cable was unnecessary. Any wire between the two parts would maintain the power circuit."

This statement brought into sharp relief how unimaginably cruelly the Latimer's captors had treated them.

Farrell's brow furrowed. "Yet they ran a current through it, you said? Why?"

"We think to disable the host," I said.

She shuddered, but continued. "The entire station is a kinetic charger of sorts, so all powered objects on the Bertram draw their power wirelessly from thousands of ports in every globe. The ports also triangulate each band, giving us the ability to track everyone inside the Station. It also requires a live pulse to remain passive."

"We discovered the Latimers' bio-bands inside their homes, still powered by a cable connector."

"Yes, so the tracking data is irrelevant, but thirty seconds after disconnecting a band, or a person's pulse ends, the protocol is to record live happenings in the immediate vicinity, the assumption being that they've disconnected because of some medical emergency or similar."

Amanda looked shocked. "So you're saying the system would have recorded the conversations and movements around the Latimers' just thirty seconds after their bands' removal?"

Farrell nodded.

"And who monitors those transmissions?" I asked.

Farrell's eyebrows raised. "Well, nobody. They're an after-measure, designed to establish circumstances in the event of a fatality or accident. They didn't design them to facilitate forensic examination as the result of criminal behaviour. The data will be here, but unless we receive an official request for access..." she shrugged and let her words hang.

"How many people on this station are aware of this?" I asked.

"A few. As the heads of security, myself and Brannon know, as do the top brass and, of course, the medical personnel, but otherwise it's pretty much unknown. It's not a secret, though. We've never needed it in sixty years, so it's a pretty benign system."

"And how long is the data kept?" asked Amanda.

Farrell shrugged again. "Until it's overwritten, but that only happens once the servers are full of incoming data. I doubt there's enough stored that'll it be over-written in a thousand years."

"Jesus Christ," I said. "You know what this means?"

Amanda nodded. "We might have the killers' voices recorded."

I turned to Farrell. "How do we get our hands on those recordings?"

"Hold on a second." Farrell held a hand up. "You said something about a sting operation? You wouldn't even be aware of the recordings if I hadn't just told you. Can we get back to the reason you came to me in the first place, and we'll circle back to the bio-bands later?"

"Well, as I said before, I think the AoG has compromised our team," said Amanda. "And I think I know how to flush out the infiltrator, but it requires careful monitoring of the entrances and exits to Globe 7."

"There are only two," replied Farrell. "The Loop and the flight bay."

"That was also our assessment," continued Amanda. "Jaxon here can have the Bay locked down without raising suspicion, so that the only route in or out is The Loop. We need to set up an incursion into a property in Globe 7 at a certain time, and then monitor the station to see if anyone from our crew turns up early to warn the occupants."

"And why can't you do that on the ground?"

Amanda bit back a touch of impatience. "Because we don't have any way of concealing ourselves, either at the station or in the street, and we don't know who's who in the residence in question. It's a block with god-knows how many apartments in, and we have no clue what the perps look like. It could be anyone."

"So you'd be blind and with no idea who you're looking for."

"Correct, and the killer or killers almost certainly know who we are, thanks to their mole."

"I understand. So you want to monitor The Loop station entrances for your own team members should one of them arrive early."

Amanda nodded.

"And you're prepared to do the grunt work yourself, but you need access to the monitoring station?"

"Preferably access to the monitors in a secure location where we're not overlooked or overheard," said Amanda.

"And you're not asking for anything else at all?"

"Like what?" I replied.

"I've no idea, but this facility is a secure area that requires highest level clearance, so nobody can just rock up and begin sifting through the data."

"Does helping us create a problem for you?" I asked.

Farrell pondered that for a moment before lifting her head and looking straight at me. "Not if I route the feeds to this room and I'm present. After all, that could just be another meeting, like the one we're having now."

"Good," replied Amanda.

"I have a question, though," continued Farrell, with her brow scrunched up. "What if nobody turns up?"

"Only three possibilities. Either they have a means of

communication that we're unaware of, or nobody on our team is a mole." She took a deep breath.

"And the third?" asked Farrell.

"You're AoG," replied Amanda, matter-of-factly.

I thought Farrell might protest, but she just looked thoughtful and nodded. "So, when do you want to do this?"

"Let's make it happen tonight. Now, how do we get our hands on those bio-band recordings?"

CHAPTER
FOURTEEN

"YOU'RE *sure there was nothing left?"*

She quelled under his gaze. "I took care of it before the forensics team had catalogued everything."

"Well, that's something. We need to be more cautious now. There is still a lot to be done before our ultimate mission can bear fruit. Is your cover still intact?"

"They suspect nothing. And they're making no headway at all. But the events of the last few days have now brought pressure upon them, so we should expect an increased presence of security everywhere."

"This monstrosity is too large for them to monitor effectively. The arrogance of these infidels might well be their undoing, marvelling at this glass prison and its enormity. We could hide for a hundred years and they'd never find us. But we shall proceed cautiously anyway. It would be prudent in the immediate aftermath."

"I will keep you updated." She watched as the screen flickered off and breathed out deeply.

Farrell spent the next twenty minutes searching the logs for the bio-band alerts, but without success.

"If you could give me even an approximate date, it would help significantly. I could do a system-wide search, but it would alert several senior personnel, so that's a non-starter. Bio-bands are disconnected en masse every day, for lots of reasons – there are hundreds of bio-docks on every level of every globe, so whilst there's very little data used, there are millions of entries in the data logs. If I search for Emily Latimer specifically, it'll show up in the logs, so I assume that's also a non-starter?"

I looked at Amanda. "Mand, we need to visit Emily Latimer. It's the only way."

She nodded. "Okay, but we need to play it very cool. She's surrounded by security after her transfer and is being monitored around the clock."

"We have a legitimate reason to see her. We found her. I think she'd want to see us." I rose from my chair. "Gemma, thank you. Sorry for wrecking your day, but I hope you can understand why. We'll be back later."

"Come straight to this office. You've already been here long enough that my team will ask questions." She held her hands up. "Don't worry, I can deal with them. Just don't announce your presence later."

"Thank you," said Amanda. We both nodded to Farrell and left her office. I headed towards the poles, but Amanda grabbed my arm and steered me left onto the main walkway.

"If her team is likely to ask questions, we need to be seen moving to other departments, so it doesn't look like we were just here to see her. We'll take the long route back."

We started the long stroll around the hamster wheel. It took just under twenty-five minutes to get to the Globe 11 mag-lifts. We discussed the plan on the way, trying to find weak spots as we went.

"We need to speak to everyone individually, not as a group," Amanda started.

"Are we still assuming Hennessey is our prime candidate?" I asked.

"I don't think we can assume anything. We need to have an open mind to prevent us from drawing conclusions we expect to draw, and not seeing what happens for what it really is."

"So, what will you say to them?"

"Nothing elaborate. We've found evidence that a residence in Globe 7 might be hiding our perpetrators. We need to meet with the entire team to discuss tactics for their apprehension or observation. That's it."

"We can't both be there for those conversations. One of us needs to be in the Hub, watching. It might take us an hour to locate every person on the team, unless we use our comms."

Amanda stopped in her tracks and thought. "You're right. Travel time from Globe 11 to Farrell's office is going to be about twenty-five minutes at the very minimum, assuming we cut through the core. Closer to forty-five minutes if we approach on foot. Getting to Globe 7 on The Loop could conceivably be quicker depending on the timings of the train."

"So one of us has to be there before we inform anyone on the team. We also need to give a couple of hours in between breaking the news and the meeting time, so that whoever is on the inside has time to get in and out of Globe 7."

We continued the discussion all the way back down to the Globe 11 command centre, which we exited onto level 5 section C, just a fifteen-minute walk to my apartment. The hospital was on the outer ring, with mag trams operating from The Loop station every few minutes. Amanda and I hopped onto a tram and continued in silence, watching as we got closer to the glass hull of the Globe.

They'd clearly given some thought to the benefits of tranquillity surrounding a hospital, with Globe 12 visible on our left and Earth directly ahead of us. The gardens leading up to the hospital grounds were beautifully land-scaped (spacescaped?), with a constant stream of people wandering around, and a few sitting on benches taking in the scenery. I felt more at peace here than I had anywhere on the station, and it brought home just how much thought had gone in to the design and layout of the Bertram.

Everything was perfect, from the beech hedges around the grounds to the areas of woodland with paths snaking past the lake towards the hospital entrance, and the flower beds rich with colour and variety that seemed to dominate the landscape as we got within a few-hundred metres of the tram station.

The tram stopped just fifty metres from the hospital foyer, on a circular horseshoe of track, ready to take it back to The Loop station. We swiped our bands to exit and wandered to the main entrance. The hospital itself grew upwards with the same titanium framework as the globe, with EM glass running in lines around the circumference of the tall, rectangular structure.

As we entered the building, I was taken aback at how busy it was on the inside. The lobby was encased in glass, but beyond that doctors, nurses, orderlies and visitors were roaming the halls with purpose, pushing patients around in chairs, or else talking between themselves as they strode. There was a buzz in the atmosphere – the sounds of thou-sands of voices within, interspersed with the gentle beeps of medical machinery and the occasional alarm.

The lobby corridor steered us towards the reception area, where we were funnelled through a row of twenty

Decontamination Portals. A couple of minutes later we were through, grateful that the hospital DECON didn't involve being dunked in freezing oil. We still had to strip and put our clothes through a separate chamber, but the sterilisation process was just a dry scanner. We entered the main foyer where a middle-aged man in purple scrubs with the BRAF insignia on his breast pocket greeted us. After a brief exchange, he tapped on his hollotab and looked up at us both with concern all over his face.

"I'm afraid I can't give you that information. The security around those patients prevents any unauthorised access."

"We were the ones that found and saved those patients. Who do we need to speak with to gain access?"

"You can ask at the security cordon on the second floor. I don't have the clearance to see that information."

We thanked him, and walked over to the stairs in the centre of the main hall, ascending silently until we came to floor two. We didn't have to look very far for the security station, as two BRMC officers blocked our path. They both saluted Amanda. "I'm sorry, Ma'am, but this is a restricted area. Nobody in or out. Colonel's orders," spoke the marine on our left.

Amanda returned their salute and replied, "Put a call in to Colonel Grealish and announce that Major Barclay and Lieutenant Leith are here to see Emily Latimer. He'll authorise it."

The two marines looked at each other, clearly unsure, having received explicit instructions to limit entry.

"Now, marine," commanded Amanda, with a fierce look on her face.

"Wait here, Ma'am," came the response, and the marine turned and walked to the security station behind him, leaving his companion to block our path forward. We stood patiently for a couple of minutes, until the marine returned and gestured for us to follow him.

He took us down a long corridor to a mag-lift, which ascended for twenty seconds, before opening onto another corridor with several doors running down the left, and a long counter on the right, behind which were a dozen medical personal, sitting at terminals and poring over charts on holloscreens.

About two-thirds of the way down was another short corridor on the left, which led to a door guarded by two armed marines, who funnelled us through a scanner on the left side. "Weapons in the box please Major, Lieutenant," said the first, as we stepped over to the scanner. Both of us dropped our Proxys into the box, along with Amanda's knife and then individually stood in front of the mirrored wall as the scanner did its work. The marine that had escorted us up saluted Amanda and left, handing us to the security detail on the ward who swiped us through into the closed room, sealing the door behind us.

There were three nurses at a small station on our left, and two doctors huddled over a bed on our right. Ahead of us was a bed with Emily Latimer on it, and just to her right, the tiny frame of one of her daughters. The doctors must be around the other twin. They both looked up as we entered, but returned to their examinations. The room was large enough for ten patients, with floor-to-ceiling EM glass, overlooking the outer dome and the grounds below us.

A woman approached from a small room to our left which I hadn't noticed, and introduced herself as Doctor Madison Keeley.

"How is she?" I asked, taking the doctor's outstretched hand.

"She's a tough cookie. Hard to believe any of them are alive, given the extent of their injuries, but they're all responding well to treatment. The Hollodoc has done the big-ticket items, so it's now mostly about monitoring and managing medication and recovery. I would think, given what they've been through, that the physical healing is the straightforward part. The hard work will come later."

"Can we talk to them?" I asked.

"Mrs Latimer, yes, if she's responsive. Until a few hours ago she was heavily sedated, so she may still be quite groggy. She needed a lot of skin regeneration on her wrists, back and ankles. The girls, not yet. They've been through things that no six-year-old should ever experience, so they need some more time to re-establish trust and confidence in people."

"I understand. Thank you." I nodded to the doctor as she headed for the nurse's station.

I strolled to the bed, with Amanda close behind. Emily Latimer looked a thousand times better than when we'd found her, with the colour returning to the skin that was almost hanging off her thin, drawn face. There were bandages around the back of her head and up both arms. They'd draped her body in a light, silver blanket, which seemed to shimmer as we approached. Her exposed feet both had what looked like inflatable boots that ran up to mid-calf.

She stirred as the sound of our footsteps reached her ears, and looked up from her partial slumber. Her eyes were ocean-green and sparkled as they widened at seeing us. A smile transformed her face from the gaunt, fragile skeleton that I remembered, to a woman with purpose and life in her. Her wavy auburn hair had been chopped away unceremoniously, leaving an uneven half-bob, that was tethered back by the bandages.

"Jaxon," she said, her eyes locking onto mine, the smile exposing her cracked lips and scuffs on her cheeks.

I stopped in my tracks and looked at Amanda, before

turning back to Emily Latimer, tears welling up in her eyes but her smile broadening.

"You don't remember," she said, her voice raspy and damaged. It was a statement rather than a question. I shook my head, confused, as Amanda walked around her bedside and handed her a glass of water, which she took gratefully. "Thank you."

She turned back to me. "Both of you. You saved my girls."

I nodded, a lump forming in my throat.

"You helped me once, in The Bleeds," she said with absolute certainty in her expression.

"You've met?" asked Amanda, looking between the two of us, consternation all over her face.

"I recognised you as soon as you walked in to the room where you found us, Jaxon. A little older, still handsome and strong," she said.

"I'm sorry. I don't remember." As I said it, images of a vague recollection were swirling in the back of my mind.

"I was Emily Harkness back then. It was two years before I met Brian." Her eyes swam with tears at the memory of her dead husband.

My brain kicked in to overdrive. Emily Harkness was a girl from The Bleeds that I saw running in to the Horsefair one day, a decade ago. She was being followed by a local man that I knew only as Boxer. I remembered so clearly watching him run after her with her purse in his hand, as she ran faster and dropped her grocery bags in panic, making a beeline straight towards two ICP officers who intervened, taking down her pursuer and cuffing me in the process, as I arrived with her spilled groceries. What she hadn't realised is that she'd dropped her purse and Boxer was just trying to return it, but the faster he walked to catch up with her, the faster she ran. I never saw her again, but had several encounters with those particular ICP officers over the ensuing years.

"You do remember," she said, looking straight into my eyes.

I nodded slowly.

"I misjudged you," she said, "and your friend. And here you are, saving me again."

"I didn't save you then," I corrected her. "If anything, I saved Boxer. I can't believe it's you."

She smiled again, that huge broad smile which lit her face up like fireworks. The transformation from the gaunt, wretched face, condemned to that filthy prison, was sensational.

"Please, sit down." Amanda and I sat in chairs on either side of her bed, as she beckoned for our hands. Amanda reached out instinctively and held her hand, as she looked back to me and I followed suit. She squeezed my hand in hers, weakly, but with every ounce of energy she could muster.

"It's okay," said Amanda. "We're just happy you're safe. And the girls too."

Emily sobbed, huge glistening tears rolling down her emaciated face, turning between the two of us, unwilling to look away in case it was all a dream and she was still back in that hellish quagmire, tied to a broken cot and left to die. Amanda continued to grip her hand and leaned over her, running the backs of her fingers gently down Emily's face, wiping away the tears and whispering soft platitudes.

It took a few minutes for Emily to gather herself and calm her breathing. Her eyes were puffy and swollen, but there was a strength behind them, shining through like a beacon.

She looked back at me again. "Colonel Grealish said you tried to save my husband?"

Again, I nodded. "I'm sorry I didn't do better." I caught

a glance from Amanda and could see her thinking the same thing. *Grealish had been here.*

She shook her head. "He did it for us. He saved his girls. Brian was a good man." Fresh tears fell from her eyes.

"We know," I said, squeezing her hand.

"Emily," said Amanda gently, "we need to ask you some questions. I know you're exhausted, and you've suffered more than anyone should ever suffer in their lifetime, but we need your help to catch these people."

"Anything," she replied. "Whatever I can do."

"What do you remember about the night they abducted you, Emily?" I asked gently.

"More than I wish I had to," she replied, simply. "It was quite late, close to nine o'clock – the girls were in bed, and I'd just finished a call with Brian. Something didn't seem right, but he wouldn't tell me what the matter was. He kept looking behind him while he was talking to me, but all I could see were holloscreens. He asked me to contact the general and request a transfer or protection, temporarily, but he wouldn't say why."

"He asked you to contact the general? Which one?" asked Amanda, her eyes wide.

"General Lavigne," she replied.

I looked at Amanda. General Lavigne was the senior officer that ordered the evacuation, and promoted me to my first rank in the military just six and a half weeks ago.

"And did you?"

She nodded. "As soon as I swiped off the hollotab to Brian, I called the general. His staff refused to put the call through, so I decided to go down there in the morning and speak to him directly."

"But you never got to see him?"

She shook her head, a little sadly. "About an hour later two BRMC officers arrived and told me they were there on General Lavigne's orders, and that we were to be moved to a secure location. I just assumed that Brian had spoken to him. They wouldn't tell me why. The girls were so anxious."

"So it was around ten when they knocked?" She nodded. "Where did they take you?" Amanda persisted.

Emily shrugged and grimaced at the movement. "I have no idea. The last thing I remember is them connecting a machine to our bio-bands. They said they were going to have to switch off the tracker, just to keep us safe. I remember my body going rigid and my fingers cramping and the next thing I knew, we were in that room where you found us and our bio-bands were gone." She shuddered at the thought.

"Can you remember the date, Emily?"

"It was the 8th June. We were counting down the days until Brian's rotation back to the Bertram." She sobbed again, struggling to maintain control of her voice which was barely above a whisper now.

"Thank you, Emily," said Amanda. "I have a couple more questions, and then we'll leave you to rest."

Emily nodded, still trying to gather her emotions.

"How many people did you meet, from that moment until the day we found you?"

She paused for a moment, clearly thinking. "There were two men that came to get me and the girls. I never saw either of them after that day. Then five others in that room. Two women and three men."

"Did you get a look at them?" asked Amanda.

Emily's faced recoiled in fear, and she shook her head vigorously. "They covered their faces, most of the time."

"Most of the time?"

"There was one man who never covered himself. He always wore a hood, though. He was the worst of them. I'll never forget his face."

The hairs on the back of my neck stood up.

"Did you ever hear any names?" I asked, gently.

"I only caught snatches of conversations, but I remember one," she replied, fear welling up inside her. "It was the day before you found us. They were talking about moving to another place. The only name I heard was 'Watkins.'"

CHAPTER
FIFTEEN

GREALISH ENTERED HENNESSEY'S office and sat down. He looked rough, having not shaved for a couple of days, and his appearance was unusually dishevelled.

"Andrew?" said Hennessey as he entered. "Is everything okay?"

"Not really, Sara," replied Grealish, removing his cap and roughing his hair with his fingers.

Hennessey walked to the coffeepot in the corner and poured them both a mug before handing one to Grealish.

"Thanks," he said, putting it down without taking a sip. He locked eyes with Hennessey. "Are you one of them, Sara?" he asked, his tone weary with fatigue.

"One of them? Who is *them*, Andrew?" she replied, eyes widening.

"One of the AoG, Sara. Look me in the eyes and tell me you're not," he said.

"Andrew, what the hell is going on?"

"Just answer the question."

"Of course I'm not bloody one of them! Why on earth would you ask me that?"

He took a deep breath and sighed. "I'm sorry for asking, Sara, but I had to. I think we've been compromised."

Her already wide eyes opened further. "What makes you say that? What's happened?"

He pushed himself out of his chair and started pacing. "I just took a call from BRMC security station inside the hospital. Amanda and Jaxon are there to see Emily Latimer."

"So? They found her. It's natural that they'd want to check on her."

"I checked the logs. After Laura's murder, the entire team had their bio-bands activated. Amanda accessed the evidence logs from the bomb lab at 02:00 after the forensic team had catalogued everything. She visited Jaxon's apartment shortly after and the pair of them went back to Globe 9, where they spent over an hour searching those two apartments."

"You think they found something?" Hennessey asked.

Grealish ignored the question. "My sources tell me they left Globe 9 on The Loop, disembarked at Globe 11 and went straight to the Hub. They spent an hour and a half inside, a significant portion of it at Unit 4 – Station Security, before heading back to 11 and visiting Mrs Latimer in the hospital, where my sources say they questioned her about her abduction."

"Your sources? Are you tracking them?"

"Not possible. Someone altered their bio-band signatures after Laura died. I can only assume it's their contact at Station Security. I've got eyes on them at all times."

Hennessey's eyes were wide with surprise. "Sir, surely you don't think they're involved in any of this? They found Laura and the Latimers. It doesn't seem likely..."

"No, no, not at all, why do you think I've had them followed? It's not some Machiavellian plot to infringe on their civil liberties. We've already lost one team member and I have no intention of losing another," he interrupted impatiently.

He paused for a moment, looking troubled. "I specifically told them not to go back to Globe 9, and they ignored the order and did it anyway. And now they're visiting the Hub and questioning our only lead in the hospital."

"So?" Hennessey looked genuinely perplexed.

"Don't you see, Sara? They're investigating without the rest of the team. Amanda has specialist training in counter-intel from god-knows-which agency, and she's chosen to exclude the rest of us from her enquiries. She knows for an absolute certainty that Jaxon is on the right side of this, because he helped her take down Eloise back in Compression, and was a casualty of the AoG bomb that Brian Latimer detonated. *And* they were together when they discovered Laura, when they found Emily Latimer and her girls, and the remains of a bomb lab."

"I think you're reading too much into this, Andrew. I haven't slept much since Laura died. Imagine what it's like for the two of them, especially Jaxon. They're probably just trying to keep busy. I expect they're both angry and just trying to make things happen now."

"But that's the point." Grealish stopped pacing and leaned over Hennessey's desk. "If they were so angry that they'd want to bring these people to justice, they'd have a much higher chance of success if everyone in this team was pulling their weight and helping."

"But they're doing this alone." It was a statement more than a question, and Hennessey frowned.

Grealish nodded. "There's only two reasons Amanda would go solo on this investigation." He counted off on his fingers. "One, she thinks we're incompetent or negligent."

"I don't think that's true, Andrew."

He held up a second finger. "Two, she thinks the AoG

has compromised this unit." He let the words hang in the air. Neither of them spoke for a minute.

Hennessey looked concerned. "Andrew, you're here talking about a saboteur in our team. I know I'm on the right side of this. There's no way Jaxon or Amanda are on the wrong side, since they're clearly taking matters into their own hands. So it's Tyrone or Amy, if there is, in fact, a mole among us."

Grealish dropped into the chair again and hung his head, rubbing his face with both hands. He sat back and looked up. "Tyrone spent the last seven weeks in and out of the hospital. He was the closest to the bomb, besides the two marines that died, and Jaxon."

"That just leaves Amy."

We left the hospital and headed for my apartment. It was a thirty-minute walk, but both of us needed to clear our heads.

Amanda eventually spoke, about ten minutes into the journey. "There's something that's bothering me, Jax. Something doesn't feel right."

"What do you mean?" I asked. My head was already swimming with everything I'd learned in the last two days.

Amanda grabbed my arm, stopped in mid-stride and pulled me around to face her. "Emily's abduction has changed everything."

"Changed how?"

"She said that her husband called her and told her to get relocated or protected, right?"

"So he knew something was going to happen." I shrugged.

"Yes, but how? He must have been leaned on and

coerced from inside Compression. He hadn't been back to the Bertram for weeks."

"We already knew that," I said.

"Maybe, but I hadn't connected the dots."

"What dots? You're losing me here."

She pulled me over to a bench in a small plaza and sat down. "We're looking for a mole in our team, Jaxon, and whilst we concentrate on what's happening here and now, we've been ignoring what happened in Compression."

"We've been through this, though. We know Brian Latimer was being manipulated, and his family held hostage. What's changed?"

"Hear me out. I'm trying to make sense of this myself. There's six of us left in Operation Echo, established on this station, right?" She looked slightly apologetic as she said the word 'left'.

"You and I, Grealish, Cooper, Sara and Tyrone," I replied. Laura's face swam into my head as I omitted her name.

"Okay, who of us could put pressure on Brian Latimer from inside Compression?"

"Well, not Grealish or Cooper. They told me they were strictly land-side."

"Correct. Compression is the sole jurisdiction of BRMC, with a small contingent of BRAF in Opps, and the occasional Navy pilots when they do a layover."

"So it's me, you, Sara or Tyrone. Except that it could be anyone in the BRMC that was in Compression."

"Perhaps, but I don't think so. We know it's not either of us, and you're correct that anybody in the BRMC could legitimately have been involved, but Emily Latimer's story raises questions."

"Such as?"

"Well, if she couldn't get a call through to the general,

how did her captors know that she'd willingly leave on his orders?"

"Someone must have monitored the call."

"Exactly. But that couldn't happen on the Bertram. Station communications security is a major priority up here. Compression is a locked-down training facility, and the only physical security is at the entrances and shuttle bay, but there's still no way to monitor calls in and out. They encrypt everything."

"So they monitored the call? How?"

"Not monitored. *Overheard*."

"I see what you're saying. It must have been someone in Compression because Emily and the girls were home alone and couldn't be overheard?"

"Absolutely. Brian lived in barracks – no personal space to himself, so someone must have been watching and listening after they coerced him in to blowing Opps up."

I was still confused, and it must have shown on my face. "That would discount Sara. Barracks are gender specific."

"Fuck's sake, Jax. He was in SECO 2 or Opps when he made that call. Emily was quite clear – *he kept looking around while he was on the call and all she could see were holloscreens.* No way he'd have made that call from barracks. Far too many people around."

"What difference does that make?"

"Very few people have access to either SECO 2 or Opps, and fewer still have access to both, so we've immediately discounted ninety percent of BRMC personnel. She said it was June 8th. That's the day after I took down Eloise."

Eloise had entered Compression in the same crew as me, Amanda, Aoife, Jennifer, Laura, Libby, Leon and Mark. She was eventually exposed as an AoG infiltrator and arrested by Amanda for Leon's murder. Nobody knew what her ultimate mission was, and she'd refused to speak at all during her incarceration.

"You think her arrest was the trigger for the next phase?" I asked.

"Seems likely," Amanda replied. "After all, we still don't have any apparent knowledge of her mission objectives, and assuming a mole inside Compression, AoG would have been immediately aware of her arrest."

"You think she was supposed to set the bomb off?" The thought that she was on a suicide mission made me shudder. But then the entire plan of the AoG was that everyone on this planet would die, so it was hardly inconceivable.

"We'll never know, but we do now know that Brian Latimer called his wife and asked her to get protection or relocation in the immediate aftermath."

"Okay, but it still doesn't point to Tyrone or Sara."

"Let me say again, I don't think it's Tyrone. I've said it before – he was very close to being killed by that bomb himself."

"Mand, there's still nothing connecting Sara to any of this."

"Maybe nothing concrete, Jax, but there's plenty of circumstantial evidence of her involvement." Amanda reeled off a list. "Sara had access to SECO 2 and Opps. She had access to the Shuttle Bay and oversight of the cargo scanners. She had communications capability with the Bertram and the outside world and was one of only two people that we know of officially able to leave Compression and enter ICP Command at GCHQ." Amanda's eyes bulged and she became more animated. "Sara had access to everyone in Crew 41, including Eloise and Mark. She knew where Laura was, received a communication that was cut off, and told nobody until the debrief after Laura's murder. Mark Hanson met with a woman – you witnessed it."

"It couldn't have been Sara. She was at the barn when I arrived."

"No she wasn't. She walked in ten minutes later with Amy."

"Maybe they're both in on it?" I asked, not really believing it.

"Come on, Jax. Amy is a nobody. Sara has more access and opportunity than anyone. What has she done about monitoring Mark Hanson, despite him being our number one suspect? Nothing! She was on the scene after we cleared the bomb lab. She has a bio-band with full access to every unused residential, agricultural, commercial or industrial building on this vessel. We know someone sanitised the crime scene after we left. Sara was there, Jaxon. She was the first to arrive after Laura's death – where had she come from? Come on, Jax, the list is endless. How could it be anyone *else*?"

I stood up from the bench and started walking back to my apartment. Amanda jogged a little to catch up with me. "Jax?"

"This is beyond us, Mand. How are we supposed to deal with this alone? We know at least seven people on this vessel are AoG, excluding our suspected mole. The two marines that picked up the Latimers, two women and three men in that hell-hole, according to Emily, one of which is probably the guy in the hoodie that Sara showed me in Compression – he was there when I boarded the transport to Echo. And now you're suggesting that Sara is also AoG? It's too much."

"Jaxon, we can't just walk away from this."

"Walk away? Mand, we're outgunned and outmatched. This might be your way of life, but it's not mine." I continued to stride home.

"But we're not, Jaxon. We know more than they realise."

I stopped and rounded on her, and she almost walked in to me. "What do we know, Amanda? Please tell me what significant nugget of information we have that'll make any difference to this investigation."

"We have a date now. June 8th. And a time – 22:00."

"And no way of recognising the voices on the bio-band recordings, even if we could find them. There's what, ten thousand BRMC on the Bertram?"

"We don't need to hear the recordings now," she replied. "Look, thanks to you, we have an ally in the Hub, and an important one at that. She needed a timeframe to find a recording on Emily Latimer's bio-band, but that same timeframe puts two marines at her apartment. We don't need their voices. The bio-band tracking data will tell us who it was."

"What if they weren't wearing bio-bands? We know for a fact that the woman who met Mark Hanson wasn't, so why would any of the others?"

"The AoG need people on the inside for their plan to work, Jaxon. For two marines to arrive on a transport that late at night can only mean that they are legitimate. They were in full uniform."

"Someone could have stolen the uniforms. For fuck's sake, Amanda. You swiped a set of white fatigues for me this week."

"Not the same, Jax." She shook her head. "The quartermaster on Globe 9 saw us arrive in a military Sigma, with a flight plan and orders, and your name stencilled on the fuselage."

"Okay," I held my hands up in concession, "assuming they were legit, why would they risk their presence being discovered by arriving at Emily Latimer's apartment still wearing their bio-bands?"

"Because it wasn't a risk. They were always going to dispose of her, I'm sure of that. They kept her alive as a bargaining chip just in case, but they were always likely to kill her. Look at the state they left her in. They had no care for her condition, and she wouldn't have lasted very much longer. With her dead, we'd be none-the-wiser about her abductors or when the abduction occurred. If by some miracle we stumbled upon information that pointed us to two marines, we'd still be in the dark. When questioned, they'd say they took a call from Emily Latimer who seemed concerned for her safety, so they drove over to check it out, but when they knocked, an hour later, there was no answer. They're there for maybe five or ten minutes, checking out the rest of the building, but when they found nothing, they left."

"And not tell anyone?"

"Tell them what, Jaxon? That they took a call, checked it out and found no suspicious activity? She could have been sleeping, or perhaps, having been denied access to the general, she took matters into her own hands and took the girls to stay with a friend. Or she left for a night out and the twins stayed with a babysitter. They'd walk out of that interview in two minutes flat."

She had a point. For them to have any real chance of success on their mission, they must have people in fairly senior positions within the confines of this space station. I wondered at the extent of the infiltration. Were we facing hundreds of spies, or just the handful that we were already aware of?

I turned and continued to walk back to my apartment in silence. Amanda kept pace by my side, but said nothing more.

We entered the building and ascended in the mag lift to my floor, walking down the corridor and entering my apartment, where Amanda immediately put a pot of coffee on and slumped on the sofa.

I took a seat in a chair opposite her. "Look, you're almost certainly right about Hennessey, which is a problem for us. We have no way of taking her out of play without actual evidence."

She looked straight at me, and a strange, wry smile appeared on her usually stoic face. "We don't have to take her out of play. At least not in any official capacity," she remarked.

"What are you suggesting?" I asked.

"We continue to stage the sting. We need to go back to the Hub and identify the two marines with their bio-bands and then create an opportunity."

I was about to ask Amanda what she meant when her comms sounded.

She looked up at me. "It's Hennessey." Her eyes flashed dangerously, but she responded to the call anyway.

"Barclay."

"Amanda, it's Sara. Grealish wants the entire team in the barn in four hours' time."

"What for? Has something happened?"

Hennessey ignored the question. "Bring Jaxon with you."

"And what if I can't find him?"

"You've been with him since 3am. And you're in his apartment. Try opening your eyes." And with that, she ended the call.

CHAPTER
SIXTEEN

MARK HANSON LEFT the hangar in Globe 10 and headed for The Loop. Despite the stress he was under, life on the Bertram had become as normal as living on earth.

His daily routine varied little; wake up, head for The Loop, skim his hollotab for the news on the sixteen-minute ride from Globe 7 to Globe 10. Descend to the hangar and perform his usual duties, servicing and maintaining the small fleet of Sigmas in the dock, whilst studying the flight, atmospheric and gravity systems of the host Globe, before making the sixteen-minute journey back to his apartment. He was on a double shift today, with a three-hour break before returning to Globe 10.

The engineering teams were multi-purposed here, overseeing anything and everything with a flight system. There were separate teams that serviced The Loop and track infrastructure, hull integrity and internal structures, but they all drank in the same bars and told the same stories.

The last few days, his boss had focussed him on the SQIID drives for the entire globe. Each level had its own system, calculated to retain a similar gravitational effect from the top levels to the bottom, linked to a hive system controlled by level 5's gravity. With each globe having an eight-kilometre diameter, the top levels required maximum intervention, as the centrifuge effect of the station rotation provided less than fifty percent of the stipulated 1.04G. The main gravity assist came courtesy of the SQIID drives, which stabilised the lateral movement of the globes and the gravitational load. It was the lower levels that needed less intervention, as the centrifugal load accounted for most of the gravitational forces.

He was just exiting The Loop at 7A when a figure stepped out of the shadows, grabbed his upper arm, and steered him into a service corridor near the mag-lifts. The suddenness of her appearance filled him with dread, and the shock showed clearly on his face.

She took a thick padded belt from her pocket and wrapped it over his wrist and bio-band, forcing him down onto his knees.

She smiled that sweet smile of hers that barely masked the contempt she held for him. "You've been avoiding me, Mark," she said, her head slightly tilted.

"N-no! I w-was just going home," he replied. His hand instinctively sought his injured ear at the memory of their last meeting. The movement did not go unnoticed by the woman.

"That's right, Mark. You'd do well to remember what happens to those that disobey me." She flashed a dangerous smile at him and he winced.

"What do you want?" he asked, with as much bravado as he could muster. He wasn't a weak man – quite the opposite, and usually difficult to intimidate, but there was a very real difference between a few guys throwing their weight around and this group of people who were quite willing to torture and kill to meet their objectives.

"Now, now, Mark. Why so hostile? You knew I'd be coming sooner or later."

He ignored the remark and remained static, staring into those piercing hazel eyes. In different circumstances she'd be very attractive, but all he saw was a sadistic monster. He thought she might be bipolar or perhaps schizophrenic. The changes in her personality were unnerving. He had little contact with her within the military complex now that they were aboard the space station, but whenever their paths crossed and she was in uniform, she'd nod and say hello; not warmly perhaps, but with an air of familiarity. He'd try not to recoil, and would splutter an acknowledgement of sorts. But then *this* version of her, in civvies, skulking in the crevices waiting for her prey; this version of her was evil, and if he didn't know better he'd swear they were two different people.

"We have a little job for you today. Just a tester to see how your skills are developing."

"What do you want?" he repeated.

"You're going back to work in a couple of hours, correct?"

He nodded. "How do you know that?"

She just leered at him. "We know everything, Mark. We also know you're working on the gravitational systems at the moment, and we'd like them to have a little malfunction."

"What do you mean, a *little* malfunction?" he asked, his eyes wide with fear.

"We need them to go offline for an hour at 11am today."

"Offline? You can't be serious. The gravity loss will have horrendous consequences. People will get hurt."

"As will you if you don't do as you're told, Mark. Or would you like me to trim your other ear?" She put a hand to her hip and caressed the handle of her knife.

His eyes widened further, and he tried to shuffle back, raising his free hand. "Okay, okay. I'll knock the systems out, but I can't guarantee an hour. They'll have a team in there in minutes to switch it back on again."

"Well then, you'd better do some serious damage to it to hold them back."

She leaned into him, her nose inches from his. "Eleven, Mark. Or I'll find you." And with that, she walked away, leaving Mark distraught in the service corridor.

———

Amanda was pacing my apartment. "I'm not sure this is a good idea, Jaxon. He's been close to Hennessey for a long time."

"Tyrone is solid, Mand. You said yourself, there's no way he's a suspect here after being hit by that bomb. And we need him."

She sat on my sofa and sighed loudly. "This is getting out of hand, Jaxon. I told you the only people we could trust were each other."

"Yes, and you also rationalised why every member of this team is innocent, except Sara. If we're to find the bastards that killed Laura, we can't do it alone. And Tyrone works with her, so his presence won't raise suspicion."

"She might still be innocent herself, Jaxon. We may have got this all wrong."

"For fuck's sake, Mand. You're the one that's convinced we have a mole and built a case against her."

"Yes, and I also said we shouldn't make any assumptions for fear it'll lead us in the wrong direction. Everything does point to Hennessey, but as you said, it's all circumstantial. We have nothing concrete."

"Do you think it's her or not, Amanda?" I was becoming impatient.

She sat still for a moment; her face a picture of concentration. "On balance, it's a high probability."

"Christ, you sound like a politician. Is that a yes?" The conversation was frustrating me.

"Yes. If it's someone on our team, I can't see it being anyone but her."

"Right, so working under that assumption, can we agree that the quickest route to confirming that is to monitor her movements?"

"It would certainly be easier than trying to tag the entire team. There's still Mark Hanson to consider."

"What happened to 'Hanson is just a low-level pleb'?" As much as I liked Amanda, she was going round in circles.

"Just because I said he's not the protagonist, it doesn't mean he's not involved. It's still likely that he's being met by AoG on board, which was the point of allowing him to embark. Right now, we have two lines of enquiry, which is one more than we had five weeks ago, and since you're so keen on involving Tyrone it gives us an opportunity to cover more ground."

We left my apartment, heading for the mag-lift to the Hub. Amanda seemed more animated.

"Okay, Jax. This is what we need to do. In three hours and forty-five minutes, we have to meet with the team. We'll brief Tyrone later. For now, we need to get things rolling."

"What do you have in mind?" I could see her training kicking in and a plan evolving.

"I think we need to pay Hanson a visit and at least ask him a few questions."

"I thought we were going to the Hub?"

She stopped and turned to me. "We are. You'd better hope Farrell is on our side, Jaxon, because I intend to shake things up. The first thing we have to do is get rid of these bio-bands."

That caught me off guard. "And how are we supposed to do that?"

"We need to pay Aoife a visit."

"What?" This was getting weirder by the minute. "Why Aoife?"

"Because Aoife teaches at that school," she pointed towards the school over by the dome edge, beyond the lake and playing fields, "and the school has a kitchen with a bio-dock. We can leave our bands there, fully connected."

"Won't that alert Grealish and Hennessey?"

"If they're looking, then maybe, but by the time they've come down here to check it out, we'll be long gone."

"But you don't think they're looking? Sara literally just called us out on our movements today."

"It doesn't matter either way, but I think not. Bio-docks are used so frequently that I doubt anyone will know. They've backtracked our movements today, rather than checking in real time, or Grealish would have known we were in the hospital before we asked the marines to put a call in to him."

We stepped onto a path that acted as a ring-road around the outer-circumference of the dome, behind the hospital gardens. The path cut through a small woodland area with raised bridges that passed over clear streams. The light above us danced and flickered as the station rotated and the sun glimmered through the canopy. It really was a beautiful sight, and I found myself captivated by the rippling light.

Six minutes later, we emerged from the woodland onto a wider avenue. Several mag-trams passed us in both directions as we stayed on the edge paths, full of passengers enjoying their daily life on the Bertram. If only they knew what we knew.

I thumbed toward a passing tram. "Are we catching one of those back to the mag-lifts?"

"Without a bio-band?" She just raised her eyebrows at me and continued walking. I supposed we weren't in any hurry, but my legs were still protesting from the surgery. I hadn't done this much exercise in a day since I'd arrived on the Bertram six weeks ago.

We reached the end of the path and the gated entrance to the school. A single security guard sat at a holloscreen in a small cabin by the gates. As soon as he saw Amanda's uniform, he stood up and came to the door.

"Help you?" he asked with a distinct American drawl, and his brow furrowed so much that his bushy eyebrows looked like they were standing on end.

"Major Barclay and Lieutenant Leith to see Aoife Hanrahan."

"Miss Aoife is in lessons at the moment." He pronounced her name "Eee-fee" and I bit back a smile at the thought of the look on her face if she ever heard him. "She won't be free for another forty-five minutes."

"Yes, I'm sure, and in forty-five minutes we need to be elsewhere, so if you'll be so kind as to put a call through we'll meet her in the foyer." She nodded and smiled at the confused guard, and walked towards the school without a backward glance.

I sped up to keep pace with her. We still had a hundred metres to cover before reaching the entrance. "'If you'll be so kind'…? Well, you've changed your tack. Does he double as your butler?" I smirked.

"Oh, do shut up, Leith," she retorted, with her poshest Surrey impersonation.

As we stepped into the foyer, Aoife came jogging down the stairs looking worried. "What are you two doing here?" she asked, glancing between us, consternation all over her face.

"Stop panicking," I replied. "We just need a favour."

She threw her arms around my neck and pulled me into a tight hug. "I'm so sorry about Laura, Jaxon." She released me and hugged Amanda, before pushing her away, putting her hands on her hips and looking fierce. "And where the fuck were you two during her wake, eh? Everyone else was there, and you two fuckers didn't even bother to show. Even that uptight princess from Compression was there." Cooper, I assumed.

Christ, this girl could flip her mood like a burger chef. She bit back a sob and continued to glare at us.

Amanda stepped forward and put a hand on Aoife's shoulder. "Jaxon was in a shit state, Aoif. He couldn't face it." She looked at me with motherly concern, like I was some sort of wounded animal. I would usually have protested, but we didn't have time to explain the whole story, nor could we even if time permitted.

Aoife looked between us, her eyes glistening, that fierce look still on her face. "You should still have been there." She turned to me. "We're supposed to be friends, Jaxon, but you seem to have forgotten us."

"Fuck's sake, Aoif. I had a drink with you and… just a week ago." I'd nearly said her name, but this conversation had brought back the rawness all over again.

Her expression softened for a moment, almost imperceptibly, before she drew herself upright and settled back to her usual challenging demeanour.

"What are you both doing here? I've got fucking lessons, you know?" The Irish in her came out so strongly when she was annoyed or trying not to be vulnerable. Which was basically all the time.

Amanda spoke. "We need to get inside the kitchens, Aoife. Without anyone knowing. We're trusting you here. We need to dock our bio-bands and then we've got… something to do," she finished a little weakly, but Aoife just stared between us.

"Is this about Laura?" she asked, searching for the answer in my eyes.

I nodded. Amanda stepped forward. "It is. But we need

to be off the grid for a few hours, and you're the only person we can trust."

There was a momentary pause, no doubt while Aoife thought of some biting comment to come back with, but in the end she just nodded and said, "This way."

Thirty minutes later Amanda and I stepped into the mag-lifts.

"Stop rubbing your wrist. You'll draw attention to us," she admonished me.

It felt alien not to be wearing it after more than three months of solid use. There was a very pale line on my wrist that hadn't been there during Compression, so presumably courtesy of the sunlight on the station.

"I've only ever taken it off to go through DECON. It just feels weird."

"If you touch it again, your face is going to feel weird as I slap some sense into you." Classy.

As we approached the Hub my stomach flipped, and I could feel myself getting lighter. The doors pinged open, and we stepped out on to the hamster wheel.

Amanda made straight for the poles and hoisted herself into the weightless arena above. I followed suit and five minutes later, we arrived at the core.

"We're going to head down to section 3 and walk back, okay?" I just nodded and trusted that Amanda knew what she was doing. At least one of us did.

We floated down to the surface, where I landed a touch more gracefully than my first attempt, but barely. Amanda reached down with her hand and hauled me upright before turning and walking to the opposite edge of the pathway.

"Farrell's office is on the other side, Mand," I said.

"Yes, I'm aware, but I don't want her team watching us

approach from a few-hundred metres away. We'll walk down this side and then cut through the security sections directly." She sped up, almost bouncing down the walkway in the reduced gravity.

The outer dome to our right just looked out into deep space. I could see the moon coming into view, vivid and bright and a third in shadow, and rotating gracefully over us as the station spun, the arc of light much slower in the Hub.

I looked up and could see the edges of the globes above us. My legs felt suddenly wobbly as my brain processed the view of the pin-prick tops of the tallest buildings, and the people, so far away that they didn't even register as specks of dust on the streets below them.

A few minutes later, we arrived at Section 4 and turned left to cross the various stations within the security section. It took another five minutes to traverse the pathway, zig-zagging between consoles and personnel, before we arrived at Farrell's door.

Amanda knocked once and entered, with me just a step behind.

We found Farrell as before, her head inches from a holloscreen desk, her hands wandering around the control panels almost autonomously. "Yes? What is it? I asked not to be disturbed," she barked without looking up. It would seem this was a daily routine.

"It's Amanda and Jaxon. We've got work to do, Gemma."

Farrell sat up and turned to face us, and then waved toward the seats opposite her.

"Okay, what have you got for me?"

Amanda explained the conversation with Emily Latimer, about the two marines that showed up at her house and the date and approximate time of their arrival.

"Do you have an address?" she enquired, looking at the pair of us.

"Err…" was all I could manage.

"No matter. I'll find her in the directory. She was 11-5-C?"

"No," replied Amanda. "BRMC accommodations in 11-5-A."

Farrell tapped away on her holloscreen for a minute or two before she looked up.

"Related to Brian Latimer?"

"That's the one," I said.

"Okay, I've got it." She transferred it to a holloscreen behind her on the wall and then entered the date and time in the search box. She then scrolled through at triple speed, watching the little red dots traverse the screen as people passed by during the evening, but nobody approached the Latimer apartment until 21.53. Two dots moved in unison from the bottom corner of the screen, near The Loop entrance, winding their way through the streets and houses until they came to a stop outside Emily Latimer's home.

"That's our perps," said Amanda, pointing at them as they approached the house. "Can you I.D. them?" she asked, without taking her eyes from the screen.

"It'll take a couple of minutes. As you can see, there's a lot of dots in the apartment complex, so I need to make sure we get the right people."

She was right. There *were* a lot of people in the building – probably fifty in all. The two dots that had stopped entered the building, and we lost them in the maelstrom of human activity inside the apartment block.

Farrell continue to scroll through the time frame at triple speed until the clock in the screen's corner indicated twenty-six minutes had elapsed since the two marines had entered the building. They exited together, more slowly than before, and spent almost seven minutes outside the apartment, presumably loading Emily and the twins into the vehicle that they'd arrived in.

The vehicle began to move, and Farrell allowed it to proceed into a more remote area of Globe 11, Level 5, Section A before pausing the feed and isolating the vehicle. She used her fingers to zoom in on the space around the two dots and then pressed an icon in the bottom corner. Immediately, the two dots lit up with the names next to them.

"Sergeants Reed Danby and Kristoffer Askey," read Amanda, tilting her head to discern the lettering.

"Do you want me to add markers to them?" asked Farrell, and then seeing the confused look on our faces continued, "It'll track all of their movements and record logs of any transactions or bio-band usage or removal."

"Yes, please," replied Amanda. "That'll certainly make our jobs easier."

Farrell nodded. "Okay, so you have your two kidnappers. Who else am I looking for?"

"Mark Hanson," I said, before Amanda could start talking about the team.

"Mark… Hanson…" she responded, under her breath as she typed his name in. "Globe 7?" she asked.

Amanda and I looked at each other. "Did you say 'Globe 7'?"

Farrell looked down at her console. "Yes, that's what I have here. Lives on Level 4 of Globe 7. G7-4-A14. 16-15-C to be exact."

"That's the address from the package in the lab," said Amanda, giving me a meaningful look.

"That changes things," I said. There was little point in staking it out if we knew who lived there.

Farrell continued as if there'd been no interruption. "Commutes to Globe 10 for work. Look, here he is now," she said, pointing at The Loop station of Globe 10, Level 5, section A, where a single red dot labelled 'Mark Hanson' was entering the globe from the level 5 station exit. "Hang on, that's weird."

"What's weird?" Amanda asked, trying to crane her neck over the desk to see the screen.

Farrell swiped her screen across onto one of the wall-mounted holloscreens to our left, and zoomed out. There were literally hundreds of thousands of little red dots all over the globe, with a healthy proportion of them clearly moving to and from The Loop. She isolated the top level and pointed at the middle-left edge of the screen. "There's your bloke, Hanson, entering the level now."

Sure enough, the red dot was moving inwards, beyond the station boundaries, towards the engineering section. She then moved her hand down, towards two white dots, close by. "And here's your two marines that we've just tracked," she said, looking up.

"What?!" both Amanda and I replied simultaneously.

Amanda looked at me, and I could see she was thinking the same thing. *He's working with them.*

"Gemma, we have to go right now, but I need you to find and add a marker to Sara Hennessey while we're gone. Lives in 11-5-A in the officer's estate. We'll be back later."

Farrell waved us off and continued to work as we left the office. Amanda dived straight for the poles and hauled herself upwards at a breath-taking pace.

I mimicked her launch and nearly propelled myself away from the pole. I wondered what would happen if I found myself floating about near the core, without a hand-hold. Nothing good, I concluded.

We arrived at the intersection at break-neck speed, and with fifty metres to go, Amanda grabbed the pole we were ascending and arrested her momentum, before spinning around and descending the pole labelled "11". I followed, at a much more manageable pace, and by the time I dropped towards the surface of the hamster wheel, Amanda was already approaching the bottom of the ladder.

I watched as she sprinted across to the mag-lifts and, without waiting for me, stepped inside. The doors closed before I'd even reached the ladder. The good news was that nobody got to see my dismount as I sent myself sprawling across the pathway before stopping in a heap at the foot of a console station. "Nailed it," I muttered under my breath.

I ran for the mag-lift, which was no easy feat in thirty-eight percent gravity. I felt more like the Easter Bunny, bouncing along without an ounce of dignity.

After a couple of minutes the lift pinged open, and I jabbed the button for The Loop. Fortunately, I didn't need a bio-band to descend. We'd used Amanda's clearance to get up here. Amanda would be close to half-way down already, and I wondered what she was going to do when she eventually entered Globe 10.

As I stepped out of the lift, I could see the tail-end of The Loop tearing off into the tunnel. "Shit!" I turned and ran for the Great Wall, and the second set of mag-lifts on the right. As the lift opened, I suddenly realised I didn't have my bio-band. I wasn't going anywhere. I was about to launch into a thousand profanities when Addison Nile stepped in beside me.

"Jaxon! How the bloody hell are you?" His face scrunched into a sad frown. "I heard the news about Laura – I'm so very sorry. Take as much time as you need before you come back, okay?"

I'd never been so pleased to see anyone in my life. "Addison, thanks. Are you going down to the hangar?"

He looked at me with a quizzical look on his face.

"Sir, please, I need to get to my Sigma."

"Where's your hollotab?"

"In my apartment. I don't have time to explain. I need to get over to Globe 10, and The Loop has already left."

"Christ, Jaxon. What have you got yourself into now?" he asked, as he pressed the button for the hangar. Then, seeing my face pleading with him, continued, "Alright, I'll take you over, but I'll have to be quick. We have a sortie in fifty minutes."

"Thank you, Sir. You're a lifesaver," I responded.

"Yes, yes, and stop with the bloody 'Sirs'. It won't make me regret this any less."

I grinned at him, and the mag-lift opened onto the hangar. We stepped out and Addison handed me his hollotab. "Prep my ride. It's in Alpha 4. I'll get us cleared and meet you on the dock."

I sprinted to row Alpha and found Addison's Sigma, 'Ocelot', parked in Bay 4. I clambered inside and slammed the hollotab into the dock, before climbing back out and running for the pushback tugs on the main dock. I jumped into the tug and swung the front end round to face the Ocelot before edging forward until the connector arm was just centimetres from the ship's towing handle. Running to the front, I grabbed the remote, extending the capture arm out until it clicked around the tow handle, and then hurdled back into the tug and reversed into the bay, with the Sigma floating behind me on its magnetic suspension. I stopped at the first docking space, unclamped and dumped the tug back into the dock where I found it, and dived back into the Sigma.

I powered up the nucleus, switched on the gyro-spheres, and watched as the screens filled up as Addison had them set, before climbing out of his seat and into the spare.

Addison came running out of the office, and hauled himself into the cockpit without the steps, punching at the door closure before taking his seat. As soon as the door had sealed, the hollotab lit up red, along with all the screens, and we waited as the bay depressurised and the gigantic doors opened on our port side. The screens went green as the doors were opening, and Addison wasted no time throttling out and powering us through the gap. He immediately swung us left and traversed the outside of the dome in the bottom portion, keeping us within two-hundred metres of the EM glass.

He really was an incredible pilot, and it wasn't until now that I appreciated just how experienced he was in that pilot seat. Usually we'd break out of the station's rotational pathway and ride in the opposite direction until the globe we required came around, but Addison had clearly understood there was some urgency here, and he silently navigated his way around the globe until he had a straight trajectory to Globe 10 bay doors. He increased our speed, momentarily putting us halfway between the two globes and then just as quickly trimmed out and crabbed backwards as Globe 10 swung upwards on its arc. Because the station was rotating with Earth to the port side, the globes at the top of the arc were travelling significantly slower than those at the bottom, relative to Earth, and we'd exited 11 just as it was phasing upwards in the cycle, catching Globe 10 in the latter stages as it began the backwards travel at the top of the circle.

He skilfully matched our trajectory with that of the Globe 10 bay doors before putting a call through to the tower and dropping it in the dock. The entire trip had only taken nine minutes, but it felt like an hour. I waited until the lights went green and launched myself out of the Sigma, thanking Addison as I left, and watched as he resealed the door and waited for me to leave the dock so it could depressurise for his return trip.

I sprinted through the airlock and up the stairs to the mag-lifts, where I was again hampered by my lack of bioband. Fortunately, Globe 10 only had a small dock, so they dedicated most of the level to industrial and commercial units, with mag-lifts extending to the levels above by The

Loop station, which didn't require a bio-band. I exited the hangar and ran for the lifts, my legs screaming at me as I powered onwards, gulping in the recycled air as my lungs protested at the sudden burst of exercise.

The mag-lift closed as I stepped in and I felt the familiar turn of my stomach as it climbed upwards against gravity, except this time the sensation pulled right at my insides, and I felt myself becoming disoriented the further we rose. I was so confused as the doors opened I didn't notice the small wave heading towards me, and choked as the water engulfed me.

CHAPTER
SEVENTEEN

MY BRAIN COULDN'T UNDERSTAND what was occurring. The negative pressure sucked me out of the mag-lift in a bubble of clear water, with the blurred flickering of fish brushing past my face. *Space fish*. What the fuck was happening?

I clipped the edge of the mag-lift column, and the water cascaded away from me, leaving me floating in mid-air about two metres from the metal pathway. I looked up and the sight that greeted me was utter carnage. Something had happened to the gravity.

I wiped the water from my face as droplets were still clinging to my eyelashes whilst trying to grab anything that could stabilise me. All around me, people were panicking and screaming.

We'd had conversations about this in the bars, as the globes would go weightless if we ever had a separation order, but what we had imagined was always bordering on amusing. The thought of thousands of people, floating about inside a globe had sparked mental images of flying cats, impossible bowling and any number of hilarious possibilities. There was nothing remotely funny about what I was seeing here.

Bodies of water were drifting up from the ponds and streams that ran through the level. It looked like the top covers hadn't closed and there were several people fighting off enormous bubbles of water, spinning freely, threatening to swallow them.

Two mag-trams floated up near the outer edge of the dome, over a kilometre above us. I supposed the magnetic systems that kept them frictionless propelled them away from the ground when the gravity failed. There were still people inside, but they were too far away to hear the screams.

Everywhere I looked was chaos. People and objects were spiralling away into the dome helplessly. Whilst not an expert in weightlessness, my experience in the Hub had given me a measure of control and calm. I looked around for the station entrance – it was three-hundred metres away to my right. Amanda would be there somewhere, looking for Mark and the two marines that kidnapped Emily. On another day I'd put a call in to Farrell and ask her to ping me their locations, but without a bio-band I had zero comms.

I heaved on the ledge I was clinging to and sent myself flying in The Loop's direction, continuing my search for Amanda, but there was so much debris in the air that visibility was down to just a few metres. I collided with dozens of people and objects, a couple of which were enough to bump me off course, so I spent a large proportion of my flight time grabbing fixtures and altering my direction.

I wondered what would happen if they restarted the gravity system. Would the SQIID drives graduate a gravitational assist or kick back in at one hundred and four percent? If that happened, people would die. Lots of people would die. There were tens of thousands, if not hundreds of thousands of people free-floating across the dome, totally unable to affect their trajectory.

Had the SQIID drives even failed? Without them, there was still a little gravity to keep everyone closer to the ground, but we were all free-floating in space. I didn't know if this was a localised failure or across the entire station. Swivelling my head, I tried to take a bearing from Earth, and sure enough, we were still rotating. So it was a local issue then. Someone had either switched the system off or it had malfunctioned. Accidentally or deliberately? Given what I already knew, I'd bet my left nut sack that this had something to do with Mark.

"Jaxon! JAXON!!"

I attempted to turn at the sound of my name, but I was mid-flight with nothing to grab so that I could pull myself round.

"Mand? Is that you?" My head was working around trying to find the source. I passed over a small building in front of The Loop entrance, and with every ounce of effort I could muster, I reached for the metal piping around the parapet.

As my fingers closed round it, another wave of cold water engulfed my head and torso. I waved my free hand furiously, trying to break the surface, flinging droplets of water in all directions but it continued to swirl around my head, working its way down my body until I was a prisoner of physics. Surface tension holds together water droplets, but with equal forces in all directions the water had no escape route, and neither did I. Not good.

I yanked on the piping and dragged myself downwards, keeping my grip on the wet metal. If I floated out into the dome with this water covering me, I would drown in a couple of minutes. My lungs were already protesting at the sudden lack of oxygen. I hadn't seen it coming, so no deep breaths before being completely encased.

My toes connected with something behind me, and I scrabbled around to lock my legs to the object so that I could free my hands to bat away the bubble. I had no idea what it was I'd kicked, but I stretched my legs out as far as I could, before bringing them back in, hoping I'd get a foothold that would stabilise me. The lack of oxygen was burning my lungs, and I could feel blackness creeping slowly through my brain.

In desperation, I searched my body for anything that could help pull me out of this bubble. I felt the edge of my kit belt with my fingers, and deployed my re-breather mask. My brain was fogging quickly and as I struggled to release the mask from my belt, I struck a solid object attached to my waist. My Proxy!

My fingers gripped the smooth surface around the top edge and sought the stippled end, closing around the shaft as I choked inside the floating pool of death. I squeezed with all my might, and then the darkness swept over me.

"Lock it down. Now!"

"Sir?"

"Don't you fucking *Sir* me. Lock the entire station down. I don't want anyone moving between globes while this shit show in Globe 10 continues."

The admiral slammed his comms against the desk and sat heavily in his protesting chair. Alarms still sounded all over the fleet control panels, with red flashing beacons every ten metres along the corridors of power.

He had the security heads, Commanders Farrell and Brannon on holloscreen one, Colonel Grealish on two and Navy Command assembled in the operations centre of Globe 5.

He addressed them all. "Someone tell me what happened, and what we're doing about it."

A navy captain cleared his throat and spoke. "Sir, we have a complete gravity failure on Globe 10. We have engineers in situ, but they're currently struggling to get to the engineering rooms that house the SQIID drives."

"That's incorrect," replied Commander Farrell and then, as an afterthought, added, "Sir." She hated the stuffiness of ranks, but the circumstances warranted a little diplomacy. She addressed the admiral. "The gravity has been reversed. If it were just a failure, there'd be enough inertia from the centrifuge effect to have some gravity, however minimal, on the upper levels. As it stands, there is zero gravity on levels three to five, so the SQIIDs are working against us."

Grealish piped up. "Could this be an accident?"

Farrell scratched her head. "Not likely, Colonel. If there was still some gravity it would indicate a failure, but a full reversal has to be deliberate, unless it's a software issue, but if that were the case we'd all be floating."

Admiral Willard addressed Grealish. "Andrew, do you think this is linked to your investigation?"

Grealish shuffled uncomfortably. The silly old fool was spouting highly classified information over an open channel. "It's unclear, Sir, but I'm not sure we should broach this subject here and now."

The admiral nearly burst a fuse. "I couldn't give a rat's arse what you're not sure about, Andrew. I've got seven-hundred-thousand people floating about in zero G inside Globe 10, and I want answers!"

Commander Brannon spoke. "Sir, we've got authorised maintenance scheduled on the SQIID drives in Globe 10 today and tomorrow. I know Gemma said it couldn't be an accident, but it seems more likely given that the systems were being worked on."

Farrell just rolled her eyes and sat back. Other people's opinions weren't something she particularly cared about.

Captain Mellors interjected. "Sir, if it's scheduled maintenance, then the engineers are already present that can resolve this. Does anyone have information on the detail, so we can get them on comms? Gemma?"

Farrell looked up. She knew very well who was there, but made a show of scrolling through her data logs, anyway. "There are three engineers on site. Theo Sadiq, Shannon Lockett and Mark Hanson, Sir."

Grealish's face looked up at the mention of Hanson. The admiral's face contorted with rage. "Well, Andrew?"

"Fuck fuck fuck fuck fuck..." was all the virtual gathering heard, as Grealish clicked off comms and ran for the control room.

Theo Sadiq looked across at Shannon and Mark. Both were floating around inside the engineering centre, looking equally fearful.

"It doesn't matter what's happened or why right now. We need to fix it, and quickly. Any ideas?"

Shannon Lockett grabbed the door handle and pulled herself back to the ground, keeping her grip so as not to float away again. "We need to shut it down now. I can isolate the breakers, but they're behind the service panel. We can't do it from in here."

Theo's comms sounded, and he connected the call.

"Chief Engineer Sadiq? This is Commander Farrell, station security. I've got you tracked to engineering on Globe 10. What's your situation?"

"Ma'am, we've got a complete polarity reversal on the SQIIDs. No diagnosis yet, but looking for ideas."

"Can you re-engage the drives to normal from there?"

Shannon furiously waved her arms at Theo.

"Hold, Ma'am," he replied, before looking up at Shannon.

"We can't reverse it, Theo. There are thousands of people free floating in the dome. If we suddenly create full gravity, they'll fall to their deaths. And that's only the ones we can see. Most of the lower levels are at least half a kilometre high, so anyone down there faces the same fate." She looked desperate.

Theo tapped his comms. "Ma'am, re-engaging the drives would result in a massive loss of life. We need to shut the system down and slow the station rotation, then re-engage gradually."

"Understood. I'll run it past station control. How long will it take you to shut it down?"

"The issue is access, Ma'am. We can knock out the breakers, but they're secured behind a panel which isn't easily accessible. We may need an engineering EVA to reach the circuits."

"Shit!" replied Farrell. The last thing they needed was to send someone outside in an EVA suit. It would take hours just to reach the panel.

Mark spoke. "We can reset the drives from the command panel, and then shut them down before they kick in to life." There was sweat dripping from his forehead and floating away into the chamber. The bandage on his ear was flapping uselessly in the weightless room.

"That's a huge risk, Mark," replied Theo. "We'd only have a few seconds to shut down after the reboot. If we missed the window of opportunity, full gravity would be in effect within thirty seconds."

"Mark's right," said Shannon. "An EVA will take too long. We can reboot the system, then shut the whole globe down before the SQIIDs restart."

"No." Mark's response was emphatic, and they both

looked over at him. "We'd be in an unlit globe, with debris everywhere. It'll be too dangerous. We need to disconnect the actual drive ports at the source."

Theo's eyebrows shot up. "But they're in the dome canopy. How would we even get to them?"

"It's zero G out there at the moment. I'll float up to the drive console and unplug them once you've rebooted the system. Then once the centrifuge winds up, I'll plug them back in."

"That's suicide, Mark. Even if you somehow secured yourself while the centrifuge does its job, once everyone is down and safe, we'll need to switch the drives back on. How would we get back up to you?"

He shrugged. His life was worthless anyway. He should never have caved to this pressure. These people were evil, and if there was a way he could save many at the expense of his own life, then, he surmised, it would be the least he deserved.

Theo's comms sparked into life again. He'd left the channel open. "Can it be done?" asked Farrell.

Theo replied. "Ma'am, I strongly recommend against this course of action."

"Can it be done?" repeated Farrell, more firmly.

Mark nodded at Theo. "Yes, Ma'am. We can do it."

"Very well," came the response. "Keep your channel open and get to work. I'll get the station slowed."

"Captain Mellors. We have a plan." Farrell looked up at Mellors on her holloscreen.

"Go ahead, Commander."

"We need to slow the rotation down to 266 metres per second. That'll reduce the angular velocity to approximately 0.1 r.p.m."

Mellors tapped away on a screen before looking up. "Christ, Gemma. We'll be operating at 0.3 G. The entire station will lose gravity."

"The SQIID drives in the upper levels will compensate enough to keep everyone's feet on the ground. They'll have at least fifty percent gravity."

"And this is the only way?" Mellors looked stressed. The station controls were his, and he'd barely had to do anything since taking command four years ago.

"It's the only way to save a few hundred thousand people on Globe 10. If we switch the SQIIDs back on, thousands will fall to their deaths. Giving them just under thirty percent gravity once they shut the drives down will at least provide most of them a fighting chance to land and regain some control."

"Understood. It'll be fifteen minutes to alert all personnel before we can start the reverse burn."

There was a dull thrumming coming back to my senses. My body felt cool, and the inky darkness around my eyes was lifting. Blurred light continued to fog my vision, and my throat felt raw. I gagged and felt a warm wetness soak through my left arm and chest. At least I was alive and hadn't succumbed to the floating pool of death, I surmised. Also, Floating Pool Of Death seemed like a glorious name for a thrash-metal band.

My right arm was being squeezed. It wasn't painful, but it felt like I couldn't properly move it if I needed to. Gradually my eyes adjusted to the light, which had now become an intermittent glow, but I still could not discern shapes. I could hear a muggy wailing noise and what sounded like an announcement, but the words weren't clear. Probably telling me to mind the gap.

More tugging at my right arm, and now some pressure on my chest. I wondered if someone was trying to pull my gloves off by standing on my ribs? That couldn't be right. Why would I be wearing gloves? The wailing noise grew louder. It sounded like the depressurisation alert in the launch bays. Fuck! Was I unconscious in a launch bay? If so, that's me bollocksed. Unless I was already outside and someone pulled me in. Nothing was making sense. I was wet. Space isn't wet. Otherwise we'd have space fish.

SPACE FISH! My eyes opened, and the world around me came flooding back. Probably not the best choice of verb. Lyrics like that would never make it into the Floating Pool Of Death album.

"Jaxon! Fuck's sake, wake up!" Amanda screamed at me.

It was like someone had removed a bag from my head. My senses were suddenly alive with information. I could see red flashing lights everywhere, and the wailing sirens were loud and immediate. Amanda was hovering over me, gripping the chest of my fatigues.

"Mand?"

I tried to reach up with my hand, but my arm wouldn't move. I looked down, and found myself tied to a railing about fifty metres from the station entrance.

"Jesus Christ, Jaxon. I thought I'd lost you for a minute." She looked genuinely relieved.

"What the fuck happened?" I croaked, my throat grating as I spoke.

"We've lost the gravity systems. Everything's gone to shit. You got swallowed up by one of the streams."

"I remember," I replied, weakly. "How'd I get free? Nothing seemed to work."

"Your Proxy. You deployed your Proxy. It scattered the bubble you were in and switched your brain off in the process. You're a fucking idiot."

"Cheers. I feel like one too. How long have I been out of it?" My throat was stinging with each syllable.

"Not a clue. At least fifteen minutes. Honestly, Jax, I thought you were done for. I saw you float past and then a body of water just rose up and attached itself to you. I watched you fighting it for about a minute before your body went inert, and just as I thought you were gone, your Proxy deployed and sent the water off in a million pieces. By the time I got here, you were rigid. I thought it was rigor mortis, but you were soaking wet and deploying an electromagnetic weapon, so I put two and two together and knocked the Proxy out of your hand. You've got more lives than a bag of cats."

I looked down and saw my re-breather tied to my arm and the railing next to it. My body was still floating at a weird angle, and Amanda was upside down above me. There were literally thousands of people beyond her, littering the skies between her and the outer dome.

"I need you to get moving. They're about to slow the station down and reinitiate the gravity system. It's going to start raining people very shortly." She looked concerned.

I reached up for her, and she stretched out for my left arm and pulled herself down to my level. Mand grabbed the railing and untied me. My brain still wasn't up to speed and I tried to gather the re-breather back into my kit belt.

"No time for that now, Jax. We need to get inside a building quickly." She pulled me around until I was almost upright and facing the other way. The railing trailed away for three or four metres and ended at a small building. "Grab my kit belt," she commanded forcefully.

I did as I was told, and let her drag us both to a building, before pulling the door open and swinging me inside. There were three people already in the room, all floating around the edges with their backs against the EM glass. I went to pull the door closed, but Amanda grabbed my hand and pulled me further inside.

"Leave it open. We might yet need to get out. If one of those mag-trams comes down on us..." She let the words hang.

A chime sounded, and I suddenly felt myself drifting towards the floor, my feet connecting with solid ground. I had the sudden urge to puke and felt my stomach flip over. I wasn't the only one. Two of the men in the room suddenly gagged, and the horrible sounds of retching and splattering filled the small cavity.

Amanda took no notice. She was looking out of the glass as masses of people descended from the dome.

I fought my way out of the room, still light but feeling oddly heavy, and looked up. It was awful to watch. Thousands upon thousands of people were cascading downwards, with very little control. Those that arrived feet first from lower heights seemed to land easily enough, although most stumbled and hit the deck. The people that were higher up were coming down much more quickly, and were hitting buildings and trees and the ground, some at horrible angles. Then there were those that came down head first, hands in front of them, desperately trying to fend off the on-rushing floor. A few rolled as they connected and found themselves alive and relatively unscathed, but the majority crumpled to the ground and remained still.

The first mag-tram hit with a force that made the ground tremble. It was like watching sped-up slow-motion. As it neared the ground, a few passengers leapt from the open doorway, taking their chances with their own mass and velocity. Those inside were less fortunate – the leaps from the escapees caused the tram to spin as it gained momentum, eventually crashing to the ground with a distressing finality. I tried to run to them, but Amanda pulled me back as bodies continued to rain down.

Those who were fortunate enough to land safely were now dealing with falling debris and people, dodging and weaving their way to the nearest shelter as the ground filled with broken bodies. It took almost three minutes before the last body hit the ground. The air was suddenly still for a moment, and then the screaming began anew.

"Jaxon, look!" Amanda twisted me around and pointed upwards. About a third of the way up the dome wall was a man, gripping a panel set into the titanium exoskeleton of the globe. His legs were hanging, and it looked like he was struggling to keep hold. The gravity was coming back now, and I stumbled under the renewed load.

"Oh my God! He's going to fall." As I spoke, he turned and looked down. It was Mark Hanson. Even from this distance, he was distinctly identifiable. No sooner had I recognised him than I felt my body dragged to the floor, bruising my coccyx on the metal walkway. I wasn't the only one. Everyone seemed to topple as the gravity system rebooted and the station accelerated.

Amanda looked down at me, and back at Mark. "Shit. How can we help him?" But we were too late. We watched as his hands faltered on the SQIID ports, and a moment later he fell from three-hundred-metres to his death.

PART TWO

CHAPTER
EIGHTEEN

"SIX THOUSAND, nine hundred and forty-one people died yesterday, when the gravity system failed in Globe 10. A further seven people died in other globes across the station, as a result of accidents caused by the reduction in gravity during the fifteen-minute reverse burn that was initiated to save the residents of Globe 10. Council sources claim that eighty-four thousand are being treated for injuries sustained as the gravity systems came back on line. Medical facilities are at capacity and officials are asking those with non-life-threatening injuries to stay away for the time being."

The news presenter was unusually sombre. The ticker-tape messages across the bottoms of every holloscreen on the station replayed the same numbers repeatedly. Amanda and I sat in Lovell's bar, in a corner booth with Aoife and Libby. None of us were really drinking. Even Aoife, who was usually two drinks ahead of everyone within an hour of arrival, was just sipping at the foam on her beer.

"Today, station chief Captain Mellors read a short tribute to commemorate the lives lost in this tragic incident, and pay special tribute to engineer Mark Hanson, who died as he attempted to reboot the gravity systems from inside the dome canopy."

I turned away from the screen. The captain's words just washed over me without meaning. Amanda and I exchanged looks and I could see she was thinking the same thing; *what do we do now?*

Aoife's eyes misted with tears, as did Libby's. None of us were close to Mark – and not for lack of effort, at least in the early days. He'd drifted apart from the crew and kept to himself for most of his time in Compression, and isolated himself completely on this vessel.

I felt guilty, mostly. Not just because Mark had died, but because it killed our best line of enquiry in the investigation. The gravity failure was a deliberate act of sabotage, although you wouldn't hear about it on the news. Even the powers-that-be believed it to be an accident, because of the engineering works that were scheduled for that day on the SQIID drives, but Amanda and I knew better.

The politicians did their part, and they wrote new protocols to prevent this ever recurring, but it did little to appease my trepidation at the challenge to come.

Once the bodies had stopped falling, Mand and I did what we could for those nearest to us. We left anyone cognitive with broken bones and bruises to their own devices. We spent an hour sifting through the corpses, looking for signs of life amongst the inert. There were hundreds of others helping too, and once the medical teams showed up from the other globes, the task of saving badly injured survivors proceeded with earnest, until there were only corpses left littered across the ground. Exhausted, both emotionally and physically, Mand and I took our leave and headed back to Globe 11.

The Loop shut down the moment the SQIIDs had gone offline, and a couple of thousand people had spent over an hour inside one of twelve trains that had locked down in the connecting tunnels, with no information, just waiting for the train to power up again. Full service resumed within thirty minutes of the gravity being re-enabled to support the medical evacuation and emergency response teams.

Thousands of animals had perished on the lower levels. Entire fields of crops had succumbed as the millions of tonnes of soil, loosened under the gravitational failure, crashed back to the floor, damaging the ground structures and framework of the hull. Hundreds of buildings suffered damaged and thousands of vehicles lay destroyed in the streets, their mag-locks not engaged when the SQIIDs powered off. They would write new software to slave vehicles to the ground in the event of future gravitational anomalies.

Several bodies we found looked like they'd drowned, and I realised how close I'd come to losing my life. The streams and ponds all had electronic covers that sealed, enabling a gravitational shift to occur when necessary, but none of the safety protocols had accounted for a SQIID failure. Our station chief and engineering teams would resolve this in the coming weeks. The deep, shimmering lakes that adorned the upper levels had their own inertia drives as a failsafe, and these had worked, thankfully. The body count would be so much higher if they hadn't. Many of the lakes had viewing panels on the underside in the lower levels, but these were closed whilst marines recovered the bodies of the deceased.

Dozens of Sigmas were patrolling the space outside Globe 10, assessing the damage. Many of the EM glass panels around the dome showed signs of fatigue, with stress fractures littering the outer dome. Teams of engineers dispatched immediately, whilst the remaining residents had to be evacuated and temporarily relocated to Globe 9. It was a huge operation, and for the next twenty-four hours, the station council recommissioned two Loop trains to travel only the short distance between Globes 10 and 9, carrying the residents to safety.

We'd collected our bio-bands from the school a short while later, by which time the news was all over the station. We both looked a mess as we walked back into the kitchen, so much so that Aoife didn't even dredge up any snarky comments to throw at us.

We wandered silently back to my apartment, our unofficial base of operations, threw our fatigues in the laundry chute and collapsed on the bed. In other circumstances it might have seemed strange, the two of us sleeping in my bed, especially so soon after the death of Laura, but we were exhausted both mentally and physically, and by the time the SQIID drives failed we'd already been working for eight hours. It was after 4pm when we arrived back and fell asleep.

The sound of the shower running woke me. My bio-band showed 7.12pm. Mand was washing the day's grime off, so I put a pot of coffee on and poured us both a brew. I jumped in the shower once she was out and sat for ten minutes in the corner, letting the hot water drench me and ease my aching muscles.

Aoife had called to ask us to join her and Libby at Lovell's. Jennifer would be down a little later, but she was training up as a medic, so her day had got busy quickly. I hadn't seen her since we left Compression, so it would be good to catch up. If only it were on a different day.

Amanda and I had missed the meeting. Neither of us had any idea if it had even happened, though we speculated it was unlikely, given the circumstances and The Loop lockdown.

We talked about what might have become of the two marines we were tracking besides Mark, but we abandoned that speculation after a while. Nothing was going to change overnight.

So, there we were, sitting quietly in a bar with our friends, trying to pretend our day hadn't gone to shit.

"Are you two fuckers going to tell us what's going on here?" Aoife piped up. I knew it wouldn't take long for her to revert to her usual cutting disposition.

"Aoif—" I began, but she cut me off with spirited arms flailing about in my general direction.

"Don't you fucking fill me with shite, Jaxon. You two have been thick as thieves since the last few weeks of Compression, having secret meetings all over the place, and now you're involving me in your shady shite. I've a right to know what's going on."

She looked at us haughtily and crossed her arms. I turned to Amanda, who just shrugged.

Libby eyed us both, that beautiful smile of hers conspicuous in its absence. "Well? Aoife's right. You sneak off together a few nights ago in a Sigma, return a few hours later with the news that Laura is dead, and now you're asking Aoife to dock your bio-bands while you run freely around the station. What the hell is going on?"

Amanda looked furious. "For fuck's sake, Aoife. We told you not—"

"—Don't fucking get all high and mighty with me! We're not stupid, and we *are* your friends. Libby, Jenn and I have been discussing your little meetings ever since you gave Eloise a kicking. Something is going on, and we're worried." Aoife was prodding her fingers at us animatedly.

"We deserve the truth, Jax." Libby was clearly just as pissed off as Aoife, but evidently less riled up. She turned to Amanda. "We know you were ICP and undercover in Compression. It's hardly a stretch of the imagination to believe your work has continued up here. After that bomb went off, you and Jaxon were called into more than one meeting. Why?" She glared at us both.

"And don't be telling us it was because you were there

when it went off, Amanda, because you were sat on your arse in Stage 2 with us."

I sighed. This was an impossible situation. We couldn't tell anyone about the gathered intelligence, and yet we'd already used our friendships to expedite the investigation. To my great surprise, Amanda spoke.

"Back on Earth, I was a deep cover operative for a specialist counter-terrorism task force embedded within the ICP. My job was to infiltrate and expose AoG operatives inside government and military departments. That's how I ended up in Compression."

"And your job was to capture Eloise?" asked Libby.

Amanda shook her head. "No. My job was to identify and neutralise the AoG infiltrators inside Compression Echo. We had intelligence from a source, inserted years previously into the AoG command structure, that they'd granted two operatives Occo status in Crew 41."

"Hold your horses. There was more than one infiltrator in our crew? But there were only nine of us. How could that be?" Aoife's eyes flickered between us rapidly.

"It's worse than that, Aoif," I responded. "Leon was an AoG defector. They sent Eloise to kill him. We never found out who the other agent was."

"Wait, what?" Libby looked confused. "But that means..."

I just nodded. Amanda filled in the blanks. "Laura and I were both law enforcement. Leon and Eloise were definitely AoG, even if Leon had turned traitor to save his own skin. The intelligence was solid. One of the remaining crew was, or is, AoG."

"Leon was one of them?" asked Libby, looking shocked. Amanda nodded.

I picked up where she left off. "So it's either someone sitting at this table, or Jennifer."

"Or Mark," Amanda added. "And we had sound reasons to believe that the AoG activity involved Mark."

"Hang on a second! We can circle back to that in a minute." Aoife sat bolt upright. "Where do you fit into all of this, Jaxon? Are you ICP too?"

I shook my head. "Just in the wrong place at the right time. Remember the bus journey to Cheltenham?" They both nodded. "Well, Laura was sitting right in front of me on the bus…" my throat caught a little saying her name out loud. Libby reached across and grabbed my hand. "… But when she wasn't in the dorm, I cornered Tyrone and told him she was missing."

"I remember that," said Aoife. "You got all the golden boy brownie points for noticing she wasn't there."

"Yes, and that Captain Hennessey was there, despite not being on the bus," I reminded her. "So at that point, they had a fledgling crew member that's spotted an imposter and a missing woman from our crew, and we hadn't even been there for twelve hours. If I'd said nothing, they'd have just swapped them out and fed us some bullshit, but I rather scuppered their plans. So they recruited me to their task force, and I ended up in the BRAF."

"But you could have been AoG too. How would they know?" asked Libby, slightly apologetically.

Amanda came back in. "They train AoG operatives to blend in. That's how they've infiltrated so many corporations and government departments. They're always the people you'd least suspect. Usually quiet, unassuming, indistinct, and unremarkable."

"Like Eloise…" said Aoife, the penny dropping. Libby frowned and looked away.

"Exactly," continued Amanda. "And within twelve hours of being in Compression, Jaxon had drawn attention to himself several times. With Cooper in the anteroom at the beginning of the process, and later on with both Tyrone and Sara. No way he could be AoG. He couldn't be more conspicuous if he tried."

I laughed. "I'll take that as a compliment."

"You should," replied Amanda, turning to face me. "You've got more balls than anyone on this station." Before turning back to Aoife. "No offence, Aoif."

Everyone laughed. "Fuck you, Amanda," came back the response, but with a smile on Aoife's face.

"So that's what all this is about? Laura's death, the gravity problem. Mark dying. They're all connected?" asked Libby.

Amanda nodded.

"So it couldn't have been Mark, then? Not now he's... dead... after what he did, surely?" said Aoife.

I looked at Amanda. We were now treading on thin ice. I wasn't sure how far we should let this conversation progress. After all, everything we'd already told them was corroborated by our actions in Compression. But we were now skirting into present operational territory, and that posed a problem for us both.

"We don't know," I said. "Mark lost his life today, saving the lives of over half a million people. We'll never know now, but it's still possible he was the other infiltrator who either had a crisis of conscience, or something went badly wrong and he had to die in order to protector a wider plot."

"But he might not have been?" said Aoife.

"Which leaves..." Amanda let the silence fill the blank.

"Us two?" said Aoife, pointing between herself and Libby.

"And Jennifer," I reminded her.

"Well, that's shite," she responded, frowning. "So now you're investigating us?" she asked, looking between us for signs of deception.

"I think you're safe, Aoif. Inconspicuous is a talent you haven't yet acquired," retorted Amanda.

I laughed, but Aoife looked put out, and Libby seemed like she was on the verge of tears.

"For what it's worth, we don't think it's you either, Lib," I said kindly, but her lips continued to tremble.

She looked up at us with sad eyes, full of fear. "I've been so stupid," she said and burst into tears.

Amanda's eyes were wide open. She looked across at me, clearly wondering if we'd truly overlooked something.

I leaned forward and grabbed Libby's hand, but she withdrew it and scrunched her fingers up in her lap. "Libby? What's going on? How have you been stupid?"

"I don't want to say. What if I'm wrong?" Fat teardrops leaked from her eyes.

Amanda spoke more urgently. "Lib, whatever it is, spill. Thousands of people died today and we're none the wiser who's behind it. If you know something that could help us, now's the time."

"You're looking for someone inconspicuous and ordinary, right?" she said.

We both nodded.

"Well, three nights ago Jenn came home covered in blood. And not just her scrubs. Her face and hands were smothered, and her hair matted with it. Our bathroom looked like a crime scene. It took us over an hour to clean it up. It was just after I'd seen you and Amanda come back in the Sigma. You were covered in blood, too. She said she'd had a rough shift at work, and I was so distraught about Laura that it didn't occur to me it might not be true. But she works in a hospital in Globe 9. She wouldn't leave without cleaning herself up, would she? I'm such an idiot."

I looked at Amanda, shock waves crashing over us both. "Globe 9? You're sure?" I said.

"Of course I'm sure," she sobbed. "We live together in Globe 7. Near to Mark, actually."

CHAPTER
NINETEEN

"YOU DID WELL TODAY."

"Thank you. It worked better than we could ever have imagined."

"We have struck a deep blow in this war, but there is much still to do. It is a pity about Hanson. The next phase will be more challenging without him."

He paced the room in thought. She just sat still, watching as he changed direction repeatedly. She had learned to remain silent until called upon to speak.

"Can they trace this back to us?" he asked.

"I don't believe so. They'd scheduled Hanson to work on the SQIIDs today. It's being reported as an accident."

He looked up, glee all over his face. "Almost seven thousand dead! What a magnificent result. We have freed them from their bondage. How are they handling the bodies?"

She shifted uncomfortably. Whilst corpses were not new to her, this sheer scale of death was on a different level and it knotted her insides. She felt guilty and resentful. "They're stacked up in hospital mortuaries across the station. The hospitals are full to the brim. They haven't made me privy to the details, but I overheard *one of the senior managers talking about a mass burial in space, rather than utilising the fusion burners."*

He nodded. "That makes sense. They will return to their earth mother, and burn up in the atmosphere en route. This gives us an opportunity."

"And the original plan? Without Hanson..."

"You will need to identify another individual with access. Someone with pressure points we can exploit."

"I've got just the person," she replied, knowing full well who he was referring to as her sister's face swam fleetingly through her mind. She would have to be brave. He'd already proven that blood ties mattered little. The cause was his mistress now, and he'd see it through, regardless of personal cost. But she would show him. She would remain invaluable, and they would die together, in glorious victory.

My brain was suddenly alive and running through a million possibilities. We'd made the fundamental mistake of following assumptions and not looking hard enough at the people closest to us. More than once, despite telling ourselves not to do precisely that. We were so focussed on Mark and Sara that we'd entirely discounted Aoife, Libby and Jennifer.

I could see Amanda mentally going through the headlines, too. What had we actually done to exonerate the rest of Crew 41? Catching Eloise had taken the focus away from the more left-field lines of enquiry. The intelligence about Mark had been enough to draw our attention away from our principal investigation objectives.

I felt like such a fool. Eloise had played me like a fiddle back in Compression, and I'd fallen for it, like the idiot I am. Yet I'd had barely any interaction with Jennifer. She was quiet and plain, attractive without being distracting.

Jenn kept herself to herself, performing adequately, but not excelling or failing. She was the very definition of middle-ground. A woman who blended in and was easy to forget.

Libby was still sobbing quietly in her chair. Aoife's eyes were wide and looking for answers. Amanda looked up. "Lib, what time is she finishing work tonight? When did she say she'd be here?"

Libby swallowed and looked at her bio-band. Why do people do that? It's not as if they wrote the answer there.

"She won't be here for at least an hour or two. She called me from the hospital earlier. They're so busy. She said she'd probably finish around 10pm."

I checked my band. 20.48. "Have we got time?" I asked Amanda.

"Depends on The Loop," she replied.

"We may have to call this one in, Mand." I got an eye roll in response. Standard.

We both stood up to leave. Amanda leaned down and put a hand on Libby's shoulder. "Lib, don't beat yourself up. These people are master manipulators. Look what happened with Jaxon and Eloise…"

"Thanks." Always nice to be reminded of my glorious fuck-ups.

"You can't tell her anything. Stay here as you would have. Have a few drinks. If she shows up, ping my comms, okay? But do it discreetly. Remember how many people died today," continued Amanda.

Fuck's sake, Mand. Way to lay it on her. Libby just looked in total shock. "I had a feeling," she said, wiping her eyes, "after the blood. I should have said something sooner." She was pleading with us, as if the day's events were all her fault.

I crouched down and pulled her into a hug. "Hey, you couldn't have known. And may I remind you, we still don't know. Right now, we just need to speak to her. We've been wrong several times before. Jennifer might be telling the truth."

"Jax, let's go." Amanda was already on her way out of the bar. I nodded to Aoife. "Look after her." Then turned on my heels and followed Amanda.

I caught up with her walking to the ring road. "Mand, what are we doing?"

"Finding Jennifer," was the simple retort.

"Hey! Hey, Mand! Wait." I grabbed her arm and stopped her mid-stride. "Listen, we cannot rush into this. We've made too many assumptions already."

"What are you saying? This is our fuck up?" She glared at me.

"No! Well, yes, I suppose it is. We've been telling ourselves not to draw conclusions all along, whilst ignoring our own principles. There are still three people from our crew who we haven't investigated. We've just left two of them in a bar."

"You don't believe it's Libby or Aoife, do you?" she asked.

"I don't want to believe it's Jennifer, either. Like I didn't believe it was Eloise. You said so yourself – these people are master manipulators. They blend in. They're unremarkable. So, when push comes to shove, what I believe is irrelevant. Only the truth matters."

"It has to be one of them, Jaxon. It's verified intelligence from a credible source."

"I agree. And I also agree it's probably Jennifer, given what we've just heard with the blood and all. We also know these people are intelligent. Doesn't it seem a little convenient that Jenn would arrive home in that condition on the same night that Laura was murdered? There could be a hundred reasons why. I just don't want to go barrelling in again, and miss something."

She turned and started walking to The Loop station,

which was at least twenty minutes away. "What's your suggestion?"

I half-jogged to catch up and then walked backwards to face Amanda. "Let's call Farrell. Get her to tag Jennifer and send us her location, at least, so we're not fumbling around in the dark."

Amanda nodded and continued to walk, whilst tapping away on her comms. A soft beep sounded, followed by a voice that neither of us recognised.

"Ensign Casey."

Amanda and I exchanged glances. "Ensign, this is Major Barclay from BRMC Command. Can you put me through to Commander Farrell, please?"

"Ma'am, Commander Farrell is on the early shift. She won't be here until 4am. Can I take a message?"

"No, no. It's nothing urgent. I'll call her tomorrow. Thank you, Ensign." She clicked off and swore at the ground. "Shit!"

"Mand, we need to call Grealish."

"What the fuck for? We've been through this."

"Because we're two people, looking for one person in a sphere with a floor area of probably two-hundred square kilometres. Without a tracker, we'll never find her, even if she's exactly where we think she is. It's hardly a small hospital. Grealish can put a marker on her."

"Too risky, Jax. What if Hennessey is with him and she sees? She could warn Jennifer, and then we really would struggle to find her."

"You still think Sara is part of this?"

She stopped and frowned at me. "You don't?"

"Well, with what Libby's just told us, I just wondered…"

"Jaxon, how did the AoG know that someone killed Leon inside Compression?"

"They had a mole on the inside," I replied.

"That's right. A mole with communications beyond the walls of Compression. A mole with access to both BRMC Opps and SECO 2, and to the ICP Command structure opposite. My mission was to find two infiltrators in Crew 41. We found Eloise."

"And Mark," I replied.

"We don't know if Mark was involved. We just know that there was decent circumstantial evidence to support making him a person of interest. But that's not the point – we're no longer in Compression, so my mission parameters have expanded to include this entire vessel. We already know there are at least seven AoG on the Bertram, possibly eight. We know that the intelligence points to at least one of our crew. And we know that someone at Echo was manipulating Brian Latimer. Sara is our best lead, given the evidence we've found so far. If we're wrong, I'll apologise to her, but right now, after everything I've seen today, I'm not feeling very apologetic. Meanwhile, Jennifer has suddenly garnered my attention."

"Okay, so what's your plan now?"

"We go to the hospital and confront her."

"No!" We were about to make the same mistakes all over again.

"No? Alright, Jax. With your many years of experience investigating terrorists, what's your suggestion?" Sarcasm. Perfect.

"I suggest we do what we were going to do before, with Sara and Mark. Right now, Jennifer has no clue that she's a suspect. Mark is dead, so he can no longer lead us to the AoG. But she can, if she is what you think she is."

Amanda stared into the distance, clearly thinking. "Could it have been her in Globe 9?" she asked.

"The night Laura died?"

"No, before that. When you saw Mark talking to a woman. Could it have been her?"

I thought about it. The woman had her back to me the whole time, so I didn't get a look at her face. Her hair was... what was it? The moment was over so quickly that I'd barely had time to register Mark's face. "It's possible, but I can't be sure. It was too quick and I was concentrating on Mark."

"Could she have been wearing scrubs?"

I just shrugged. I couldn't remember.

Amanda thought for a moment. "Emily," she said, simply.

"What?"

"Emily told us there were two women in the house where they were captive. Maybe she can identify one or both of them?"

"She said they covered their faces. And if they hadn't, surely she'd have already identified the perps to Grealish?"

"If they'd intended to kill them, they may have been a little less cautious about it, but I take your point. She definitely heard them, though. She told us."

"Yes, she did. Maybe that'll be enough. She spent nearly two months in captivity. I doubt she'll ever forget any of their voices." A plan was forming. I could see it in Amanda's eyes, too. There was only one problem.

"Libby," I said, breaking the momentary silence.

"Oh, shit," replied Amanda. "There's no way she'll hold out living in the same house as Jennifer. She's not cut out for this."

"Let's go back to the bar and get her out. She can stay with me in the meantime. Or you," I added, seeing the look on Amanda's face.

Amanda thought about it for the moment. "They're friends, Jaxon. We'll need to get her reassigned under some emergency provision following today's incident. And we'll have to get Jennifer pulled into double shifts for a couple of days, so they can legitimately avoid each other."

"Okay. So now can we call Grealish?"

———————

Grealish sat opposite the admiral, resigned to the oncoming eruption. Admiral Willard leaned forward in his seat. "This is a fucking mess, Andrew. Your prime suspect, still moving about unencumbered, despite our previous conversations, and now we've got nigh on seven thousand bodies piled up in the hospitals."

"Yes, Sir, including Mark Hanson's. He saved thousands of people today and died for the privilege. None of us know what actually happened. For all we can ascertain, it may well have been an accident."

The admiral stood up. "If you believe this was an accident, you're unfit to run this investigation, Andrew."

"Sir—"

"Shut up, before you embarrass yourself further." He slammed a hollotab down on the desk, tapped a Navy emblem and pushed it towards Grealish. "Open it to page ninety."

Grealish picked up the hollotab. The screen was adorned with a navy crest on a light blue background, under which was the title *Gravity Control*. He tapped the corner, and navigated to page ninety.

"What am I looking at, Sir?" Grealish asked.

"You're on page ninety, yes? Now swipe to page one hundred and three."

"Okay." Grealish did as instructed and then looked up at the admiral.

"Thirteen pages, Andrew. Thirteen pages of instructions to get from normal gravity to reverse polarity without shutting the system down. Miss any of these steps, and the system locks for ten minutes, and resets the sequence."

Grealish looked back at the manual, swiping through

the pages, and then up at the admiral, who was lowering himself into his seat for a second time. "Shit." Then his comms sounded.

———

"Sir, it's Amanda."

"Amanda! Where the hell are you? I've been trying to contact you and Jaxon for most of the day."

"We removed our bio-bands, Sir."

"And why would you do that?"

"So you couldn't track us or contact us. I don't have time to explain now. We have a time pressure here and a sensitive situation. I need you to listen, not interrupt, not question me, and action what I ask of you when the call ends. Understood?"

"Amanda—"

"Sir! Time pressure. Do you understand?"

He sighed audibly. "Of course, yes. What can I do for you?"

"Are you alone, Sir?"

"I'm with Admiral Willard."

"You are? Okay, that may actually prove useful. Can you open the channel for him?"

She heard a click, and then the admiral's voice. "This is Admiral Willard. Who are you?"

"Amanda Barclay, Sir. We met at Echo a few weeks ago. Admiral, you need to code me in."

"You're CTI?"

"Yes, sir."

There was silence for a few seconds, and then the response. "Wait." Another momentary pause, and then the admiral came back. "Designation?"

"Leah Mori." She spelled out the surname.

"Code in."

"23024, Sir."

"Wait one."

Amanda and Jaxon could hear a holloscreen being tapped through the speaker.

"Agent, are we on a secure line?" replied the admiral.

"No, Sir. Belt comms. But we don't have time for anything else."

"Okay, what's your sitrep?"

"We have a situation. A viable lead, but a potential conflict of interest. I need several things actioning. Please let me read them out and save the questions for later."

"Understood. Proceed."

"Libby Baxendale is a flight engineer that works in the BRAF hangars on Globe 11. She currently lives with Jennifer Edgecomb on 7-4-A. We need Baxendale reassigned to Globe 10 recovery and repair detail with immediate effect, and her shift pattern amended to ensure no contact with Jennifer Edgecomb. We have temporary alternative accommodation already sorted in 11-5-C, but we need to make it as legit as possible without raising suspicions with Edgecomb."

They could hear the admiral furiously scribbling away on his hollotab, without once asking Amanda to slow down or repeat her instructions.

"Jennifer Edgecomb is a trainee medic on Globe 9, level 5. We have reason to suspect that she's AoG, but it's essential she is unaware. I need a marker on her bio-band and also on Baxendale." She paused and thought for a moment. "And while you're at it, put one on Aoife Hanrahan. Colonel Grealish has all of their details. Don't take action from Admiralty. Wake Commander Gemma Farrell – she runs station security for Globes 9 and 10."

"I know Gemma. I'll get her on to it," replied the admiral. "Anything else?"

"Yes. Tell Gemma the order has come from me. She'll

understand why. And get me a full background on Edge-comb, including mandatory assessments. Then we need to send a BRMC crew to get Baxendale's essentials from the house. It'll add to the legitimacy if they arrive while Edge-comb is home. And be careful who you choose," she added as an afterthought.

"Understood."

"Check back please, Admiral."

"Markers on Baxendale, Edgecomb and Hanrahan via Commander Farrell, specifically on your orders. Switch detail to Globe 10 recovery for Baxendale, and amend both Baxendale and Edgecomb's itineraries to ensure no contact. Send trusted personal to retrieve Baxendale's possessions. FBC on Edgecomb to deliver to you. That about it?"

"That's it. Thank you, Sir. Colonel Grealish?"

"I'm here."

"Sir, I'm sure this goes without saying, but this conversation must remain between the four of us."

"Four?"

"Yes, Sir. Jaxon is on comms with us as well. It is imperative that we do not inform the rest of the investigations team about this, under any circumstances."

"Amanda, surely—" Grealish interrupted, but Amanda talked over him.

"Colonel Grealish, Sir, I cannot emphasise that heavily enough. There is a mole in our team. Jaxon and I have a bead on them, and we'll happily discuss it with you at a more appropriate moment, but right now, this has to stay between us and us alone. Any breach of this will be viewed as a threat to our security and will result in your removal from the station. Am I making myself clear?"

Grealish sounded outraged. "Have you any idea who you're speaking to, Amanda?"

"Yes, Sir, I do. But you don't. The admiral does, though, and he'll confirm my authority. This is now my investigation, and you're either in the team or you're not. Let's not start a pissing contest. Have you understood my requirements, and will you action them immediately?"

"I'll take care of it, Amanda," boomed the admiral's voice.

"Thank you, Sir."

"WHO THE FUCK is Leah Mori? And what the hell was that all about?" I felt like I was standing next to a stranger.

"It's complicated, Jax."

"Fine. Simplify it for me. You've been harping on about being able to trust each other ever since Laura died, and three days later you're making threats to BRMC Colonels, with the support of the station commander. What is going on? What is CTI?"

She sighed, but continued to talk. "I told you I was a deep cover operative, Jaxon. I may have glossed over the finer details, but everything I've told you so far is true. CTI is Counter-Terrorism Intelligence. Think old-school MI6, except we're a unit inside a unit. You shouldn't even know it exists, but I trust you and there wasn't any other way to get this done without relying on Grealish and Co. There are protocols in place for my extraction, but they can only be initiated by me. My unit has no way of knowing where I am, hence deep cover. I can't tell you more than that."

"But the admiral knows?"

"Yes, and no. The admiral is one of the joint intelligence committee chiefs, and has special access to deep cover operations and agents. When I'm operational, I would usually put a call in to my base, but that's on Earth and comms between here and there are heavily monitored. There are ways, but I don't have time to exploit them."

"And Leah Mori is your real name?"

"Leah Mori was my year-eight English teacher. It is a name I'm only supposed to use when under duress or in trouble. I can only use in exceptional circumstances. And only once, so it's now burned."

"So you are still Amanda?"

"Yes, Jaxon. But using the designation and code tells the admiral that I'm in trouble, and need help. It's a last resort, usually, but in the current circumstances I needed a no-questions-asked response. I'll probably get a bollocking for improper use later, but that's not important right now."

Christ. This was proper James Bond stuff, and I was well out of my depth.

"What was all that about with Grealish? Can you really remove him?"

"I can. If I deem him to be a threat to our security."

"And does anyone have the authority to remove you?"

"Sure," she replied smiling, "if they've got a big enough gun."

I didn't doubt it. "So what's the plan?"

"You heard the call. We're about to get Libby out of there. Like you said, she can stay at yours for now. I will stall Jennifer at work for the time being, and then BRMC will collect Libby's spare fatigues when Jennifer arrives home."

"What's stopping her from calling Libby?"

"Nothing at all, which is why Libby is going to leave her a message explaining her temporary relocation."

"Do you think she's up to it, Amanda?"

"I've no fucking idea. We'll cross that bridge when we come to it."

"Why move her off Globe 11 engineering to Globe 10? Surely she's safer here surrounded by BRAF?"

"Because we haven't cleared her yet, as you so delicately pointed out ten minutes ago, and I'd rather she wasn't working in a military hangar if there's even the smallest possibility that her little display back at Lovell's was an act. Besides which, The Loop is closed during the day between Globes 9 and 11 while they make the repairs, so she'd have to go the long way round, which gives us a good reason to relocate her without raising suspicion."

She looked around, in thought for a moment, and then headed back towards Lovell's.

My brain was running in circles. I felt like a rookie working with Amanda, probably because I was. I'd already seen her in readiness for combat, and the way she'd stormed the apartment when we found Laura, and later her methodical approach to clearing the surrounding buildings, and the bomb lab. She was only a year older than me, but had clearly made something of herself whilst I'd been drifting along in The Bleeds.

I've always been quite confident in myself, but Amanda made me feel like I was well out of my depth. I also had a huge amount of trust in her guidance and capabilities. She could be a bit of a hot-head, but I suspected a lot of that came from the pressure she was under. There was no doubting her training or abilities, though.

We closed on Lovell's, and Amanda stopped.

"Jaxon, Libby is likely to be second-guessing herself for the next few days. We need to make sure she stays at yours for at least forty-eight hours."

"I thought she was being reassigned to Globe 10?"

"She is, but it can wait a couple of days. For now, we just need to keep her safe long enough to do some digging."

"What about her bio-band? Surely they can track her with that?"

"They can, but why would they? She's not a player here. Nobody is looking for her. And if they were, your apartment is hardly suspicious. I just don't want her bumping in to Jennifer accidentally."

"Is that likely?"

"I've no idea. If Jenn turns out to be nothing more than a medic then probably not, but if she is AoG, who knows what she gets up to outside of work hours? I know Gemma can track any location on the station, but she can't backtrack people's movements without a mark—oh!"

She paused suddenly and tilted her head, before her eyes widened and she looked up. "We don't need a marker! We have a location and a time. You saw Mark with a woman in Globe 9, remember? Sara was supposed to track Mark to see who the woman was."

"Holy shit! We'll have to get Gemma on to it. That's another nail in the Sara coffin."

She nodded. "We're going to have to deal with her quickly. Sara being on the inside is too dangerous for us now."

We walked for a bit, my brain running at a million miles an hour trying to piece together everything we'd learned in the last few days.

"What Libby said, about Jenn…" I turned to face Amanda. "She'd come home covered in blood the night they killed Laura. She worked in a hospital, so blood on her scrubs was probably commonplace, but would she go home without changing first?"

Amanda seemed to sense my thoughts. "There's no way she'd leave a hospital in that state. I don't know what the protocols are, but I'd bet if we checked her shift on the day we lost Laura versus the time she came home, that she didn't go straight home from work, even if they allowed her to leave covered in blood."

"Jenn just seems so unlikely, Mand. I can't imagine her as a killer."

"Jax, I've been investigating these people for a long time. They come in all shapes and sizes, and they're trained to blend in. She ticks every box. I was watching her and Eloise closely in Compression, but their actions were that of ordinary women. Eloise was so close to getting away with murder. She should have been caught long before I got her, but someone higher-up deliberately fudged the investigation, so I turned my attention away from the crew and focussed on BRMC command. That's on me. Now we need to finish the job I started."

We picked up the pace as we walked back towards Lovell's, neither of us breaking the silence until we reached the door. I looked nervously across at Amanda. We'd only been gone twenty minutes, but I opened the door with a feeling of trepidation.

Aoife and Libby were exactly where we'd left them. Aoife had her arms around Libby, who was clearly in some distress. She looked up as we approached.

"What the fuck are you two doing back here? I thought you were going to find Jenn?"

Libby raised her head and looked at us through puffy eyes. Her face was blotchy and wet, and she was still sucking in shallow sobs as we took our seats.

"Change of plan," replied Amanda, surveying the room for prying eyes or eaves-dropping. Satisfied that we were suitably isolated, she reached over to Libby and held her hands in a rare display of affection. "Lib, you're going to stay with Jaxon for a few days. You're being reassigned to the Globe 10 recovery with immediate effect, but we want you to stay in Globe 11 for a couple of days before you join the recovery detail. Okay?"

Libby nodded, still hiccoughing from the effort of crying.

I looked at Libby and realised there was no way she'd be able to hold it together in a communication with Jennifer, so I turned to Aoife.

"Aoif, we need you to message Jenn and tell her you're heading home. Tell her Libby's been called in to work, so there's no point in her coming over. If she asks why, tell her you don't know. She got a call through comms and had to leave."

Aoife nodded.

Amanda looked up. "I don't have to tell you how important it is to keep this conversation to yourselves. Jax and I have been working hard on this investigation, and the one thing we've learned is that there's no knowing who to trust. We're going out on a limb here, trusting you, because we're running out of options."

Aoife protested, but Amanda just talked over her.

"It's not personal. These people are professionals. They know just how to blend in, how to get the access they need to further their cause, and they are ruthless and deadly."

Aoife was still bristling. "Aoif." I called her attention. "Eloise snagged me hook, line and sinker. That entire display in the shower block – she hoodwinked all of us. Then weeks of helping her with her conditioning assessments, meanwhile, she murdered Leon. Never forget that. And she lost no sleep doing it."

"I'm not Eloise," she retorted, but there was a significant de-escalation in her tone. "Could Jenn really be involved in this? She just doesn't seem the type."

"Any less likely than Eloise?" replied Amanda.

Aoife just shrugged.

"These people killed Laura, and she was a professional with military training. Look at what's happened today on

Globe 10. Nearly seven thousand dead. We have to put an end to this before it's seven million dead."

Libby and Aoife looked genuinely shocked. I thought Amanda might have overplayed her hand, but it clearly had the desired effect.

"Are we going to die?" sobbed Libby, her eyes welling up again.

"Not if I have anything to do with it," replied Amanda. She was about to elaborate when a tone sounded throughout the globe, and our bio-bands vibrated.

Instinctively, we all looked at our bio-monitors to check the message.

It was a station-wide directive from Admiralty.

CITIZENS OF THE BERTRAM RAMSAY. BIO-
BAND TRACKING HAS BEEN ENABLED ON
EVERY OCCUPANT OF THIS STATION. FROM
MIDNIGHT TONIGHT, NO OCCUPANT WILL BE
ABLE TO DOCK THEIR BIO-BAND WITHOUT RE-
CONNECTING HOURLY. THIS IS A NEW
SECURITY PROTOCOL INSTIGATED WHILE
INVESTIGATIONS CONTINUE INTO TODAY'S
GRAVITY FAILURE ON GLOBE 10. OUR
INTENTION IS ONLY THE PRESERVATION OF
THE SAFETY AND WELLBEING OF ALL
OCCUPANTS AND WE ASK THAT YOU
RESTRICT YOUR MOVEMENTS TO WORK
COMMUTES, AND FACILITIES WITHIN THE
GLOBES IN WHICH YOU RESIDE.

USE OF THE LOOP AND ALL MAG-LIFTS, MAG-
TRAMS AND COMMUNAL FACILITIES WILL
REQUIRE BIO-BAND SWIPE TO ACCESS UNTIL
FURTHER NOTICE. COMMUNICATIONS WITH
EARTH ARE CURRENTLY SUSPENDED WHILST
THE RECOVERY CREWS MAKE NECESSARY
ESSENTIAL REPAIRS TO GLOBE 10.

AS A CITIZEN OF THE BERTRAM RAMSAY, YOU
ARE OBLIGATED TO REPORT SUSPICIOUS
BEHAVIOUR, AND WE ASK THAT YOU REMAIN
VIGILANT WHILST PREPARATIONS CONTINUE
FOR OUR DEPARTURE FROM EARTH'S ORBIT.
IF YOU HAVE QUESTIONS OR CONCERNS,
PLEASE DIRECT THEM TO YOUR GLOBE
OPERATIONS CENTRE ON LEVEL 4 OF ALL
GLOBES, EXCEPT 5 AND 11. OCCUPANTS OF 5
AND 11 SHOULD DIRECT ALL
COMMUNICATIONS TO ADMIRALTY ON
LEVEL 3.

FINALLY, WE WISH TO REASSURE YOU THAT
THESE MEASURES ARE PRECAUTIONARY, AND
THAT THERE IS NO REASON TO BE ALARMED.
PROTOCOLS ARE IN PLACE PRECISELY TO
HANDLE SITUATIONS THAT ARISE BOTH
LOCALLY AND GLOBALLY, AND WE ASK FOR
YOUR PATIENCE AND COOPERATION WHILST
INVESTIGATIONS CONTINUE INTO THE TRAGIC
ACCIDENT ON GLOBE 10.

ADMIRAL H. LEIGH WILLARD

Conversations erupted around the bar. I could see everyone looking at their bio-monitors with stunned expressions. Amanda and I exchanged glances, and I could see she was as conflicted as I was.

The problem with the new protocols was that it restricted our movements as much as it did the AoG, and with a mole in our team that was a real problem. No sooner had we both come to that conclusion when our bio-monitors pinged again. Not everyone's though, just mine and Amanda's.

The message you've just received is false.
Keep this to yourself and don't let me
down. Grealish.

I could see the look on Amanda's face. Neither of us spoke. Nothing needed to be said. Amanda just nodded and then between us we coaxed Libby up, said goodnight to Aoife and made our way back to my apartment.

TWENTY-ONE

I WOKE up the next morning on my sofa, slightly confused. I looked across at my bed, and saw the covers had been kicked off, and no sign of Libby. It was only as the fog cleared from my brain that I heard the shower running.

Amanda had left Libby and I shortly after arriving back here, and then headed for the Hub to meet Gemma. We agreed it was best if we were discreet about our movements, and with Libby around it made it difficult to explain why the two of us would be heading out at 11pm when the order from Admiralty was to restrict our movements. As far as Libby was concerned, Amanda was going home.

Aoife had messaged us with a copy of her comms with Jenn.

Jenn, Lib's been called in to work and so has Amanda. Lieutenant Golden Balls is being a pussy and going to bed, so fuck-all reason for me to hang about here like some lonely bitch sipping on desperation martinis. Hope work was ok. Catch up soon. A x

Subtle. I had to hand it to her. It was about as 'Aoife' as any message could get. I wasn't particularly enamoured with my latest nickname, but it was still an improvement on 'egg-timer'.

Jenn's reply was short and sweet.

Okay babes x

I smiled at the thought of how Aoife would react if *I* called her 'babes' and made a mental note never to find out. Whilst the coffee was brewing, I collected up the bedclothes and the filthy flight suits from yesterday's excursion into zero gravity, and threw them into the laundry chute before extracting clean-everything from the cupboard.

Libby wandered out with a towel wrapped around her and damp hair plastered to her face and neck. She looked so different without the little ringlets that usually bounced jovially against her flawless skin. Her eyes were still puffy, and I expected she'd been crying most of the night. She gave me a weak smile as she walked across to the bed.

"Jaxon, where are my clothes?"

"I've ordered you some more. They'll be here in a minute." I'd barely finished the sentence when a soft tone sounded from the wardrobe, and a fresh set of women's fatigues and underwear arrived alongside replenishment flight suits and bedcovers.

I handed the fatigues and underwear to Lib, and poured us both a coffee.

"What are you up to today, Jax?"

Honestly, I didn't know, but given recent events, I supposed I had better show my face in the flight office. Mand would call me if anything came up, but until it did, there was little we could do. With the entire station on alert, using Jenn as our new bait would have to sit on the back-burner whilst we solved our Hennessey problem.

I wasn't relishing the prospect of business as usual, but the last few days had been intense, and both Amanda and I had been in the thick of it. We'd continued our investigation unhindered since Laura had died, but we were now at risk of attracting too much attention to ourselves, especially amongst those on the inside of Operation Echo. Whilst Grealish had a good idea of what we'd been up to, Amanda and I had been careful not to draw attention to ourselves beyond finding Laura and the Latimer family.

I showered, dressed and headed out, leaving Libby on the sofa with a coffee. She smiled as I waved her goodbye, but it appeared forced and cold and I could see she was second-guessing herself. No sense me worrying further – I couldn't babysit her all day.

I walked across to the Great Wall and took a mag-lift to the flight office, where I found Todd and a few others milling about, awaiting the morning briefing. I shook his hand and said hello to the others before pouring myself a lukewarm coffee from the corner pot and taking a seat for the briefing.

"Where have you been, mate? You were only here for a day and then disappeared!"

I was pretty sure Todd wasn't fishing – there was no reason to suspect he might know of my involvement in the previous day's activities, and he certainly wouldn't know about Laura and the Latimer family, so I improvised.

"I'm still working with the medical team to get back to full fitness. They're continuing assessments whilst I recover from my injuries, and then Globe 10 went to shit and I got a bit banged up again."

"Jesus Christ, you were on 10 went the gravity systems failed? What was that like?"

"Total shit-show. Never seen anything like it." Before I could elaborate, Addison walked in and waved everyone down before people started saluting.

His eyes locked on mine and there was a flicker of surprise, but he didn't draw attention to me, instead leaning against the briefing desk and beginning his morning address.

"Morning, everyone. Busy day ahead. We've got two inspection protocols around the Globe 10 recovery, the usual missions in advance of our orbital breakaway, and a shuttle escort this morning."

There was a collective groan at the mention of the shuttle, and I looked at Todd with a question on my face, but before he could say anything, Addison continued.

"Settle down. I know the shuttle escorts are dull but they're necessary, and today even more so as we're taking the Pilgrim down to Earth for parts to patch up Globe 10. It's ugly down there at the minute, now that we've abandoned the final stage of the evacuation, so we'll be on full alert with back-up protocols for crews flying the orbital routes."

"Armed, Sir?" asked a female pilot from behind me.

"To the teeth, Captain. Full security protocols."

There was an outbreak of murmuring following this statement, but Addison ignored it and continued to brief us on the day's flight plans. I half listened for the next fifteen minutes, making the occasional note on my hollotab, before Addison divvied out the assignments and dismissed us.

I was on the shuttle detail, so I scooped up my kitbag and headed for the launch bay. Addison collared me just as I left the briefing room.

"Sir?"

"Don't look so worried, Jaxon. I'm just tagging along with you today." He looked around as if scoping the area for prying eyes, and had clearly concluded we were alone.

"You're flying with me, Sir?" So that's why I was on the shuttle detail, so Addison could pry me for information.

"Cut the crap, Jax. Yes I'm bloody well coming with

you. My Sigma is all banged up thanks to the gravity fail on Globe 10, a globe which I shouldn't have even been on if I wasn't playing taxi to you, so you'll do me a favour and indulge my presence."

"I don't understand – they designed Sigmas for zero gravity and they have their own SQIIDs and a magnetic landing gear. How'd you get banged up?"

"Because shit was flying all over the place. The dock was closed, but the bay entry was open where we'd disembarked and nothing in the bay was secured. I'm bloody lucky I didn't get bludgeoned to death by unsecured cargo. I managed to get myself into the control room, where I spent an hour waltzing about in zero gravity with a fucking filing cabinet. They're fixing my Sigma as we speak, but with most of the engineers helping with the effort to repair Globe 10, I'm out of action for a few days. So, today you're going to be a taxi for me."

He nudged me forward into the mag-lifts and we descended to the launch area. My Sigma was still being brought through – apparently they weren't expecting me.

"How are you holding up?" asked Addison as we watched the tug guiding my Sigma through the bay entry doors.

I had to think for a minute. The last few days had been emotionally intense, and I wasn't entirely sure how I felt. I settled for, "Knackered."

"What the bloody hell is going on, Jaxon? You seem to be neck deep in shit every time we meet these days. I called into Admiralty the first day you didn't show up and I got told to drop it and crack on."

"It's complicated, Addison. There's a lot happening, but I can't really talk about it."

"For fuck's sake, Jaxon, it's me. At least tell me what happened on Globe 10. You clearly knew something was going down."

I shrugged. "I didn't know what was going down, to be honest. Only that something might. Let's just say that more than one person-of-interest was in situ on Globe 10 when it all went to shit. It wasn't a system failure, it was a deliberate act."

"Jesus." Addison's eyes were wide.

"That's privileged information, Sir. Keep it to yourself." He raised his eyebrows at me but said nothing.

We climbed into my Sigma when it arrived and watched as the bay doors sealed and the huge docking doors began their upward sweep. I released the mag-dock and powered the spheres, drifting sideways towards the exit behind five other Sigmas and the Nova Pilgrim.

"That's a lot of firepower."

Addison leaned back in the co-pilot's seat. "We don't know what we'll find when we get to Cheltenham. Better safe than sorry."

"We're going back to Echo?" I asked.

"You seem surprised."

"I thought they'd closed all compression sites in the bomb's aftermath?"

"They did, but there's still a crew there that is operational. And it's the most secure compound in the wake of the attack. It's also nearest to the shipyard in Berkley, Gloucestershire, where they built Berty."

"And our job is just to escort the Pilgrim?"

"And provide security."

"Are we expecting trouble?"

"We closed off an evacuation that stranded two million souls on Earth. There are fifty Compression centres around the world, eleven of which are in Cheltenham, so there are likely several thousand people that we abandoned either in Compression or nearby. The big worry is a breach of the security cordon and the Pilgrim being overwhelmed with bodies."

I swept out of the hangar and into formation behind the Pilgrim. Two Sigmas headed the squadron, with two others flanking either side and two at the rear. We pulled out of the rotation and drifted back and away from the station. The enormity of it still blew my mind and whilst you could see other globes from within your own, nothing compared to the sight of the entire station. It would be ten minutes before it was far enough away to fit into our viewing windows.

"Are we picking up more crew while we're there?"

"That's down to the Navy, but I suspect we will. There are four thousand seats on the Pilgrim. It makes no sense not to fill them, but I've had no official word that there's an ongoing plan for crew evacuations."

"Four *thousand*? I thought it was four hundred, based on my journey up here."

"Four hundred? Jaxon, how the fuck did you think they were going to evacuate nine-million people on a bus that only seats four hundred? There are six decks on the Pilgrim, split into two cabins each, and each cabin holds four hundred."

"Right." I felt like an idiot. Of course it held more. A round trip to the Bertram was at least two hours, not accounting for loading and unloading, which probably added an extra hour, so with it running twenty-four hours a day that would be eight pick-ups, which is twenty-four-hundred passengers, maximum. That's seventy-two thousand passengers a month, which is less than nine-hundred-thousand a year. It would take a decade to evacuate everyone. I decided to deflect, especially since Addison was looking at me like a disappointed father.

"And there's been no mention of picking up those that we left behind?"

"Nobody's told me of a plan."

"But you think there is one?"

"I think it's a political mine-field right now. We expect the crew at Cheltenham to provide comms and load the Pilgrim, but they have zero motivation to do so if it's going to mean they remain on Earth. So, yes, if it were my call, I'd be buttoning down the site and evacuating the remaining crew."

"Christ."

"I see you've grasped the perilous nature of our predicament, Jax. Knew you'd get there, eventually." He turned back to face the console and muttered, "Four hundred" under his breath, whilst shaking his head.

I ignored the sarcasm and swept right, as the formation rotated through thirty degrees, taking station on the starboard flank of the Pilgrim. We were about to enter the atmosphere above the Coalition so I deployed the front EM shield and swept away from the Pilgrim. The EM shield on the Sigma was pretty efficient, but it wouldn't withstand being in the re-entry wash from the Pilgrim.

The other Sigma pilots followed suit until we were loosely formed up two-hundred metres either side of the shuttle. I watched as the EM shields did their job, the thick atmosphere burning white at the edges, with huge fire trails stretching hundreds of meters in our wake. It took just over a minute to enter Earth's atmosphere before we reformed around the shuttle as we escorted it down to Compression Echo.

The skies were white below us, and thick with cloud. Only the tops of The Bleeds were visible, ninety miles in the distance to the east of Cheltenham, and I felt a pang in the pit of my stomach as I thought about my home. We broke through the cloud at thirteen-thousand feet into a deluge of rain and lightning. My aircraft rocked and twisted as the winds and heavy rain buffeted it, and for the first time I think I truly understood what we were losing. Inside the Bertram, they contrived the weather to suit the population and farmlands. It was perpetual, static and clinical in its precision, unlike Earth where the elements were unpredictable and chaotic and could unleash a furious tirade at a moment's notice.

As we swept closer, the ground looked blackened and dead. We circled the tower and took in the devastation below. I could see the temporary wall erected over the airlock where the bomb had gone off just a few weeks ago, and the launch bay on our left, but beyond that was a level of destruction that I could barely comprehend.

The ICP Command structure at GCHQ had been reduced to ashes. The smouldering remains of the outer circle were being doused by the pounding rain and washed into streams that ran through the streets, carrying the debris of this famous old building.

There were groups of people wandering over the ruins. Not rescuers, but scavengers, looking for morsels of value to ease the burden of their expiring lives, but as we passed overhead the steady thrum of our gyro-spheres turned heads. They looked like savages. For all the world ordinary people, but in this moment the hatred was palpable. I couldn't hear them but they looked to be screaming at us, some waving their fists, others reminding us which finger is longest.

To our left was Echo, and further back I could see the Delta and Charlie sites still fortified and awake, with lights around the perimeters and patrols pacing behind the gates. We skimmed the top of the Stage 2 building and hovered over the launch bay.

"Tower, this is the Red October escorting the Nova Pilgrim, requesting permission to land." I waited for the Tower to respond and wondered why the Pilgrim hadn't put in a request.

"Red October, this is Pilgrim. Just get us on the deck."

I looked at Addison, who just shrugged and nodded. It

was against all protocols to approach an *LZ* without seeking clearance, but I guess following protocol wasn't a priority for those on the ground.

I put down close to the gantry and the other Sigmas followed suit, except two that remained hovering and rotating over the landing site. I guessed they were our exit security and suddenly felt like I was under-briefed for this assignment.

I went to stow my controller when Addison grabbed my arm and shook his head. "You keep this bird powered and your finger on the trigger, got it?"

I just nodded, a small tingle of fear creeping into my stomach.

"You're certain they will come?"

"They have little choice. They cannot manufacture the glass in time for the departure, so they need to resupply from our earth mother."

"Very well. We will take care of it."

"No. The shuttle must survive any attack. It is imperative to our mission."

"Then how are we to proceed?"

"You must keep the shuttle in the launch bay at all costs."

"And the escorts?"

"They are unworthy of your time or attention. You cannot replace their pilots, so they serve no purpose. Dispose of them if it will not harm your extraction, otherwise they can be ignored."

We sat in the cockpit for the next forty minutes while the crews loaded huge sections of EM glass onto the shuttle. Addison left briefly to talk to the Navy pilots, presumably to get the lay of the land on a continuing evacuation effort, but he returned after a few minutes and said nothing.

There was a hive of activity around the loading bay of the Pilgrim, with enormous crates being marshalled from the warehouse into the fuselage. Streams of uniformed workers – mostly marines – fought through the unrelenting downpour, moving the heavy cargo with little enthusiasm or care.

Addison was getting twitchy beside me, continually looking out of the open hatch at god-knows-what.

"For fuck's sake, Addison. Can't you sit still for a minute?"

"I'll relax when we're off the deck and back on Berty." He looked skyward and aft before going completely still. "Shit!"

"What it is it?"

"Air Force. Not ours," he said.

"What do you mean *not ours*? How many bloody air forces are there?"

"There is still a military command establishment on Earth, Jaxon. What did you think, that the moment we left they'd all stand down and relax until the world ended?"

"Okay. So what's the problem?"

"Jesus, Lieutenant. You really do live in your own little bubble, don't you? What do you think the presiding senti-ment is for those of us escaping on Berty? You think they're happy for us? Joyous that others will live?" He shook his head at me in deep disappointment, for the second time since we boarded.

He wasn't wrong. I did live in my own little bubble. The politics of Earth had never really interested me. Until nine months ago I was going to die, just like everyone else, so I didn't waste my time and energy reading up on public sentiment. The first time I realised that there was anger and resentment was on my journey from The Bleeds to Cheltenham. There were crowds at Abingdon, jostling their placards and shouting hate at those of us boarding the buses, but they were nothing compared to the scale of violence we witnessed as we arrived. Tens of thousands in the streets, throwing petrol bombs, rocks and whatever else they could get their hands on.

The evacuation had become a civil war, contested between those charged with ensuring the continuity of our species, and those left behind to suffer the anguish of annihilation. Cheltenham had become the latest in a long list of human battlefields.

I must have been zoning out, because Addison punched my arm and said, "Get us in the air. Now!"

No sooner had he said it, than the comms sounded. "Bertram Ramsay Defence Force, this is the Coalition Air Force. Do not attempt to take off. You are being detained for an unauthorised incursion into sovereign air space. Power down your vessels and exit into the hangar."

There was a brief click, and then the comms sounded again. "Sigma pilots, this is the Nova Pilgrim. We need you in the air punching a hole through their defences. We are two minutes from being able to take off. Get to it. Pilgrim out."

"What is he talking about, Addison? How is this 'unauthorised'?"

I looked at Addison, and I could see genuine fear on his face. He'd obviously expected some sort of trouble, but it was clear as day that a military response was not in the morning briefing. I throttled up the spheres and brought the Red October to a hover ten metres above the dock. I started my rotation, as is standard protocol, but Addison just shook his head. "No time. Just get up there."

I opened the throttle, and we leapt to three-hundred metres in under a second. Three of the other Sigmas followed suit, and the other two were still in the first stage of power up. The surrounding group splintered and formed a loose circle around the site. I tapped on my HUD and brought up the targeting systems in my central window. The scope showed aircraft everywhere – it was impossible to count them.

I rose further into the air, spiralling upwards whilst nose down, so I could monitor the Pilgrim and assess the emerging threats around us. As I was turning in to my second rotation, a CAF Guardian thrust through the middle of our formation before stopping a hundred metres away and turning to face us.

"This is the Coalition Air Force. You are in violation of Earth's air space and instructed to set down immediately or you will be fired upon. There will be no further warnings. You are outnumbered."

There was a brief pause and then a response from one of the other Sigmas. "Coalition Air Force, this is the BRAF. We are here for supplies only. There are no hostile intentions. We are, however, in faster, more heavily armed and armoured air craft with hypersonic speed and deep space capabilities. If we perceive a threat of any kind, we will respond in kind. Your numbers are irrelevant – you simply do not have our flight capability or firepower. Please stand down your weapons – we do not wish to engage."

A small beep followed and the VOX light flickered on my command console. "Chaps, we're off VOX. Let's give them a little taster to discourage any hostile act. On my command, take up a position over an enemy aircraft and deploy your EM shields. On three, two, one… mark."

I swivelled my nose down and throttled in VTOL mode, flying vertically relative to the position of my Sigma, but horizontally relative to Earth. The CAF fighter that shot between us was just over to my left, so within a couple of seconds I was stopped dead above and pointing downward into his cockpit at a distance of less than ten metres. I deployed the EM shield as instructed and looked out.

The force of the EMS pressed the Coalition fighter downward. They'd designed the EMS as high velocity repellent for re-entry, so the pulse wall expands and retracts as it meets resistance. The fighter below us was a big blip on the screen, and the EM shield was pushing it away. I could see the pilot fighting with his controls to stabilise his aircraft.

I looked around and three of my colleagues were similarly positioned over three of the Guardians, but the fifth and sixth were still not fully airborne. Instead, they were positioned to the starboard side of the Pilgrim, whose bay doors were besieged with evacuees streaming into the hold.

There was a moment when everything just stood still, and I thought we might be OK – then everything went to shit. At least thirty CAF Guardians emerged from the clouds above us and opened fire.

"Get us out of here, Jaxon!"

I wrenched the control console closer to me, opened the throttle, pitched the nose up and let fly. In less than a second, I was a three-hundred metres above the melee. There were CAF Guardians everywhere, like a swarm of locusts, ripping through the heavy air at Mach 3, weapons hot and fury guiding their sights. I could see the other Sigmas manoeuvring around the flock, EM shields deployed on all sides.

Nothing was getting through the shields, but the pack was circling. There must have been forty Guardians closing the noose on the Pilgrim below. I hit my comms.

"Guys, I'm going to punch a hole through for the Pilgrim. Pull up and away to draw those Guardians off."

"Wilco," came the singular response. I dived at breathtaking speed, straight through the middle of the swarm. I didn't deploy my weapons, as I simply didn't want to be the reason this turned into a shit fight. My EMS was pulsing ten metres from the fuselage, and as I approached the centre of the pack I could see them being shunted back. The Pilgrim was powering up below me as I hurtled to the ground – I could see the stanchions dropping as the spheres glowed blue in the gloomy light.

I pulled left just as the Sigmas next to the Pilgrim shot vertically upwards at full pelt, closely followed by the Nova Pilgrim. She opened fire as she spun through her vertical ascent, sending the Guardians around us scattering outward. *Game on.* The pulse weapons on the Sigmas were powerful and I'd only had a single occasion to deploy mine, when a meteor collision was imminent, but they were safe around other Sigmas, designed to be absorbed into the Quirillium Nucleus.

The Guardians couldn't cope with the firepower, though, at all. That's why they'd deployed in numbers. The Pilgrim blasted through the opening and I swung round and towards the underside of the shuttle, spinning to port whilst holding down the trigger. I watched as several of the Guardians took fire, billowing smoke from their wounds and spinning hopelessly towards Earth.

There were aircraft everywhere, like flies, zooming about in an impossible pattern, weapons firing in all directions. The Pilgrim, not designated as a combat vessel, only had forward shields for re-entry so as a group we formed up under the belly of the beast as it hastily retreated to the relative safety of space. I could feel deep, violent vibrations as the EMS absorbed the impact of the Guardian's weapons.

We were climbing at full throttle now, the Guardians in pursuit but losing the race, weapons frantically firing off and pounding our shields in the thousands. I felt like my bones would rattle out of my body as hit after hit pummelled the EMS. As we passed sixteen-thousand metres' altitude, the VOX pinged and the voice of the Navy Commander rung through my cockpit. "We are hit, I repeat, we have been hit. We cannot maintain altitude."

Instinctively, I looked up. The Nova Pilgrim was pitching strangely to the left and slowing its ascent, as the drag from the gaping wound now visible on its port flank halted its progress. The Sigma on the port side had to take evasive action to avoid a collision, as it was close to wiping out both aircraft.

"Nova Pilgrim, what can we do to help? Over."

"We are out of options, Sigma One. We need to return to Echo for a hull patch. Can you escort us back to the launch bay?"

"Sir, Echo is compromised. Repeat, you wish to return to Echo?"

"No choice, Captain. We cannot maintain pressurisation. And we need an escort to get us back down there in one piece."

There was a pause, and then the captain of Sigma One spoke sombrely. "Patrol units form up around the Pilgrim and protect. She is dead in the water and needs safe passage back to Echo."

"Aye, Sir," came the response from the other pilots. I was about to chime in myself when Addison laid a hand on my control panel. "No, Jaxon. We can't follow them in. We need to go back for reinforcements and devise a plan to repair and repatriate the Pilgrim with Berty."

"But, Addison, the Pilgrim..."

"Jax, listen to me. We have zero comms with the Bertram whilst in Earth's atmosphere. They won't even know there's been a problem until our deadline to return passes. It serves no purpose to follow them back. Admiralty needs a sitrep and a plan of action. Take us back."

I looked at him. The fear in his eyes had been replaced with determination. This wasn't a cowardly act of retreat, but a calculated move from an experienced combat pilot. I just nodded and hit my VOX key. "Nova Pilgrim, this is the Red October. We're heading back to the Bertram for reinforcements. Stay safe, and we'll be back soon to bring you home."

"Roger, Red. Be seeing you."

CHAPTER
TWENTY-TWO

AS WE BREACHED the atmosphere and entered space, Addison put a call through his comms to the station chief. Twenty-five minutes later, when we arrived back at the dock in Globe 11, BRMC officers greeted us and escorted us through DECON. Once through and still wafting the foul aroma of the cleansing oil, they marched us straight to Admiralty and into a bustling operations centre I hadn't seen before. There was an enormous conference table in the middle, and holloscreen walls bathed the assembled officers in a blueish light.

The admiral entered from a door to our right and bellowed, "Take your seats, people," as Addison and I skirted the table to the far corner. Grealish was present, as were a couple of officers I'd met previously in Echo, but most faces were new to me.

We sat and Addison gave me a meaningful look, but before I could say anything, General Lavigne addressed him.

"What happened, Addison?"

"It was an ambush, Sir. They waited until we landed at Echo before making their move." Over the next few minutes he explained what had happened, to rapt attention from the sea of faces at the table.

Admiral Willard turned to General Lavigne. "Can they repair the shuttle at Echo?"

General Lavigne, in turn, gesticulated to a man on my right. "Nigel?"

He nodded. "Yes, is the short answer. Obviously, it depends on the extent of the damage. The signals conduits throughout the shuttle all have ten to the power of twelve redundancies, so there'll be no loss in flight capability even if they just patch the hole and make it pressure-ready."

"And what sort of timescale are we looking at?" asked Admiral Willard.

"Hours, probably. The panels are all glass-reinforced nylon, so they'll print replacements on site, and fuse with an aluminium exoskeleton and an outer aluminium skin. The harder part of the task is cutting away the damaged edges and replacing the framework, but even that is minimally laborious. I would expect flight readiness by nightfall with the right engineers, but no later than morning."

The admiral nodded. Everyone looked to him for answers.

I needed to understand what had just happened, and since nobody seemed keen to fill the silence, I decided I might as well ask the question. "Admiral, why are our own people firing upon us? This was supposed to be a routine supply mission."

General Lavigne spoke. "If I may, Sir?" He looked at Admiral Willard, who nodded imperiously, before continuing.

"Our sources on Earth confirm that the AoG, or at least organisations that we know to be funded by them, have begun an intense campaign to sway public opinion in light of the evacuation closing and the imminence of their destruction. Many of the top brass in military command share their views on those of us fortunate enough to live on the Bertram Ramsay, especially those that were abandoned after the evacuation halted. Whilst we were still in the process of training and evacuation, there was a degree of unification – preserve life, culture and humanity etcetera – but that time has passed and now we are a vessel filled with humans, orbiting a few-hundred miles above Earth who no longer face the greatest threat to the planet that we call home."

"So that automatically makes us a threat?"

Admiral Willard spoke. "Not a threat, Lieutenant, just an enemy of circumstance. Their mission on Earth, now, is to survive the impossible. They have no incentive to help us when they are so helpless themselves. Until the evacuation halted, I think there was still hope, however minimal, amongst the populous, that they may get an opportunity to evacuate. That hope has evaporated."

I remember well the talk in bars and coffee shops and in the shadowed corners of The Bleeds. The fantasy of survival, the speculation about life on a space station. The wonder as it traversed the skies above, visible momentarily in the glimmers of blue and black between the towering structures.

"What you have to remember is that the very last people slated to join the Bertram were the senior military command personnel heading up the ICP, CAF and other military and government infrastructure. These are the people we have left behind. They are capable, and intelligent, and not at all happy about being stranded on Earth." This from General Lavigne. "Obviously we had planned to effect further evacuations once we were days away from our orbital breakaway, but we had decided against sharing this with senior personnel on Earth, in case it didn't happen."

Grealish spoke. "Do we have a plan, Sir? I mean, are we looking at a rescue and retrieval?"

"No choice, Andrew. We cannot break from our orbit without the EM glass."

"I thought we manufactured our own glass?" he replied.

"We do, but not in large enough quantities that we can fix such extensive damage in the time available. There are thousands of panes of EM glass in storage on Earth. By far, the simplest solution was to resupply. We will, of course, given the current circumstances begin a larger scale manufacturing and storage within individual globes, but as it stands we need the panels that are complete and on board the Nova Pilgrim."

I was getting a prickling sensation on the back of my neck. Something felt very wrong, and judging by the faces around the table it was a sentiment shared throughout the room.

"The problem," the admiral continued, "is that the shuttle is now a *Trojan Horse*."

His words rang through the silence. The occupants of the room were still and focussed.

My comms pinged, and I looked down at my bio-monitor. It was a message from Amanda.

Lovell's, after your meeting.

Addison looked at me, one eyebrow raised. I shook my head imperceptibly and refocussed on the room.

"So, we need two plans." General Lavigne looked around the table. "We need a viable rescue plan, for both the shuttle and the Sigmas, and a plan to repatriate them all at zero risk to the colony."

There was an outbreak of chatter around the room as they contemplated and discussed the seriousness of the situation. The Admiral kept us there for a further hour, during which they grilled me, along with Addison, Grealish and the senior officers from Compression sites Alpha to Kilo, about our knowledge of the facility and the connecting pathways and tunnels to the Echo launch bay. I was of little use, to be honest, having only been on site for seven weeks. I hadn't explored the site at all, given the turbulent nature of Crew 41's progress through Compression, but I nodded my head, and responded where I could until the meeting was called to a close.

"We will meet again at 06.00 to finalise the plan. Please continue to consider alternative options – nothing is off the table until we launch our counter-offensive." With that, we were dismissed, and I headed back to my apartment.

I messaged Amanda when the meeting ended and told her I'd be there after a quick pit-stop at the apartment. I showered and changed into my civvies and looked out of my window at the vast landscape below. The sun was rolling over the back of the great wall, sending a vast shadow across the paths and buildings on my right, sweeping gracefully round as the station rotated.

Libby was unusually quiet. She'd nodded to me as I walked in, but she looked strained and there was a redness to her cheeks that gave away her emotional state. I didn't have any crumbs of comfort for her. And I didn't know how to handle this at all. Seeing her here just reminded me that Laura wasn't. That pain was still raw, although with everything else going on around me, I'd done a half decent job of compartmentalising it until I had more time to deal with how I felt.

I missed her, was the truth of it. More than anything, I felt a deep sadness. We hadn't known each other very long – just a few months, but Compression is an intense process that forges relationships, good or bad. I felt like I'd known her for years, but already I was mentally trying to move on from her presence in my life. It felt like I'd lost a friend rather than a lover, and I felt worse still about admitting that to myself. There were moments when my throat swelled and my stomach knotted, and I wondered what could have been, but these were slowly dissipating as the days wore on.

I'd always been on my own, back in The Bleeds. I'd learned from an early age that people are less reliable than me and so I forged an existence of relative isolation and self-sufficiency. Of course, I had friends, of sorts. People I liked and, occasionally, hung around with in town. But everyone was at arm's length, never encroaching upon my ability to exist at my pace, under my rules.

And despite all evidence to the contrary, I was unconvinced that any of us would survive the next four years.

I looked over at Libby. The same was true of our relationship. She'd been quiet but happy at Echo, just soaking up her responsibilities and keeping her head down. She'd smiled a lot and cried a lot. Saying goodbye to family and friends is always hard, but when it's this permanent – well, it just made everything more poignant for her.

I'd left no one behind. Not really. Being here with these guys made me realise that I'd missed out on genuine friendships, on a normal life. But I had one here and I was determined to preserve it, at least until the inevitable cataclysm. I needed to work harder to maintain these relationships, especially now that I'd been drawn into this secret war. When it was all over, they'd still be here, I hoped, and it wouldn't bode well for me if I kept myself in exile.

I took a seat next to her. She looked surprised, but gave me a weak smile and lay her head on my shoulder.

"How are you doing?" I asked, putting my arm around her.

She sniffed a little and replied so quietly, "I'm okay. Just second guessing everything and feeling completely helpless."

"I've been there," I said. "That's a bottomless pit that leads nowhere. You've done the right thing. If Jenn is innocent we'll know soon enough, and you can blame me for peeling you away."

"That's the thing, though. I don't think she is. I've been going over conversations and moments in my head constantly, and there are just so many little red flags everywhere."

I sat up and turned to face her. "Like what?"

She rubbed her face with both hands, as if trying to invigorate herself to speak. When she did it was more like the Libby I knew – confident and animated. Like she needed to get these cancerous thoughts out before they drove her to despair.

"She was so secretive in the last few weeks. I thought it was a boyfriend at first. God knows she's flirted with enough guys when we've been out. But then she'd get a message pinged to her comms and her face would change, and if I asked if she was okay she'd put on a brave face and brush it off. Sometimes she'd even get irritated with me."

"Did she ever leave after getting a message?"

"Nearly always. That's the other thing. She'd say she had to go to work and I believed her, but sometimes she seemed agitated."

"Agitated?"

"Yes. I don't quite know how to describe it – you know, a little frantic and snappy? I assumed it was work-related stress, but something about her just seemed a bit more urgent and aggressive."

She paused for a moment, and her face changed to one of contemplation and deep concern.

"What is it, Lib?"

"What if she's being manipulated and threatened? Would you help her? What would you tell her to do?"

It *had* crossed my mind, given what happened with Brian Latimer, but there was no way to tell until we confronted her, and Libby was completely oblivious to the ongoing investigation into the capture and torture of Emily and the girls. She'd never even heard the name Brian Latimer, and now wasn't the time or place, so I answered her question with a question. "Is that how it seems when you look back at those moments?"

"Honestly, I don't know, but the change in her manner was always immediate and negative. She'd get snappy and irascible if I asked her what was wrong." She looked miserable, as if she were betraying her friend. "Would you help her?" she asked, again.

"Of course I would. I'd ask her to tell me everything, so I could try and do something about it."

She went still for a minute, her eyes unfocussed and brimming with tears.

"Lib, you knew her better than all of us. I need you to really think about some of those moments and challenge them in your head."

"I have, Jax, that's the thing. I knew it couldn't have been a boyfriend. She went out with a guy she met on the shuttle shortly after we arrived here – came in bouncing and jabbering away at full speed, like she was on cloud nine. She was like that for a couple of weeks, going out with him, staying at his apartment in Globe 11, coming home all hours with a shit-eating grin, smelling of sex and margaritas. And then it was suddenly all over. No explanation at all. She seemed totally cut up at first. More than once, I saw her crying, but she refused to talk to me about it. I saw him a few days later, and he just seemed really put out. He told me she'd changed her mind and had become quite stroppy with him when he asked why."

She walked to the windows and looked out over the artificial landscape. She stood there, silent for a moment, and then turned back to me with those sad eyes of hers. "It didn't make any sense to me at all – she'd dumped him, but she was upset about it. I asked her about it when I got back to the apartment, but she just shrugged and said 'Plenty of fish in the sea, Lib. No sense tying myself up in the first month of being here.'"

"After that, she stopped all the flirting. I'd see a guy in a bar and point him out, and she'd smile and play the game, but she had zero interest in them. I got the impression she was just pandering to me."

"What about other friends, Lib? Did she ever hang out socially without you?"

"All the time, Jax. I mean, we're both shift workers, and both working in different globes. We didn't really see each other that often."

"Did she mention any other friends? Any names?"

She just shrugged, and her face clouded with sadness again. I had no idea what to say, so I just pulled her into a hug and then left to meet up with Amanda, my brain full of thoughts and questions.

My mind was agitated with buzz and hyperbole as I stepped into the mag-lift. Jenn had dated a guy who lived in Globe 11, so he must be BRMC or BRAF. If Jenn was really AoG, that would make her boyfriend an asset or a complication. If she'd had orders to break it off, it could only mean that either he was a potential threat to the AoG, or she lacked the composure to keep him at arms' length from their plans. The latter didn't really make sense though – she'd flown completely under the radar for twelve weeks so far. It was only in the last two days that we'd actually considered the possibility that she might be involved.

The other option was that Libby's hunch was right – Jenn was being manipulated. But then she'd shown no outward signs of distress throughout our time in Compression, to my knowledge at least, so she was either a sleeper, only activated once on board the Bertram, or something had happened just a few weeks after we'd arrived here that had changed the complexion of her tenancy.

Or she was completely innocent, and Libby was either paranoid or deliberately misleading us.

It was all so complicated that it made my head hurt. I stepped out of the mag-lift and walked straight into Tyrone.

He grabbed my arm before I fell over my own feet, and pulled me into a bearhug.

"Jesus Christ, Tyrone. You're going to break my ribs!"

He dropped me, laughing.

"What the fuck was that all about?" I brushed the creases out of my uniform, courtesy of Tyrone's mass.

He grinned at me and slapped me on the shoulder. "I'm just glad you're okay, mate. Your little skirmish down at Echo is doing the rounds at BRMC HQ. I don't know how much to believe, but it sounds like you were lucky to get away." He raised his eyebrows at me.

I gestured towards the door. "Let's walk and talk. I'm just going to meet Amanda."

"I wanted to talk to you about that, too." He looked sideways at me as we walked.

"About Amanda?"

He breathed in, one of those deep sighs that people do when they need to get something off their chest. "I want to know what you two are up to."

"Tyrone..."

"Jax, don't fob me off. It's obvious to everyone in the team that you two have paired off and are sneaking about on your own. Amy and Sara are both royally pissed off with you, and Grealish keeps muttering about it under his breath." He scrunched his features in a mixture of anger and confusion. "I know Amanda's type – her entire career is shrouded in secrets and information, so I understand her isolating herself, but I don't get what it has to do with you. So, what's the score? And don't insult me by denying it. I'm your friend and you saved my life."

Fuck it. I'd been championing Tyrone to Amanda since before the gravity fail on 10. Might as well put my money where my mouth is. Reluctantly, I explained to Tyrone everything that had happened so far, leaving out our suspicions about Hennessey and Jennifer. I wasn't quite ready to broach that yet. Not without Amanda to back me up, anyway. He listened attentively, only stopping me to ask the occasional question as the need arose.

When I got to the part about discovering Mark and the two perpetrators of the Latimer's kidnap being on Globe 10, he physically grabbed me and pulled me around to face him. "So that's why you were on 10 when the system went down?"

"How did you know?"

"Sara Hennessey," he replied, without further elaboration. "Answer the question."

"Amanda had already beaten me to the mag-lift and made it down to 11 by the time I made it out of the Hub, so I hitched a ride on Addison's Sigma over to 10. It all went to shit as I was coming out of the mag-lifts on level 5."

I looked at him, and despite his brief outburst all I could see was concern.

"Never seen anything like it, Tyrone." I shook my head, mentally reliving the events of that day. "It was an absolute shit-show. I'd have drowned if it weren't for Mand. We saw the whole thing as it played out. When the station started to rotate again, I was terrified. There were people and vehicles and all sorts of shit falling out of the sky, like gravity bombs, just hitting the grounds and buildings. There were bodies everywhere."

"What about Mark and the two perps? I only know what they've said on the news. I thought it was a coincidence at first, but now…" He shook his head.

"We watched him die, Tyrone. He saved all those people, and we watched him die. There was nothing anyone could do. If he hadn't rebooted the SQIIDS, he could have stayed there until rescued and thousands more would have died, but with full gravity and nothing to hold…" My words trailed off, and Tyrone looked at me with worry all over his face.

"You don't think he was in on it, do you?" he asked.

I took my time answering. It had been a question bouncing around in my head ever since I'd seen him fall. "I don't think there's any doubt he was involved. Everything we've seen points to him resetting the gravity system, regardless of the fact that he also fixed it. But I don't think he was doing it voluntarily. I think he was being threatened, otherwise why sacrifice himself to switch the drives back on? The only reason to do so was that his life was in serious jeopardy either way, so he did the only humane thing and took the fall. Literally."

We walked on for a while in silence, until we reached the corner of the street that Lovell's was on.

Tyrone broke our short reverie. "So, what are you and Amanda working on now?"

"Come in and find out," I replied, opening the door and ushering him inside.

Lovell's seemed unusually dingy, but it was quite full and we were met with a blast of chatter as we stepped inside. Amanda was at a corner booth and waved me over, but faltered when her eyes clocked Tyrone beside me.

We ordered some drinks en route, which they promised

to bring over, and joined Amanda. She raised a single eyebrow at me – a sure sign that I was in for a bollocking.

"Jaxon, I really needed to speak to you alone," she started, looking entirely unapologetic.

"Save it, Mand. I've brought Tyrone up to speed on everything, except our current line of enquiry."

She looked between us, half anxious and half furious. I could see a gasket about to blow, but couldn't decide which way she'd sway. Tyrone headed her off before she could start.

"Amanda, I want to help. I'm here to help. The whole fucking team is here to help." He looked at the pair of us. "What's with the lone crusade? We all miss Laura, and we're all focussed on ridding this station of the current threat."

"Not all of us," replied Amanda, much more calmly than I'd expected.

"What do you mean, *not all of us*?" asked Tyrone.

She sighed and looked at me without blinking. "Fuck you, Jaxon. You had no right to tell him anything without talking to me first."

"I talked to you, Mand. Several times. I told you Tyrone's solid. You even conceded that during our last conversation about it."

"Will you two stop this pissing match and tell me what the fuck is going on? Please!" he added, as an afterthought.

I sat back and gestured to Amanda to bring Tyrone into the conversation. Better that he hears it from her. Judging by the look on her face, anything I said was going to be too much, anyway.

She sighed and stared at Tyrone. "There's a mole in our team."

CHAPTER
TWENTY-THREE

THERE WAS some back and forth to begin with between Amanda and Tyrone until she told him to shut the fuck up and listen. He dutifully obliged and for the next twenty minutes, Amanda brought Tyrone up to speed on our investigations so far.

"Wait a minute." He held up both hands. "You think the mole is Sara?"

"You don't?" I replied.

"No, I don't," he responded, looking at us. "There's no way. I know Sara."

"Come on, Tyrone." Amanda looked aghast. "Everything points at her. The botched investigation for the first five weeks we were here, leaving Mark Hanson to roam unhindered all over the place, the comms between her and Laura on Globe 9, and she's monitoring our bio-bands to track our movements."

"Of course she fucking is!" He shook his head.

Amanda banged her fist on the table, nearly taking my beer with it. Before I could complain about going through enough tragedy without losing my first beer in days, she pointed straight at Tyrone's face and leaned across the table. "She had the means and opportunity to scupper our investigation inside Echo. She had access to air and land sides, and communication with the Bertram and the outside world."

"So did I!" he shouted, standing up and glaring at her. There was a moment when the voices in the bar seemed quieter than we would have preferred, and both of them looked around at the faces glancing in our direction before settling themselves back in their seats.

Tyrone lowered his voice. "It's not fucking Sara. I've known her for years."

"Come on, Tyrone..." I replied, wearily.

"I'm telling you, you've got this wrong. And I know you've got it wrong." He looked down at his bio-monitor and tapped away on the screen. A moment later, a soft tone sounded and he looked up. "She'll be here in twenty minutes."

"What the fuck, Harris?" spat Amanda. "Have you listened to a fucking word I've said?"

"Yes!" he replied, leaning forward in his seat and staring straight at Amanda. "And now it's time you did some listening. I can't tell you what's going on – it's not my place, but she'll be here soon and then you can hear it for yourself."

"Jesus Christ, Tyrone." Even I was exasperated. "We've been investigating the team since Laura died. Sara was..."

He cut me off angrily. "Sara Hennessey was going out of her mind with worry when you were back at Echo escorting the shuttle and it all went to shit. All she cared about was you not getting hurt with everything you've been through. You should have seen the state she was in when the gravity systems went down and she found both your bio-bands docked in Aoife's school. She knew you'd be on 10."

If my face looked anything like Amanda's, we were both stunned.

"But..."

"But nothing. Sara suspected there's a mole in the team while we were still at Echo, and her fears were confirmed after they cut her comms when Laura called in from 9. Her primary objective since has been to keep you alive."

"Her comms were cut?" asked Amanda.

"Totally jammed," replied Tyrone. "She's already changed the digital signatures on both of your bio-bands, so nobody can track you. We've had no idea what you two have been getting up to, save for monitoring your movements, but we both agreed it was for the good of the mission and not some self-serving quest for revenge over Laura."

Amanda looked confused. "But if she knows neither of us is the mole, why not bring us in and talk to us? Why keep us in the dark?"

"Are you taking the piss?" he hissed at Amanda. "She's not keeping you in the dark. Neither of us have seen you to talk to you since the debrief. You've been gallivanting all over the place doing fuck knows what, and getting yourselves caught up in every incident that happens on this station, and you've got the audacity to suggest *you're* being kept in the dark? Behave."

He crossed his arms and leaned back in his seat, glaring furiously at both of us.

Amanda and I exchanged glances, and after a minute of silence Amanda opened her mouth to speak, but Tyrone cut her off before she could get a word out. "Save it. I'll be back when Sara gets here." And with that he necked his beer, stood up, and left the bar.

———

Amanda and I passed the next ten minutes talking about everything we'd just heard. Tyrone's revelation, if he was right, changed everything. On balance, we both agreed that he probably was, and whilst this should have been some comfort, in reality we'd made zero progress on the team investigation because we'd been so focussed on Sara. We'd both assumed that she'd ignored Laura's last message, to enable her captors more time, but this latest intel turned that on its head. If she couldn't communicate, she'd have done the only thing she could and made her way over to Globe 9 as quickly as possible, which is probably why she was the first on scene at the hospital.

She arrived with Tyrone in tow, right on cue, and sat down next to Amanda. "I hear you two have me pegged as an AoG infil?"

"Sara…" I started.

She waved me off. "Forget it. I can see why you'd come to that conclusion. I can't say I'm enamoured at being a suspect, but I'll get over it. Honestly, I'm just glad you're safe after what happened to the Pilgrim."

Amanda spoke. "So, bring us up to speed. What don't we know?"

"Hold your horses. You first. I need to know what you've been doing at the Hub and why Libby is currently living at Jaxon's apartment."

"How do you know about that?" Amanda asked, looking shocked. "I had to call that in at Admiralty level to make it happen. The only other people aware of that are Admiral Willard, Colonel Grealish and Aoife Hanrahan."

"And how, may I ask, are you able to call anything in at Admiralty level?" Sara raised her eyebrows. There was a lot of that happening today.

Amanda sighed and held up a hand.

Sara spoke again. "Before you consider selling me some bullshit story, you should know that, until this morning, you were both being followed 24/7 and I've gone to some considerable lengths to repeal that order to allow you the freedom to move about uninhibited."

"What?" I asked. "Why are we being followed?"

"*Were*," corrected Sara. "Grealish's orders. I switched out the digital signatures on your bio-bands so you'd be untraceable. Amy had every person in the team pinged after Laura died," she faltered for just a moment as her eyes locked on mine, "so I took matters into my own hands and changed your band coding. You're not the only one with contacts at Station Security. If someone in our team is AoG, they'll be looking to retire the pair of you. As soon as they alerted Grealish that you were missing from the tracking system, he had people placed around you for your protection, I think."

"You think?" asked Amanda.

"Well, there's a mole in our team and since it's not either of you, or Tyrone or myself, that only leaves Amy and Andrew. If it's Amy, the people following you are for your protection. If it's Grealish, then they're tracking and looking for an opportunity to neutralise you." She was completely matter-of-fact about it. "Given that they've had a few days to slot you, and haven't, I can only assume that Grealish is not the mole."

"Okaaaay… " Amanda shook her head. "How the fuck were they following us without being seen?"

"Drones and security cameras. They didn't even need to be in the same street. We'll circle back to that in a while. I need you to answer my question, please Amanda. How are you able to call the shots at Admiralty level?"

Amanda looked at me. I just shrugged. At this point, I was so confused I didn't know what the boundaries were.

Amanda muttered under her breath, "Fuck's sake." She looked up at Tyrone and Sara, took a swig of her beer and spoke. "Most of what you already know about me is true, but at a layer below where I actually operate."

"What's that supposed to mean?" asked Tyrone, looking confused and exchanging looks with Sara.

"You were told that I was ICP, in a special division investigating the AoG infiltration of Compression Echo. That was true to an extent, but it was a cover story for a much bigger mission. I'm actually a CTI field agent, inserted into ICP to investigate the ICP's role in the infiltration of the Bertram Ramsay."

There was a stunned silence at this.

"Jesus fucking Christ." Tyrone sat there, shaking his head. Sara was frowning.

"So, you *knew* there was an ICP leak at Echo?"

Amanda nodded. "Not just a leak, and not just at Echo. People we know to be AoG and many, we suspected, were routinely selected to enter Compression but only at Cheltenham. We don't know how far-reaching the AoG is at other sites, but they wholly compromised Cheltenham."

"For how long?" asked Tyrone.

"My head of department brought me into the team eighteen months ago to work on this, so whilst I can't give you an accurate answer, my guess would be three to five years, but more likely three, given the timescale for the beginning of the evacuation."

"*Three years!?*" exclaimed Sara. "So we've been letting AoG infils onto the Bertram for *three years*? For fuck's sake!"

Amanda shook her head. "I don't think so. For the AoG it's all about the long game. It's like chess – you spend years moving your pieces into position, and then you strike. We got wind of it through Grealish's friend, Andrea. She was ICP Special Ops. We collected her dead drops before the ICP picked them up, and used her intel to insert me and others into the program."

"How?" Sara asked. "Andrew told us they had teams of

agents patrolling the dead drops to affect collection as soon as they occurred."

Amanda nodded. "And he did. But in the very first month, we inserted devices into the drops to record and transmit the data the moment the drops happened, without ever removing the items. We knew what was going on before Grealish did."

Tyrone let out a low whistle.

"Okay. So what about Crew 41? Why were you inserted then? Because of Leon and Eloise?"

She shook her head again. "We didn't know who the crew infils were. We knew about Leon, because he's a moron, but he wasn't active at the time he entered and Mark's service record flagged the moment he got his ticket punched. The whole business about his parents and the Valiant was discussed at the highest levels of our intelligence community." She paused for a moment, as if gathering her thoughts.

"The next rotation was eight weeks out, and all intelligence pointed us to a major attack that would halt the evacuation, giving us a limited window to investigate from within. Someone inside Echo was pulling the strings, and it was my job to find them and neutralise them before moving on to this vessel to take out the AoG already inside."

"For fuck's sake, Mand." I couldn't believe what I was hearing. I thought she'd been straight up with me about everything.

"Don't be so fragile, Jax. I told you I was CTI before anyone else."

Sara continued. "So it didn't do you any favours when we outed you in Compression?"

I recalled that moment vividly. For weeks the team had kept a close eye on Amanda in Compression, after her early skirmish with Leon, assuming, incorrectly it transpired, that she was an AoG infiltrator. Somewhere along the way her behaviour triggered a different thought process, and Amanda was pulled into Amy's office and confronted. That's when we discovered she was actually ICP.

Amanda replied, "Actually, it did. It gave me an opportunity to check out the ICP land side, albeit at an arm's length, which I couldn't do inside Echo."

"And?" asked Tyrone.

"And what?" replied Amanda.

"And what did you find out?"

"Look, as fun as these questions are, I'm not saying anything more until I know what you know. So now it's your turn." She turned to face Sara directly.

Sara looked stern. "I've asked you once, and I'll ask again. What were you doing at the Hub, and why is Libby living with Jaxon?"

My turn to chip in, or we'd be going round in circles for the next hour. "We've been investigating the kidnap of Emily Latimer and her daughters. We traced back all bioband data to the night of the abduction, and have identified the two BRMC officers that took them. Incidentally, those two officers were on Globe 10 with Mark, just before the gravity system failed, which is why we were both there chasing them down. We never got round to finding them, because it all went to shit."

Sara nodded. "And what was your next move if you had found them?"

I looked at Amanda and shrugged. I hadn't thought that far ahead.

"I was going to interrogate them. With a lump hammer." She threw it out like some casual statement at a PTA meeting.

Both Tyrone and I looked up, eyes wide, but Sara just looked thoughtful. "What about tracking them back to other AoG operatives?" she asked.

Amanda shrugged. "Killing the two Marines would

have flagged with AoG, which would have either forced them to dig in, or change their plans. It was fifty-fifty that it might flush them out. We still had Mark. We'd put a marker on his bio-band already, so we could trace his movements and see who he interacted with on the station."

"But the AoG are unlikely to even have working bio-bands, so how were you supposed to do that?"

"I set us up to receive real-time data on Mark's where-abouts directly from the Hub, allowing us to follow him around and see who he was meeting, but that lasted a whole hour before we watched him die. And the two Marines both had bio-bands on, so not every AoG infil on this station is walking around without one. They must have operatives who are above suspicion because they're working normal jobs and living normal lives."

"Hiding in plain sight." It was a statement rather than a question, and Tyrone looked thoughtfully at Amanda. Amanda just nodded.

"Okay. And Libby?" Sara looked back at me.

"We have intelligence that suggests Jennifer is AoG."

"*What?*" both Tyrone and Sara exclaimed simulta-neously.

I spent the next ten minutes recounting our conversation in this very bar just a couple of nights ago. They both listened in silence while I went into detail about Libby's suspicions, and our course of action since.

"Which leads me to my conversation with Libby this evening, after the meeting ended," I looked at Amanda, "which was on my agenda to talk to you about before this idiot bear-hugged me in the lobby." I kept my eyes on Amanda, but jabbed my thumb towards Tyrone.

I explained about Jennifer's boyfriend when she first came on board, and the vague conclusions I'd drawn based on her behaviours according to Libby.

"Well, we'd better keep a closer eye on Libby then," said Amanda.

"You think she's not safe at mine?" I asked, slightly confused by her response.

"No, I think she's perfectly safe at yours, but I also think pointing the finger at someone else is a great way to deflect attention and in my experience you share your concerns once. The whole story. Not in dribs and drabs. We can't discount her yet. What she said may well be true, and if it is it's more likely that Jenn is just another dupe, and being manipulated into doing things against her will. But after everything we've seen so far, we'd be foolish not to keep our minds open. She's at your place now, so you're well positioned to keep an eye on her."

I hadn't thought about that at all. The four of us looked at each other, all contemplating the current scenario.

Amanda broke the silence. "Okay, so that's everything from us. Now, can you tell us where your investigation is going? After today we're down to Grealish, which is problematic, and Amy who we had concerns about before Echo."

"You suspected Amy?" Tyrone looked concerned. "Before coming to Echo?"

"*Suspected* is too strong. We certainly looked at her closely. She was the ranking officer overseeing the mandatory assessments and ticket distribution. There was nobody better placed to manipulate the data and falsify selection. We'd been investigating her for six months prior to my insertion."

Sara looked up. "Did you find anything?"

"Nothing concrete, and very little circumstantial. Her father was a colonel in the UCoB Army, and he was definitely on our radar having been photographed with people we *know* to be high ranking acolytes, but he went missing in action before we could arrest him. Then something happened with his family, but the file on that is completely redacted, so fuck knows what that's about, but it's definitely unsavoury. We've got nothing connecting Amy to any illicit activity, and the 'guilty-by-association' argument doesn't fly with the brass, but as I've already pointed out to Jaxon this week she's an intelligent woman that's made zero progression through the ranks and seems quite content to stay exactly where she is. She either has no ambition at all, or she's trying hard not to be promoted."

"Grealish thinks it's Amy, too," replied Sara. "He confronted me after you found Emily and the girls and asked me outright if I was AoG. It was during that conversation that he let slip that you were being followed. He thinks your visit to the Hub was to meet the person who had re-coded your bio-bands. He doesn't know it was me."

"But you said they followed us to the Hub, so that doesn't add up. According to you Grealish had us tailed because our bio-bands had been re-coded."

"No, he assumed you already had a contact and were going to meet them at the Hub. He's not thinking straight at the minute. Willard tore him a new arsehole last week, and he's been flapping ever since."

"And what about Mark? Why didn't you have him monitored the moment we arrived?" Amanda asked. "That was the first step that led us to think you were the mole. You had five weeks, and he was our prime suspect and you did nothing."

"Do you really believe I did nothing?" Sara snapped. "You're not the only one that can put markers on people, Amanda," she bristled, "and I had two of my people reassigned to the Globe 10 hangar."

"So how did he meet a woman on Globe 9 without your knowledge?" I asked, before Amanda could get there.

"Who said it was without my knowledge? I may have heard it first from you, but that's only because I was on my way to the team meeting. They followed him all the way, but there was no way they could pursue him into an empty globe without being seen." She pulled a hollotab out of her pocket, navigated through a couple of screens, and tapped a corner. "That doesn't mean we didn't hear him."

W: "You are late."
M: "I don't want to be here."
W: "What you want is not relevant. You agreed to help us, and now you are here you wish to back out?"
M: "You approached me after my selection for this evacuation. My presence here is not indicative of anything you have achieved."
W: "And yet you have seen first-hand the consequences that befall anyone who acts against us, and before you tell me you have no intention of acting against, it would be prudent to remind you that refusing to act for us amounts to the same thing."
M: "If I help you, I will die along with you. If I do not, you will kill me. I would rather die without the guilt of murdering millions."
W: "There is no escaping death, that is true. But there are worst things than dying, and you do not want to find out what they are."
M: "Why me? I'm nobody. You don't need me here."
W: "Ah, but we do. We have a plan that requires your particular expertise."

There was a momentary pause and the distinct sound of The Loop passing overhead, before she continued.

W: "You will get your instructions shortly. You are lucky we need your fingers to work or you'd be losing them now for being so weak and pathetic. Still, it doesn't hurt to have a reminder of what you face if you defy us further."

The recording ended with a slashing sound and a scream, then footsteps fading into the distance.

There was a collective intake of breath around the table.

"Well, that explains the blood I found on the ground when Jaxon and I were looking around."

"You found blood?" asked Sara.

Amanda nodded. "On the ground. When Jaxon and I were looking around," she said, sarcastically.

Sara looked at Tyrone. "You've heard this before?"

Tyrone nodded. "I have. Why didn't you mention the blood in the debrief?"

Amanda gave a small shrug. "We saw it, which added to our intrigue, but then we started hearing noises which lead us to Laura. With everything that happened after, it didn't seem relevant. It could have been anyone's."

"That didn't sound like Amy, did it?" I asked, which furrowed a few brows.

"It's difficult to tell. His sleeve is covering the band. I didn't think it sounded much like Mark, either," said Tyrone.

Sara spoke. "We can get some analysis done. The key takeaway here is that we now know for certain that they approached Mark prior to his insertion, after receiving his ticket."

"We also know that they planned the gravity fail. But to what end?" asked Amanda. "Did you monitor all of his conversations?"

Sara nodded. "He actually rarely spoke to anyone. The few conversations he had were pretty meaningless. There's a three-minute gap on the day the gravity systems failed. My guys saw him taken into a service corridor off The Loop, but they were keeping their distance and by the time they reached it, he was leaving. One of them stayed on him while the other checked the corridor, but it was empty. All we got on the recording was static for three minutes."

"And you think that's when they tasked him with the gravity outage?" asked Amanda.

Sara nodded. "They planned it well."

"You think that was the job they needed Mark for?" I asked. "There must be fifty engineers in every globe – why would they need Mark for such a mundane task? I'd always assumed it was his flight engineering they needed him for."

"We'll never know now," replied Sara, "but Amanda's right. We need to work out why they even initiated the gravity fail."

"Surely the death of nearly seven-thousand people is a good enough reason?" said Tyrone. "Seems to me that's a hell of a victory for the AoG."

Amanda answered, shaking her head. "Their plan is to kill everyone. Unless they're plotting to do it in bite-sized chunks, it makes little sense to cause this much disruption just to kill a few thousand occos."

"So there's another motive for the attack," I mused.

"And we need to find out what it is," replied Sara.

CHAPTER
TWENTY-FOUR

THE FOLLOWING morning I made my way down to Admiralty for the briefing. I wasn't sure why I was involved at all, save for the fact that I'd been the only pilot to return. I had nothing else meaningful to contribute, but Willard and Grealish wanted me there, so who was I to argue?

I'd intended to leave Libby asleep in the room. It still felt a little strange having another woman in my bed, but she seemed totally at home with it. I tried not to wake her up, but she opened a bleary eye as I poured myself a coffee. "You got an early flight?"

"Just a briefing. No idea if we're going out today."

"Something to do with the Pilgrim being shot down?"

"It wasn't shot down. It was hit, and unable to proceed into orbit."

"Okay. So shot down then."

"How do you even know about that?" I asked, perplexed.

"Everyone's talking about it. Aoife messaged me to ask if you were okay. Why is she asking if you're okay?"

"Long story, Lib. I have to go. Enjoy your first day back

at work." I was about to walk out when she sprang out of bed, flung her arms around me and kissed me on the cheek. "Thanks, Jax," she said, simply, before walking off to the shower.

I walked across the grounds in the muted light of the EM glass. We were in Earth's shadow at the moment, so it was darker than normal. I strayed off the main road onto one of the woodland paths. The needles of the tall junipers dampened my footsteps as I trudged wearily to the Great Wall. The lake on my right looked dark and ominous in the half light, with small ripples breaking the surface. I crossed an inlet stream and re-joined the main footpath, aiming for the nearest mag-lift.

My brain was waking up and trying to make sense of everything I'd heard yesterday. Sara Hennessey had been the object of our suspicions ever since Laura died, so to discover that she was actively working against the mole to keep Amanda and I hidden and safe came as somewhat of a surprise.

I was lost in my thoughts for a moment and moving on autopilot, but as the mag-lift doors opened into the Opps centre the internal lights shook me from my reverie. I grabbed a coffee from the pot in the corner and made my way to the end of the corridor, and over to the mag-lift into Admiralty. There was a buzz of activity on the floor as I exited and turned left towards the conference room, but Addison cornered me.

"Morning, Jaxon. We're not in the conference room today. Follow me."

"Where are we going?"

"To the War Room," he replied.

"Sounds serious. Things escalating?"

"No idea. I guess we'll find out shortly."

We walked to the end of another corridor, where two marines stood guard by double doors. They escorted us through scanners over to our right, and then through an airlock into another corridor.

"Why did we just go through an airlock, Addison? What the fuck is this place?"

"The War Room has its own eco-system. The command hierarchy can detach from the primary structure within this complex, and retain control of the station remotely, should the need arise."

"Should the need arise? What the hell is that supposed to mean?"

"It's just precautionary, Jax. We've been at war with the AoG for a long time, however suppressed the media coverage has been. Berty is a lifeboat, with seven million people on board. It needs a command structure and a governing body. The War Room is just a last resort should the station come under attack."

I was about to press him further when we stepped into an impressive room with high ceilings – more of a hall, really, with its own spherical exoskeleton. There must have been a hundred people in here. A mixture of civilian and military personnel, all stationed at terminals and desks that filled two-thirds of the space. At the far end was a conference room with floor to ceiling EM glass, and that was our destination.

"Why am I here, Addison? This is well above my station. I'm just a pilot, remember?"

"Oh, come on, Jaxon. We both know you're working counter-intel. You've been caught up in this at every step. You and I were the only ones to return from the mission to resupply. That's why we're here, but I expect you to know more about what's really happening than I do."

I didn't know how to respond to that, so I opted to say nothing. The doors slid open as we approached, and a marine captain ushered us to our seats, two-thirds down the table. Over the course of five minutes, everyone that was at the previous meeting entered the room, along with a few that weren't.

Admiral Willard entered, and everyone stood up. He waved a hand lazily, indicating we should sit, and lowered his gigantic frame into a protesting chair at the head of the table. Two marines closed the outer doors and then tapped on a control panel, which misted the internal glass until it was opaque and white.

Willard nodded at General Lavigne, who stood up and addressed the room.

"Good morning. As you are all aware, yesterday the Nova Pilgrim was ambushed and forced back to Cheltenham, along with five Sigmas and their pilots. We received a communique from the Opps Centre at Compression Echo, shortly after 10pm last night. They are threatening to destroy the Pilgrim and its cargo, and the remaining stocks of EM glass currently being stored at Shipyard Berkley."

He paused for a moment and looked at the assembled personnel. "We have one-hundred-and-fourteen damaged EM panels on Globe 10, and four damaged panels elsewhere because of the gravity system outage and subsequent rotation hold. That's after we have depleted our own inventory and repaired the most compromised panels on the structure. So, we need that cargo."

"Who are *they*?" I asked.

"*They* are the Government of the United Coalition of Britain," replied General Lavigne. "They are requesting the further evacuation of six-hundred officials and military personnel, all of whom were supposed to be on this vessel, anyway."

"Sounds like a fair trade, Sir," said Addison.

The general nodded. "On balance, it does, but we have been unable to verify the message from official channels, which means it could also be a ruse to bring AoG agents on board, or an explosive device capable of ending our mission."

There was an outbreak of chatter around the table.

"Settle down, please," barked Admiral Willard. "Continue, General."

"We have no choice but to accept their terms at face value, but we need an alternate plan once the Pilgrim is in low orbit." He turned to face the wall of holloscreens to the right side of the conference table. The full-wall display showed the Bertram orbiting Earth in real time, and the location of Compression Echo.

"We need to execute this plan precisely, in stages. The first stage will be to send seventy percent of our remaining Sigma fleet to Cheltenham, as a protective escort for the Pilgrim, and a visible deterrent to the CAF. The fleet will affect re-entry over the Atlantic, four-hundred kilometres west of Reykjavik, heading south before turning east towards the Irish Sea. At this point, the majority will spiral up to take positions, whilst seven Sigmas stay low until they land at Echo and surround the Pilgrim."

"Seven, Sir?" came the response from a man in BRAF uniform sat opposite Addison.

General Lavigne nodded. "The launch bay at Echo can hold a maximum of twelve Sigmas alongside the Pilgrim. There are five already down there, so the most we can send is seven. The remaining squadrons will form a perimeter around Cheltenham at five and fifteen miles, staggered at altitudes of one thousand, five thousand and ten thousand metres."

"What about the remaining Sigmas on the Bertram?"

Admiral Willard spoke. "They will mobilise and rotate around the Bertram at a distance of fifty kilometres."

Lavigne pressed a corner of his hollotab and drew everyone's attention back to the screen wall. The display changed to show a closer view of Echo with the Sigmas surrounding it. There must have been three hundred Sigmas on the screen, all rotating the site at different altitudes and distances. It was a display of force that I could barely comprehend.

"Two of the seven Sigmas will carry Navy pilots to command the Pilgrim as a precaution. We don't know the condition of the personnel that were forced to return to Echo yesterday after they hit the Pilgrim. The other five will carry senior BRMC commandos, whose job it is to confirm the payload on the Pilgrim. We will equip them with scanners and they'll sweep the shuttle for explosives and incendiaries prior to the evacuation."

"If the all-clear is given, the six hundred people listed in the communique will board the Pilgrim and once this is complete, the shuttle will ascend with the Sigmas and join the fleet who will escort them to low earth orbit, just above the Kármán line at one-hundred kilometres."

The Kármán Line was an attempt to define where Earth's atmosphere ended and outer space began. It was the altitude at which a satellite would decay before completing a single orbit, due to the sudden increase in atmosphere.

"And if the all-clear is not given?" I asked.

"Then, Lieutenant, we will take it by force. I will ask the fleet to fire upon the structures surrounding the launch bay, whilst the commandos take control of the Pilgrim and allow the navy pilots to launch." He paused.

Admiral Willard chose this moment to speak. "We have requested that the Pilgrim remain empty of personnel until we can inspect it, and that the shuttle and Sigma pilots be waiting for us by their ships as we arrive, but these requests have gone unanswered."

"How do we know the Pilgrim is flight worthy?" asked Addison.

"We don't," replied Willard, "but it seems unlikely they

wouldn't have repaired it. Either their demands are genuine, and this mission turns out to be nothing more than a rescue mission and a further evacuation of personnel, or the Pilgrim is a trojan horse filled with god-knows-what, designed to incapacitate the Bertram and effectively end our mission. Either way, they need a working shuttle, so we are continuing on the assumption that they've carried out the repairs and checked the shuttle for departure."

"Why don't they just fill the shuttle with the people on the list and take off?" I asked. "Why wait for us to come down there?"

"This is the question that has kept us awake all night, Lieutenant. Either the Navy pilots are incapacitated – unlikely, given that they haven't requested more pilots, or there is a wider plot that we are yet to establish. Or they realise that any approach made to the Bertram would be dangerous, given the circumstances. The launch might even be treacherous, with other aircraft patrolling that we're not aware of. We simply don't know."

There was a moment of silence around the table. The concern was palpable. Every person present in that room understood the importance of the retrieval of the Pilgrim, but this mission was not straightforward.

General Lavigne walked over to the holloscreen wall, and pointed at Echo as it slowly rotated to the opposite side of Earth, relative to the Bertram. "We cannot fail this first stage of the rescue, which is why we are taking such a vast fleet with us. We need a show of strength, long enough to give them pause whilst we affect the rescue of our men and women pilots, and the precious cargo stored inside the Pilgrim. Globe 10 is damaged. We have switched off the atmospheric systems inside and everyone working on it is doing so in pressurised suits with their own oxygen supply, because continued pressure will eventually lead to a hull breach that will cause irreparable damage to this station."

"Can we repair it in time for our orbital breakaway, General?" asked an older woman in civilian attire, sitting next to Grealish, who had been unusually quiet.

"Probably not," replied Lavigne, "but our engineers have assessed the damage and agree that we can continue repairs once we are free of Earth's gravity. As long as we can seal the hull prior to the breakaway date, we can replace the EM panels in the following days. The four hull panels damaged on Globes 11, 9, 8 and 6 must be repaired prior to breakaway though, as these are at critical structural points of the station and the panels are on board the Pilgrim. We cannot evacuate these globes."

So there was damaged to Globe 11. It made sense, I suppose. Debris from 10 would naturally float into the path of 11 as a consequence of the station's movement. Addison and I exchanged looks. 'Critical structural points' didn't sound good. I was glad I didn't live on any of those globes. *Oh, wait…*

Addison looked at Lavigne. "Okay, so assuming everything goes to plan and we extricate the Pilgrim from Earth to low-earth orbit, what's next, Sir?"

Lavigne looked uncomfortable. He walked back to the table, and leaned over with both hands on the table-top to look around the room. "This is where it gets complicated."

He lowered himself back into his seat. "At this stage we will have a shuttle with six-hundred souls on board, and an unknown payload. The scanners we're sending in with the Marines are handheld and designed only for a minimally penetrative scan to identify any obvious risk items in the hold. They can detect explosives and incendiaries, but there are hundreds of tons of cargo in that hold and many opportunities to hide things that may be harmful."

He sprang back to his feet and walked back to the hollo-screen, swiped across and pulled up a scale diagram of the Nova Pilgrim.

"There are several access doors to the shuttle. Eight on the port side of the upper deck and eight on the starboard side, plus four on either side of decks two and three, two on either side of the cargo hold, and the main cargo bay door. As most of you will know, when loading personnel we usually marshal everyone up the cargo ramp and use the internal stairs and corridors to reach the upper decks. What we are planning to do is launch the Nova Palmer and bring her alongside the Pilgrim, and dock with her, to affect the transfer of all passengers. The Palmer will have full body scanners at the entrance to check every individual as they enter."

"I thought the Palmer was out of service," I said, and then remembering my place, added, "Sir."

A man in navy uniform to the right of Lavigne's empty chair shook his head. He looked at Lavigne. "If I may, Sir?"

Lavigne nodded. "Go ahead, Captain."

The navy captain looked back at me. "The Nova Palmer cannot enter Earth's atmosphere due to damage to the EM shield generators sustained whilst docking. Previous damage to the hull and flight systems has been repaired. Operationally, it's perfectly functional."

"Oh, Jesus," said Addison, uncharacteristically. He wasn't the only one that looked deflated by this news.

"Quite," replied Lavigne. "I cannot understate how dangerous this will be without shields. The Pilgrim will need to power its shields down, to enable docking and cannot power up until the two craft separate."

"That being said," continued Lavigne, "we will have a squadron of Sigmas form up with shields deployed behind the two shuttles to protect them from any debris or stray meteors. This is why we need to do it in low-earth orbit. The debris floating around at that altitude is travelling far slower than the debris at the altitude of the Bertram, so whilst there's more of it, it's less lethal."

There were some nods around the table, but still one or two looks of concern.

"Sir?" A woman at the far end of the table wearing BRAF fatigues raised her hand.

"Wing Commander Nevis?" came the reply.

"CAF, ICP and Allied EU Guardians are capable of low-earth orbit, Sir. As are US ICP Pegasus Fighters."

"Yes, they are, and that's what makes this mission so difficult. We don't know whether to expect a confrontation, and there's a lot of sky for pursuit." He paused for effect. "*But*, they cannot penetrate the Mesosphere significantly as they do not have the shield capability or the airframe density for re-entry, which is why it is essential that we reach a minimum altitude of one-hundred kilometres. They can follow us up, but any attempt to do so would be a suicide mission. Three-to-four minutes is all we need. Not only are they out of weapons range at this point, but the moment we break the stratosphere at fifty kilometres, we will outrun them."

"Sir," I spoke, "why would they engage us if the plan is to repatriate six-hundred top-brass? Or even if the plan is to destroy the Bertram. Surely, their best course of action is to make our retreat easy and safe?"

"That's true, Lieutenant, but we cannot rule out the possibility of attacks from other regions, or even rebel units inside the Coalition. We have no idea of the presiding senti-ment amongst the military brass of the US, Brazil or AEU countries. Our only point of contact has been with the government of UCoB. We're potentially repatriating six hundred from Cheltenham. There were two million left behind, so today's rescue mission is little more than a token gesture."

You could hear an ant fart. The stunned silence seemed to engulf the room.

"Now comes the challenging part," said Lavigne,

moving across the holloscreen wall towards the far end of the table. All eyes followed him. "Because of the risk to life by devices stowed within the Pilgrim's cargo, we are going to unload the EM panels outside of Globe 10 while it is depressurised, at a distance of one kilometre, inside the shields. Any explosion that may occur will be far enough away in the vacuum of space, that no further damage will arise to the Bertram except from potential debris. Each crate of panels will be opened in the cargo bay, inspected, and then towed from the hold by Sigma and deposited on the Palmer, which will hold station half a kilometre away. We have the equipment to do it, but it will be time consuming and dangerous. Once the Palmer has a crate on board, they will dock in the forward bay of Globe 10, where unloading will begin. Each crate holds ten panels, and there are twenty crates."

"And once that's done, what happens to the Pilgrim?" asked Addison.

The general sighed and shook his head. "We'll enter the cargo hold with a team of inspectors who will study every inch of the vessel, looking for anything that may harm the Bertram. If they find nothing, then the Pilgrim will routinely dock in Globe 10, and assist with repairs as necessary."

"And if they find something?"

"They'll scuttle the Pilgrim."

CHAPTER
TWENTY-FIVE

AMANDA CROSSED the main street from her apartment in 11-5-A, and walked towards the Great Wall. This side of the globe was more crowded than 11-5-C, where Jaxon lived, because the BRMC outnumbered the BRAF ten-to-one. This side was bigger, of course, but the architecture was denser and the greenery scarcer. She made a mental note to request a transfer once this shit-show of an investigation was behind her.

As she approached the mag-lift, her comms sounded. Jaxon.

"Jax, what's up?" she asked as she stepped into the lift.

"Mand, in two and a half hours, we have full mobilisation. Most of the fleet is heading back to Echo."

"What?!" she exclaimed.

"You heard me. It's crazy the amount of firepower they're committing to rescue the Pilgrim."

"So, every air force unit is being deployed *today*?"

"That's correct. Make of that what you will. I just thought you should know, as it takes me out of action until it's over. I have to go. Stay safe."

Her comms beeped softly as the call disconnected. She

stepped out of the lift into the command centre and made straight for the office in the corner by the outer dome, where she knocked twice before entering.

Sara Hennessey looked up from her desk as Amanda entered the room.

"Amanda? I thought we were meeting later?" she said, checking her bio-band for the time.

"We were, but something's on my mind and Jaxon's just told me they're about to mobilise the entire fleet, so we have a limited window before our military might is no longer on this vessel."

Hennessey looked alarmed, but shook it off quickly. "What's on your mind?" she asked.

"Jennifer," replied Amanda simply. "I want to confront her now."

"To what end?" asked Hennessey. "The whole point of the catch-and-release order on Jennifer was to enable us to track her whereabouts back to the AoG. What do we gain by compromising her today?"

"There is no order. It's just something Jax and I looked at and got squared away with the brass. Something isn't right, Sara. I think we'd be better to know now, so we can concentrate of the remaining loose ends in the crew and investigations team. If Libby is right, and Jenn is AoG, then it stands to reason that her assessment of Jenn being pressurised or coerced is likely to be correct, so she'll not be able to lead us to anyone. She'll just be another asset that they're using to achieve something."

"And if Libby is wrong?"

"Then we'll do the same with Libby. I doubt it'll be two hours out of our day, and we'll have either discounted two crew members, or we'll have enough probable cause to detain them and remove them from this vessel."

Hennessey nodded and looked thoughtful for a moment. "You know, ever since Jaxon mentioned Jennifer being a suspect, it hasn't sat right with me. She opted to do medical training and become a nurse. Wouldn't she pick a more penetrative occupation, something with actual access to things the AoG need?"

"Maybe they need medical supplies. Or drugs. Or chemicals," said Amanda.

"Maybe," replied Hennessey, scrunching her face up. "Even if that's true, I just can't see it being Jennifer."

"Could you see it being Eloise?" Amanda asked.

Hennessey shook her head. "Point taken. Okay, let's go."

They exited the building on the BRMC side and walked up towards The Loop. Amanda tapped her bio-monitor and put a call through to Commander Farrell, who answered before it had barely beeped.

"G'day."

"Gemma, it's Amanda Barclay. Need a quick favour."

"Shoot."

"Can you give me the whereabouts of Jennifer Edgecomb, please?"

There was a brief delay and the sound of a screen being tapped. "She's at her residence in Globe 7. We flagged her schedule. She's not due at work until this evening."

"Thanks," replied Amanda. "If she moves in the next thirty minutes, can you ping her marker to my bio-monitor?"

"No worries," came the response as she clicked off.

"Did Jaxon tell you what's happening with the fleet?" Hennessey asked.

Amanda shook her head. "Just that it is a full mobilisation. He said *most* of the fleet will head to Echo, which I assume means they will leave some to patrol the space around the station."

"Makes sense," replied Hennessey. "I haven't seen Andrew since yesterday afternoon, so I'm totally in the dark about what's going on. If it wasn't for Jaxon telling us, we probably wouldn't ever know about it."

Amanda stopped at the entrance dome to The Loop. "Grealish wouldn't tell you?" she asked.

Hennessey shook her head. "He's kept his cards very close to his chest since the gravity failure. I don't know if it's pressure, or he's deliberately keeping me at arm's length, but something changed a few days ago." She thought for a moment and looked back at Amanda. "Given that you suspected me as AoG, it's not a stretch of the imagination that Andrew has come to the same conclusion."

"We'll go and see him after we've spoken to Jenn. It won't help matters if he's investigating you, while we're investigating Jenn and Amy."

The Loop pulled into the station, and the two women stepped into the packed carriage where they remained silent until they exited at Globe 7-A. They left the station and weaved through the crowded streets, across a wide plaza and into a park. The grass was soft underfoot, and felt alien to the two marines, both of whom had spent the majority of their time on the station, pounding the nylon-coated metal walkways.

There were people playing ball sports in all directions, and others sitting around in groups talking and laughing. It was like a summer's day in Hyde Park, with forty-eight minutes of subdued light in every ninety-six, as the station traversed the planet. At that precise moment, the sun was in full effect, throwing long, graceful shadows across the grass and ponds, bathing the assembled masses in a warm, orange light. The Arctic circle was visible through the domed glass of the outer hull around the perimeter of the level, glimmering white in the morning sun.

They left the park through the southernmost gates. Whilst compass directions were irrelevant up here, each globe had the same directions designated as a means to navigate internally. Section C was always to the east, whichever the level, and A to the west. The Loop stations were east and west of each globe and all had northerly and southerly exits.

They crossed the street into a wide avenue, with tall apartment buildings on either side, all the way to the dome edge. The population density on this level was higher than most on the station, as most of the lower levels were industrial and agricultural. They turned into a street about a third of the way down and crossed diagonally to the second apartment building. It looked to be about thirty stories high, with a small garden frontage skirted by vehicle access ramps which led to underground levels for deliveries and utilities.

Hennessey swiped her band to access the main doors, pulling them open and then holding them in place. Amanda pressed the entry bell to Jennifer and Libby's apartment and waited. Jennifer answered after about ten seconds. Amanda dominated the camera's field of view, looking directly into the lens.

"Mand?" Jennifer asked. "What are you doing over here?"

"I was on patrol in section C and thought I'd drop by. Can I come up?"

"Sure!" came the reply, and the door sounded entry.

They crossed the spacious lobby to the mag-lift which took them up to the eighteenth floor, where Jennifer was waiting for them outside her door.

She smiled as Amanda stepped out of the lift, and then her gaze faltered slightly as Hennessey followed. She ushered them inside and closed the door. They walked through a small entryway into an open-plan living area, with floor to ceiling EM glass filling it with light. She'd modestly decorated the space with the few knick-knacks that they'd brought with them, minus Libby's, which the BRMC had collected and deposited at Jaxon's apartment.

Jennifer sat on the sofa and motioned the two women to the chairs on either side of the coffee table, looking confused and apprehensive.

"Have I done something wrong?" she asked nervously.

"Why would you think that?" asked Hennessey, eyeing her curiously.

"Well, it's just, you know – after Compression, I never thought I'd see you again. You were in charge of our training, so I just assumed..." Her words tailed off as she shrugged, still looking confused.

Amanda adjusted her position to face Jennifer directly. "We need to talk to you about the night of Laura's murder."

If Jennifer was surprised at the sight of Hennessey, it was nothing compared to the look on her face as Amanda's words washed over her.

"I don't understand," she said, almost stuttering as the words left her mouth.

"You were seen covered in blood, returning home on the night of Laura's murder. How do you explain that, Jennifer?" asked Hennessey.

"Blood?" she asked. "Why would I be covered in blood?"

"That's precisely the question we've been asking ourselves, Jenn," replied Amanda. "Why would you be covered in blood?"

"I wasn't... I haven't!" she stammered, looking utterly bewildered between the two marines.

The two women made eye contact. They had both expected some sort of hastily assembled excuse or far-fetched reasoning, but Jennifer's reaction seemed both genuine and plausible.

Jennifer took gulping breaths to calm herself, her chest heaving as she struggled to regain control of her emotions.

"How could I come home covered in blood?" she asked. "We're not allowed to leave the hospital in scrubs, and I don't help patients wearing my civvies. I've had no accidents. It's just not possible. Who would tell you that?"

"You're not allowed to leave work in scrubs?" asked Amanda.

"Of course not! The station is a sterile facility. I have to go through a Decontamination Portal to get into and out of the hospital."

Amanda looked at Hennessey. "Jaxon and I both had to go through a DECON Portal to see Emily Latimer, and they wouldn't even let us inside the hospital when Laura died because of the blood on our fatigues."

"Of course they wouldn't!" said Jennifer. "Patients that arrive covered in blood are the only exception to that rule, and unless their injuries are life threatening, we immediately remove their clothes and send them to a sterilisation laundry. Then they're wheeled through a portable DECON scanner."

Hennessey paused a beat, and then said, "Someone in your building told us you'd come home absolutely soaked in blood."

Some of the colour had returned to Jennifer's face. She controlled her breathing and spoke. "Captain Hennessey, if you've just walked from The Loop to here, you'll know how far I have to walk every day, to get to and from the station. It's always busy on this level. There's no nine-to-five here. Everyone works shifts. The bars and leisure facilities are open twenty-four-seven and you can see people playing sports and sitting around in the plaza at all hours. The strip of bars at the dome edge is known as 'Buzz Vegas'." She looked at each of them. "It's always heaving. There's just no way I could do that walk soaked in blood, and the only witness is one person in this building. How many people did you see when you entered?"

She was right, thought Amanda. They stepped inside the lobby and across to the mag-lift, a whole five metres, before exiting the lift and walking another five to the door of Jennifer's apartment.

Amanda decided to gamble. "It was Libby that told us," she said.

Jennifer scowled. "That little..." she retorted. "The number of times she's come home with bruises and blood on her, ranting about her boss, blaming the injuries on the tools and men in the Hangar, and she has the audacity to make up stories about me?" Her face was furious.

"What do you mean? She's come home covered in bruises and blood?" asked Hennessey.

"All the fucking time!" Jennifer was regaining her composure and there was a steeliness in her voice that had so rarely manifested itself during previous conversations. "She's so moody half the time that I stopped asking after being totally ignored the first few times I mentioned her injuries. I thought she was being roughed up by a bloke at first and asked her straight out. She told me to mind my own fucking business, which really wasn't her way at all. She was usually a bit more amiable and mostly she'd talk about problems with the Shuttles and Sigmas, and her time spent fixing and upgrading them. And then when she came home after the gravity failure on 10, she was in a shit state, crying for hours and refusing to talk about it."

"She was crying after the gravity failure? Why?" asked Amanda.

"I've no idea. She was fine that morning. In fact, she seemed back to her usual self. Laura's death seemed to knock the wind out of her. She was in pieces about it after she saw you and Jaxon."

"And she didn't say what had upset her?"

Jennifer shook her head. "She seemed scared if I'm honest. She was just shaking and crying for hours, and then she pulled herself together and went off to meet Aoife and you."

Hennessey and Amanda exchanged glances.

"Then she just moved out." She paused, wide-eyed and looked up at them both. "Did you know she didn't even have the decency to tell me? Sent two marines to collect her stuff. I don't know where I stood with her at all. Something happened that day. Good luck finding out what it was," she said sarcastically, before making a sad face and gazing out of the windows.

"I thought you two were friends?" said Hennessey.

Jennifer shrugged. "I did, too. Things were okay in Compression. She was warm enough towards me, but we didn't have an awful lot to do with each other. Then we arrived here, and they paired us up because we were sitting together on the shuttle, and we ended up living here. The first couple of weeks were okay – to be honest, we saw very little of each other during that time. We both had new jobs, and were meeting new people, and learning the station geography. Then something happened at work, I think – I don't know what, but she became irascible and moody, crying all the time and biting my head off at the slightest thing, or locking herself away in her room. She was definitely going through something, but whatever it was she wouldn't share it with me."

Amanda thought back to her conversation with Libby. It was like the same story in reverse, with a few different details.

Amanda looked at her. "Sorry, Jennifer. We had to follow up. We're still no closer to finding Laura's killer, and we're now scraping about trying not to let this case go cold."

Jennifer looked sad for a moment. "I'm sorry about Laura. She was always nice to me. We never really talked much, but she was always pleasant. How's Jaxon taking it?"

"He's doing okay," replied Amanda. "Throwing himself into his work, and trying not to think about it, mostly."

There was a pinging sound, and Jennifer looked down at her bio-band. She stood up and walked to a hollotab on the wall. "Sorry, ladies. I've been called in to work early. Has to be something big – I'm not even on call this week." She looked irritated and apologetic simultaneously. "It must be about the burial," she said, more to herself than anyone else.

"Burial?" asked Hennessey.

Jennifer nodded. "We've got nearly seven thousand bodies piled up in hospitals all over this station. Apparently we're moving them to a single location to be ejected into the atmosphere where they'll burn up. Most of them haven't even had autopsies, it's so sad."

"Do you know where they're being moved to?" asked Hennessey.

Jennifer just shrugged. "There can't be many places on this station large enough to house seven-thousand corpses. Probably one of the hangars, if they're planning on ejecting them in to the atmosphere."

Amanda and Sara stood up and thanked Jennifer for her time, apologising for the insensitive nature of their enquiries before leaving.

"Please keep this conversation to yourself, Jenn. At the moment we're still trying to piece everything together," said Amanda, giving Jennifer a hug.

As they stepped out on to the street, Hennessey stopped and looked back at the apartment building. "What the fuck just happened?" she asked Amanda.

"I think we've been duped. It's weird though. Libby was on Globe 11 before and after Laura's murder. She wasn't anywhere near Globe 9."

"But why lie to us about Jennifer coming home covered in blood?"

"Everything we've just heard is so similar to Libby's version of events, but reversed. It doesn't make sense. Why would Libby lie to us when it's so easy for us to disprove?"

They walked for a while, going over what they'd just heard, stopping at the plaza. Hennessey walked over to a bench and sat down. She looked up at Amanda who was standing a few metres away, looking deep in thought.

"You were in Compression with Libby. What were your impressions? You must have looked closely at her, given your brief."

Amanda shook her head and sat down. "Not close enough. I was there for the BRMC and ICP connections. Libby seemed nice though, if I'm honest. A little emotional. She was nearly always smiling and was quick to laugh. She was in the group without commanding attention the way Aoife and Leon did."

"So why would she sell Jennifer down the river at all? I mean, why even bring her to our attention? Did she seem the spiteful type?" asked Hennessey.

"Not at all. And when she told us about Jenn at Lovell's, she seemed wholly unwilling to do so, like she was second-guessing everything. She was so careful with her words."

"Could Jennifer be lying to us just now?"

"I don't think so, Sara. Her reactions were genuine. Shock, anger, frustration, confusion. Plus, it would take about two minutes to get the policy on scrubs being worn to and from the hospital. They wouldn't let Jaxon and I inside covered in blood, so I can't imagine she could leave in that condition, especially having to go through DECON. Come to think of it, I don't think I've seen a single person in scrubs since I've been here, except when Laura died. How many hospitals are there on this station?"

"Two on each Globe that has residents. There's a small

unit in the Hub with very basic facilities. Only one on Globe 11 because of the lower population, but that's a specialist facility."

"So there must be at least ten thousand medical personnel here."

Hennessey nodded. "We'd have seen people in scrubs for sure."

"So Libby is definitely lying. We need to speak to Jaxon."

———

I spent the next hour getting the Red October set up properly. I hadn't had time to do it before. The entire system was modular, so I could move my controls and hollodock into more comfortable positions before going through the painstaking process of setting up the screens.

Once that was done I powered down, double-checked the undercarriage and mag-dock and made my way back to Command. There were a few pilots milling about, checking the screens and talking amongst themselves. I checked the holloscreen where they were standing and found my name next to the designation *1 Bravo*. I was about to head to the briefing when Addison entered the command centre.

"Addison," I called to him as he exited the mag-lifts. He acknowledged and walked over to me.

"You all set?" he asked.

I nodded. "Addison, is it me or is every stage of this plan built entirely on facts we don't have?"

He looked thoughtful. "It's not the best plan I've ever heard," he conceded. "It's not the worst, though. Our biggest concern is hostility. We'll have three-hundred Sigmas in a confrontation with potentially a thousand or more aircraft. Our EM shields can withstand most things, but sheer numbers could overrun us, hence the emphasis on altitude."

"What about the docking and transference of people from the Pilgrim to the Palmer? Can they really do that?"

"It's never been attempted to my knowledge, but both shuttles have docking tunnels and airlocks, so the capability is there."

"Okay," I said, "and what's stopping someone walking halfway between the two and blowing both shuttles up?"

Addison stopped suddenly. "Everyone is being scanned before boarding."

"Sure," I replied, "but if someone knows there are explosives already hidden on the shuttle, they could easily retrieve them in the crowd. There's only five marines to control and marshal six hundred people."

"Shit! I need to go back and talk to the general. Convince him to set the screening up on the Pilgrim. It's the only way." He turned and walked back.

"You're welcome," I muttered to myself before heading back down the corridor.

I made my way to the mag-lifts and down to level 1 at the very bottom of the globe, exiting into a bizarre building almost entirely constructed of EM glass. There was arable land around on all sides, stretching to the very edge of the globe with machinery moving about in the distance, and a few people. The floor was also EM glass, with the titanium exoskeleton holding the structure in place on five sides. I looked down and felt my legs give way. The single-storey building was suspended from the ceiling of level 1, with the ground some five-hundred metres below us.

I looked back up and saw twenty rooms neatly spaced around the edge of the main hall, each with glass entry doors and walls, and designations illuminated on the hollo-screen walls. There was a kitchen with a coffee machine directly opposite me, so I refilled my flask before making my way into the second room on the east side, 1 Bravo.

As I sat down, my comms sounded.

"Mand?"

"Jax. Sara and I have just paid a visit to Jenn."

"I thought you weren't doing that until this afternoon?"

"We weren't, but something's been bothering me ever since Libby told us about her."

"So what did she have to say? Do you have her in custody now?"

"Libby lied, Jaxon. About all of it. Jennifer can't leave work in scrubs, and this globe is so populated that it's impossible she could have walked from The Loop to her apartment covered in blood without others noticing."

"What? But why would Libby lie?" I asked.

"That's what we need to find out," replied Amanda.

"She couldn't have killed Laura, Mand. She was at the dock when we left and when we returned from Globe 9."

"I know. I've just been talking to Sara about it. It makes no sense. These are such easy lies to disprove."

"She said something weird to me this morning, too," I said. "Asked me if my flight today was something to do with the Pilgrim being shot down."

"How could she know about that?" asked Hennessey.

"That's what I asked her. She told me everyone is talking about it. Apparently, Aoife messaged her to ask if I was okay. I didn't have time to talk about it."

"Where are you now?" asked Amanda.

"I'm in one of the briefing rooms in command. They're putting the plan together for mobilisation. Everyone has been called in."

"I'll call you back in a minute, okay?"

"Okay, but be quick. Briefing starts in ten and then we're all systems go for launch."

CHAPTER
TWENTY-SIX

AMANDA CLICKED off and looked at Hennessey. "How could Aoife have known about the Pilgrim if you didn't?"

"There's no way it's public knowledge. Earth attacking the Bertram on any level would instigate panic."

"We need to get back to 11 and speak to Aoife. I don't want to do this on open comms."

"Let's go," replied Hennessey, and the pair of them increased their pace back to The Loop.

It was twenty minutes before they were back in 11, having got off at the second stop, 11-C. Amanda steered Hennessey down the main path, before crossing the wood-land walk to the gardens in front of the school.

The same security guard stepped out to stop them, but scrunched his face up when he saw Amanda. She just waved nonchalantly at him and walked through. They arrived at the front entrance and stepped into a wall of noise. The sound of children echoed around the building, but muffled, like they were outside, and there were more adults walking around than Amanda had seen during her first visit with Jaxon.

"Can I help you?" came the voice of a woman behind a desk in the left corner of the entrance hall.

The two marines strode over to her, and Hennessey spoke. "We need to speak to Aoife Hanrahan. It's urgent," she added, just in case this woman decided to be a jobsworth.

"She'll be in the staff room. The kids are on lunch break outside." That explained the noise. "Down the corridor, third on right," she said, pointing to her left beyond the staircase.

They walked down the corridor as instructed and entered the room behind the third door. There were about twenty people in here, all in various stages of conversation or sitting with a hollotab.

"Amanda? Captain Hennessey?" Aoife stood up from one of the armchairs around an ornate glass coffee table. "Is everything okay?" she asked.

"We just need a few minutes of your time, Aoif," replied Amanda. "Is there somewhere we can go to talk?"

"Sure, sure," she replied as they left the room, several pairs of eyes following them out of the door. They walked down the corridor to the end and entered a spacious room on the left side, full of musical instruments.

"Aoife, we need to ask you about a conversation you had with Libby yesterday."

"I haven't spoken to Libby since that night at Lovell's a few days ago," came the response.

"Libby said you told her about the shuttle being shot down and asked if Jaxon was okay."

"Jaxon's been shot down on the shuttle?" she asked, looking shocked and concerned.

The two marines looked at one another.

Hennessey spoke. "You know nothing about the Pilgrim being shot down? Yesterday?"

Aoife shook her head slowly, her eyes welling up with

tears as she explored theirs for an answer. "I saw it leave yesterday – we all did. The main dock is a level below us and right underneath this school," she replied. "We see launches every day through the glass." She pointed to the dome behind the playing fields where a couple of hundred kids were currently running about, terrorising the few staff that were out there with them.

"I had no idea Jaxon was on board. Is he okay? Please, you're worrying me."

Amanda put a hand on Aoife's shoulder to reassure her. "Jaxon's fine. He wasn't on the shuttle. And the shuttle is fine. It's coming back today."

Aoife visibly deflated and sucked in her breath, trying to regain control of her emotions. "What the fuck is going on, Mand? Has this got anything to do with what we talked about?"

"I don't know. Honestly," she added, seeing the look on Aoife's face. "We have to go. I'm sorry to have barged in on you, but I had to ask you about it."

They left Aoife where she stood, looking emotionally wrung out, and stepped out of the building. Amanda tried to raise Jaxon on comms but he wasn't answering. "Let's pay Libby a visit," she said, heading towards Jaxon's apartment building.

Over the course of the next fifteen minutes, 1 Bravo filled up, as did the other twenty rooms. By the time the last person filed in, the entire glass structure was full of pilots and senior command. I kept checking my bio-monitor for Amanda's call-back, but it never came.

Addison walked into the room last, with General Lavigne. There was a strange assortment of characters in here – ten pilots, most of whom I'd met before, four navy pilots and eight marine commandos who looked like they could kill me with a paper cup.

Lavigne took a seat in the corner, and Addison stood in front of us. He pulled out a hollotab, misted the glass and opened up an image of the Echo facility and the downed aircraft on the launch pad.

"1 Squadron. You are the tip of the spear on today's mission. Yesterday, during a routine re-supply mission, CAF Guardians attacked the squadron and shuttle."

There was an outbreak of chatter in the room. Clearly, nobody knew anything about it. I wondered how Libby and Aoife had heard about it, and my brain started meandering through previous conversations with them both, looking for any signs of deception, coercion or anything that could suggest either of them was on the wrong side of this. I'd completely zoned out when I heard my name.

"… and Jaxon is the only pilot that returned to the Bertram."

Every face in the room was looking at me. I felt like I was dropping below the Kármán Line as my face started burning up. I settled for a weak smile.

"The footage from that fly-over is incredible. In the wake of the evacuation closing, whilst Echo remains standing, most of the ICP building has burned to the ground." He stood back as they screened the recording of our fly-by.

There were some grumblings as the people in the room took in the sheer scale of destruction at GCHQ.

"As of right now, there are upwards of six hundred high-ranking officials waiting to be repatriated, plus the Nova Pilgrim and five Sigmas. Our mission is to retrieve the Pilgrim, its cargo, the Sigmas and all seven pilots. Priority one is the cargo. Without it the Bertram cannot leave orbit, which means saving the Pilgrim. Our secondary mission is to save the pilots, and our tertiary aim is the repatriation of six hundred souls."

Over the course of the next hour, they laid every manoeuvre out for us, step by step. It was a fairly simple objective, with a complex interpretation of the rules of engagement. All aircraft were considered hostile, until proven otherwise, including the five Sigmas and the Pilgrim. We were to skim the Atlantic at just five metres, staying below conventional radar. We'd be visible via satellite, but those images would be delayed in transmission, assuming they were even being watched. It was a risky strategy, but there were no other solutions forthcoming.

I was to drop my Sigma to the deck, let my passenger out and then retract my landing gear ready to move instantly. They changed our call signs to mission signals, 1 Alpha, 1 Bravo, etcetera. I was 1 Bravo, with Addison taking the lead sign. I'd be carrying one of the navy pilots with me. Addison and I were to hover above the launch bay whilst the other five landed and dropped off the marine commandos, who were to secure the launch area before signalling to us to release the navy pilots who would perform a visual inspection of the Pilgrim. The commandos would then sweep the Pilgrim internally before admitting the pilots, securing them in the cockpit and then opening the bay doors, scanning the six hundred souls that would join the Bertram, one at a time. The commandos would board the Pilgrim to maintain order and initiate the hard-docking procedures of the Pilgrim and Palmer.

We'd have three further Sigmas holding above launch with a navy pilot and two commandos for redundancy, in case any of the advanced team suffered losses.

Somewhere in this mess, we hoped to secure the release of the previous navy pilots and Sigma pilots, who were to join their respective vessels and accompany us home. We were to make a hard exfiltration, with a vertical climb to twenty-thousand metres before pitching up and accelerating into the stratosphere. The fleet would surround us like a huge, moving funnel and fend off any attack until we reached the Kármán Line at an altitude of one-hundred kilometres. From there we were to escort the Pilgrim into the Bertram's orbital pathway at five-hundred-and-fifty kilometres altitude, holding station fifty kilometres out, supported by the remaining fleet while the Nova Palmer docked. We would stay on point with the fleet assembling at the rear of both crafts, acting as a shield to deflect and destroy space debris and meteors that may stray into the path of either shuttle.

Upon completion of the personnel transfer, we would escort the Nova Palmer back to the forward dock on Globe 11. Another squadron would take the Pilgrim inside the shield where work would begin on unloading the cargo, whilst the remaining fleet returned to the forward dock on 11.

There were a lot of unknowns on this mission, and we had done very little preparation on handling other combat vessels in the arena. Our mission was purely to escort and exfiltrate. The fleet would be in the fight without us.

Amanda and Sara entered the south tower of the BRAF accommodations, crossing the lobby and taking a mag-lift to the fifty-first floor, where they turned left and walked down to Jaxon's apartment. Amanda swiped her bio-band across the entry pad and entered, with Hennessey close behind. It was immediately apparent that Libby wasn't home.

The apartment was messy, with Jaxon's spare flight suit thrown haphazardly on the floor and the wardrobe doors left wide open. The bed was unmade and unkempt. There was a fresh pot of coffee, still hot but untouched in the kitchen, and wet footprints from the shower to the apartment door.

"Something's not right," said Amanda, looking at Hennessey. "I've spent the last couple of weeks with Jaxon, and a lot of time holed up here talking about the mission and the team, and I've never seen so much as a sock out of place."

"Maybe Libby isn't the domesticated type?" asked Hennessey, eyeing the wet floor and frowning.

"She always made her bed back in the dorm and tidied her things away. I don't think she did this."

"You think someone else has been here?"

Amanda paused for a moment and walked to the EM glass. She scanned the pathways below before turning back to Hennessey. "Everything's wrong. This is too messy. I think Libby's been abducted. Why would she make fresh coffee and then not drink any? Who gets out of the shower soaking wet and immediately heads for the exit?" She shook her head. "I think someone came here, pulled her from the shower, grabbed her fatigues from the wardrobe and marched her out of the door."

Amanda knew Libby was scheduled to join the maintenance crews inside Globe 10 today, so they closed up and left the apartment. Hennessey tapped her comms, but Amanda grabbed her wrist.

"Amanda, we need to call this in and find her," said Hennessey, pulling her hand out of Amanda's grip.

"We can't. Right now, we don't know who's who. We need to find her ourselves. The coffee is hot, so she can't have left very long ago and she's due back at work today, in Globe 10."

"Call Farrell. See if she can track her," replied Hennessey.

Amanda tapped her comms and Farrell once again answered after barely a single tone.

"Gemma, it's Amanda again. I need you to find Libby Baxendale for me."

Farrell acknowledged the request and punched away at her hollotab, scrolling through the data.

"That's odd."

"What's odd?" Amanda responded.

"Well, her bio-band is showing as *inactive*. Last location recorded was 11-5-C. Floor 51 of the south tower."

"That's where she's been staying. We've literally just been in – she's not there. Indications of a possible abduction."

"It makes no sense, though. Her bio-band is still recording her vitals and still connected to comms, but I'm not getting a location. It just says *inactive* on screen, even though it clearly is still active," replied Farrell. "It's like someone has reprogrammed her band to withhold the GPS signal. I've never seen a status like this."

"So she's definitely alive?" asked Amanda.

"No question," replied Farrell. "It's coded to her DNA and showing a strong pulse."

"Is that something you could do from the Hub?" asked Hennessey. "Re-program the band?"

"No, no, definitely not," said Farrell. "At least not remotely. You'd need physical access to the band. Someone has actually removed the lines of code that connect the band with the station. It shouldn't be possible."

"Okay, thanks Gemma. If she turns up, can you send me her location please?"

"I'll monitor it. I'm not going anywhere for a few hours."

Amanda clicked off and looked at Hennessey. "Something tells me we don't have a few hours."

CHAPTER
TWENTY-SEVEN

I WAS GETTING BUCKLED in with my navy pilot passenger in tow, when the lights around the dock flashed red. On the way up from 1 Bravo, I'd walked past the main hangar. Every single Sigma that could fit was being towed into one of two docking bays on this level. The dock itself was enormous and could house about sixty aircraft, but we were launching just over four hundred, so they had battened everything down and were opening the two internal hangar doors before depressurising the entire level and releasing the bay doors. I could see the far dock, just about. It was almost eight kilometres away. Once empty of aircraft, I'd be able to fly right through the heart of Globe 11 and come out the other side, if I were so inclined.

Hundreds of aircraft would mobilise through the two docks and convene just outside of the station at a distance of fifty kilometres, following the orbital path of the Bertram until signalled to make re-entry. I powered up the nucleus and gyro-spheres, checked my screens and waited for my hollotab to light up green, which it did in just under a minute.

I disengaged the mag-dock and followed Addison's

Sigma out of the bay. Nobody was calling in to the tower for pre-launch authority. There were simply too many units being mobilised for that to be efficient.

Addison took his Sigma out half a kilometre before pitching downwards and taking us fifty kilometres out, where we held steady at an altitude of five-hundred-and-thirty kilometres until the entire fleet had caught up. As the last call-sign checked into the fleet holding pattern, I looked out of my starboard window. The sight of four-hundred Sigmas was awesome to behold. A hundred of them peeled away and began surrounding the Bertram.

Two squadrons of twenty Sigmas flew ahead of our unit and turned into the re-entry path, slowly descending to the Kármán Line. We followed in close formation, with Addison in the lead, and the rest of us splayed out like a pyramid behind him.

My altimeter pinged, and I deployed my EM shield, watching as the nose of the Red October glowed orange. The re-entry phase took just under ninety seconds before we broke free of the Mesosphere and my HUD switched to atmospheric data, as we slowed to thirty-five-hundred knots.

We were back inside Earth's airspace. Game on.

———

Amanda crossed the woodland path at a slight jog, with Hennessey close behind. They made another two-hundred metres progress towards the command structure when a pulsating roar distracted them.

They turned to face the dome between the two BRAF accommodation towers.

"Look!" pointed Hennessey, as hundreds of Sigmas exited the bay on the level below. It was awesome to behold the might of the entire fleet.

"Jesus fucking Christ," said Amanda, shaking her head. "What the fuck is going on?"

"Not a bloody clue," replied Hennessey, "but we have bigger concerns at the moment."

They resumed their jog towards the Great Wall when Amanda's comms pinged.

"Amanda, it's Gemma. Ms Baxendale's bio-band was just pinged, entering a mag-lift to the command centre. ML19 at the northern end of the Wall."

"That's why they abducted Libby, it has to be! Because they need her access to the command centre," said Amanda.

"No," came the response through her comms. "They didn't use her bio-band to get inside. The command centre scans anyone entering, and Ms Baxendale's bio-band was one of them."

Amanda and Sara looked at one another. Hennessey spoke. "Gemma, it's Captain Sara Hennessey. Are you able to isolate who she is with or whose bio-band was used to gain access?"

"That'll take a little while, but yes, I can do it."

"Thanks, Gemma."

Hennessey looked at the Great Wall. "If they don't need Libby to get inside, they must be active BRMC or BRAF personnel."

The two Marines picked up the pace and turned north, skirting the wall boundary at thirty metres.

"ML8," said Hennessey, pointing at the nearest mag-lift.

Amanda pulled up and stopped. "What's at that end of the command centre?" she asked.

"Several cargo holds, the training arena, the range and the light-weapons armoury," replied Hennessey.

"The armoury!" said Amanda, eyes wide open.

"They can't get in there," stated Hennessey with absolute certainty. "Libby definitely doesn't have access. The only place Libby's bio-band would get them is inside the hangar, which is a restricted area, and they're at the wrong end of the command centre for that."

"We already know they've had access," replied Amanda, "or they wouldn't have been able to manufacture bombs on this vessel."

Hennessey shook her head. "The light weapons don't include explosives or incendiaries. It's mostly Scorpion Rifles and Proxys. Anything combustible, including armaments for the fleet, is stored in the bay armoury, which can only be accessed when the doors are closed and the bay is pressurised."

"Okay," said Amanda, taking a deep breath. "But we know they must be command centre personnel. We don't know what access levels they may have. We still need to get there and it's just over four kilometres away."

Hennessey looked around. "We need a vehicle. There!" she pointed at a maintenance building behind The Loop station.

They ran over, and Hennessey swiped her band across the garage doors on the south facia. Inside was an assortment of vehicles, mostly trucks loaded with equipment for the gardeners and cleaning crew. She vaulted into an AethervoX with the words 'Forestry' stencilled onto the sides. Amanda ran around the back and jumped in the other side.

"Hey!" came a shout from the corner of the building, but Hennessey ignored it and gunned the accelerator, launching out onto the street before turning right and driving straight at the Wall. A hundred yards out, she turned right again onto a wide boulevard that ran the width of the level. The AethervoX bounced on its magnetic suspension as they weaved around the afternoon traffic and pedestrians at a pathetic thirty-eight kph. The speed limits on the station were twenty-five kph everywhere, and they passed more than one concerned BRMC officer tapping into their comms.

"Vehicle eighty-one. This is the BRMC. You are violating station laws. Please stop immediately."

Amanda hit the VOX button on the dash. "Captain Sara Hennessey and Major Amanda Barclay responding to an emergency," she replied.

"Please state your emergency," came the response. "You are not allowed to use civilian vehicles."

"In pursuit of a civilian hostage. Please call Colonel Grealish and relay this message. He'll confirm."

"I'm sorry. Did you say *civilian hostage*?"

"Just do it. We don't have time for this," replied Amanda, hitting the off button.

They got another twenty seconds further up the boulevard, when the vehicle died on them.

"For fuck's sake," said Hennessey. "They've overridden the system and manually stopped us. We'll have to do it on foot."

The two marines jogged up the outside wall. It took them sixteen minutes to run the remaining three kilometres.

Hennessey pulled up, holding a stitch in her left side. "ML19." She pointed at the mag-lift. They were only three-hundred metres from the dome edge. There was nothing beyond the glass – just space and the very edge of the new moon as it crept into view.

They were both sweating in their BRMC fatigues. Amanda's hair was sticking to her forehead, but she was fit and in better shape than Hennessey. She tapped her comms.

"Farrell."

"Gem, it's Amanda. We're at ML19. Any idea which level they headed to?"

"I'll check. Hang on." There was a pause while Commander Farrell searched for the lift logs. "They went down to the hangar level," she replied.

They were about to step inside when Farrell spoke again. "The logs say the last person to enter was a Lieutenant Amy Cooper."

We were descending above the Artic circle, moving slowly south to our entry point west of Reykjavik. As we dipped below twenty-thousand metres, I heard the awesome thrum of three-hundred pairs of gyro-spheres vibrating through the hull of my Sigma, making the hairs on my arms stand up.

We were radio silent until our final approach so I stayed in the wake of 1 Alpha, matching his pitch and roll as he followed the forward squadrons down to sea level, before pulling up and skimming the Atlantic Ocean.

The ocean rushed below us at unfathomable speed, as we thrust into the edges of the storm around the British Isles. Meteorology had flagged the inclement weather during our briefing. Modern aircraft were less affected by poor weather than our historical counterparts, but the buffeting wind and driving rain still made the conditions tricky. Visibility was under thirty metres, and at the speed we were travelling we'd be bang in trouble if anything suddenly loomed out of the darkness, but the scopes were clear ahead.

We skirted the southern tip of Ireland, less than forty kilometres from the coast, before slowing to sixteen-hundred knots at the Severn Estuary and following the path of the river between Lynton and Porthcawl.

As we neared our target, the two squadrons leading the fleet pulled up and spiralled into the sky, accelerating to three-thousand knots. Addison's Sigma stayed true to the target and the ten Sigmas of 1 Squadron proceeded to Cheltenham alone. We had just trimmed thirty-five degrees to port to proceed over Portishead towards Cirencester, when all hell broke loose.

A squadron of CAF and AEU Guardians broke through the cloud cover six-thousand feet above us and opened fire. I barely had time to acknowledge their presence when they were engaged by one of the Sigma squadrons at our rear.

"Maintain course," came the call from Addison to 1 Squadron as Filton and Patchway flashed below us in the afternoon gloom. The plan was to bank left to a heading of three-hundred-and-forty-eight degrees as we reached Cirencester and breach Cheltenham from the south.

"1 Alpha, this is 1 Delta. We're taking fire. Shields deployed."

The rest of us followed suit and deployed our EM shields as we made the last turn towards Echo. The skies lit up with lightning and explosions as the battle above us commenced, but we remained resolute in our trajectory and turned in unison for the final leg of the infiltration.

The sight that met us as we made the turn was like nothing I'd ever seen. There were hundreds of aircraft engaged in an epic battle in the skies above England. Explosions flashed in the darkness, illuminating the swarm as war played out in the thunderous rain.

My comms barked as Addison calmly relayed his orders to the squadron. "This is 1 Alpha. Take your positions on my mark."

There was a chorus of "roger" and "ten-four" through the comms, before Addison called "Three, two, one, mark!" and the squadron deployed.

I pulled up to one-hundred metres, and briefly turned starboard, before slowing and rotating back around Compression Echo. There were black rivers of filth and ash running through the broken roads around the destroyed GCHQ building. To my left I could see the launch bay, and in its centre the imposing bulk of the Nova Pilgrim.

I swept back around and positioned myself under the wings of two Sigmas at the rear of the Pilgrim, between the cargo bay and the terminal building, descending to five metres from the deck and holding steady as I watched the five Sigmas transporting the commandos dip to the ground and open their hatches.

There was a sudden crash on the right as the building above Echo took fire, followed by the screech of metal as tons of titanium exoskeleton and EM glass plummeted to the launch bay, crushing one of the inbound Sigmas. The commando that had been inside was already free, and forming up at the rear of the Pilgrim with his teammates, but the pilot had not emerged from the cockpit.

The cargo bay opened and the five commandos sprinted up the ramp, scanners in hand and disappeared into the bowels of the shuttle. The rain came down even harder, drowning out the sounds of the battle above. I looked at my scopes. What I saw was unimaginable.

There were aircraft everywhere. A thousand metal wasps cluttered the skies above us, thrashing about and peppering each other with plasma cannons. Our comms in 1 Squadron were isolated from the fleet so I couldn't hear the carnage above us, but I didn't imagine there was much chatter between pilots.

It took three long minutes before the commandos emerged from the rear of the Pilgrim and gave the signal to proceed, during which I could hear Addison frantically trying to hail the downed Sigma pilot. I dropped my Sigma and popped the hatch before we'd even hit the deck. The navy pilot next to me jumped out without a word and swung himself from the frame before dropping to the metal dais three metres below.

He sprinted for the loading ramp and vanished inside. I looked across at the Sigma buried under the rubble but couldn't see any sign of the pilot emerging. Without thinking I idled the Sigma and launched myself through the hatch, swinging down and dropping to the platform, falling hopelessly on my arse as my flight boots slipped on the wet metal in complete contrast to what the navy pilot had done moments before. I ran towards the rubble on the right side of the downed Sigma, soaked through on one side of my suit, and getting wetter with every second. I could hear Addison's voice calling to me through my comms, petering out as I put distance between myself and my cockpit.

The left side of the Sigma was open, with the hatch hanging from its mounts. Rubble buried the starboard side, and half of the fuselage had staved in. There was a fire at the rear where the gyro-sphere stanchion had wrenched from the frame of the aircraft, sending blue crackles to the shredded titanium exoskeleton of the partially collapsed building. The windows and screens were smashed, and the pilot was unconscious, lulling clumsily into the harness.

She was too high to get to and her concealed entry ladder was a twisted mess of titanium and aluminium. We rarely used the on-board ladders to enter or leave the Sigmas, because the launch bays here and on the Bertram have ground crews with moveable steps, but we'd all used them today to mount up and leave the station. There was no saving this one, or the aircraft. I ran to the hangar and grabbed the steps, wheeling them at top speed towards the stricken vessel.

As I pushed the steps back across the platform, the doors to the terminal building opened and a mass of bodies flooded out. The commandos had set up a makeshift checkpoint for entry to the Pilgrim, but it was going to take several minutes to get six-hundred people on board.

I got the steps into place and scaled them carefully until I reached the cockpit, which was filling up with smoke. The rain was beating down harder than ever, and I stumbled more than once as I rushed to the top of the steps. I heard the steady throb of gyro-spheres close-by and looked up to see our three redundancies circling the launch bay, getting lower and lower.

I slapped the centre of the pilot's harness, releasing the magnetic clasps and hauled her unceremoniously through the hatch and onto the steps. I draped her awkwardly across the side bars and top platform, but her comfort wasn't the priority. There was blood dripping from several gashes on her face and head. I jumped down the steps, grabbed the handles and wheeled her as fast as I could back towards my Sigma. I had to go under the belly of the shuttle, as the stream of bodies from the terminal building was blocking my path in a straight trajectory.

I could hear hundreds of footsteps tramping up the metalwork of the cargo doors above me, and the unrelenting patter of rain pounding the Pilgrim and the metal dais on which she perched. My feet were sliding as I tried desperately to turn the steps at speed, the weight and momentum of the metal stairs dragging forwards as I tried to steer left. It took two hard tugs to pull it round and shift it toward the Red October.

I made it to the base as another explosion ripped through the air to my right, and the sudden rush of atmosphere billowed into me from the gaping wound in the Opps centre as the airtight facility decompressed over the launch bay. Flames were flickering from the walls and I could feel the heat intensifying as the rush of escaping oxygen fed their fury.

The boarding process looked to be almost complete, with about another hundred queuing to enter the Pilgrim. They looked like drowned rats as the rain pummelled them in a merciless deluge. I pushed the steps to meet the edge of my Sigma, without bothering to line it up particularly well, before pulling the lever on the side and engaging the mag-lock on the base. I hauled myself back to the top, stepping over the unconscious pilot.

There was a gap of about half a metre between the top of the steps and the hatch of my Sigma, but I couldn't worry about that – time was of the essence here. I stepped across, and then leaned back and grabbed the collar of the injured pilot, turning her over on to her back, before hooking my hands under her arms and dragging her over the gap. I wedged my legs into the edge of the open doorway, and my heels slipped as I tried to lever myself backwards with the dead-weight of the pilot in my arms.

I eventually dragged her through, just as the gyrospheres on the Pilgrim started spinning up. Hauling her into the first seat, I grabbed the harness and fastened it across her chest, missing the left shoulder and right leg. I was up against the clock and figured she'd rather have a bumpy ride than no ride.

I stepped into the pilot's seat and hit the hatch close and mag-dock release simultaneously. The door swung down as water cascaded in from the storm and the elegant metal wasp rose above the dais, waiting for the command to launch.

Addison's voice was still coming through on VOX, but I hadn't been listening. It was only as the hatch finally closed and my controller was in hand that I heard Addison screaming into the comms.

"1 Bravo. Are you secure? Jaxon, for fuck's sake, respond!"

"This is 1 Bravo. I'm battened down and ready to go, Wing," I replied as my stanchions angled back and the surrounding sky lit up blue, reflecting the gyro-spheres of fourteen Sigmas and the Nova Pilgrim.

"This is the Nova Pilgrim, ready for launch."

CHAPTER
TWENTY-EIGHT

"GET us out of here 1 Alpha," was the command from the Nova Pilgrim.

"Affirm," came the response from Addison, "1 Squadron, full shields, go vertical."

I hit the VTOL button, pulled down on the throttle and the Red October leapt into the sky. She'd barely made it to three-hundred metres when weapons loosed upon us from all directions. I could see plasma criss-crossing from every angle as the swarm of Sigmas fought off the antagonists to protect our exfiltration. Explosions happened all around me and, more than once, my screens lit up red as their weapons hit my aircraft. I could feel myself being buffeted by the wind and plasma fire as we climbed faster and faster.

It took less than twenty seconds to breach the cloud cover and power into the bright glare of the afternoon sun. If I thought the skies would be clearer above the storm, I was sorely mistaken. If anything, my screens looked even more cluttered, with every Sigma, Guardian and Pegasus visible in my forward displays. Two CAF Guardians thrust into my path, but my shields propelled them backwards.

My displays flickered and my shield energy flashed.

Nineteen percent. I was down by eighty-one percent in under thirty seconds. The nucleus was desperately trying to recharge the shields, but with full throttle applied, the energy was going into the gyro-spheres and thrusters. The Pilgrim was directly below and slightly forward, and the ten Sigmas of 1 Squadron alongside the four from the previous day's mission were crowding the top of the Pilgrim's hull, protecting it from the onslaught in the skies above.

Faster and faster we flew until we reached the limit of our VTOL capability. "Pitch up!" came the command from the Nova Pilgrim, and we rotated upwards, maintaining momentum. This was the most dangerous part of the plan. The Pilgrim had forward shields only, and as it rotated upwards the pilots exposed the underbelly of the beast to lateral enemy fire, from which it had no protection. As a squadron, we feathered back from the Pilgrim's path, and formed up on the underside to protect the shuttle.

Only a minute had passed. We were skirting twenty-five-thousand metres and gaining altitude and velocity with every passing moment. The battle below intensified as Earth's protectors desperately fought to ground the shuttle permanently. We'd been naïve to assume our path home would lack peril, but whilst this revelation was bad news for the present situation, it was good news for the crew and passengers of the Pilgrim. It seemed, given the circumstances, the passengers were probably legitimate and not a threat to the safety of the Bertram.

Higher and higher we flew. My HUD read *3670 knots* and climbing steadily as the air thinned and the unwieldy aerodynamics of the shuttle became less of a hindrance. Seventy-thousand metres passed, and the conflict below had shrunk on screen. The fleet disengaged and formed up thirty-thousand metres down. I wondered how many we'd lost in the fight. I could never have imagined an aerial battle that intense. No sooner had I thought about it than the Red October shuddered and lurched, impact warning alarms sounding. The Sigma's nose immediately twitched right, and I had to fight the controls to compensate for the yaw with my left thrusters.

The hissing on the lower port flank by my left foot was worrying, and my screens flickered as the hull warning lights illuminated and a master alarm sounded. I could feel the pressure and temperature dropping inside the cockpit. I reached my hand down to my hip to release my rebreather. As I pulled the mask out, I looked across at the pilot slumped in the passenger seat. Her kit belt was gone.

"For fuck's sake." Deftly, I locked off my throttle, released my harness and took my kit belt off, laying it in the lap of the female pilot. I pulled the bag over her head and hit the inflate button, and watched for a moment as nothing happened. I briefly wondered if she was already dead when the faintest patch of mist from her breath caught the inside of the mask. Relieved, I grabbed a box from behind the bulkhead and pulled the patch-repair foam spray from the inside. I couldn't see the breach in the rapidly diminishing light, but I could hear it, so I leaned around my console, threw a glass-reinforced-nylon patch towards the sound of the escaping air, pushed the nozzle into the corner and emptied the contents onto the inner hull.

The surrounding sky darkened considerably as the stars above began to twinkle and shimmer in the inky blackness of space. I switched off the master alarm, and waited for the flashing red lights to turn off as the pressure inside equalised, but they never did. It took another minute for us to reach the Kármán Line, and as we did my comms crackled and the navy commander of the Nova Pilgrim hailed us all. "1 Squadron, this is the Nova Pilgrim. Steady to five-hundred-thousand metres now. Take us to our stand-off point, 1 Alpha."

"Wilco," came Addison's dulcet tones. "You heard the man. Let's go home."

I could still hear hissing from the corner of the hull by my feet. It was getting colder with every passing minute, but I could still breathe. My oxygen showed seven percent on screen. Not good.

"1 Bravo to 1 Alpha."

"Go ahead, Jax."

"Addison, the Red October is bleeding. I'm losing oxygen and pressure."

"Put your mask on, Jaxon. Can you find the leak and patch it?"

"The mask is on my passenger. I lost her kit-belt during the exfil. She's unconscious but breathing. I've tried to patch the hull, but she's still bleeding. Oxygen at seven percent. Make that six percent."

"Okay, Jaxon. Recommend you leave the fleet behind and make haste for the Bertram. We've got this. Just get back safely."

"Roger," I replied and pushed my throttle up to max, skimming the underside of the Pilgrim and thrusting until my displayed showed 27,450kph. The Bertram was about fifteen minutes away at this speed and my oxygen level was worrying. The temperature inside the cockpit was showing at -4 Celsius and dropping quickly.

My heart was racing as I looked at the dials and watched the ice creeping into the corners of my hollo-screens. I tried to keep myself calm and breath more slowly, but panic was gripping me as we approached the station. "Mayday, mayday. Bertram Ramsay Tower, this is Red October – I mean 1 Bravo – requesting emergency assistance. Over."

"1 Bravo, this is Tower. What's your situation?"

"Ma'am, I'm losing oxygen. Showing three percent and icing up inside. I have a hull breach and an unconscious pilot beside me wearing my rebreather. I need an open hole and a quick docking, over."

"Understood 1 Bravo. Proceed on your current trajectory, slowing to fifty-above station limits whilst we calculate your docking procedure and destination."

"Thanks Tower. Awaiting further instructions." I looked across at the pilot next to me. I'd seen her in my first briefing, but we hadn't spoken. She'd seemed fairly relaxed and confident, and I was glad I had been able to pull her from her Sigma. I unclipped my harness and stood in front of her, detaching her harness and re-seating it over both shoulders, across her lap and through her legs. It wouldn't be great to have effected her rescue, only to kill her with a crap landing. She was definitely breathing, so I took that as a win, but I watched as the blood seeping from her wounds gathered at her neck where the rebreather sealed the oxygen in.

My comms flashed and the Bertram Tower interrupted my thoughts, which at that precise moment were mostly about how fucking cold it was. *-31 Celsius*. If I still had testicles when we landed, they wouldn't be big enough to plug the leak.

"1 Bravo, we can put you in the rear bay of Globe 11."

"Negative Tower. I can see 10 directly ahead. Put me in there."

"We've depressurised 10, so not a possibility. It's going to be tight but 11 is coming down now. Be advised: the rear bay is stacked full with crates. There's very little room, but you can make it."

"Wilco, Tower. Initiating trajectory control burn." I waited until I could see the underside of Globe 11 bearing down from the top of the rotation and hit my rear thrusters. The Red October shuddered under my feet and I felt my stomach lurch as I came out of my seat, which wasn't good. Clearly, the SQIIDS were knackered. Perfect. The inertia of the controlled burn sucked my eyeballs forward, and I felt myself gag as I tried to remain in control. Another master alarm sounded, and I looked at my port display. *Oxygen, one percent.*

"1 Bravo, you are still too fast. We need you to slow it down and bring it starboard for entry."

"Tower, I am out of air. If I trim off more speed, I will not make it. Is the bay open?"

"That's affirm, 1 Bravo. We need you to make starboard entry and initiate mag-dock immediately you're inside so we can close the doors and pressurise. Please confirm."

I was trying not to be sick. My fingers and toes were numbing up in the cold. *-54 Celsius* on my forward screen, and red lights flashing. The Bertram was coming up fast, and I could feel my eyes blurring at the edges as I trimmed over to the starboard quarter of the bay. I needed to time this perfectly, but with every second, I felt lighter and less in control of myself. My limbs felt like someone else's, vaguely attached to my dysfunctional brain.

"1 Bravo, please confirm."

The huge bay door of the rear dock on Globe 11 swung into view above me. I was travelling way too fast. I could hear the Tower asking for a response, but I barely had enough focus left to fly the aircraft. If I didn't control it now, I'd impact under the bay and it would all be over. I mustered every ounce of mental strength I could to manoeuvre the Red October into position, but she felt sluggish and was trying to rotate right with every subtle movement I made to the controls. The escaping pressure was fighting my trajectory and threatening to send the Sigma into a lateral spin. Fucking marvellous. At least the centrifuge effect would recover my gonads.

I pitched up and lowered the landing gear just one-hundred metres from the bay, still travelling too fast. My eyes blurred and I could just about make out the dark chasm of the open bay doors as the dock slowly arced downwards to meet me. I trimmed back on the throttle – tiny adjustments to slow my forward progress.

"Oxygen level critical," came an announcement from my holloscreens, which were no longer functioning as visual displays, as the windows cracked and the electronics froze. *No shit*, I thought, as I struggled to move my hands around the control console. I could barely see the bay enveloping us as we swept inside, too fast to be fully in control. I hit the mag-dock button and felt the inertia pull me over the console. The aircraft thumped the deck at break-neck speed and way too heavily. The sound of metal twisting and splitting filled the void, and the hissing grew louder as the impact ripped the pressure seal open. I fell into the front cavity behind the nucleus and my head smashed against the hull. Ice was forming on my lips and eyelashes as my lungs protested the total absence of oxygen. Then everything went black.

———————

"Amy Cooper?" said Hennessey. "You're absolutely sure?"

"Yes – but it's strange," replied Farrell.

"Strange how?" asked Hennessey, her breathing still laboured from the exertion of running three kilometres.

"Her bio-band says there's a mismatch on her DNA. It must be an error."

"I don't understand," said Amanda.

"Bio-bands are coded to DNA."

"Yes, you told us that."

"Right, but it's not her DNA. It's very similar, but not hers."

"But it's definitely her bio-band?"

"According to the logs, yes," replied Farrell.

"What the fuck is going on?" asked Hennessey.

"Only one way to find out." Amanda shrugged as she entered the mag-lift and clicked off her comms.

"Amy has access to command levels, but not the hangar," said Hennessey, as they stepped out of the mag-lift onto the hangar level. They were in a small hallway, with corridors extending in three directions.

"That's why they need Libby," replied Amanda.

"No, that's why they needed Mark Hanson," corrected Hennessey. "Libby is their redundancy. That's the corridor to the main hangar," she said, moving towards it.

"Wait," replied Amanda. "If they were going to the main hangar, they'd have used ML8. Why come all the way to the edge of the dome to enter? It doesn't make sense."

"The armoury?" suggested Hennessey. "Amy would certainly have clearance to book out a weapon."

Amanda nodded, and Hennessey pointed to the northern corridor. "This way," she said.

Amanda unclipped her Proxy, and Sara followed suit. They jogged up the corridor, checking the doors for any sign of movement, but the rooms were mostly empty. They passed the range on the right where twenty BRMC officers were training, discharging Scorpion rifles at digital targets.

As they approached the end of the corridor, a set of glass double-doors slid open for them, and the sound of several-hundred voices greeted them. To the left was the training arena, which stretched four kilometres west. Assault courses, tenement housing and sports pitches were amongst the features being used by an entire company of Marines. Each area was denoted by a grid position hanging from the roof, fifty metres above them. They watched as a small squad made dynamic entry into C2, the tenement block, clearly simulating a hostage situation.

"Help you?" came a voice to their right. A BRMC officer in his early fifties, with neatly trimmed grey hair in a flat-top style with shaved sides, peered at them through a hatch behind an EM glass screen. Hennessey walked over to him and checked his insignia momentarily before addressing him.

"Staff-Sergeant, we're looking for Lieutenant Amy Cooper. She's an ICP transfer and we believe she might have come up here in the last forty-five minutes."

The staff sergeant pulled out a hollotab and scrolled back. "I have her. She booked out three Scorpions and the Hangar sim in E7."

"How many with her?" said Amanda, before Hennessey could respond.

He shook his head. "I didn't see, but hang on." He leaned back and around, out of sight, and called someone. "Nate! Come up here a minute."

When he reappeared, he was with a young Marine who couldn't have been much older than twenty-two. "Nate, Major Barclay and Captain Hennessey would like to know how many people were in Lieutenant Amy Cooper's company when she booked out the Scorpions and E7."

The Scorpion rifle was an exoskeletal combat weapon that clamped around the user's forearm, with six silicone-dipped titanium legs. The tail looped back over and housed the plasma chamber, so it looked like an actual scorpion. A cable ran from the forward casing to a trigger handle, gripped by the wearer. They were formidable weapons and incredibly light, and only required the user to point their arm towards the target, making them highly accurate.

Nate looked confused, but the staff sergeant swiped through the hollotab until Amy's picture showed. His face lit up. "Oh yeah, I'd remember her anywhere. Me and the boys have a sweep-stake on who can ask her out first," he said with glee, in a strong New York accent, until he caught sight of the serious look on the surrounding faces.

"There were four of them. Three marines and pilot." He nodded enthusiastically.

"A pilot?" asked Hennessey.

"Yes, Ma'am. I didn't get much of a look at her, but no mistaking the black flight suit."

"Libby. Probably one of Jaxon's suits," said Amanda to Hennessey.

Amanda pulled a hollotab out of her kit bag, and tapped away on the screen, before turning it to show the young marine. "Is this the pilot?" she asked, showing Libby's photo.

Nate shrugged. "Sorry, Ma'am. She was at the back of the group. I didn't really see," he said, apologetically.

"Were they carrying anything?" asked Hennessey.

Nate nodded. "The pretty one had a backpack."

Amanda raised an eyebrow, and Hennessey looked at the staff sergeant. "I need to book out two Scorpions."

CHAPTER
TWENTY-NINE

"LIEUTENANT." *Beep, beep, beep*.

"Lieutenant, open your eyes." *Beep, beep, beep*.

My body was numb, but I could hear the words echoing in my head.

"Lieutenant Leith." A man's voice for sure. *Beep, beep, beep*.

I felt something touching my face and then a bright blur before it went dark again. The sounds were muffled. An alarm was going off somewhere.

"We need to get him in a pressure suit," same a female voice to my right. "His body temperature is dangerously low."

I could feel myself moving, and a tingling sensation on my lips.

"Lieutenant Leith," the male voice said again, "if you can hear me, we're putting you in a pressure suit. We need to cut away your flight suit, so just stay still for a minute."

Beep, beep, beep.

Many hands were on me. I could feel them, but not feel them, which made no sense. I could feel the sensation of movement but not touch.

My head was rolling to the side. Another hand on my face, and that bright light again. *They're checking my eyes*, I thought.

Beep, beep, beep. Suddenly, the alarm stopped. I could faintly hear the sounds of mechanical movement behind me. I didn't know what to make of it.

I felt pressure on my back and a scraping sensation, like fingernails down my spine. My toes were hurting. I didn't know why my toes would be hurting. And then they weren't.

"Lieutenant Leith." Another flash of light, but brighter this time. And a shape. "Lieutenant Leith, I'm Major Adán Nishimura. Do you know where you are?"

The last thing I remembered was the crushing cold as Globe 11 approached. My lips felt like they were vibrating, and the words hurt my throat as I tried to speak. "The dock. I was trying to land."

I felt something on the back of my head, and then a dark line through my vision. There was a small hiss, like a pressure seal, and then a warm sensation in my arms and legs. I felt like I was being lifted, and then lowered. Then a buzzing sound and a strange clicking.

"Lieutenant Leith," came the voice again, but different now. Like it was on comms.

"Jaxon," I replied, my lips cracking.

"Jaxon, okay. You should feel your body warming up. Can you feel that? Squeeze my hand if you can feel that."

My hand. Something was in it. Or maybe nothing. There was warmth at my fingertips, and a light pressure on my palm. I tried to move my fingers.

"That's great, Jaxon, you're doing great." There was a muffled conversation occurring, but I couldn't make out the words.

I thought I could hear a woman, and then I remembered the other pilot in my Sigma.

"The other pilot," I said. "Is she okay?"

My comms crackled, and the voice replied. "She's pretty banged up and still unconscious. We're trying to bring her round now."

"She was unconscious before," I said.

"She was already unconscious, Jaxon? Did I hear that right? Squadron Leader Navarro was already unconscious?"

"Yes. She was hurt at Compression Echo." I didn't know that was her name. I wondered if she outranked me. Stupid. 'Course she did.

There was a flurry of activity behind me, and I could hear a conversation happening, but it was too muffled. I was regaining some vision, although it was still blurry. It looked like I was inside a helmet.

"Jaxon, we want you to stay still for a minute whilst the hollodoc scans you, okay?"

"Okay."

There was a sliding sound and a thump, and then more of the buzzing and clicking noises. I lay still and looked up. All I saw was the roof of the dock and to the left, the black tunnel of The Loop. My eyes were focussing now, and the lights were bright and stinging.

A moment later, I saw a line slide over my head. The hollodoc canopy, I presumed. Or maybe a guillotine. It was a shit landing, and they'd probably be doing everyone a favour.

"Jaxon, you're doing great." His voice was reassuring, and low and calm. *We'd be friends*, I thought, unless he was the one operating the guillotine. I felt a slight pressure on my back, and a stabbing sensation in my fingers and toes.

"It hurts," I said.

"What hurts, Jaxon? Where is it hurting?" asked the major.

"My fingers and toes are stinging." I could see his face

through my helmet. He had a kind face, maybe early forties, jet black hair and eyes like pools of tar.

He smiled at me. "That's the blood beginning to recirculate, Jaxon. It'll sting for a little while, but it's good news so you should try to enjoy that." Sure, who doesn't enjoy pain? Idiot.

"What happened?" I asked. I turned my head a little. All I could see were giant pallets of blankets, which was weird.

"Easy does it, Jaxon," said the major. He lifted me gently into a sitting position. "We're going to lift you down from the hollodoc, okay?"

"Okay." I felt pressure on my back again, and then the sensation of hands gripping my thighs and under my arms. There were maybe four people around me. They placed me on the floor and leaned me back into something soft. I looked to my right and saw I was leaning against one of those giant pallets. The woman in front of me made a face. I wondered if I looked as shit as I felt.

"You're a lucky man, Lieutenant," said the major, smiling at me. "Your cockpit briefly peaked at minus sixty-seven Celsius when we pressurised the bay, and you'd been without oxygen for a shade under three minutes."

"How's my ride?" I asked.

The major laughed. "She's pretty banged up too, Lieutenant."

"Jaxon."

"Jaxon, okay. The flight office recorded you engaging the magnetic dock from sixteen metres. That's a hell of a fall. The flight deck team got the bay doors closed within a minute, and we were waiting in the airlock for you."

"Thanks," I said. My eyes could focus now, and I looked to my left. The Red October was a crumpled wreck on the bay floor. The front undercarriage had collapsed completely, and the nose twisted against the deck. The starboard stanchion was hanging off, and the gyro-sphere was barely attached.

"We need to keep you in that pressure suit for a little while until your core temperature stabilises. How are you feeling?"

"Cold, except my hands and toes. I can feel them getting warm. My chest hurts."

The major nodded. "You were lights out in the footwell. You've probably got a few bruises to show for it, but according to the scan, nothing more than a couple of broken ribs. Why weren't you in your harness?" he asked.

"No time," I replied. "She wasn't strapped in properly, and I knew we might crash. Needed to secure her before landing, but ran out of time. And oxygen." My throat was still scratching but easing up. The major must have read my mind because he replied. "There's a tube just below your lips and fresh water in the hydra-pack, Jaxon."

I nodded and found the tube with my lips. The water was icy, and I could feel it soothe my throat as I swallowed.

"How long have I been here?"

"A little over fifteen minutes," came the response. "You've had a hell of a day, Jaxon. We're going to keep you here for a while longer until you get more sensation back in your limbs. There's nothing more we can do for you while you're in that suit, and we can't get you out of it until your core temperature reaches thirty-six degrees, so sit tight. Once your blood is flowing, we'll fix you up and move you as soon as we can."

I nodded as he stood up and turned to speak to another officer. A female officer in military scrubs started fussing about my legs. She was squeezing my calves and digging her thumbs into my muscles. "What are these pallets?" I asked, looking around. There were hundreds of them, neatly stacked in the dock, and people working all around them.

The officer frowned at me. "You don't need to worry about those, Lieutenant. Let's concentrate on getting you on your feet."

"What are they?" I asked again. I'd never seen anything other than aircraft in here.

She frowned again, and there was a brief moment of sadness on her face. "They're the bodies of those that died when the gravity systems failed, Lieutenant."

"What are they doing here?" I asked. I could feel her hands working more urgently on my knees and thighs.

"Major," she called out. "The lieutenant is asking questions I'm not authorised to answer, Sir."

The major crouched back down beside me. "What's up, Jaxon?"

"Why are the bodies here on pallets? We're in the rear dock of 11, right?"

"Yes, we are. They've scheduled the bodies for burial shortly. Once released from the dock, they'll burn up as they're pulled into the atmosphere."

"Why today?" I asked. Given the scale of the operation this afternoon, it made little sense.

"Because today this entire level is empty."

———

Hennessey weaved through the various sections of the training arena, with Amanda close behind. The troops in the area saluted the two officers several times as they jogged around the connecting paths, but they ignored this and continued to the far wall of the arena.

Hennessey waved her bio-band over the pad by the double doors on the back wall and stepped through as they slid open for her. Amanda tapped her comms. "Gemma, can you give us a location for Amy Cooper?"

"She's in the main dock at the rear," came the reply.

"Thanks, Gemma." She was about to close comms when Farrell spoke. "Amanda?"

"Go ahead."

"Those two marines we flagged abducting Emily Latimer – they're with her."

"Okay, thanks."

"Well, that's a confirmation," said Hennessey. "I need to call this in before we go any further."

They slowed to a walking pace, whilst Hennessey raised Grealish on comms.

"Sara? What's going on? I had a call about a stolen forestry AethervoX twenty minutes ago. By the time they'd patched me through, you were gone."

"Sir, it's Amy. She's AoG."

"Jesus Christ. You have confirmation?"

"Yes, Sir. No doubt about it. She's abducted Libby Baxendale from Jaxon's apartment. Amanda and I are hunting her down."

"Okay. I'll put out a station-wide BOLO for her and Baxendale."

"She's armed, Sir, as are two other marines with her."

"Where are you both?"

"We're in the command centre, lower levels near the training arena, Sir, but her bio-band shows Amy is in the rear dock."

"They've sealed the dock off at the moment. We have medical personnel and flight safety officers attending to an emergency. Jaxon is hurt."

"What the hell?" exclaimed Amanda. "What happened to Jax?"

"I don't have all the details, but he made an emergency landing and crashed his Sigma into the dock about twenty minutes ago."

"Is he okay?" asked Hennessey.

"I'm not sure. Medics are still in attendance. He'll have

to be moved to a hospital soon, though. They're evacuating the entire level for the mass burial. Before the fleet returns."

———

The medics continued to work on my legs and arms, massaging them as I tried to move them. I experienced really odd sensations in strange places on my body as my blood circulated properly once more.

"Jaxon, we're going to get you on your feet. Do you think you can do that?" asked the major.

"I can try."

"That's all we can ask. There's another gurney on the way down, but we didn't know about Navarro and we have some time pressures, so we need to get you moving. Slowly does it." He took my hands as the female officer on my right, and another male officer on my left, put their arms around my back, and attempted to lift me up.

I was part way through standing then everything went black again, and I stumbled sideways into the arms of the male officer.

"I've got you," he said. "Are you feeling dizzy?"

I tried to nod, unsure if anything actually moved. "I think he has a concussion, Sir," said the female medic.

"Jaxon, can you hear me still?"

I opened my eyes again, and the lights above swam across my field of vision. "I'm okay, sir. Just light-headed."

"I understand, but we need to get you moving. We're on a timetable here." No sooner had he said it than the amber warning lights flashed to clear the dock. They helped me to my feet again, and I staggered with the medics on either side supporting me. My body felt cumbersome, like I was wearing chains around my ankles. My arms flopped stupidly by my side. I wiggled my fingers and toes, trying to get some sensation back in to them.

"That's good, Jaxon. One step at a time. We just need to walk you out. It's a fair trek to the airlock, so we need to get moving."

I walked, slowly and gingerly at first. I was still shivering, but that sensation was retreating with every passing second. My legs felt like they were someone else's and my feet were hitting the floor before they should. We stepped around the first row of pallets, and I tried not to look at the shapes inside the fabric wrapping. There were pallets as far as the eye could see in every direction, and the low hum and clanking of heavy machinery at the Hangar entrance.

Another medical team jogged passed us, heading for Opps, with a gurney and Squadron Leader Navarro strapped down, still unconscious.

"Will she be okay?" I asked.

Major Nishimura shrugged. "She's in good shape, all things considered. She has two dislocated shoulders and she'll have a couple of cracking scars on her head, but otherwise our biggest concern is her concussion. They'll prep her for surgery as soon as they get to the hospital and bleed the pressure from her brain. No adverse effects from the crash, and her oxygen levels are good thanks to you. I'll know more once we get you to the hospital, and you can be sure I'll keep you updated."

We walked for another few minutes, still slowly, but the feeling was returning and I was more confident in my steps. My body ached all over, and I could feel bruising around my ribcage and shoulders.

"We need to keep this pace up, Jaxon," said the major. "This level is clear now. We're the last ones inside."

I nodded and continued to walk, looking around at the pallets. It was unreal, the sheer scale of death that surrounded us. I'd seen first-hand hundreds of people dying as they crashed into the grounds and buildings of

Globe 10, but it seemed immaterial compared to the devastating loss of life around me.

I picked up the pace a little as the feeling returned to my muscles. My body still felt heavy and my limbs seemed unwieldy, but improving as the minutes wore on.

We had about two-hundred metres to go to reach the command centre, when the female medic on my right shouted, "Sir, there's someone down there!"

She pointed over to the left, between a row of pallets about fifty metres long. Sure enough, at the very end was the silhouette of a woman, sat on the floor with her back to the pallets. Her body shape looked all wrong, even from here.

I turned to walk down the row, but the medics grabbed me. "Jaxon, we'll send someone else. We need to get you off this level."

I shook my head. "There's no time. They haven't started the countdown yet but the lights are amber, so it's imminent. They won't decompress with us inside, but if they don't know about her..." I tried to give him a meaningful look, but couldn't be sure I pulled it off from inside the helmet. "I'm okay. Get down there and help her."

"Jaxon, we can't." The major grabbed at my arm but I pulled it away, wincing as my shoulder protested. I continued to walk down the makeshift corridor, getting closer to the inert form. It was a woman, I was sure. I could see tiny movements, but it was strange and constricted, unnatural.

"Jaxon, I'm ordering you to make your way to the airlock."

"Sir, there's someone down there that could die if we don't get them out now. You can pull rank all you like, and bollock me to your heart's content later, but we're going to help her."

He glared at me for a moment, and then cursed under his breath and ran.

As I picked up my pace, the station rotated and a beam of sunlight from the upper wall shone through the lines of pallets queueing to be released into space. As the light hit the woman, I could see her dark ringlets and her eyes full of fear as she turned towards me.

Libby.

CHAPTER
THIRTY

HENNESSEY AND BARCLAY were running for the
dock. There were people everywhere, moving between the
various command centres dotted along the main hall to the
hangar. The mass of bodies was moving away from the
dock area and into the path of the two women.

They battled through the crowd, desperately hunting
down their quarry. Amanda's comms sounded.

"Gemma?"

"Amanda, Amy Cooper has disconnected or removed
her bio-band. Last pinged location was as before; the main
dock at the rear of Globe 11, twenty minutes ago."

"Understood. What about Libby Baxendale?"

"I'm unable to get her location, but her vitals are still
recording. She has an elevated heart rate, but that's all I can
tell you from here."

She clicked off and the two women continued down the
hall as fast as they could, making little headway through
the crowd. Amanda's comms sounded again. She looked at
her bio-monitor and back at Hennessey, her eyes wide in
surprise. "It's Jaxon."

"Libby!" I tried to run, ignoring the protests and the slight dizziness that threatened to engulf me. The major reached her first. She was in a shit state, half tangled in the off-white fabric of the pallets, leaning strangely downwards to one side. Her right arm was tethered at the wrist to something inside the pallet, awkwardly warping her body, like she'd fallen out of the stack of corpses.

She had something tied around her head, gagging her, which the major removed before gently lifting her and turning her round, releasing her painfully distorted arm.

She locked eyes on me through the helmet. "Jaxon?"

"You know this woman?" asked the major.

"Libby, I'm here," I said, ignoring the major. "Who did this to you?" The other two medics were busy trying to free Libby's arm from the pallet.

She looked at me with a mixture of relief and fear, and clearly wondering why I was inside a full space suit. "That woman from Compression – can't remember her name. She was ICP. After the gravity system failed. I'm so sorry Jaxon, I should have told you but she said they were listening to everything."

Whilst I had suspected Amy after the last few days of revelations, the words still shocked me. I looked down at Libby, her face swimming in tears, her eyes pleading with me.

"Don't worry about that now, Lib. We need to get you out of here ASAP." I took a step back whilst the major and the two medics fussed about freeing Libby from her bondage. I tapped my comms panel and put a call through to Amanda.

"Jaxon?"

"Mand, we need to find Amy now."

"Are you okay? Grealish told us you'd crashed your Sigma inside the dock."

"No time right now. I've found Libby tied to a pallet of corpses in the bay. She said Amy took her."

"We already know, Jaxon. We're in pursuit now. Did she say anything about the bomb?"

"Bomb? What bomb?"

"Amy had a backpack with her, and we think it's carrying another device. She's with the two marines that we tracked to Emily Latimer's house. They're armed with Scorpions."

Jesus fucking Christ. I gingerly walked back to Libby. "Lib, Amanda's asking me about a bomb. Do you know anything about it?"

"A bomb?" asked the major, alarmed.

I ignored him again and implored Libby to respond. She looked terrified. "It's here, Jaxon."

"It's where, Libby?"

"Somewhere in here. I didn't see her place it. She just told me there'd be an explosion so big that the body count in the bay would seem irrelevant, compared to the damage she was about to do."

"Amanda, did you hear that?"

"We heard," she replied.

"How big is the device, Libby?" asked Hennessey.

"She said it was inside the backpack," replied Libby. "I never actually saw it."

"How can a device as small as a backpack cause that kind of body count?" asked Amanda.

"There's nothing down here. Even if she blows the main entry doors to the dock," I said. "The fleet is deployed, and this whole dock is full of corpses. She can't kill them twice."

"Oh, Jesus," said Hennessey. "The armoury."

"Yes!" said Libby. "She mentioned the armoury before."

"Jaxon, you need to find that device," insisted

Hennessey, a note of urgency in her tone. "She doesn't need a large bomb because her plan is to detonate the explosives and combustibles in the armoury."

"Where is it?"

"The armoury is on the south wall of the dock. If that bomb goes off, it'll start a chain reaction that'll destroy this globe and every person inside."

For fuck's sake. I turned to the major. "Major, I need you to get Libby and your medics out of here."

He protested. "Lieutenant, you're in no condition to—"

"Major, I don't have time to argue. I need to find that device. If the bay depressurises, I'll be fine." *Fine* was relative, I thought. I was still a fucking mess under this suit, but the bomb was more pressing than my recovery. "I'm in a pressure suit and my oxygen is still ninety-seven percent. Get them out of here."

I turned left and hobbled along another pallet-corridor, loosely scouring the pallets for any odd protrusions. As I neared the end of the corridor, the amber lights changed to red.

"Sixty seconds to depressurising," came the announcement, and a siren sound.

"Jaxon, you need to hurry," said Hennessey.

The depressurisation didn't worry me. The crash had banged me up pretty badly and my head was still fuzzy, but I was upright and mobile and my eyes were working. I was in a full pressure suit, with comms, so if the bay opened my biggest concern was drifting out of the gigantic doors in the weightless cavity. If that happened, I'd get dragged down into the atmosphere by Earth's gravity, where I'd burn up like a human burrito with the rest of the bodies. *At least it won't be cold*, I thought.

I worked my way through the pallet maze until I hit the south wall. I was only two-hundred metres from the internal hangar, so I looked left to the bay doors, a kilometre away. The armoury was only fifty metres along, on the right side, so I gritted my teeth and tried to jog.

"I've found the armoury," I said, through my comms.

"Can you see a backpack, Jaxon?" replied Amanda.

"Negative." The armoury front was a metal grill which could retract into the ceiling, enabling pallet trucks and forklifts to access the special weapons visible through the mesh. The surrounding wall was smooth, with no place to hide anything, so I checkout the pallets opposite. They were only three metres away from the armoury door. I probed them one by one, running my hand between the corpse stacks to see if the bag was hidden in the gaps. As I reached the third pallet I noticed a step down on the opposite wall, into a door to the left of the metal grill.

I cursed myself for wasting time on the pallets. Of course, she wouldn't plant it there. If the depressurisation occurred before the bomb detonated, it would just get sucked out of the doors, exploding uselessly in the vacuum of space. I crossed to the step and reached into the shadowed channel under it. There was a handle sticking out from under the aluminium standoffs. I yanked it and extracted a black nylon backpack with the BRMC Insignia stitched to the top.

"I have the bag," I said, through my comms.

"Careful opening it, Jaxon," said Amanda.

"Can you get it to the bay doors?" asked Hennessey.

I unzipped the main compartment and opened the bag fully. Inside was a device that looked identical to the bomb that Brian Latimer had detonated in Compression, except this one had a timer in place of the dead-man's switch.

"No can do," I replied, as the realisation swept over me. "There's nineteen seconds left on the clock."

"Jaxon, get out of there!" screamed Amanda.

"I can't outrun this," I replied.

"Jaxon, throw it away from the south wall and run back

to the armoury. There's a panel on the right side of the doors."

As I launched it sideways and watched it sail through the air, I glimpsed the timer. *Fifteen seconds.*

Moving as quickly as my broken body would allow, I backtracked along the armoury shutter to the flat wall with a holloscreen and a console. "Found it!" *Twelve, eleven, ten...*

"Jaxon, press and hold the right side of the console. It has a failsafe in case of an accident at the armoury," said Hennessey, with even more urgency.

I pressed my gloved hand to the panel and held it there. *Eight, seven, six...*

The panel glowed red, and a question flashed up on the screen. *Five, four...*

Emergency decompression:
ACTIVATE / ABORT

Three, two... I just prayed the Major Nishimura and the medics had got Libby out of the dock, and hit the ***ACTIVATE*** button as hard as I could.

There was an explosion and a huge sucking noise, like a giant plug hole in a bath. Fire ripped through the pallets, and, for a moment, I felt it envelop me. The blast catapulted bodies and body parts across the bay and sent me careening towards the inner hangar. There was a rush of air, and I was lifted off the ground and struck by a pallet which propelled me back towards the outer doors. The collision knocked the wind out of me, and in my disorientation I tried to grab something, but the wall was flat and I was moving too fast. I bounced off the steel panelling into the back of another pallet, which slowed me down but did nothing for my ability to breathe.

Gasping for air and desperately clawing to consciousness, I saw the mammoth bay doors hinged outwards like old-fashion saloon swing doors. The doors usually retracted into the hull, but I stared as they pivoted under the pressure of millions of litres of escaping air, sucking hundreds of pallets of corpses out into space.

Globe 12 was visible through the bay doors, but my view quickly became obscured by the giant pallets and carnage ripped from the floor of the bay.

I tumbled across the dock, unable to control my flight, spinning end over end, which made me nauseous. Every fibre of my body protested at the sudden force exerted upon it. I could hear voices through my comms, but the rushing air and explosions were too loud to decipher them. Objects and pallets flew by and I tried to reach out and grab something, *anything*, to steady my rotation and arrest my momentum, as the bay doors loomed larger and larger.

I could feel intense heat as flames from a burning pallet licked the edges of my suit, the powerful explosion dragging it beyond my grasp. The whole bay was like an asteroid belt, thick with debris, bathed in a flickering orange glow. For a moment, I saw a flash on the starboard quarter; a reflection of metal amongst the carnage.

And then, just as suddenly, the flames went out and a deathly quiet settled over the massacre around me. I was still inside the dark bay, drifting towards the doors, when I saw her. The Red October loomed out of the shimmering light from the distant globe, between the floating pallets. Still magnetised to the dock, but severely damaged by the escaping pallets, the cockpit appeared crushed and caved in, and the fuselage looked like something had ripped it in half.

I flailed about, uselessly, trying to find some means of thrusting myself towards the stricken aircraft. It was the one thing in the entire dock that was fixed magnetically. She was in tatters. Shot to shit, wrecked by the forced landing and further brutalised by the onslaught of debris and bodies.

The decompression was over now and the rush of air had subsided, but there were thousands of objects floating in the dark void, still on a trajectory into space, exacerbated by the rotation of the Bertram Ramsay. I searched for a handhold, object or surface I could use to change my direction. The remains of the Red October clung to the starboard quarter, right inside the doors, whilst I was drifting hopelessly towards the exit on the opposite side of the dock by the southern wall.

Everything ached. The explosion had been akin to pressing hard on a bruise, if the bruise was the size of my entire body and the pressing finger was a pallet of corpses. The burst of adrenaline was subsiding, and I could feel a tinge of panic creeping in. My stomach lurched and I swallowed, trying not to be sick inside my suit. I was in free-fall now. There was no escape. I imagined this was how Mark Hanson felt as he held tight to the SQIID ports in the upper dome of Globe 10.

I was still half a kilometre from the bay doors, completely out of control and spinning slowly. The dock was almost empty, the bulk of its contents sucked out in the initial decompression. Globe 12 was conspicuous again, between the last bits of debris drifting aimlessly about in the vacuum, in a slow waltz towards the infinite desolation of space.

I'd never been inside most of the globes in my short, seven-week tenure on board the station. The bottom levels of Globe 12 crept into my peripheral vision. The top levels were not visible to me this far from the bay doors. I could see a lot of greenery in the bottom two levels, but very little else, being over eleven kilometres away. It looked peaceful. I wondered if I'd drift out of the doors into the path of 12, hitting the glass at almost four-hundred metres-per-second, and dying like a bug on an AethervoX windscreen. Classic.

Pain was permeating my thoughts. My ribs felt like an advertisement for cushioned dashboards, if I was the crash-test-dummy. I closed my eyes for a moment, trying to suppress the nausea as I spun relentlessly, and in the absence of sight I was suddenly aware of how I smelt in the confines of the space-suit. Unsure of what I should have expected, it was mostly sweat, coupled with what I could only describe as *aged flatulence.* If I lived, which at this juncture seemed unlikely, I just hoped they wouldn't rescue me near a naked flame.

I was getting closer now. The gaping entrance was looming, huge and formidable in front of me. Earth was visible for the first time, creeping into view at the bottom edge of the doorway. She looked beautiful. I hope she'd be the last thing I saw as the oxygen in my suit expired.

The Red October was over to my left, still magnificent even in death. I'd only flown her a handful of times, yet I felt connected to her in a manner I'd failed to find with most humans. If her injuries were anything to go by, I was fucked anyway. I watched her in the gloom as I drifted past, through the giant bay doors and out into space, until the shadows took her from me.

ADDISON WATCHED as the two shuttles docked. Despite the challenges the Nova Palmer engaged the Nova Pilgrim in less than five minutes. The fleet had spread out around the rear of the two vessels, with shields deployed, protecting them from orbital debris.

The two vessels connected for just under fifteen minutes, a testament to the efficiency of the commandos and crew on board. As the tunnel retracted into the Palmer, Addison's comms sounded.

"1 Alpha, this is the Bertram Tower. Proceed to station at two-fifty-above limits, at an altitude of five-hundred-and-sixty-five kilometres. That's five-six-five, confirm."

"Wilco, Bertram Tower. Five-six-five at plus two-fifty." He tapped away on his hollotab and then hit the VOX button. "Bertram Fleet, this is 1 Alpha. Tower has initiated our recall. Proceed to an altitude of five-six-five kilometres at station-plus-two-fifty. Steady as she goes until final approach. 6 and 7 Squadrons, you're tail-end Charlie."

The fleet moved en masse, in a graceful arc as it increased its altitude and velocity, until the entire ensemble was stretched out over several kilometres. The Bertram was one-hundred-and-eight kilometres ahead and slightly below, so it would be fifteen minutes before they'd break formation and begin final approach.

As the enormous station filled the forward screens, Addison reflected on the success of the mission. Reports from the other squadrons suggested few casualties in the conflict, but few was not none. Only Jaxon's Sigma had sustained damage in the exfiltration, and by now he was on deck and probably in a bar somewhere, he mused. The rest of the fleet had suffered casualties, with six Sigmas lost in the conflict, which, given the sheer scale of the battle, was a miracle.

Admiralty would no doubt consider the death toll *reasonable* in the circumstances, and the thought angered Addison. It wasn't just the loss of life to the Bertram that bothered him. Many of Earth's pilots would also have succumbed, and for what? It was a needless battle, fought by brave men and women who were only following orders. He suspected his grief was reflected in all cockpits, both here and on Earth, and it was this alone that had minimised the bloodshed. Whilst well-trained in combat, the pilots would wonder why they were shooting each other.

His comms crackled, waking him from his melancholy thoughts.

"All stations, all stations. This is Bertram Tower. Be advised that a mass burial is occurring on Globe 11 in the next two minutes and expected to last for five further minutes. Please slow to station limits and hold until advised."

He pressed VOX and responded. "Bertram Tower, copy that. Station limits and holding."

At this altitude and distance, he could see each of the globes rotating as the Bertram orbited Earth. He watched as Globe 11 swept slowly past, the huge stencilled number *11* adorning the doors of the rear bay. He waited for the doors to open, spilling its precious cargo into the atmosphere as the fleet slowed and compressed in his wake.

Without warning, the bay doors exploded outwards – an emergency depressurisation. At first, he assumed they were using the internal pressure to slingshot the bodies into space, but then a ball of flame emerged and died unnaturally as debris spilled haphazardly into space.

Addison hit the VOX button for a third time. "Mayday, mayday. Shields up! Nova Palmer, take station behind the Pilgrim. Squadrons closest form up on the Palmer's nose with full shields." He briefly looked at his scopes and kept one eye on the Palmer as it slowed and turned into the wake of the Pilgrim.

"Mayday, Bertram Tower. We are seeing an explosion and emergency depressurisation."

The Bertram started to list and accelerate as the bay depressurised.

"Mayday, Bertram Tower. We are seeing a large procession to the port side. Are you receiving, over?"

The Tower was in Globe 11, and Addison's initial concern was a hull breach beyond the dock. As he watched, thrusters fired on all twelve globes, and the Bertram slowed. It was still marginally off-axis, but even as he noticed this, the skilled pilots of the navy corrected the wobble, and regained control of the Bertram's trajectory.

"All stations, this is Bertram Tower. We've had an emergency depressurisation in the rear dock of 11. Recovery in progress, and emergency personnel in attendance. Please remain in your holding pattern until we can reset the outer doors."

"Roger that, Tower. Awaiting further instructions. Can we help? Are there any casualties?"

"That's a negative, 1 Alpha. We've got this at the moment. No casualties reported so far. Thanks for your concern, out."

Globe 11 looked magnificent from out here. I remembered, as a kid, reading about space-walks whilst they were constructing the Bertram, and the elation on the faces of the engineers and astronauts who got to experience EVAs. The view wasn't much different from the inside of a Sigma, but there was something ethereal and pure about the feeling of weightlessness in just a suit as I gazed upon the station.

The scattered debris floated in all directions, some of it impacting Globe 12 as the station rotated into its path. There were bodies flying out in to deep space, and others towards Earth. They would all get pulled down eventually, even those that had catapulted to a higher altitude. There's no escaping the might of Earth's gravitational pull.

Out here, the planet was more beautiful than I'd ever seen. We were currently traversing North America. I could see the snow-capped peaks of Alaska, the arid desert landscape of Nevada, and everything in between. I'd probably appreciate it even more if I wasn't slowly spinning to my death.

As I continued to tumble away from the station, I glimpsed the fleet returning from Earth. *Took you long enough*, was my first thought. For a moment, I considered waving, but there was absolutely no way they'd see me this far out. I could barely make out the individual aircraft. It looked more like a swarm surrounding two queens.

I took a swig from the hydration pack and felt the cool water soothe my throat. Not that that mattered anymore. My comms were silent, save for the occasional click of static. The fear had dissipated to a large extent, replaced by annoyance and frustration. I could be back in The Bleeds right now, scrounging for a meal and living my best life for another four years.

I thought about Laura. She wasn't right for me, I knew

that now. I ought to be devastated at her passing, but with everything that had happened since, she'd diminished to little more than a dull ache, and the feeling of guilt that accompanied it. I couldn't pinpoint the guilt. It was for not saving her, or for not missing her more. I couldn't decide which. Probably both.

I'd miss Amanda and Libby the most. Amanda had trusted me and put her faith in me to get the job done. Those many hours and days spent together, with only the briefest glimpse of her personal life, thanks to a brief excursion on the Red October. And Libby. Sunny, beautiful Libby with her ready smile and effortless warmth. I didn't know why she'd lied to us, but I sensed no malice or mischief in the story she'd told. I hope she'd made it to the airlock.

I'd miss Tyrone, too. For all of his maddening, cantankerous ways he was genuinely decent and hardworking, and always wanted the best for those around him. He pushed me constantly to be better. Not just in conditioning, but in everything.

And Addison. He'd changed the course of my life. Given me a purpose, and a sense of pride.

The others were nothing more than bit-parts in my life story. Casual interactions that shaped a small period of my life. Emily Latimer would live. It was a strange coincidence that we'd met before.

I was mentally eulogising myself to pass the time when my comms pinged.

"Jaxon. Please respond. Jaxon!" Amanda was almost pleading. Her voice was like a bucket of ice to me. My immediate reaction was to turn around and look for her.

"Jaxon, if you can hear me, please respond."

"I'm here, Mand."

"Oh, thank fuck you're okay," she said, the relief palpable in her voice.

"Define *okay*."

"You're alive, aren't you? Don't be a drama queen." Her words sounded forced, like she was pulling herself together.

"I'll try to look on the bright side, shall I?"

"For fuck's sake. They've got a team inside the dock and they're manually closing the doors shortly. You'll be fine."

"Mand…" She clearly thought I was still inside.

"Jaxon. I've got some good news, and some bad news."

I sighed. "I'll take the good news."

"Well, Libby's okay. They've taken her to the hospital. She's under guard at the minute until we figure out why she lied to us."

"That *is* good news. What's the bad news?"

"In all the commotion, Amy slipped past us."

"For fuck's sake!"

"I know. There's a station wide alert, and every BRMC officer is looking for her. We got her accomplices, though. They weren't smart enough to ditch their bio-bands, and Gemma tracked them trying to board The Loop. They timed it badly and got arrested standing on the platform waiting for a train. Idiots," she added.

"Mand."

"Jaxon."

"I've got some good news and some bad news," I said, smiling at the irony of it all.

Sara replied, "We'll take the bad news first. It can't be any worse than Amy getting away."

"Hey, Sara," I said.

"Hey, Jaxon," she replied.

"Well, don't keep us hanging," said Amanda. I could almost hear her eyes roll through the comms.

"Well, I'm not inside the dock," I said.

"What the fuck? Jaxon, where are you?"

"I'm just approaching Globe 12. Maybe a kilometre out."

"Jesus fucking Christ. Stay there. I'll alert the deck chief," replied Hennessey.

"I'm not sure *staying here* is a viable option for me, truth be told," I said.

"How's your oxygen level?" asked Amanda.

"Well, that's the good news. It's at ninety-four percent. And I have a full hydration pack, so at least I'll still be breathing and well hydrated when I burn alive in the atmosphere."

"Don't even joke about that, Jaxon."

"Come on, Mand. I'm drifting into space. I've accepted it at this point."

"Fuck you, Jaxon. Don't you give up on me."

"Jaxon, it's Sara. I've got Addison on comms with me. The entire fleet is still out there."

There was a crackle, and then Addison's dulcet tones permeated my helmet. "Jaxon?"

"Sir?"

"Don't start with that *Sir* shit. Where are you? Be precise."

"I'm under a kilometre from Globe 12, but it's passing me now. If you're leaving the dock on 11, I'd say maybe two o'clock high."

"Stay there. We're coming to get you."

"Can everyone please stop telling me to stay here? I'm floating. In space."

"I'm sorry, Jax. I didn't mean it like that. But if you wouldn't mind shutting the fuck up for five minutes, I'd be eternally grateful," he replied sarcastically.

"Bertram Tower, this is 1 Alpha. We have a man overboard from the decompression. Permission to breach the perimeter with the Nova Pilgrim and affect a rescue, over?"

"1 Alpha, please repeat."

"We have a pilot floating away from the station. Lieutenant Leith was inside the dock when the emergency decompression occurred. He's on the peripheries of Globe 12, but I think we can rescue him if we depressurise the Pilgrim and catch him in the cargo hold."

"1 Alpha, give us a minute to process."

"Tower, we don't have a minute. I'm proceeding to enter station limits with the Pilgrim. I'd appreciate your blessing, but I'm going in either way."

The comms went silent. Either Addison had switched off VOX, and was putting the world to rights, or the Tower had muted the entire conversation.

I continued to roll through space as I passed Globe 12, and I was close enough to see inside. The upper level looked like a forest on one side with hills and streams, and even a waterfall that flowed into a lake. On the other side of the lake was a town, much like the one on level 4 of Globe 7, but less utilitarian. The high-rise apartments were taller, but interconnected, with sky-bridges straddling the gaps between them. There were boats on the lake and people walking along the beach, oblivious to the chaos of the last hour on Globe 11.

It was unlike anything I'd ever seen, here or on Earth. The forest and lake looked tranquil, and the town had a serenity about it whilst still feeling fresh and vibrant. There were restaurants and bars along a promenade facing the lake.

"Jaxon, does your suit have a torch or a light?" Addison burst into my eardrums.

I felt around the suit for anything I could use as a light. I could see the Pilgrim now, approaching from the left.

"Negative. All I have is my bio-monitor. But I can see the Pilgrim coming around. If they hold where they are, eventually I'll drift into them."

"Roger. 1 Alpha to Nova Pilgrim. Hold in place."

It took fifteen minutes before I was close enough for them to see me. Addison kept me talking the whole time.

We watched from different vantage points as the doors to the dock finally closed, and the fleet passed the starboard flank of Globe 11, landing in batches in the forward bay.

The fireworks started shortly after. Thousands of bodies burning up in the atmosphere below, leaving fiery trails as they entered the Mesosphere at twenty-five thousand kph.

"Nova Pilgrim, I'm about two-hundred metres from you. Eleven o'clock, and low."

"We don't see you yet," came the response. The problem was the darkness. I'd drifted out and away from the station. Globe 6 was closest now, but at least three kilometres away. I could see every globe from here, and the Hub in the centre, holding them all together. In the distance, I could see half the fleet still waiting to land. The docks had to take them in batches because of sheer numbers. It would take a few hours to sort out.

"1 Alpha. Jaxon, can you see the Ocelot?" asked Addison.

I was still rolling through space, so it was difficult to get my head around inside the helmet to check every direction.

"Negative. All I see is the Pilgrim."

"Nova Pilgrim, be advised, I'm coming under your port flank," said Addison.

"Roger, 1 Alpha."

And then I saw him. "Addison, I can see you. Turn about fifteen degrees to port and nose down."

I watched as the Ocelot's thrusters pitched the nose down and rotated to the left.

"I'm directly ahead now. One hundred metres."

Addison switched on the forward lights, and I tried to make myself wide and visible.

"I've got you. Hold tight, I'm coming."

There he goes again with the *hold tight*. I was freely spinning through space. I would have facepalmed, but I was wearing a helmet.

I saw the Ocelot approach, more cautiously than he needed to, and over the next two minutes I watched as Addison used every ounce of his skill to bring the nose of the Sigma into my path of drift.

As I got closer he fired the reverse thrusters to match my velocity, until I was just metres away from the nose. It took about twenty seconds for me to catch up to the Ocelot, and as I did I reached out with both hands and tried to arrest my momentum. I scraped my way over the nose to the forward screens and grabbed the top lip of the port window. I was lying on the roof of the Sigma with my helmet dangling over the front screen looking directly at Addison, who winked at me and said, "Need a ride, Lieutenant?"

CHAPTER
THIRTY-TWO

IT WAS another three hours before I was back on board the Bertram. Addison had asked the Tower if he could land with me still on the nose, but they refused entry.

"They've seen my landing skills, and they know you taught me," I quipped.

Addison laughed and held station whilst the Nova Pilgrim manoeuvred until the cargo bay doors were directly ahead. As the loading bay opened, I saw two commandos in pressure suits standing on the rear ramp, with tethers attached.

I shuffled to the screen edge, ready to push myself into the path of the Pilgrim, but Addison told me to hang tight while the commandos came to get me. One of them launched from the ramp towards the Ocelot, still tethered to the reel inside the Pilgrim's hull. It was slow progress as he drifted the twenty-metre gap between the two vessels, but as he approached he held his arm out, and I grabbed it.

He clipped me into his tether and hit his comms. "I've got him, Scott. Reel us back in." We both jolted and bounced as the tether tightened and reeled us back to the Pilgrim. In my usual graceful manner, I missed my landing and dragged the commando into a whole crate of EM glass, but I didn't care and as we came to a standstill, I could see him grinning at me through his visor. There were hugs and backslaps and even the occasional aristocratic whoop from Addison over the comms.

After that, I took a seat in the cockpit with the navy pilots whilst they took the Pilgrim out to one kilometre and a small fleet of utility tugs dispatched from Globe 10 to unload her. I tried to get the pressure suit off, but the medical staff on the Bertram insisted I keep it on until they could get me in to the hospital and check me out fully.

"Hurry up. It smells of arse in here." I ached all over, but mostly I just felt relieved and happy to be alive.

Addison didn't stop jabbering on my comms the whole time. He'd saved me today, and for that I could never thank him enough. Sara, Amanda, Tyrone and Grealish met me as they wheeled me into the hospital. They fussed over me for a little while, and then the subject changed.

"So, what's happening with the investigation?" I asked.

Hennessey responded first. "The two marines we caught are being interrogated by CTI. They're not the brightest, but we're making some progress. Amanda's heading off to talk to them shortly."

"What about Libby? Is she okay?"

Amanda nodded. "She's fine. I spoke to her while Sara was dealing with the marines. She says they first approached her a month ago, well before Laura died and said she was being watched and they'd call upon her when the time was right. She freaked out when you returned from 9 covered in blood. Then they got to her within an hour of Mark Hanson dying. Told her that her bio-band was being monitored and that they'd hear anything she said. Threatened to kill Jennifer, too, if she didn't do as they asked. They knew exactly where she worked and without Mark, they needed access to the hangars and the docks."

"Why tell us it was Jennifer, though?" I asked.

"I think she was genuinely concerned and embellished the details to get us to confront Jenn, so she'd be safe until she could blow the whistle. Brave girl. Clever too," said Amanda. "She thought you might read between the lines."

"Seems ambitious, expecting someone with diminished intellect like Jaxon here, to decipher that," said Tyrone. Hilarious.

"What's going to happen to her?" I asked. I was used to having Libby at mine, and felt a sudden pang of sadness at the thought of her going back to Globe 7.

"She's still hurt. They treated her pretty roughly and her right arm is a mess, so for now she's a floor below you in room 1018. We've got guards on the door for her protection, but she doesn't know enough to be useful. She's pretty wrung out from being interrogated," answered Hennessey.

I was about to speak when Grealish piped in. "Amy's in the wind, Jaxon, but we'll find her. I'm just sorry I didn't bring her in when I first suspected her."

"When did you first suspect her, Sir?" asked Amanda. "Jaxon and I were convinced it was Sara. There was nothing to suggest Amy's involvement."

"The day after you found Emily Latimer," replied Grealish, to everyone's astonishment.

"After you cleared the building, the investigations team entered to catalogue the contents. Amy was with them, and prior to you leaving she looked really stressed out. By the time they'd transported everything back to Command, she was much more relaxed."

"She was there to make sure nothing pointed to her, or gave away the location of the AoG safe house," said Sara.

Grealish nodded. "That's the current working theory. She was also our head of comms in the team, and when Laura's communique to Sara was interrupted we all assumed it was just a system outage. I think it's fair to say that it was probably a deliberate act. As you know I had everyone's bio-bands tracked after that, and went through the logs to clarify the team's movements so we didn't trip over our own cover story during the debrief."

He paused. "According to the logs, Amy didn't move from the barn, which gave her a solid alibi, except it literally didn't move at all. It remained absolutely still for the duration of the events that played out on 9, with a steady, unwavering pulse until ten minutes before you found Laura. It suddenly sprang to life and rode The Loop from Globe 6 back to Command. Initially, I assumed she was just working in the meeting room. When the call came in about Laura, my pulse, Sara's and Tyrone's all changed to reflect the stress we were under. Amanda's and Jaxon's were already off the charts, but Amy's didn't change at all."

He looked at Amanda. "Then you discovered Libby was missing, and identified Amy as the perpetrator, so I went to Commander Farrell to find out how Libby's bio-band could have been altered outside of the Command structure. It seems Amy could manipulate the data locally, which is how she retained an active pulse and GPS data whilst not wearing it."

"And how she changed her DNA profile on the band," said Amanda.

"She what?" replied Grealish. "Why on earth would she change her DNA? That doesn't make any sense."

"Well, we're not on earth, are we? Who the fuck knows what's going on in her head?" said Hennessey.

"It also explains how the AoG is getting around on board the Bertram. There's no way they can walk around without bio-bands – they'd have no access to mag-lifts, The Loop, currency, food or anything," said Grealish, his brow still furrowed.

Sara spoke. "Wait, so you think they're putting the

bands on to move about, and then removing them some-where secure before returning to their hideout?"

"That's exactly what I think," replied Grealish.

"Why bother with the gravity system sabotage?" I asked. "I thought we agreed they had an ulterior motive for it."

Hennessey responded. "Amanda and I were talking about that earlier. We think they used the fall-out as a distraction to move locations. It would be much easier with the entire station on general alert, and everyone focussing on Globe 10, to transport their entire operation wearing BRMC uniforms. Nobody would give them a second thought."

"So they're not stationed on Globe 10," said Tyrone, "and 11 would be too risky."

"And they can't have switched globes, with The Loop suspended," I reminded them.

Hennessey nodded. "We came to the same conclusion. There's limited access and far too few structures on 6 and 3 to be of any use, and 5 is Navy so they won't be there for the same reason as 11, so that leaves six potential globes, although I think we can discount 7. Otherwise why bother meeting Mark in Globe 9 when they could knock on his door anytime?"

"Still, that's a lot of ground to cover," I said. "And nothing to stop them moving again when the Bertram is fully operational."

Amanda looked at Grealish. "Why can't Farrell search for any bio-bands that are operational, but completely still?"

"She can, and she is. The moment she finds them, she'll let us know, but there are almost seven million people on this station, and we don't have a specific timeframe or loca-tion, so it's going to take a lot of man-hours, even if we focussed on the five globes you've isolated as most likely."

"Amy removed her bio-band, though," said Hennessey. "Farrell told us whilst we were trying to track her."

"That makes sense," replied Amanda. "She probably discarded it in the dock, so that when the bomb exploded, we'd assume she was dead. Except now she can continue her mission outside of the BRMC controls."

"And take out the entire investigations team at her funeral," I said. I'd seen that in a movie once.

"Why would she need to?" asked Tyrone. "If that bomb had detonated the arsenal in the armoury, this entire globe would have gone and the Bertram Ramsay would be dead in the water." He shrugged. "Mission accomplished."

He had a point. So much for my movie theory.

"So she must have had a plan to get off this station," said Hennessey. "If it was a suicide mission, she needn't have left the dock."

Grealish shook his head in disgust. "I can't believe it was Amy. Seven years she's worked for me."

Tyrone put a hand on his shoulder. "Don't dwell on it, Sir. She fooled us all."

———

The doctors insisted I remain in hospital overnight, at the very minimum. They strapped my ribs up, which was uncomfortable, but they seemed more concerned with my feet and hands which had suffered extensive frostbite.

Major Nishimura dropped in to see me the following morning, and gave me the bollocking I'd been expecting, but ruined the effect with "Good call yesterday, Jaxon. Ms Baxendale would not have survived otherwise." He shook my hand, which caused me to wince, and grinned at me without an ounce of sympathy before turning his back and leaving.

I popped in to see Emily and the girls mid-morning. The

transformation was huge. The girls both hugged me (I tried not to wince), their tiny bodies still wrapped in bandages but their eyes bright and alert, the colour back in their skin and their smiles warm and innocent.

I looked at Emily, still bed-ridden but in much better shape than the last time we'd met. She still looked emaciated, but there was a glow about her that suggested recovery and healing. Her eyes were still sad, and a little empty. She'd lost her husband, after all, and had barely processed and grieved his loss.

"We got them, Mrs Latimer. The two marines that abducted you. They've been detained and are being questioned by the authorities as we speak."

She smiled, and it filled the room. "That's great news, Jaxon. What about any of the others?"

"We're not sure yet, but we think we know who one of them is." I pulled my hollotab out of my kitbag and showed her a picture of Amy Cooper.

She scowled and then frowned, as if two conflicting thoughts were fighting for space in her mind. "That might be her, although she looks different there."

"Different how?" I asked.

She tilted her head and examined the photograph for a moment. "I can't quite put my finger on it. She just looks different. Please understand, Jaxon, they all wore masks around the girls and I so we only ever saw partial faces, right up until the last time I saw her. And at that moment she was soaked in blood from head to toe and told us we wouldn't see anyone again. That was the day before you found us."

I nodded. That made sense. I felt sick at the thought of it, but if Amy had seen Laura get off at Globe 9, she could easily have followed her over there and disposed of her. She could have showered in the apartment, changed into fresh fatigues and left with the bomb lab.

We chatted for a little longer, and then her eyes closed so I hugged both the girls again and headed up to the tenth floor. Even if I hadn't known which room Libby was in, it was fairly obvious with two armed marines at the door. I was clearly on the list this time, as they didn't challenge me when I went inside.

"Jaxon!" Her eyes lit up before filling with tears and her face crumpling. "I'm so sorry, Jax. I didn't know what else to do," she said, before I even opened my mouth to speak.

I put my arms around her and squeezed gently, trying not to damage my ribs further, before taking a seat next to her bed.

We talked for a little while, about everything and nothing. She was carrying a burden that wasn't hers to carry. I tried to console her, but she wouldn't have it.

"They told me they were listening to everything I said," she sobbed. "They knew where I worked and lived, which made me wonder if it might be Jenn. The way you were talking about Eloise, I don't know…" Her words tailed off as she looked at me through sad eyes. "But then they threatened to kill her, and I didn't know how to get her safe. I knew you'd talk to her eventually, but I didn't know how you'd react. I was so scared."

She was just another pawn in this deadly game, and I could feel the anger building inside me.

Hennessey interrupted after twenty minutes with news that they'd processed the order for Libby's release. Libby had given statements already, and the two marines that aided Amy were in custody and being interrogated. Whatever happened, they'd pay for their part in this. For the suffering and death they'd so callously caused. For trivialising life, and marginalising those tasked with prolonging it.

The medical staff released me from the hospital later that day and confined me to light duties for two weeks. I found Libby in my apartment, curled up on the sofa, sleeping.

Jennifer had been over to see her in the hospital, and the two of them had cried for ages. Their friendship had grown, despite the forces tearing them apart. I tried not to wake her, but she stirred as I pushed my loaned fatigues into the laundry chute.

"Jenn's said I can go back to hers whenever," she said, looking at me so intensely that I felt I was being x-rayed.

"That's great," I said, feeling a lump form in my throat. In just a few days I'd got used to having her around. She was beautiful and funny, fragile and casually carefree in a way that was so fresh, and so endearing. I hated the thought of being here alone, though I'd never admit that to anyone. I fussed about the coffee pot with my back to her, desperately trying to suppress my emotions. I was so conflicted about Laura's death, and Libby's attention, that I couldn't get anything straight in my head. I felt horribly guilty for even looking at Lib, but a rather loud voice in my head was cheering me on, which just made me feel worse.

"I didn't commit," she said, and an unnatural stillness filled the room.

I turned to face her. "What will you do if you don't go back there?"

She tilted her head to the side and made a small shrug with one shoulder. "I was just getting used to being here with you," she said, her shining brown eyes wounded yet defiant.

I didn't know what to say. I must have opened my mouth to speak a couple of times, but I couldn't muster the words.

She looked suddenly panicked, and her eyes widened. When she spoke, her voice was shrill and forced. "Oh, sorry, yes, of course. Laura..." she said, looking away from me.

"No, Libby..."

"Jaxon, it's fine. I understand. I didn't mean... I'm not, you know..."

"Libby, I want you to stay." The words spilled from my idiotic head.

She looked at me, eyes flickering between mine, looking for any sign that I didn't mean it, or that I was saying it to appease her.

"Really?" she asked, so quietly.

"Really." I felt my face reddening, and looked down just in case I'd conjured up the earthquake I so desperately needed at this moment, but it refused to materialise. Fuck's sake.

She launched herself off the sofa and threw her arms round my neck, probably re-breaking the ribs that I'd worked on healing, fat tears leaking from her face as she buried her head into my chest. We stood there, clinging to each other for the longest time, in total silence save for the occasional soft sniff.

CHAPTER
THIRTY-THREE

THE ENTIRETY of fleet personnel lined up in the grounds of Globe 11-5-A at the edge of the woodlands, by the lake facing the dome. Earth was just disappearing from view, beautiful as ever, to be replaced by the moon, splendid and bright over Earth's horizon.

General Lavigne and Admiral Willard stood saluting with the six-hundred BRAF pilots, flight engineers and command centre personnel, as well as over four hundred civilian attendees. The Station Council stood to the side, looking sombre and detached, like some alien delegation, important but irrelevant in that moment.

This was the service to honour the fallen. The six BRAF pilots lost in the mission to bring back the Nova Pilgrim, the six-thousand, nine-hundred and forty-one civilian casualties of Globe 10's gravitational system sabotage, Mark Hanson, for his heroic efforts to restore the gravity, despite being in mortal peril, and Laura Watkins, the brave BRMC staff sergeant, murdered by the AoG. As far as I was concerned, they were all murdered by the AoG.

I could see Aoife and Jennifer wiping tears from their eyes to the side of the main procession. Libby was somewhere in the BRAF ranks, still wracked with guilt over nothing, really. I stood within my squadron, flight suit neatly pressed and my Victoria Cross pinned ceremonially to my chest in place of the solitary ribbon. I would have given anything to not wear it – not here – but Addison insisted I be the very best version of myself, as the station celebrated those who had lost their lives.

Much later, and thankful that it was over, I sat quietly in Alpha Centauri, surrounded by my friends. My family, really. Tyrone looked back to his physical best and was quick to laugh as we talked about everything and nothing. Sara and Amanda talked animatedly, with ready smiles and drinks flowing. Grealish was lurking somewhere, but he'd been out of sorts ever since Amy had fled. He blamed himself for not seeing her for who she was, and refused to hear the placatory voices offering solace and comfort.

Libby, Jenn and Aoife were all sat in a booth in spirited discussion, giggling the way that girls sometimes do, and it was wonderful to see their joy. Addison was conspicuous in his absence, but he'd sent me a message to say he'd been called into a briefing about our orbital exit in the next couple of weeks.

I watched them all, drinks over-flowing and laughter filling the bar in every corner, from the relative tranquillity of the balcony that overlooked the infinity pool to the edge of the dome. It had been two weeks since the mission to Earth. Two weeks since they'd lifted me from the crumpled remains of my faithful Sigma. Two weeks since Libby's abduction, and my slow, solitary drift into space, alone but for the voices in my helmet.

I knew the job was incomplete. That despite my best efforts, and those of the investigations team, the AoG threat remained credible and real, empowered and encouraged, no doubt, by their devastating victory. The BRMC had rounded up four other AoG infiltrators following the arrest of the two marines responsible for Emily Latimer's kidnapping, but despite them providing actionable intelligence they were nowhere near the inner circle. They were just puppets in the game, manipulated to believe they were serving a higher purpose yet ultimately considered expendable by the AoG hierarchy.

Amanda and I had stayed in contact with Gemma Farrell and introduced her to both Tyrone and Sara. As a team we'd abandoned the barn in Globe 6 – it seemed foolish to revisit places which Amy knew about. All eyes were on the lookout for her. The holloscreen stations had been broadcasting her image everywhere for the last two weeks, in the hope that she may be spotted somewhere on the station.

We concluded she had not departed the Bertram Ramsay. No escape pods had launched, and all sorties now returned to the Bertram without going anywhere near Earth so there was little point stowing away in a Sigma or Nova Shuttle. There was a slim chance that she'd concealed an escape pod amongst the pallets of bodies, enabling her escape when the dock depressurised, but we discounted that theory quickly. It was simply too high a risk for her to be in that dock. If the bomb had detonated as planned, and ignited the ordnance in the armoury, there wouldn't be a dock left. Or a Globe 11, for that matter.

Admiralty revoked her access, and the next time she attempted to use her bio-band, the terminal would wipe it and an immediate alert would sound.

They'd frozen her accounts too, so she had no funds at her disposal; at least none that we knew about. With her recently discovered skills in bio-band manipulation, there's no telling what she could do to increase her access or fiscal scope.

The team had met up in Sara's apartment in 11-5-A just

two nights ago. Amy was the only topic of conversation – understanding her role and how she'd deceived us all.

"Okay, so this is what we believe has played out in the last twelve months," said Grealish, leaning casually against the window. "Amy was altering the data in our systems, particularly candidate selection, in order to facilitate the infiltration of this vessel by the AoG. As the overseer for the entry documentation and process, she had access to all systems, communications into and out of Compression sites Alpha, Bravo, Charlie, Delta, Echo and Foxtrot. She also had full communications with ICP Command, Whitehall, and with the Bertram Ramsay Station Council, Admiralty and Station Security."

"Not to mention we tasked her with investigating the leak from the ICP side," injected Hennessey. Grealish shuffled uncomfortably. He'd been hoodwinked in a way that was almost impossible to recover from.

Admiral Willard had torn him a new arsehole for an hour in the days following the dock explosion, but had stopped short of removing Grealish despite several calls for him to do so from the Station Council and many senior personnel in Admiralty.

"You're fucking lucky to still be standing here, Andrew. I've got councillors and generals breathing down my neck and calling for your head. The only reason I'm not kicking you to the kerb is that Lieutenant Cooper is still at large, and despite your biblical failure to recognise someone in your own ranks as an AoG mole, you are still the person most likely to find her, because you knew her better than anyone."

Whilst he'd escaped any serious repercussions, they'd demoted him to lieutenant colonel with a reduction in pay, privileges and access.

"We also believe she was the person you saw talking to Mark Hanson on level 4 of Globe 9, Jaxon," continued Grealish. "We can't confirm this, because her bio-band shows as being in the barn in Globe 6 at the time, but we also know she arrived late with Sara to that meeting, so the bio-band data is clearly false."

"It's fairly safe to assume that she followed Laura into Globe 9 and blocked communications before killing her," said Hennessey. "After that, it gets a bit more speculative."

"We *think* she used the distraction to help move the bomb lab, but it's also possible that she was in no condition to do so because Emily Latimer's testimony is that her fatigues were stained with blood, which we assume to be Laura's," said Grealish, looking apologetically at me. "There's only one real possibility, and that is that she showered and changed in Globe 9, then took The Loop back to the barn and re-connected her bio-band before heading to the hospital. None of this can be corroborated, though." He sighed. "The timing is also ridiculously tight. There's no footage of her getting on The Loop, and she'd have had to be on the same train as Laura, Amanda and Jaxon in order to have had time to carry out her orders, but there's also no evidence to suggest it *wasn't* her."

"She sanitised the bomb lab, too," added Amanda. "Jaxon and I cleared it and saw documents that were not included in the inventory taken by the investigators. Amy was present during that investigation and had several opportunities to enter any of the apartments in that building and remove evidence of her involvement."

My mind drifted at this point. I was angry and exhausted and still nurturing broken ribs. It seemed so unlikely to be Amy Cooper, after everything I saw of her in GCHQ. We knew someone had been sneaking information out to her from inside Compression Echo, but that investigation was a non-starter. It was now impossible to make any reasonable assumptions about the identity of that mole, and pointless even thinking about it. For now, it was all about finding her and decommissioning her. The sound of Tyrone's voice brought me out of my daydream.

"Sara and I have searched her apartment, but it's clean. Too clean, in fact. It doesn't look like she was even staying there."

"So, what's our next move?" I asked.

Grealish sighed again. "Honestly, Jaxon, I don't know. The problem we now face is that the AoG is, and has been totally aware of this team from day one, yet we are unknown to our own security services, outside the chain of command."

"Well, it's not like we have the option to change that," I remarked. "Right now, we know our team is air tight and on the same side, for the first time ever. Before, Amy must have reported every action, every meeting and every discussion. Now, they're out of the loop."

"That's precisely what I told the admiral," said Grealish, pulling a face as if the mere mention of Willard was enough to sully the room. "So whilst they are setting up an official task force to tackle the AoG problem, we are to continue operating as before, under the radar."

The meeting continued like that for another hour. Half of it was spent cooking up a plan of action, and the other half connecting historical dots. We made little headway and left the meeting feeling frustrated.

Libby was at the apartment when I arrived back. Things between us were more settled, but a little odd. She was good company, smiled a lot and spent most of her time walking around in her underwear or a towel, so I had no complaints, but there was an invisible barrier between us. I suspect Libby was overthinking things, because Laura had only died a month ago, and I continued to feel guilty about not feeling worse over her death, but the reality of it was simple; we'd only known each other for three months, and another three would pass in the blink of an eye. I was sad about Laura, truly, but not in the way I felt like I should be.

Libby was much easier going. She was likeable and friendly, and less prone to mood swings, although Jenn had confessed to me she'd seen a different side of Libby since she started working in flight engineering. I promised Jenn I'd keep an eye on her, and I made Libby promise she wouldn't keep anything from me if it was bothering her.

I was still on light duties, so I spent most of my days working on the flight deck, and organising daily sorties and mission briefs. The broken remains of the Red October were in Hangar 4, alongside the Nova Palmer. The engineering team were working diligently on both aircrafts, but they refused to give me an answer when I asked outright if she'd fly again. They joked they were renaming her 'Lemming' because it looked like I had dropped her off a cliff. Priceless. I must have scowled because the senior engineer patted me on the back and said, "We'll do our level best to put her back together."

The rear dock was still closed whilst they repaired the bay. There was a little fire damage, but mostly it was just dents to the walls and ceiling panels from the floating debris, so the squadrons were having to fly from the front dock, which presented other challenges.

Globe 10 was close to being re-pressurised. They'd replaced the EM glass panels, and now a rigorous process was underway to test everything before pressurisation. A bunch of artists and sculptors were creating a monument to those who died when the gravity went out, which they would install in a woodland clearing by a waterfall on level 5. It was a nice touch, but a painful reminder of our failure.

I spent more and more time sitting alone at the edge of the woodland, looking out through the dome and just thinking.

"She likes you, you know?" said Aoife, walking up behind me and plonking herself on the bench.

"Who likes me?" I asked.

She rolled her eyes at me.

"Oh," I said. "Libby."

"What's holding you back?" she asked.

I shrugged. "I don't really know, Aoif. So much has happened."

"Look, Jaxon, I know things have been a bit shite—"

"A bit?" I asked with mock incredulity.

"Yes, for fuck's sake, a *bit*. I know you and Laura were a thing, but that was never going to last. If she hadn't been horribly murdered, I'd have won the sweepstake on that."

I smiled. Aoife was an appalling diplomat, whilst simultaneously being a rather decent human being.

"I'm just not ready yet," I replied.

"Jesus fucking Christ, Jaxon. You're sleeping next to each other every night. You've probably seen her naked a hundred times. What more does the poor girl have to do to get your attention?"

"She had my attention in Compression, Aoife, but I've got a target on my back now. They've already tried to kill her once."

"And you saved her. She skipped the Stockholm Syndrome and moved straight to falling in love with her rescuer."

I turned to look at her. My eyebrows must have looked like the gravity had failed on my forehead.

"Look, Jaxon, you're a decent bloke and a nice-looking guy, but in approximately three months, given your track record for attracting disaster, you're likely to be hideous and then nobody will want you, and you'll probably die alone, friendless and pathetic. And really ugly," she added.

I laughed, and so did she. For all her brashness and lack of filter, she was pretty astute and refreshingly honest.

"Just make your mind up," she said, before getting up and walking away. She halted briefly after five metres and looked back. "If it makes you feel better, you'll always be a pathetic loser in my eyes." She winked and disappeared into the subdued light of the evening.

EPILOGUE

JOHN LENNON

I CAN FEEL the walls around me closing in, like a relentless march towards inevitability. There is an artificial levity around the station, as if everything we're doing is justifiable and humane, but it isn't.

Earth seems smaller now that we're in a higher orbit. Just a blue marble in the rear windows of this grotesque den of iniquity. We're abandoning them. Removing their hope. Condemning them to oblivion, and for what? So we can live out our days inside this glass and metal cage?

My thoughts have become more morose over time, as if my perpetual gloom is penance for our collective immorality. The obscenity of our good fortune, *our prosperity* others are calling it, weighs heavily on my shoulders as if I, alone, am responsible for our escape. More than once I've been told I am, but even I can't ignore the truth; fortitude, coupled with blind luck, is a more accurate assessment of my influence on recent events.

"What's with the glum face?" asks Libby, her head resting on my thighs as she sprawls out casually on the sofa.

"Oh, nothing," I reply, absentmindedly stroking her hair.

She sits up, analysing me with a frown that wrinkles her forehead. "Jaxon, you promised you wouldn't keep anything from me."

"Really, it's nothing. I just feel shitty because of the people we're leaving behind."

"Oh," she says, as my darkness envelopes her in a crushing sorrow.

I ought to rescue her from my selfish damnation, but all I can think about now is Amy Cooper, and how we all missed it. The signs. The secrecy. The subterfuge. The Croydon facelift.

I laugh out loud and Libby glares at me, startled from her aching despair.

"Come on," I say, grabbing her hand and hauling her off the sofa.

"Where are we going?" she asks, as if we ever go anywhere other than Lovell's.

"Who the fuck knows?" I reply, opening the door and pausing for a moment to get a last glance at Earth, before the pair of us turn and leave.

...TO BE CONTINUED in BOOK 3 of
THE ROGUE SERIES

ACKNOWLEDGMENTS

There are so many people to thank for their efforts with this book, that I barely know where to begin.

Firstly, and most importantly, to my wonderful kids, Evie and George, for making every single day better. I'm so proud that Evie read *Rogue* for her school English project, and gave me the feedback I needed to hear from the perspective of a 14 year old daughter; "It's really good, dad. I mean, I didn't really understand some of the words, though. Oh, and you swear too much."

George's response, at the age of 11, to being asked if he would read it was almost as perfect; "Sure. Maybe. Like, when I'm 40 or something. Can I have two pounds?"

My lovely Leanne, who has had to suffer my selfishness when talking about my books, and keep my feet on the ground on the days when I get too excitable about plots, characters, and childish jokes that I've shoehorned in at inappropriate moments. I was in a rut with Enemy, and it was Lea that dragged me out of it, and gave me a kick up the arse. Thanks babe.

So many people contributed to the story line. Jenny Avery was a font of knowledge with military ranks, flight protocols and teaching me how to speak "Aussie". Her feedback massively shaped the direction of one of the sub-plots, and made the book so much better.

Robin Price, for his continual support, encouragement and the gentle nudges in the back to pull my finger out and do something with my books. I'm at the "offering bribes to convince him to be my agent" point.

Next-door-Mark (Pattison) stuck his neck out and read the whole kit and caboodle, and allowed me the self-indulgence of talking over the plot lines with him down the pub, and during the footy, which must have been infuriating. Being that he's an Everton fan I can only form the conclusion that I was preventing human rights atrocities by distracting him from a disastrous season.

The brilliant Andy Weir, who gave me the **worst advice ever** about researching bombs and their explosive effects in space;

I just google whatever I want. If I end up on a list I end up on a list. Who cares?

-ATW

I care, Andy. But cheers anyway.

My excellent team at 3 Legged Thing – particularly Alison Barclay who is always the first to volunteer to read my stuff. Unlike Rogue, Enemy took nearly two years to write, so it had no impact on my working life, but they all encouraged me and kept me feeling positive about it.

Liz Ward, my editor, who totally gets me, but was mean to me in the margins of the manuscript, and forced me to remove more references to testicles and farts, thus ruining the entire novel for everyone. Booooo *mimes throwing cabbages*.

To be fair, my dialogue punctuation is so appalling that I pretty much got my revenge before she even started. Plus I added a thousand 'fuck you' commas, which I'm still laughing about. Despite this, the book wouldn't be what it is without an amazing editor. She keeps me on track, tells me when I'm crap (often), and shunts me towards the right conclusion when I'm digging my heels in over something irrelevant.

I still don't know how it will end. Amy's story took on a whole new pathway after I wrote the fourth book in The Bleeds series (The Cylume). I had to rewrite so much of Enemy, but it was totally worth it.

Laura had to go - she was doing my head in. Even Liz wrote, "I'm glad you killed her off. I forgot how annoying she was."

Lastly, a massive thank you to all the indie authors in the world today, diligently plugging away, trying to find that elusive publishing deal, whilst trying not to let the rejections drag them under. Keep bringing your wonderful books to the fore. You deserve so much more, but you're appreciated regardless.

ALSO BY DANNY LENIHAN

THE BLEEDS

A series of dystopian shorts, prelude to THE ROGUE SERIES

The Bleeds series act as a prelude to Rogue & Enemy, documenting the early life of Jaxon Leith in the build up to the apocalypse. There are currently four stories (with more planned) and these are available only in eBook format as a compendium edition (The Bleeds) or individual stories for download.

FAGAN

Coming 2025

Haunted by his sister's death at the hands of a drunk driver, Mason Winward spirals into despair, intent on revenge. A stranger named Fagan saves him from the brink of committing murder, and under his guidance, Mason finds a new purpose.

The two become close until one day Fagan suddenly vanishes, leaving no trace that he ever even existed.

Along comes Alex, Mason's best friend, and fellow idiot, who, despite his astounding immaturity, happens to have invented a time-portal.

Together, they honour Fagan's

legacy by dedicating their lives to travelling back in time and rescuing kids from the brink of irreversible despair. They are the better Samaritans. The pioneers of our generation.

Until they save the wrong child.

Fagan is a tale of redemption—a testament to the indomitable human spirit that rises from the depths of grief and anger and becomes a saviour of those who cannot save themselves.

ABOUT THE AUTHOR

Danny Lenihan was born in West London, raised in Chessington and now lives in the Shires with his two children. A former press photographer and stand-up comedian, Danny spends his days writing and designing for his global brands, 3 Legged Thing and Toxic Bags.

A passionate writer, Danny has contributed to several books prior to publishing his debut novel, Rogue in 2021. For over three decades he has written for newspapers, magazines, TV, film and radio, and hosts the cult comedy podcast "Faces for Radio".

For fourteen years, Danny toured the world as a stand-up comedian, during which time he starred in three movies, numerous television shows and was a frequent panellist and contributor to BBC Radio. An accomplished musician and songwriter, Danny composed the musical score to British director, Pat Higgins' debut horror movie, Trashhouse.

His current projects include TRAITOR, the third novel in the Rogue Series, and FAGAN, a brand new concept about a time-travelling psychologist set in Chessington, where the author grew up. Both novels are expected to release in 2025.

facebook.com/DanLenihan

instagram.com/dannylenihan

linkedin.com/in/dannylenihan

bookbub.com/authors/danny-lenihan

tiktok.com/dannylenihan

goodreads.com/dannylenihan

threads.net/dannylenihan

www.ingramcontent.com/pod-product-compliance
Lightning Source LLC
Chambersburg PA
CBHW010315100726
47906CB00006B/998